COLORADO CUTIE

Spur heard a noise and looked up. The robber was on top of the rock less than six feet away! Spur lifted the Winchester and fired. The unaimed round skidded off the stone breaking up and splattering some of its hot lead into the robber who dropped out of sight.

"Don't be a fool," Spur called. "You're hurt and I'll kill you if I have to, just like I did Varner. You ready to die?"

There was no answer.

A stick of dynamite with a short fuse sailed over to the granite boulder and Spur drove away from it, rolling as far as he could toward the open space behind the rock.

The blast went off with a cracking roar.

TEXAS TEASE

Yankee carpetbaggers, murderous rebels, and hot-tempered women—that was what McCoy found when he rode into Johnson Creek, Texas. But Spur had stepped into vipers' nests before, and he knew there was only one thing to do—gun them down before they got a bead on him.

Other Spur Double Editions:

**GOLD TOWN GAL/RED ROCK REDHEAD
SAVAGE SISTERS/HANG SPUR McCOY!
INDIAN MAID/MONTANA MINX
RAWHIDER'S WOMAN/SALOON GIRL
MISSOURI MADAM/HELENA HELLION
ROCKY MOUNTAIN VAMP/CATHOUSE
KITTEN**

SPUR DOUBLE:

COLORADO CUTIE

TEXAS TEASE

DIRK FLETCHER

LEISURE BOOKS NEW YORK CITY

A LEISURE BOOK®

April 2007

Published by

Dorchester Publishing Co., Inc.
200 Madison Avenue
New York, NY 10016

ISBN 10: 0-8439-3207-4
ISBN 13: 0-8439-3207-2

The name "Leisure Books" and the stylized "L" with design are
trademarks of Dorchester Publishing Co., Inc.

Printed in the United States of America.

Visit us on the web at www.dorchesterpub.com.

COLORADO CUTIE

1

Two black horses thundered out of the side street, their eyes wild, foam flying from their mouths as the desperados on their backs spurred them viciously. The men fired deadly six-guns at anyone who moved on the small Kansas town's Main Street as they pulled up at the Newtown bank.

Two other bank robbers inside the venerable establishment burst through the big doors carrying carpetbags stuffed with all the paper money in the safe and tellers' cages. The second pair of ne'er-do-wells leaped on board waiting chargers and emptied pistols at the men from the bank, and others foolhardy enough to oppose them.

"If any of my men are wounded, I'll come back and kill every man in town!" the leader roared. The man on the silver gray stallion was Big Red Ryerson, the scourge of the plains, the most wanted bank robber in a dozen states, and now taking his deadly toll on this small Kansas town of no more than two thousand souls.

Sheriff Johnny White pushed his hat back on his head from where he crouched beside the hardware store, his Remington repeating rifle at the ready. Slowly he lowered the rifle. He would not endanger the men of the town by shooting up the bank robbers now. He would wait until they were well out of town, then with a selected posse he would throw down on them while they camped, and capture every man without spilling any blood.

The outlaws laughed and shot out two store windows as they thundered out of town, making Sheriff Johnny White look like a coward in the eyes of the citizens of Newtown. Johnny didn't worry about that, he could live with criticism until he brought Big Red Ryerson to justice.

But he hoped that Caroline Caruthers did not think ill of him. She was the prairie flower he loved, and soon he was going to tell her.

Sheriff Johnny White ran into Main Street, fired three shots into the air.

"All right, the town is safe now. I need six volunteers who can shoot straight to form a posse. Who is with me?"

Willard Kleaner looked up from the short story he had been reading. Wow! There were the men, that was the action he thought he would find in the West. The pages of *Amazing Western Stories* told what the Wild West was really like! He'd read every one he could find when he could talk his father out of a dime.

But his father had been killed in a runaway buggy six months ago and now Willard was here in Johnson Corners, Colorado living with his Aunt and Uncle. But this *couldn't be the West!* Nothing was the same. He hadn't seen a single Indian. There were no big herds of buffalo, and the only cowboys he had seen were short, dirty, foul-mouthed and about as colorful as a slab of brown bread.

This couldn't be the Wild West!

Willard looked out from the porch of a clapboard house where he sat reading the dime western. He was fifteen years old, had finished the eighth grade of regular school and one year of higher school in Chicago. He was tall and new-corn thin, with a mop of carrot red hair, dark green eyes and a face full of freckles.

He'd had a fight for every one of his freckles and had won most of them. Now he stared in silent anger at the poor excuse of a real Western town that cluttered along the main street. They called it Johnson Corners. Now wasn't that a colorful name for a western town!

His uncle, who ran one of two small hotels in town, said there were over two thousand people in town and the surrounding valley.

"Yes sir, Willard," his Uncle Ronald Lewton said. "We're building something good here. Johnson Corners is going to be a big town someday. We're not a hundred miles from Denver, and we get a lot of traffic through here along the trail west. We've got a good bit of cattle ranching already, and being so close to the railroad, we'll do right fine with farm products too.

"This is a town to grow in, to grab opportunity and shake it by the throat and beat a living out of it. Right here in Johnson Corners!"

Willard sighed. He put his finger in the dime novel and tried to imagine Big Red Ryerson thundering around the corner on his horse, shooting out the windows in the stores, robbing the bank and laughing as he rode out.

When he opened his eyes, Big Red Ryerson was well out of town, the sheriff was chasing him, and Willard wondered if he had been born twenty years too late. Here it was 1877 and most of the Wild West wasn't all that wild anymore. If he'd only been here back in the mid sixties! Right after the Civil War, before the railroad came! That would have been the really great time.

Willard could almost imagine it. Only pockets of people, a few fences, lots of horses and cattle and buffalo. Those would have been the days! He would have been a foreman on a cattle ranch, where he could ride and rope, and make trail drives down to the rail head in Kansas.

Yeah! He couldn't even ride a horse. Maybe he could get a job as a swamper down at the livery and learn to ride there. He'd ask his uncle.

"Willard!" a thin, whinish voice came from the parlor. "Willard, it's time you were getting to the hotel if'n you want your allowance. Nobody gets paid around this house for sitting on his fanny all morning."

"Yes, Aunt Zelda. I'm leaving right now."

His aunt's thin, frowning face appeared behind the front screen door staring down at him.

"Willard, be sure to leave that horrible dime novel here. I don't want anyone decent seeing you reading that trash. The very idea!"

"Yes, ma'am," he said. He held the soft paper dime novel as far as the door when his aunt whipped it out of his hand.

"Had my way I'd burn this for kindling." She sniffed. "But your uncle says its little enough we can do." Her scowl deepened. "Lord knows we try."

"Yes, ma'am. I'll be going now."

Willard hurried off the porch, anxious to get out of

the sound of her irritating voice. Willard knew that his father had left him some money when he died. He didn't know how much, or where it was. His uncle was his legal guardian now, but the money was in a "trust" whatever that was. But his uncle did get twenty dollars a month to pay for "food, clothing and shelter" for Willard's keep.

William knew that twenty dollars a month was more than some working men made. That was two hundred and forty dollars a year! What he could do with that much money!

Still his uncle said he had to work around the hotel to help pay his keep. He did get fifteen cents a day for every day he worked cleaning the hotel, working in the laundry and mopping down the hallways.

As Willard came around the corner into Main Street, he saw the stage pulling in. He ran. The stage came twice a day, east toward Chicago in the afternoon, and west toward Denver in the morning. The arrival of the stage was usually the most exciting event to take place in Johnson Corners on any day.

The big Concord coach rolled along like a prairie schooner, rocking on the heavy leather straps that helped absorb some of the jolts of the roadway. The Concord was the biggest and best of the stage coaches, and William was fascinated by them.

He ran now, caught up with the coach and trotted alongside it as the team of six began to slow so the rig could stop exactly in front of the Overland Express office.

Willard checked out the big coach to see if it was one of the new ones. He knew a lot about the big coaches. Most of them weighed more than a ton, stood eight feet high and often cost as much as $1,500 to buy. They could carry as many as twenty-one passengers—nine seated inside and the rest hanging on while sitting on the roof.

The driver's box up front was usually shared by an express company messenger riding shotgun over his often precious cargo. Under the driver's box was the boot, a leather covered area that held mail and express items and a strongbox with valuables. Personal baggage and larger express parcels were carried in another leather enclosed boot in the rear.

A Concord might use four or six horses, depending on the hills that had to be climbed. Most Concords that wheeled into Johnson Corners came with six.

Willard looked with interest and saw that this Concord had the two throughbraces, the three-inch strips of leather that served as shock absorbers for the ride. The writer Mark Twain said the straps made the coach ride like a cradle on wheels.

For a moment the coach outdistanced Willard, so he ran faster, caught up and then had to stop quickly as the driver put on the hand brake on the big rear wheels and the Concord from the Ben Holiday Overland Express Company came to a sudden halt at the express office.

Willard moved back against the side of the building and watched in open amazement as the stableman rushed forward and unhitched the six horses. Helpers led them down the alley and brought back six fresh horses for the run on toward Denver.

He fantasized himself hitching up the horses, backing them into the tongue, then hitching the second pair and the third in front of them. Black leather harness shining, the steel connectors sturdy and sure.

Then he would trade places with the driver and go dashing out of town, eager to get his cargo and passengers into Denver where there would be a layover for a good night's rest and some fine food.

Willard turned and watched the passengers getting off. Some might even be staying. A woman with red hair stepped down, looked around, saw him and waved. Willard wasn't sure she waved at him, he didn't know her. When she laughed and pointed to a big suitcase that the shotgun guard lifted off the top of the rig for her, he turned away.

He watched the next person get off, a tall man with a moustache and sandy brown sideburns well below his ears. The man wore town clothes, a brown suit and white shirt with a black string tie. He carried a battered brown hat with a low crown and a row of Spanish silver coins as a headband.

Willard knew at once that the man was a famous outlaw. One look at the six-gun worn low and tied down to his thigh proved to Willard that he had been right. Nobody in town wore his holster tied down that way. A gunsharp!

Maybe they would have a shoot-out!

Maybe a call-out and a gun duel on Main Street!

Maybe a bank robbery by the man and his gang of cutthroats who steal horses and thunder out of town shooting out the store windows and . . .

The man he had been watching motioned to him.

"Son, could you take my bag over to the best hotel in town? I'm thirsty and can't wait to lift a beer or two."

The tall stranger dropped a medium sized carpet-bag at his feet and stared down at Willard.

"Son?" the stranger said.

"Huh? Oh, yes sir. Sorry, I was thinking . . ."

"Could you take my bag over to the hotel? Give it to the desk clerk and tell him I'll register when I get there. My name is Spur McCoy."

"Yes, sir! You bet," Willard said. He wanted to ask him if he were really a gunsharp, a fast gun, an outlaw maybe! But Willard simply nodded and picked up the bag. He had taken two steps toward the Aspen Hotel when the man called.

"Hey, son."

Willard stopped and turned. The man tossed a coin at him and Willard caught it smoothly. It was a quarter!

"Here's something for your trouble. Tell the clerk that bag better be there when I come or he's in for some trouble. What's your name, son?"

"Willard, sir. Willard Kleaner. I work at the Aspen Hotel. Your bag will be there."

The tall man nodded, turned and watched the redheaded woman talking to the shotgun guard for a moment, then walked quickly across the street to the biggest drinking establishment he could see on Main Street, the Evangeline Saloon and Gaming House.

Spur McCoy saw the sign of the Aspen Hotel half a block down the dirt street of Johnson Corners, waved at the young redheaded boy, and walked with a thirsty purpose across the street, avoiding the horse droppings. He stepped up to the boardwalk built in front of the business establishments and pushed through the swinging doors into the Evangeline Saloon.

He was interested in a cold beer or two to start, then he would check in at the hotel and have a late midday meal. When he came back to the saloon he might try his hand at some poker. It had been some time since he had indulged himself with the pasteboards.

As soon as he stepped inside the Evangeline he knew it was a different kind of saloon. The floor was clean, oiled and well scrubbed. More than a dozen coal oil lamps already lighted the place with twenty more hanging ready to be lit. The chairs and poker tables were in good repair, varnished and orderly.

The voices were subdued and he didn't notice any men wearing guns. He had a quick look at a woman who stepped from behind the bar and vanished into a rear room. There were no dance hall girls in sight.

A huge man four inches taller than Spur's six-foot two inches, stopped three feet from Spur. He had a barrel chest, arms the size of railroad ties and looked as if he carried 280 pounds of solid muscle.

He looked straight into Spur's eyes.

"Miss Evangeline asks you to check your six-gun," the man said in a surprisingly soft voice.

Spur looked around and saw now that none of the men wore gunbelts. He shrugged.

"Why not?" he said, and took off his leather and the .45 with the long barrel and handed it to the big man who gave him a poker chip with a number written on it.

When Spur turned toward the bar, the woman was there again. He smiled automatically and stepped up to the polished mahogany that glistened even in the lamplight. The only thing Spur saw was the woman behind the bar. She was short, delicately formed with soft brown hair on her shoulders and a alabaster complexion with two dimples and a pair of darting black eyes.

Spur smiled. She smiled back and he saw the heavy gold chain around her neck outside the chin high white blouse. The chain had in the center the largest pearl Spur had ever seen.

"You must be Miss Evangeline," Spur said.

She smiled again and the dimples deepened. The pretty woman nodded slightly. "True, and you must be Spur McCoy. You look thirsty, how about a cold beer?"

2

Spur McCoy was jolted when the beautiful bar maid called him by name. He had never been in this small Colorado town before. From long practice, he had not shown surprise at the woman's use of his name.

"That's right kindly of you, miss. I certainly could use a cold beer. Ice house?"

"Sam built a big one at the edge of town and supplies us all summer. Lower his supply gets, higher the price." She opened a bottle of beer and pushed it toward him, her dark eyes curious.

"You didn't seem surprised when I called you by name. Why?"

Spur grinned, tipped the bottle and took a long pull. When he let it down he wiped his mouth and looked at her. "Are you always so outspoken, so direct?"

"Usually, unless I'm playing poker, then you won't ever know what I'm thinking."

"Sounds like an interesting gamble."

"You are interested to find out how I knew your

name, I can tell. But you didn't let on, not even a flicker of an eyebrow. So, that makes you a railroad agent, or maybe a Pinkerton, or just possibly a U.S. Marshal. Now that we're a state I don't know if the U.S. Marshals work around here."

"They do, but I'm not one." He pulled at the beer again. "That tastes good after eating dust for forty miles. And it's served by the prettiest lady I've seen in town."

She pouted for a moment, lips thrust out, eyes almost closed, chin up. Then she laughed, "Sir, that is no compliment, since you just got off the stage and the only woman you've seen is our redheaded Lotty, who is one of our town's few ladies of ill repute."

"Lotty is not much of a talker. She didn't say three words to anybody on the stage."

"Lotty has other talents and skills."

Spur chuckled. "I would guess. Now, I am curious. Are you Evangeline?"

"Guilty. I own the place and run it straight and clean. No house rules, no cheating, no gunplay. Every card dealt comes off a deck laid flat on the table. Haven't even had a fist fight in here in six months."

Spur finished the beer and pushed the bottle back to her. She took it and put it below the bar. It was a little before noon but already four poker tables were busy.

Spur had a dozen questions for her, but he also was hungry, felt grimy from the long ride, and wanted a bath. He tipped his hat and pushed back from the long bar.

"I'll count on talking to you later," he said.

"Anytime, McCoy. I'm always here." She smiled and both dimples popped in. "I'll look forward to our next little chat."

Spur collected his gun belt and iron from the big man near the door and walked into the sunshine. It was high country in the Rocky Mountains, the air clear and crisp, the sun beaming down warm, and at night the stars so close you could reach up and play jacks with them.

The town had about two thousand people, Washington had told him. The man he looked for couldn't be too hard to find. But there was a curious proviso in his orders. He'd go over them carefully when he got into his room.

Spur dropped off the boardwalk and into the dust of the street, dodged one farm wagon with the driver already asleep, counting on the team of horses to take him safely back to his ranch. The team probably knew the way better than he did.

On the far boardwalk he passed the Weber Brothers Clothing House and the McNamara Bakery. Then came Bill Johnson Groceries before he reached the Aspen Hotel. Spur went up the six steps to the lobby. Three old men sat in chairs on the small front porch. They nodded at him and he waved back, then walked inside.

The redheaded boy he had seen in the street was sweeping the lobby. The youngster nodded and kept sweeping. At the desk Spur gave his name and the clerk's interest picked up slightly when he saw Spur in a town suit.

"Yes, sir, Mr. McCoy. We've put you in Two-C, right in front and just down from the stairs."

"Good. I'd also like a bath. Do you have separate bathrooms or do I get a tub brought to my room?"

"Sir, we have a bath on each floor. You'll be just across from the bath on two. I'll have some big towels sent up. Will there by anything else you need?"

18

Spur shook head, signed the register and gave the man six dollars for six nights.

"There is a fifty cent charge for the bathwater," the clerk said apologetically.

"Best half a dollar I ever spent," Spur said, took the key and walked up the open stairs to the second floor.

Inside Two-C he found his carpetbag on the bed. He checked carefully but it had not been opened. Before he had his bag unpacked and into the small dresser, a knock sounded on his door. Spur touched his Colt .45 on his hip and walked without a sound to the door. He pulled it open suddenly.

A young woman stood there with two large, fluffy white towels over her arm. She was sturdily built with broad shoulders, long blonde hair and large breasts pushing against a white blouse she had outgrown.

Brown eyes evaluated him as she grinned. "You wanted some towels for a bath?"

"Yes, thanks."

"I'll put them in the bathroom for you. Willard has already brought up the hot water. Better hurry before it gets cold." She smiled at him and walked toward the bath down one room and across the hall. He could see the smooth operation of her hips under the skirt.

Spur closed the door. Now there was a healthy young woman, who would not try too hard to chase away a man. For just a moment he thought about his orders. He should check them again. Gen. Halleck had told him in a wire to proceed to Johnson Corners, Colorado and determine if one Horace Olson was in town. He was reported to be living here under the name of George Slocum. He was about thirty-five and was wanted in Washington D.C. for murder and counterfeiting.

Spur pulled off his jacket, and his tie. He took a stack of clothes he would put on and walked to the bathroom. The door was ajar and inside he saw three steaming buckets of water as well as one that was probably cold.

Spur closed the door and began taking off his shirt. Before he could react, soft woman's hands reached around his chest and helped him undo the buttons. Then he felt her press against his back, her breasts warm, her hot breath on his neck.

"Thought you might need some help with your bath," she said. She slid around until she was in front of him. The white blouse was unbuttoned and pulled out of the dark skirt. Soft white flesh showed through the opening and the blush of a pink areola on one breast.

She grinned up at him. "I'm Tessie, Spur McCoy, and I'd just love to scrub your back."

She watched his face for a moment. The first surprise had been replaced by a smile and she reached up and kissed his cheek.

"I don't give just anybody this kind of special service," Tessie said. "Maybe we better lock the door." She moved away from him, threw the bolt on the bathroom door and when she turned she took off the white blouse.

Her breasts were high, full, with bright red, thumb-sized nipples on discs of pink areolas. Tessie shook her shoulders so her breasts bounced and jiggled.

"I don't want to get my blouse wet while I scrub you," she said. "We better get the water in the tub before it goes cold." She lifted the first bucket and emptied it into the tub, then the other two hot ones. She put her hand in the water and pulled it back quickly. Tessie dumped in half the bucket of cold and smiled.

"Bath time, Spur, now don't be bashful. It may be hard to believe, but I actually have seen a man's good parts all bare and hard!"

"You are serious, aren't you?"

"Hey! I don't show my titties to just anybody." She covered her eyes a moment with a hand. "But you're about the most handsome man I've ever seen. And I don't mind washing backs . . . or fronts for that matter."

She moved up to him and finished undoing his shirt buttons and pulling it off him.

"Yes, lots of black chest hair! I like some hair on a man's broad chest, helps cover up his man titties." She reached in and kissed both the buds on his chest.

"Now, the pants. You gonna wear a gunbelt when you're soaking in the big tub?"

The tub was one of the new ones, almost six feet long, and made of heavy, nickel plated metal, and had four sturdy claw legs.

Tessie pulled off his gunbelt and opened his fly.

"Oh, yes, the good stuff!" she shrilled. She tugged down his pants and then the short underwear and sat back on her heels in surprise. "Lordy, lordy, lordy! Would you look at him!"

Tessie bent quickly, kissed his throbbing erection, then took off his boots and the rest of his clothes and led him to the tub.

"In you go, and save room for me!"

Spur stepped into the tub of hot water and gingerly sat down. As he did, Tessie stripped out of her dark skirt and the drawers she wore that came to her knee. She stood there naked for a minute watching him, then stepped in the tub and sat down in the steaming water facing him.

"Watch out where you put your toes!" she said and they both broke up laughing. They both grabbed wash cloths and bars of soap and sudsed each other seriously. Spur used only his hands to wash her breasts and Tessie rolled her eyes and grabbed through the water at his crotch.

"That does me furious fast that way!" she panted. She pulled Spur down in the tub until she could straddle his crotch, then held the sides of the tub and lowered herself toward him.

"You're gonna have to aim that lance of yours, sweetie!" she said. Spur adjusted and with a groan felt her lower onto his throbbing penis.

"Oh, glory!" Tessie squealed. "I never done it this way before. Just glorious!" She began lifting herself by the sides of the tub and dropping back on his turgid member. A dozen drops and Spur was thrusting upward in the water to meet her. Their union was under the water now and waves threatened to break over the top of the tub on each stroke.

Tessie's face turned red and her breathing was so fast and ragged she sounded like a panting steam engine.

"Do me! Do me!" she rumbled. "Oh, damn! Oh shit! Oh fuck! That is so wonderful! I've never been touched like that inside before. Oh glory! I'm dead and done gone to heaven for sure. No fucking has ever been so marvelous, so great, so fucking wonderful!"

Tessie shrieked then and Spur brought his hand over her mouth to hold down the sound. Her face turned purple as her whole body shook and rattled and vibrated as she kept dropping again and again on Spur's lance. He met her quickened strokes and just before she fell forward on top of him, he reached his own climax and jolted upward until his breath billowed out in raw steam. He thrust her naked form a foot off the bath tub.

Tessie lay against Spur's chest, her legs around his waist and in back of him. For a moment he wondered if she had died or only fainted.

Then Tessie giggled.

"Glory, we done fucked in the bathwater!"

"About the size of it," Spur said. He eased her away from him to a sitting position.

"Going, going . . . gone," Tessie said. "You just deserted me."

"He has a way of coming down to size after an outing," Spur said.

"Otherwise you'd have trouble walking!" Tessie laughed and pulled away from him. She used the cloth and washed him off and then herself and stepped out of the tub and brought the two fluffy towels.

"When I came to your door, you didn't get any ideas about doing me?" she asked.

"Ideas? Most men, from time to time, look at a pretty, sexy girl and wonder what it would be like. But wondering is usually as far as it gets."

"Did you wonder about me?"

"Yes, especially that tightly filled white blouse."

"My best features. I mean every girl's got one between her legs, but nobody can see that. Tits are right up there and if a girl's got them, it's a lot easier."

They began drying themselves with the big towels.

"You like making love, Tessie?"

"Oh, yes! Who doesn't? Girls I know who have done it, like it, unless they got raped the first time or it was bad. Sex is great. Part of the fun of working here. I get first look at the most handsome men who come to town. Once I flirted with this young guy and he didn't give me a glance. So that night I unlocked his door and slipped naked into his bed. When he finally woke up I had him half inside and he couldn't stop. That was a wild one the rest of the night. He couldn't get enough once he got started."

Spur put on his clothes, a brown western plaid shirt and jeans.

"What happens when you get pregnant?"

"Lordy, I worry about that if it happens. I talked to the doc and he said there are ways. I do him now and then, kind of in payment for his services. He told me ways. Like right after the curse is over is the best time."

Tessie put on her drawers and her skirt, then stood there near him bare topped.

"You like my titties?"

Spur stroked each one, then kissed them and she groaned.

"Let's do one more, right here on the floor!"

Spur laughed and stepped to the door with his clothes. "Tessie, maybe later, right now I have to go and get some business done."

"What business you in, McCoy?"

"Business. I'm looking for a small business to buy. Might stay in town."

"Good, let's do this again."

Spur smiled. "Never can tell, Tessie. Just never can tell. Say, you might know a man I need to see, George Slocum."

Tessie laughed. "Why you want to see him, you get the crotch itch or something? I didn't give you nothing. George is the guy I was talking about before. George is the town's only doctor."

3

Spur watched Tessie closely. She was telling the truth. The man he had come to find was the town's only doctor. That would make arresting him ten times as hard. He'd seen whole towns close ranks behind a doctor and lie like Indian squaws to keep the man in town.

Spur opened the bathroom door, carrying his travel weary clothes and smiled. "You asked why I have to see Doc Slocum. Same as the rest of it, just business." He winked. "You take care of those twin beauties, you hear?"

A few moments later McCoy closed his door and dropped the clothes on the bed. Time to start laying his cover story. He combed his hair, trimmed his moustache and shaved fresh, then went down to the first good sized store and went in to talk to the owner.

Before closing time at six p.m., he had canvassed six stores. None of them were for sale, but one couple was willing to listen to a price. By morning every merchant in town would know he was there with the idea of buying out an existing business. Then he would be able to get down to his real work.

He had a quick, uneventful meal at the Aspen Hotel dining room and discovered it was not going to be the best place in town to eat. Upstairs in his room he lit a coal oil lamp, put it on the dresser and lounged on the bed reading a telegram from his boss in Washington D.C.

Spur McCoy was a United States Secret Service Agent, working directly under the command of Gen. William D. Halleck. The general gave the orders for the number one man, William Wood, the director of the agency appointed by President Lincoln and re-appointed by each succeeding president.

Spur opened the telegram he had picked up in Denver and read it again.

McCOY. PROCEED TO JOHNSON CORNERS, COL. LOCATE AND DETAIN ONE GEORGE SLOCUM. SAID TO BE RESIDING THERE UNDER THAT ALIAS. WANTED FOR MURDER AND COUNTERFEITING. MAY BE DANGEROUS. ARREST SLOCUM, TRANS-PORT HIM TO THE FEDERAL COURT-HOUSE IN DENVER FOR ARRAIGNMENT AND TRANSFER TO WASH. D.C. FOR TRIAL. SPECIAL CIRCUMSTANCES: WE HAVE NO HARD INFORMATION ON THIS SUSPECT. WHAT WE KNOW COMES FROM AN INFOR-MANT. INVESTIGATE CAREFULLY BEFORE TAKING ACTION.

REPORT PROGRESS WHEN POSSIBLE,

AND REPORT DISPOSITION WHEN THE CASE IS FINISHED.

The orders had come addressed to Spur McCoy, Investigator, Capital Investigations Inc. at the Denver Overland stage office. His trip here by stage had been difficult, tiring but spectacular visually along the rim of the highest mountains in the nation. Now he stared again at the seemingly contradictory parts of his orders. One said bring Slocum in for trial, the other paragraph said go easy, be careful, this might not be the right man.

The saloon lady might have some information on his man, if he went about it right. Spur changed shirts, put on a pair of town pants and a brown leather vest, string tie and his new brown low crowned hat and headed for Evangeline's.

There was still a half hour to sundown when Spur came out the hotel door. The same redheaded boy who had carried his bag to the hostelry, sat on the steps. When he saw Spur, he jumped and walked toward him.

He came slowly at first, then when Spur glanced at him he pushed out his chin and strode ahead with determination. When he was six feet away, the youngster's steps slowed, his face worked and he frowned for a minute.

Then he blurted out what must have been thought out and rehearsed.

"Mr. McCoy. Are you really a United States Marshal the way folks say you are?"

"Well, now, Willard, who says that?"

"The desk clerk. He said it. You are a lawman, ain't you, since you got a tied down gun and all?"

Spur smiled and shook his head. "Sorry, Willard,

I'm not a U.S. Marshal. I'm a businessman, here to look for a good opportunity. You know of any?"

Willard frowned and took half a step back. "Well, no I don't, Mr. McCoy, but I'm just a kid."

"A kid? Out West kids grow up in a rush. How old are you, fourteen?"

"Most fifteen and a half, Mr. McCoy."

"See what I mean? Western boys get to be men at near sixteen."

"But I'm from Chicago. Only been here in Johnson Corners for a month now."

"Don't matter, Willard. You're almost a man. Now, I got one more business call. Oh, your dad run the hotel?"

"No, sir, Mr. McCoy. My father's dead. That's my uncle who owns the Aspen."

"Oh, I'm sorry. Well, Willard, I have one more business call to make."

Spur continued across the boardwalk and into the dust of the street.

Willard watched him go. He figured Spur McCoy was at least six feet and two inches, maybe two hundred pounds. And his gun was tied low on his right thigh. It reminded him of the story about Forty-Four Jones in *Lonesome Rider on Dead Sage Mesa*.

Now there was a man! But Spur McCoy looked just as good. Tall, and lean with powerful shoulders and that deadly six-gun.

Willard walked along the street for half a block before he turned down to go to his uncle's house. He was reliving the shootout at the south range water trough from the current Western dime novel he was reading, when he went past the alley in back of the Main Street businesses.

It was getting dusk now. Half light could affect the way a person saw things, but Willard knew for certain that there were two men on horses in the alley. That was a bit strange. Most men hitched their nags at the front of the store. There were only a few houses that backed up to the alley from the other street.

Willard faded behind an aspen tree growing near the alley and waited, watching in the long dark strip. He knew there were two desperados in there waiting to rob some saloon! Or maybe planning a bank robbery! Yes. The Concord State Bank was on that block!

Willard could almost see the men.

Then he did, as two men came walking their horses from the alley directly toward him. He froze in his boots.

The men came from the alley and turned toward Main Street, failing to see him, but Willard had a good look at them.

The first one led a gray with a saddle and saddle bags and a Remington Repeating rifle in the boot. He had a bedroll and another sack for grub tied in back of his saddle. The pair had just come in from a long ride.

The first man was in his twenties, Willard guessed. He was clean shaven except for a moustache that drooped around his mouth and gave off twisted strands two inches longer that had been waxed and nurtured. He wore one of those long coats that outlaws used to hide their shotguns under!

The second man led a black. He had a dark crushed hat with almost no crown, a swarthy face under a full beard. He wore what almost looked like a Rebel officer's coat and he walked as if his feet hurt. He was much taller than the first man.

Willard turned and watched the pair go past the lamplight coming out the saloon on the corner. Both were desperados, he knew! Should he run back and try to find Mr. McCoy and tell him that bank robbers were in town?

Willard turned and shuffled slowly toward his uncle's house. No, he couldn't tell Mr. McCoy, although Willard was sure the man was a peace officer of some kind. The tied low gun proved that. Only lawmen and outlaws wore guns that way, and it was plain that Mr. McCoy was no outlaw, gambler, gunsharp or robber.

The first week Willard had been in town he thought for sure he saw a killing take place and he'd run to the sheriff and led him back to the alley, but it was only two drunks shooting at whiskey bottles. The sheriff rawhided him good about that.

Willard's head sagged as he came closer to his uncle's house. Maybe he wasn't cut out to be a Westerner. Maybe all this reading he was doing had turned his head around.

Willard scowled at a mulberry tree. Danged if he was going to believe that! No sir! He could be just as good at being a Westerner as anybody. He'd learn to ride and rope and even shoot a gun when he could afford to buy one!

He'd have his own horse and saddle and even spurs!

Willard walked into his uncle's house with his head high and more sure now than ever that he *had* seen two bank robbers slipping into town. Maybe he could find Mr. McCoy and at least report the chance that the men were robbers.

Yes, that sounded like a good plan. It was the way young Billy Roberts handled that problem he had in *Death Rides The Range.* It worked for Billy.

Willard let the screen door slam as he entered the house. It was June and plenty warm even in the evening.

"Willard! When on earth are you going to learn not to let that screen door slam? You know how it hurts my head. Sometimes I think you do it just to aggravate me."

The voice came from the parlor, where Willard knew his Aunt Zelda sat in the rocker fanning herself and nipping at a bottle of wine. She said it was medicine for her bad back, but he knew better.

"Sorry, Aunt Zelda, I forgot. I'll go right up to my room."

"You have supper, boy?"

"Yes, ma'am. Uncle Ron and I ate in his office."

"Well, all right. See to it that you don't read those horrid dime novels all night. I threw that one away, but you probably have more. Don't bother about me, I'll be fine."

Willard heard the start of the slurred words. She would be unconscious in the rocker by the time his uncle Ron came home. They certainly were a strange couple. Not at all like his parents had been.

Willard went up the steps quietly, so Aunt Zelda would not hear and call to him again. He was still wondering about the two bank robbers. Should he tell Mr. McCoy about them or not? He would have to figure it out by the time he went to work tomorrow morning. What should he do?

McCoy had worn his six-gun out of habit as he left the hotel, now he took off the leather and handed it to the big man inside the front door of Evangeline's. The saloon was not only kept clean, it was well appointed, with decorations and even oil paintings on the walls that Spur was sure most of the men never noticed, let alone appreciated.

The place was almost full. All of the poker tables were busy, with men waiting for empty chairs. A game of black-jack thrived at the end of the bar. Two men with white aprons around their waists hoisted beers behind the bar and poured an occasional whiskey.

Evangeline was not to be seen.

Spur ordered a beer and watched the crowd. No women, not even dance hall girls. Evangeline ran a pristine clean operation. She probably didn't even cut the whiskey.

He turned to look down the bar the other way and found her standing beside him.

Evangeline was not a dazzler, rather she was a presence, a picture of everyone's mother, daughter, sweetheart. Her soft brown hair swirled around her shoulders and for a moment her dimples popped in.

"I wondered when you were coming back for our talk," she said softly with just a hint of concern in her gentle voice.

"Would now be a good time?"

She smiled and dimpled. They held in place. Her delicate features softened, and she nodded.

"I know the management and have a reserved table." She turned and led the way through the poker players and wheels of chance to a raised platform near the back of the saloon. On the two foot high mesa sat a carved black walnut table with a snow white cloth on it decorated with lace. A single white candle sat on top near a slender vase that held one red rose.

Fragile leaded glass stemware for two rested on the linen cloth. They stepped up and he held the chair for her. It was a fine dining room chair to match the small table. He sat across from her and as he sat down, one of the barmen brought a bottle of champagne and opened it. He set the bottle beside Spur and left.

"Now we talk," Evangeline said. "To answer your question, I do have a last name, but few here remember it. I came to town almost seven years ago with my husband Frederick. He was a gambler, and a good one. He won this saloon in a game of five card stud.

"We fixed it up, cleaned it up, renamed it, and made it into the best gaming house in town. Then one night Frederick took on the Pascal brothers in a poker game. He beat them both, and as he scraped in the last pot, one of the brothers shot him with a hideout derringer. That's why I don't allow any guns in my saloon."

She watched him as he poured the champagne. It was imported from France.

"Now, who is Spur McCoy, and why are you here?"

Spur chuckled and lit a thin black cheroot. He sucked in a mouthful of smoke and then blew it out slowly.

"You are one of the most direct people I've ever met. Which is surprising but not unpleasant. I'm a businessman. My father has several stores in New York City and does importing, but I wanted something a little less hectic, where there was less pressure. So I came west."

Evangeline swirled the champagne in her tall stem glass and then sipped at it. "Then it is true, you are here looking for a business to buy."

"Or I might start one if nothing touches my fancy." He smiled at her and stared around. "I must say that I am totally amazed at this place. You know the reputations most saloons have, the rougher, the more fights the better. A killing a day keeps the whiskey flowing. You take a different approach."

"And it works. After my husband died I swore I would never let guns in here again. I sent the three fancy ladies packing and did a lot of construction and redecorating and put in absolutely honest gaming tables. If I catch one of my dealers or operators cheating, I tar and feather him and run him down Main Street."

"It seems to work. Are you filled this way every night?"

"Most of the time. If it thins out, I'll bring in a woman singer. They come out of Denver now and then. A good one can boost profits tremendously. But right now I don't need that kind of trouble."

Voices raised two tables over. Spur looked around as two men leaped to their feet glaring at each other. Spur never saw her move but the next moment tiny Evangeline stood between the two big cowboys and in her hand was a short whip with burs in the tails of the nine strips of leather.

She cracked the whip on the top of the table sending chips and paper money flying. The two angry men stared at each other a moment. Then both stopped yelling and looked at the small woman between them.

Evangeline said something that Spur couldn't hear and the men shot angry glances toward each other. She talked to them a moment longer and slowly both men sat down at the table, the chips were arranged, and Evangeline stood beside the table as the rest of the hand was played out. There was no sign of the whip.

When a new hand had been dealt, the proprietor came back to the elevated table. Spur poured fresh champagne for her after he seated her at the fancy table.

"You should be a diplomat. We could use you in Washington, or maybe France."

"I don't like France, it's too damp and wintry. At least here we have three months of warm weather."

"Were you a diplomat in France?"

"No, my father was. They don't let ten year olds be ambassadors." She paused, sipped at the wine, then her darting black eyes looked up at him. "Have you found a business you like here yet?"

"Just starting. I did see a sign that I must have read wrong. Did it say Doctor Slocum? Could that be George Slocum?"

"Yes. Doc Slocum. Do you know him from somewhere else?"

"Must be a different man. One I knew wasn't even a doctor. Has he been in town long?"

"He was here when we came through and decided to stay. He's good with the bedside manner, but he says he doesn't do operations any more."

"Must be a different man. I don't want to buy a doctor's practice anyway. Do you know of any businesses in town that are for sale, and what's the best way to make a living in this small community?"

As he said it Spur reminded himself to get some local greenbacks to check. Once a counterfeiter, always a counterfeiter. It was a tough habit to break. He'd check some local bills to see if there was any funny money around.

4

Evangeline took out a deck of cards from a drawer in the table and began shuffling. She knew how to handle cards.

"Want to play some twenty-one while we talk?" she asked.

"The way you work those cards?"

"No money to change hands." She dealt a hand of twenty-one and beat him with two cards. She won five out of the first six hands.

"See what I mean, you're a real gambler, Evangeline, I'm just a beginner."

She smiled and her dark eyes tracked him. "For now. You could be setting me up for later. What kind of a business are you looking for, retail, service, banking? We could do with a better bank in town, that's for sure. Bart Concord knows almost nothing about banking. I don't see how he makes a go of it. But he does."

"I'm not the banker type. How's the livery stable?"

"First rate, and room for just one. Be hard to compete with Josh."

"Could I get some change, Evangeline? I may try the poker tables later and I hate to start a game with double gold eagles." He put two on the table. They were so new that the saw tooth edges were still sharp and clean. No one had taken a dozen of them, put them in a leather pouch and rattled them together to mint himself a half ounce of gold as the edges wore down.

Evangeline motioned to one of the house men watching play and he gave Spur ten ones and six fives.

"Now I'll be ready to play if I decide to," he said. Spur spun his hat on his finger, then eased it back on his head. Most of the men in the saloon wore their hats, cowboy fashion.

"Miss Evangeline. Would it be proper for me to ask you out to dinner tomorrow evening?"

"Might be, might not be. But it really doesn't matter. I don't go out much. Some of the snootier women in town think that I'm a fallen woman, a harbinger of doom, and the handmaiden of the devil. Although they don't really believe that I'm a maiden running an establishment such as I do."

Spur chuckled. "Sounds like you have a batch of God-fearing women in this town."

"Deed we do, Mr. McCoy, and two fire and brimstone preachers who do their best to scare each other and their respective congregations every Sunday morning and every Wednesday night at prayer meeting."

"Just so they won't be totally disappointed, I'll

play one hand of serial number poker with you on one of those fives you have. Deal?" Evangeline smiled sweetly and dimpled both cheeks.

"Deal. And after that?"

"Next I have some business things to do in my office. I am running an establishment here. I have twelve employees and bills to pay and items to order. You know about a business."

"Do you need any help?"

She started to smile, then her face shifted into a stern mask to cover her feelings.

"Mr. McCoy. I may run a saloon, but I am not a saloon girl. I don't go to bed with men for money. I don't invite men up to my bedroom on a whim. I was happily married for six years, and until I find a man I love and want to marry, I'll smile a lot and dress conservatively and make every effort to keep my knees pressed firmly together and my dress buttoned up to my chin."

"You've said that before."

"Twice a day for the past five years. More times on Saturdays." She looked up quickly. "Once in a great while I don't really mean it. Sometimes it gets lonely even in a crowded saloon."

"Lonely I know something about," Spur said. He cleared his throat and tried to change the mood. "Now, you said something about a hand of five dollar bill serial poker. Do I get to pick one my six?"

Evangeline smiled, the somber mood broken. "Not a chance. Draw one out from the green side so you can't see the numbers. I'll do the same." She opened the drawer, leafed through a stack of bills until she came to the green side of some fives and pulled one out.

Spur picked one of his fives and turned it over to

the side where the serial number was. It read: 86617165. He had sixes over aces, a full house.

He looked at her and saw only a slightly serious poker face that told him nothing. "I'd really like to bet on the hand, but all we bet is the bill, right?"

"True," she said. "This would have been a great hand to play with. Would you believe I have a full house?"

Spur laughed. "That's what I've got. Can you top three sixes?"

"Can't top it but I can match it, and then throw in a pair of aces! No way you can beat that hand!"

Spur felt a shot of energy surge through his body. That was the exact serial number of the five dollar bill he held. That meant trouble. He tried to cover his concern.

"I'll be damned! That's the same number I have. Let's see."

They compared the bills on the table. They were exactly the same.

"How can that happen?" Evangeline asked.

"Doesn't happen often. Once in a while a printer forgets to move up the counter on the press. Whammo . . . two with the same number. Which means collectors will pay twice the face value for such a bill. I'll give you ten dollars for that fiver."

"Really? Best deal I've made all day. You'll probably sell it for ten times its face value, but I doubled my money." Spur gave her a ten dollar bill from his wallet and tucked the twin fives safely away.

Things were getting more interesting. Slocum must be dispensing medicine and counterfeits from the same location. Spur had asked for the five dollar bills because they were the denomination most widely counterfeited. Twenty dollar bills were too hard to pass. Lots of merchants hesitated to take them.

But a fiver was more standard. Lots of men worked for a week for five dollars. Counterfeiters found they could buy something for twenty cents and pass a fake five and get back four dollars and eighty cents in clear profit. A good buyer could pass a hundred fivers in a small town in a day and be on his horse heading for the next town away from the telegraph the next morning before anyone discovered the funny money.

Evangeline was laughing. "Hey, you were a million miles away there for a minute. You want to try one more game?"

Spur grinned but shook his head. "I think I better quit while I'm only out ten dollars. Truth to tell, I'm about asleep on my feet. That stage ride was wild, and sleep is one item I'm short on. If you don't mind, I better try to find my way back to the hotel."

"I could send a guide with you," she said.

He looked at her quickly and saw she was laughing at him. Suddenly she leaned in and kissed his cheek.

"There, that's to help scare away the lonelies. Stop by tomorrow and we'll talk again. I grew up just upstate from New York City a ways. We can do some old home talking." She stood and was gone before he could get to his feet.

Spur had started to rise, now he dropped back in the chair and checked the remaining five dollar bills he carried. Three more of them had the same serial number, counterfeit. The town must be flooded with them.

Tomorrow he would visit Doc Slocum about the

cough he had nights and mornings. Tomorrow he might also wrap up this case and get headed out for Denver.

He sipped the champagne in his glass. It wasn't his favorite drink. He picked up the bottle, stepped down from the platform and set the champagne on a table where four men were engaged in some serious beer drinking.

They looked up and then three of them grabbed the bottle at the same time.

At the bar, Spur caught the attention of the apron. "How much for the champagne?"

The bartender shook his head. "That's Miss Evangeline's table, sir. Never any charges there."

Spur nodded and walked out of the saloon and gaming house, wondering just now he could trip up Doc George Slocum into giving away where his printing press was. That was vital, he had to have the press and the plates for a conviction.

Outside, Spur turned down Main Street, walked two blocks to where the stores thinned out an occasional house showed. The third one on the left was Doc Slocum's office. The lower floors were dark, but there were lights on in the top floor. Office? Home?

Maybe an office, home and printing plant. Spur hoped so. He had no desire to spend any more time in this little town than he needed to.

Spur headed back for his hotel room. He guessed the hot-blooded maid would be through with her duties for the day. A grin spread across his face. She had been delightful, such a healthy young thing and so eager. If he stayed in town more than three or four days, he made a small bet with himself that she would be back to see him.

He thought of the teenager, the redheaded boy

who thought Spur was a lawman. The kid was closer to being right than Spur wanted him to know. Spur remembered his own youth. Growing up was harder than adults remembered.

Especially it would be tough for Willard, moving here from Chicago, leaving all his friends, and coming into a rougher, more action oriented society. Spur wished Willard all the good fortune he could get.

Willard sat in his room at the small desk and finished the last chapter of the Western dime novel. Big John had been beaten in a shootout and the ranch was saved for the widow Beluchi. She asked Lew Hardison in for supper. Lew had killed Big John and saved the ranch for her. Willard knew that Lew was not going to be out on the trail that night. It was all very straightlaced in the book, but Willard knew what would happen.

"Blow out that lamp, Willard!" a shrill voice came up the stairs. "Past your bedtime."

"Yes, Aunt Zelda," Willard said. His mother had been dead almost five years. He missed her. She hadn't been as cranky and mean as Aunt Zelda. She acted like she wished he had never come. Willard never mentioned the twenty dollars a month his aunt and uncle got from his estate, but he wondered what they did with it. Hardly any of it was spent on him.

He slid onto the bed. He wouldn't need covers for some time yet. The afternoon heat was still in the attic and seeping down into his room.

Willard kicked out of the bottom half of his long johns and lay there naked. For just a moment his imagination flashed back to the end of the dime novel story. He wondered what that cowboy was going to do with the widow. He had ideas. He'd heard about it, about a man and a woman doing it.

His hand brushed his crotch.

Oh, yes! Willard had an instant erection, hot blood pounding and pounding. That made him remember Chicago. One week he had walked around school all day with a hard-on. It just wouldn't go away.

That was the week Martha had kissed him behind the band shell in the park. She had kissed him and then let him touch her breasts through her dress.

But just for a moment. Then she ran back with the three girls she was with and wouldn't even look at him. He had made a mess in his pants right there before he could move.

It had felt so good!

Willard's hand closed around his hard pole and he knew it would feel good again.

But he shouldn't do it.

Why not? Who said? He'd seen guys have a contest once and neither of them grew hair on the palm of his hand. That wasn't true.

He stroked it once, then again. He really shouldn't. He remembered Martha and how soft she had been. Were all girls tits that soft? Willard let his imagination take over then. Martha was there and they kissed again, then she let him touch her and he pulled her dress open and pushed his hands inside.

Her breasts were so warm! So soft and warm. She had shivered and said she liked the way he felt of her. She put her hand down lower and pressed it against his bulge. Then she opened his pants and tried to pull him out.

Willard helped. Then her breasts were bare and

she told him to kiss them. He did and his hips bucked and she shivered and shook and he pushed her down, his hips pounding against hers even though she still had her dress on.

Willard heard his aunt and uncle walk by in the hall and his hips stilled. When they were in their bedroom he turned over and rammed his erection against the sheet. He was with Martha again and she was helping him and spreading her legs, and then . . . then . . .

He didn't have to imagine any more. His hips bucked spasmodically six, seven, eight times and he shot his cream all over the sheet.

Willard panted and gasped for breath. Someday he wouldn't have to imagine what it was like. He would have a girl and they would do it and it would be wonderful!

He found an old handkerchief and wiped up the sticky goo from the blanket and threw the handkerchief in the back of the closet.

Then he lay on his bed thinking about Martha, and about the lawman he had met today. He was positive that Mr. McCoy was a lawman. But he shivered when he remembered the two desperados who had sneaked into town. They were going to rob the bank, he was sure of it!

Tomorrow he would get up his courage to go tell the sheriff. He thought about that for a minute. No, the sheriff wouldn't believe him. He'd see Mr. McCoy. Willard was sure that Mr. McCoy would be interested in bank robbers.

Every lawman was duty bound to protect the banks and to stop any bank robbers they saw.

Willard nodded and wavered toward sleep. He thought of Martha, and for just a moment she was

naked. Standing in front of him without a thing on!
Then she smiled and faded away, and Willard
Kleaner slept.

5

Spur McCoy slept in the next morning. He woke at his usual 5:30, turned over and went back to sleep. He was up at eight o'clock, dressed, shaved, had a leisurely breakfast at a small cafe and arrived at Doc Slocum's office promptly at nine.

He worked up a small cough and would keep clearing his throat. There was no one else in the doctor's office when he walked in and a small bell rang over the door.

A moment later a man about five-six came through the connecting door. He wore a white shirt and red suspenders. Dr. Slocum was slightly on the chubby side, with pink cheeks and alert brown eyes. He had a full head of dark hair.

Spur heard chairs scraping and small feet running upstairs. So Slocum had become a family man.

"Are you Doc Slocum?" Spur asked.

"Guess you're out of luck, that's me. You look healthy enough."

"Wish I was, Doc. Got this cough that's been hanging on. You help me lick it, Doc?"

The brown eyes sparkled. "Toughest medical problem I had all day. I got a jug of cherry cough syrup back here that'll knock out any cough. Don't say for sure, but I'd guess it's got some laudanum in it. I used some once and for a couple of hours I didn't *care* if I had a cough or not!"

Spur coughed again and Slocum waved and went into the back room. Spur looked on the office walls, but saw no framed medical diplomas.

Lots of the far West doctors didn't have complete medical training. The pioneers in the West took what doctoring they could get and were glad for it.

The doctor came through the door carrying a small bottle that had a white label.

"Two teaspoons full of this as needed," Doctor Slocum said. "Any other problems?"

"Just a small brown haired lady that I'm going to have to handle myself Doc. How much do I owe you?"

"Fifty cents'll be fine. I don't get a lot of cash money in payment these days. Lot of chickens and loaves of bread and a quart of milk a day. That comes in handy. You be from the east, Boston, I'd say by the twang."

"Went to school a while there," Spur said. "Thought I'd lost it. You sound more from Virginia or maybe Washington, D.C."

Slocum looked up at Spur but saw that the big man was only making conversation.

Spur handed the doctor one of the fake five dollars bills. The medic stared at it and shook his head.

"Sorry, don't have change enough. Just owe me like everybody else in town does."

Spur put the fiver back in his wallet and fumbled in his pocket until he found two 1875 minted twenty cent pieces and a dime. He handed them to the doctor.

"Think these new twenty cent pieces will last?" Spur asked. "I keep getting them mixed up with the quarters."

"Won't last. A damn nuisance. Won't last more than two or three years. Then the collectors can make money on them. My advice, keep all you can find and give them to your grandchildren. Be able to put themselves through school with them."

Spur tossed the bottle of cough syrup in the air and caught it. "Thanks, Doc. I just got into town. You know of any businesses for sale? I'm looking for something."

"Always one or two available. Just so you aren't another doctor."

"Not a chance. Thanks, Doc." Spur went out the front door and walked quickly down the street. Slocum had not taken the five dollar bill. Had he guessed it was fake, or was he simply out of change? He did know about coins, but everybody had something to say about the new twenty cent piece.

Spur hesitated about taking the local sheriff into his confidence about the fake money. He didn't want to start a panic. The quieter this could be kept the better. If he could scoop up Slocum, his plates and press in one bunch, then he would go to the banker and they could begin gathering up the bad bills without anyone the wiser.

To lay a foundation for that move, Spur walked toward the bank. It was nearly ready to open. He toured two more stores and talked to their owners. Neither wanted to sell. They knew about him though, and were pleased that he had asked them. Always nice to be asked to dance even though you have a broken leg.

At the bank he asked to see the manager. The man turned out to be Barton Concord. He was a tall man, and slender, with a thin face, protruding eyebrows and deep set eyes that reminded Spur of Abe Lincoln. Concord wore a banker black three piece suit with a stiff collar and carefully tied cravat.

He was cautious, friendly, reserved. He seemed to be the form they used to turn out bankers these days.

"Mr. Concord. My name is Spur McCoy and I'm looking for a business property here in town, as I'm sure you have heard by now."

Concord smiled. It was not a banker's smile. "Yes, Mr. McCoy, news travels fast in a small town. Everyone knows by now. By the time Hans Walker gets his paper out you'll be old news."

"That's one of the reasons I want to settle in a small town. Everyone knows everyone else." Spur chuckled. "Of course that means you have to be a bit careful with your public conduct." Both men laughed.

"Well, Mr. Concord. Being a merchant I handle a lot of paper money, and I found a bill in my change that didn't look exactly right. Would you take a look at it for me?"

Spur handed the banker one of the counterfeit fivers and sat back. Concord turned it over, rubbed it between his fingers and crumpled it up. When he straightened it out on his desk top he nodded, then handed it back to Spur.

"Far as I can see it's a one hundred percent guaranteed U.S. banknote. Looks genuine to me. Course

I have been fooled once or twice, but I'm pretty good at bills."

"Good. That was my one concern. I certainly wouldn't want to start a business in a town where there was bad currency. No, no I won't start any rumors. That's why I came to see you first. It has been a year or so since I had my own store, so my fingers have lost the touch. I used to be able to tell by the quality of the paper when I got a bad bill. Didn't happen often, of course."

"Mr. McCoy, when you locate the right business and make a purchase, I hope you'll do your banking here with us. We're not the oldest bank in the county, but we think the most friendly. We could even arrange some kind of a loan or a mortgage on property, that sort of thing to get you started."

"Thanks, but I have more than adequate financing. Well, thanks, Mr. Concord. I have some more ground work to do. You'll be hearing from me in due course."

They shook hands and Spur left the solid brick building. He was puzzled. On close comparison with a genuine bank note there was no doubt that the bill was a counterfeit, even without the proof of the serial numbers.

Concord must not know his business. Of course he didn't handle the actual bills much on a day to day basis from the looks of the bank. He had three tellers and a bookkeeper. Adequate. He'd put Bart Concord in the uncertain file for now.

Spur stopped at two more stores, talked to the owners, hinted at what he might offer for one store and was turned down. He had to keep his offers low enough to discourage a sale.

Where would Slocum do his printing? Newspaper.

Every newspaper in the west had a small job press or two for stationery and business forms. Spur found the newspaper office where the *Johnson County Voice* was created once a week.

As soon as he opened the door, a familiar and slightly nostagic odor assaulted him. It was a combination of the smell of newsprint and all kinds of paper goods, mixed with the slightly acrid odor of printer's ink and the cleaning fluids they used on the presses. Every newspaper in the country had that same smell.

There was a chest high counter across the front of the office. Behind it a man sat at a desk stacked with papers and galley proofs. Beside him at a second desk a woman looked up, rose and came to the counter.

"Good morning. You must be Spur McCoy, the gentleman in town looking for a business to buy. How about a newspaper? I've been trying to get Hans out of here for three years now."

"This establishment is not for sale," the man at the desk said without turning around. His pencil made a correction on a galley proof and he pushed it over to the next desk the woman had just left.

She smiled at Spur. He smiled back. She was attractive, in her late twenties and not yet ground down by hard work.

"Now that we have that out of the way, what can we do for you, Mr. McCoy?"

"I find I need some cards, twenty-five, maybe fifty, with my hotel address on them. You do commercial printing?"

The man stood quickly and turned.

"Damn right! That's how we stay alive in this god-forsaken hole. Certainly not be selling advertising in the *Voice.*" He pulled out a type sample book and began showing Spur the typefaces.

"Mr. Walker I would guess," Spur said.

The man grunted, held out his hand. "Yes, and you're McCoy. We can give you fifty cards by four o'clock this afternoon. Just pick out the type style you like."

"Mr. Walker, you're far more skilled at those matters than I am. Make me a card you'd be proud to give out yourself. I'll put down my name, the Aspen Hotel and say, businessman. That will do it."

Hans wrote down what Spur told him, then he took another sheet of newsprint. "You looking for any particular type of business, Mr. McCoy?"

"No, but in the retail field I think."

"Been looking long, in other towns as well?"

"Yes, I'm working west. Denver will be my next stop I think. But I'd rather be out here."

The interview went on for another five minutes. Spur said nothing about his real purpose for being in town. He asked how much the printing would be and the man gave him a price without any figuring.

"Three dollars."

Spur handed him one of the counterfeit bills and Walker took it without hesitation. He didn't even examine it as he put it in a small money box under the counter and handed Spur two singles.

"Thank you, I'll be back at four." Spur tipped his hat to the woman and walked out. He had been able to see in the back room of the newspaper plant. It had a sheet fed press as well as two smaller job presses, platen type. Either one was good enough to print the currency. Another spot to watch.

Spur moved slowly down the street to the Moon's General Store where he spotted four captain's chairs next to the outside wall. Two men sat in them. They were old men watching the world sail by now instead of doing the rowing.

Spur eased into one of the vacant chairs and tipped it back against the building. The sun came down warm on his face. He slid his hat down over his eyes so it shaded them, but left him a small area of vision.

For the next hour he sat there, watching Main Street, checking every now and then the front door of Dr. George Slocum. He had seen three women go in, and one man, then two kids and their mother. The doctor did not go out for a noon time dinner. He probably ate upstairs with his family when the office emptied.

Spur wasn't sure if he were really expecting the doctor to leave in the middle of the day, or if he just liked sitting there in the sun.

This was the craziest assignment he'd ever had. His orders were to go get a guy who might not be the man the Service was hunting after all. Bring him back to Denver, but first be sure he was the right man.

It certainly didn't make it any easier. In five minutes he was going to get up and take the next step in his investigation, whatever that was. Maybe Evangeline. She probably knew a little about almost everyone in town, and the habits of some of the men better than most. Yes, in just five minutes he would have another talk with Evangeline.

Willard Kleaner walked down Third Street toward Main. He looked again. Nope, no hair grew in the palms of his hands. He thought about the night before and grinned. Martha had looked so great all naked that way, but the picture had faded out too quickly.

Just thinking about the vision started action at his crotch and he deliberately moved his mind to something else. The robbers! He had decided last night that he was going to tell Mr. McCoy about them. How did he find the lawman?

He was half way to Main when he saw a lone rider coming in from the Denver trail. The man was slouching in the saddle, a sure sign that he had been on a long ride. He had a dirty bandage around his left arm, and as he came closer, Willard could see a patch over one eye held in place by a black band around his cheek and over his forehead.

Willard turned up an alley and crept back to watch the man pass. The desperado had hired killer written all over him. On his right thigh a hogleg was tied low, the way killers did it. A rifle rested in the saddle boot. No bedroll, no grub sack. The man was traveling light and fast, the way Kirk Dawson did in *Killer on the Run.*

The man was a vicious desperado alright! Willard followed him down the street well back, and when he turned right on Main, Willard was sure about him. That was where most of the saloons were. The first thing a killer did when he was running from a dastardly deed was to get drunk.

Willard came around the small saloon at the juncture of Main and Third, just in time to see the killer get off his horse and limp heavily as he went into the Three Aces Saloon. A morning drinker, a limp from long days in the saddle, and a tied down gun. Not even counting the eye patch the man had labeled himself a desperate killer of the worst kind.

Willard stood there pondering his moves. He could go directly to the sheriff. But that might not work. He could hire one of the ten year old's hanging around Main Street to take a note to the sheriff.

Or he could try to find Spur McCoy. Willard decided on the latter plan and walked down Main Street toward the hotel. He had five minutes before he had to be to work at the Aspen. This was more important anyway. A killer in town should not be tolerated. He had to be routed or captured quickly before his evil ways would spread.

Willard stopped as he passed the hardware. There in front of the General Store sat Spur McCoy. Willard recognized him by the string of silver pesos serving as a headband around his hat.

Now all he had to do was go up and talk. Willard suddenly felt that his hands had no connection whatsoever with the rest of his body. He didn't know where to put them. They hung like dead appendages on the end of his long arms.

For a moment he wasn't sure if he could walk. Would he have to think of every motion, tell his legs how to walk?

Willard turned and stared into the hardware. Maybe he shouldn't bother the lawman. He must be in town on a highly secret and important case. The killer might be running away from a murder like the guy in the novel was. Of course the killer in the story really didn't do it, he had been framed.

But this guy, with the wounded arm, the limp and the patch over one eye . . . there was no doubt about him being a killer.

Willard set his jaw firmly. Mr. McCoy said that in the West fifteen and a half was almost a man. He had *to act like a man!* He took the first step and then the next, gaining confidence with each one as he marched straight for Spur McCoy sitting leaned back against the General Store.

6

Willard Kleaner stopped abruptly in front of Spur McCoy's chair where he had tipped it back in front of Moon's General Store. Willard was shaking now, he was on the delicate point of turning to run when Spur pushed his hat back on his head and grinned.

"Willard, good morning. You look all fired up and full of purpose this morning. What's on your mind?"

"There . . . there was a man . . ." He tried to go on, couldn't and turned.

"Willard, just relax and take a deep breath or two," Spur said standing beside the boy. "Easy, relax a minute. You have nothing to be worried about. Now where did you see this man?"

Willard wiped sweat off his forehead. His hand still shook. He pushed both hands into his pockets.

"The man was on Third, coming into town."

"Yes. Why did you notice him, Willard?"

"He looked sneaky, and mean. He had a rifle and a pistol tied low on his thigh and . . . and he had a black patch over one eye. I'm sure he's a killer running away from some foul murder!" At last he got warmed up and had raced through the last sentence.

"This man rode into town?"

"Sure did. Went into the Three Aces Saloon. He even had a bloody bandage on his left arm. All bloody!"

"You think I should go down and see if he's an outlaw?" Spur asked.

Willard nodded. "Yes."

"Fine, Willard. I'll drop down that way. Are you going to be late getting to your job?"

Willard lifted his brows, turned and ran toward the Aspen Hotel. Spur adjusted his hat, put it back on his head exactly right, and walked toward the sign of the saloon Willard had mentioned.

For an Eastern boy, Willard had a good eye for detail. Inside the Three Aces Saloon, Spur bought a cold beer and saw the man Willard had mentioned. He was at the end of the bar talking with a man wearing a dark gray town suit and string tie over a white shirt.

When the men parted a little, Spur saw a sheriff's star on the town man. Spur motioned to the barkeep.

"Who's the Jasper talking to the sheriff?"

The bar man shrugged, then laughed. "Hell, that's the sheriff's top deputy without his badge. Looks like he was in a real showdown with somebody. I better give him a free beer. You want another one?"

Spur declined, finished the one he had and went out to the boardwalk.

Willard stood near the front steps to the Aspen

Hotel as Spur came striding up.

"The joke is on us," Spur said.

Willard looked up, anxious.

"Turns out the man you saw coming into town was a lawman himself, just back from a tough fight with a bunch of outlaws. He's one of the sheriff's deputies."

"Oh." Willard said. "Guess I was wrong. Thanks . . . Mr. McCoy. I'll be more careful next time."

"Willard, nothing hurt. You see somebody you think might be doing wrong, it's your duty to report it to the sheriff, or to me if I'm around. Now, you best be getting yourself inside before your uncle sends the sheriff out looking for you!"

Willard grinned. "Yeah. I guess so. Thanks . . . Mr. McCoy." He ran up the steps.

Spur wished his problem could be solved so simply. He remembered where he was going when he first saw Willard. His supply of .45 rounds was getting low, he needed some more. Spur walked across the street and down to the Johnson Mercantile. It was one of the smaller stores, but Spur figured they would have pistol rounds.

Windows on the boardwalk showed off displays of household items, as well as bolts of cloth and sheves of hand tools. Inside it was cool and dim. He paused a moment to adjust his eyes, then saw a well arranged display of counters and islands filled with merchandise. It reminded him of some of his father's stores in New York.

"Yes, may I help you?" a strong, woman's voice sounded from near the back of the store. Spur moved that way and soon saw a tall, slender woman standing behind a small counter.

"Morning, ma'am. I'm looking for some .45 rounds, Remingtons if you have them."

"Yes, we have them, over here."

Now he could see her better. She had long black hair that flowed over her shoulders and down her back. It framed a thin face with high cheek bones and from a quick look, he thought green eyes. She walked like a dancer going across a stage.

A smile flashed across her round, pert face.

"Hear you're in town to buy out a business. This one is for sale."

"Interesting," he said following her to a case near the far wall where an assortment of handguns were displayed and behind them rifles and shotguns in a wall rack. "How much are you asking for the business and the stock?"

"I own the building, too. I need seven thousand five hundred for the whole thing." She stopped and put one hand on her hip in a defiant pose, as if she were challenging him to try to bluff her down.

"Interesting. I'm not sure what I want to buy yet. I'll take two boxes of the .45's, please."

She pushed the rounds across the counter to him, took his money and gave him change. Then her whole attitude seemed to change. Her smile was warmer, her arms were not defiantly posed. He thought she held herself so her breasts pressed tighter against her dress.

"Could I show you around? We have a good sized storage room in back for downstock, and there's a rear delivery door on the alley. Yes! Let me lock the front door and I'll give you a guided tour. I haven't thought too much about selling but I know I should."

She walked quickly to the front, snapped a night lock and put a sign up that said "Closed, Be Back Soon."

Back at the counter she waved at the stock. "I

have a good general merchandise variety. I try to keep up on the catalogs and what people like. Here we have items for the house and kitchen and even the yard and workshop. We have a good variety of tools as well."

She waved at islands on either side of the main aisle.

"Now, Mr. McCoy, if you'll step this way to our storage room, I'll show you what else we have. I'm sorry, that 'we' is not right. I said that for so long it's hard to break the habit. You see, my father built the store, ran it for almost twenty years. I can't remember him not being here when I was a little girl.

"The big pox epidemic five years ago just rose up and hit our town hard. We had eight people die, all within a week of each other. Daddy just couldn't fight it off. Not even Doc Slocum could save him, but he tried hard.

"Oh, excuse me. My name is Priscilla Davis. Everyone in town knows who you are. We don't have a lot of strangers in Johnson Corners."

"Thank you, Miss Davis, but I really have to be looking at some more stores."

"You've hardly seen anything here yet. I insist." She caught his arm and pulled tightly against him. He was strongly aware of her breasts pressed against his arm.

"Now, behind the counter is the storage and back stock area." She led him through an opening in the wall into the next room. It had stacks of unopened boxes. Some rolls of barbed wire and some heavier hardware items such as pipe and roofing and kegs of nails.

She kept his arm tightly imprisoned by her hand

and her breast. He could feel the heat of it through her dress. The blue gingham was prim and proper, buttoned to the chin with long sleeves and ruffles at her wrists. The dress swept the floor as she walked showing not even a hint of ankle.

"My father was an excellent merchant. He taught me how to stock and how to display the goods. He told me over and over again that you can't sell a washtub without showing washtubs."

She stopped and watched him a moment. "Mr. McCoy, you look like an intelligent, kind, understanding man. I have a problem that I think you can help me with, if you only will."

Spur grinned. "I often help damsels in distress, Miss Davis."

"Good." She smiled then a frown stained her face. "This is what my mother would call a highly personal problem. It embarrasses me to mention it, but I have to grab the opportunity while I can."

They went around a stack of boxes and found a walled off section of the storeroom.

"Oh, I built a small apartment back here to help save money. I don't need much room. Could I make you a cup of tea?"

Spur frowned for a moment, then shrugged. "I'm never likely to turn down tea with an attractive lady."

Priscilla smiled. "You've very kind. Come in, it isn't much but it's all I need."

The small room held a bed, a tiny wood stove with a chimney, a wash stand and a dresser. The single bed was covered with a beautiful spread and three pink pillows. There was only one chair.

"Sit down while I light the fire and put on the teapot. It won't take but a minute."

He chose the chair and when she had the fire lit, she moved to the bed and sat down.

For a moment she looked straight at him, and Spur was struck by the honesty in her eyes, in her whole manner.

"Mr. McCoy. I told you I have this small problem. You see, there's a wonderful man in town who has asked me to marry him. I said of course, but he put one condition on it. This gentleman is . . . I don't know the word, but he is unable to perform sexually."

She turned away and he saw a blush on her neck and cheek. "This is difficult for me, and I ask your patience." A minute later she looked back at Spur. The fire crackled in the stove.

"He was open and frank with me. A war wound, he said. His heart's desire is to have children, at least to let the community think that he has children."

Priscilla took a deep breath, and then rushed ahead. "He said the only way he can marry me is if I will get pregnant first!" She hurried on. "Yes, I know, shocking. But when you think of it, practical. How else could we have a family? I told him I would try. But in a small town, talk gets around. The whole idea is to let the town think the child is Milton's."

To cover her embarrassment she went to the stove and took off the boiling pot and poured tea. Then she turned. She had unbuttoned half of the fasteners of her blouse and now walked toward him slowly. She undid more buttons.

"Mr. McCoy, I would be so unendingly grateful to you if you could try to . . . you know . . . to make me pregnant. I told you this was a highly personal and a delicate problem."

She had the buttons open to her waist. Quickly she shrugged out of the top of the dress letting it fall, then unhooked a binder that covered her breasts and slowly let it slide down. Her twin mounds of flesh were revealed slowly, first the rounded swell, then the breasts and at last the small nipples of pink, set in large areolas of darker pink.

Spur shifted in the chair. She stood directly in front of him, her bared breasts at eye level.

"Miss Davis, I don't see how . . ."

She moved forward, caught the back of his head and brought his mouth slowly toward her right breast.

"You are an attractive woman, Miss Davis. Beautiful. But I don't see how . . ."

Then her nipple brushed his lips and with a small moan he opened his mouth and accepted her offering. He licked her breast, chewed on it, nibbled at her nipple until she began to writhe in delight.

She moved so he could minister to her left breast, and then she sat down on the bed and pulled him over beside her. She flipped up the skirt of her dress and lifted it over her head. She wore the kind of underwear that fit tightly down to the knee.

At once she began taking off Spur's clothes. He hesitated, caught her hands and watched her. But she pulled his hands to her breasts and he laughed softly.

"All right, all right. I'll help you with your small problem. With a lady as beautiful as you, I wouldn't think you would have any trouble at all."

"Getting pregnant? Oh, but I don't want to let just any man father my first child. He must be tall and strong and handsome like you." She pulled open his belt and then his town pants and pushed them down.

For a moment she worked at his underwear, then she yelped in joy as his stiff penis popped out slanting up at a forty-five degree angle, hard and ready to perform.

Without a moment's hesitation, Priscilla bent and kissed his throbbing tool.

"Oh, yes, just perfect! So big and long. He'll plant your seed deep inside me so they can make me pregnant this very morning!"

Eagerly she slipped out of the tight, white cotton drawers, and squirmed naked on the bed, her black pubic triangle quivering.

"Hurry, hurry!" she said.

Spur pulled off his boots, then the rest of his clothes and lay down beside her.

"Quickly, quickly! I don't want to lose another minute. Push it inside me right now. I want to get pregnant this very moment!"

She was soft and moist and open. Her legs had spread and knees lifted and Priscilla watched him with glistening, bright eyes.

"Yes, Spur McCoy! Oh, yes, push it in me hard and fast. I want it right now. All of it! All of you!"

Hell, I'm only human, Spur thought as he went between her legs and eased forward. She accepted him with a squeal. Her hips shot up to meet him and she lunged and moaned with each thrust.

"Yes, yes! Harder, faster! Plant those seeds of yours deep! I want to be pregnant in two minutes!"

Spur grinned. He could never remember being in quite this situation before. Below him, Priscilla became totally erotic, reacting to every movement with a shout or squeal or moan of satisfaction and fulfillment.

She slammed through two climaxes so close

together that they blended into one and all the time she encouraged Spur to reach his own satisfaction.

By that time Spur was so worked up he knew it wouldn't take long, and he panted and then gasped and grunted as he felt the floodgates opening and he pounded fast and furious into her eager body. She lifted her legs over his back and locked them together, accepting his thrusts with a shout of joy each time.

"I know this is the one!" she called. "No, this time, this is the time I get pregnant!"

When Spur fell on top of her with a long wheezing sigh, and began gasping for breath, she smiled and locked her arms around his back.

"Wonderful!" she whispered in his ear. "Now, twice more today, just to be sure."

Spur heard her in the fuzzy haze of his mini death, and shook his head. "I have business to take care of, Priscilla."

"Not as important as this," she said. "Hush now and rest up, I need you again, soon."

Fifteen minutes later, Spur got up and dressed, over her protests.

"I have to make sure. Once is fine, but three times is best. That's what all my lady friends tell me."

"Priscilla, I told you I have important business. The first time is always the most potent. That's the best I can do. Now you better open the store, don't you think?"

"This way?" She stood up and twirled around. She was still naked. Her breasts bounced delightfully. Spur almost weakened.

"However you think you can make the most sales, Priscilla," he said. "I'll let myself out the back way."

"No! You can't go!" She jumped in front of the

door. Spur picked her up by her waist and moved her out of the way.

"Good luck on your quest, Priscilla," Spur said, then he went out the door, and slipped through the door on the alley and walked around to Main Street. He wanted to watch the newspaper office. As far as he knew that was the only printing press in town.

7

For the rest of the day, Spur watched the newspaper office and printing plant. He lifted a cold beer in a saloon where he could look out the window at the place. Later he walked around to the alley and peered at the rear door. Nothing happened. Nobody went in or out. The press was not working. The newspaper would be out Thursday morning.

By mid afternoon he gave up and began talking in saloons about Doc Slocum. He found out little about the man's background. Almost nobody knew much about him. A few men said he was in town when they arrived. One barkeep said he heard the doc came from back East somewhere.

There was agreement about one thing. Doc Slocum was the only doctor in town, and they would fight to keep him from leaving. They might even consider paying what they owed him to keep him in Johnson Corners.

Spur stopped by at the barber shop, sat in the

chairs until it was his turn and got his neck trimmed and his thick reddish brown hair thinned out a little. The moustache clip was free.

"Hear we got a good doctor in town," Spur ventured.

Slim of Slim's Barbershop snapped the long barber scissors twice near Spur's ear and stared at him.

"Only damn one we've got. Don't matter none how good he is. He's here and he's ours. Belongs to the town you might say. So good don't matter."

"About the size of it," Spur agreed. "Know where he came from? Seems like most folks here come from somewhere else."

"Don't know, don't care." Slim snipped some more. "Just so he stays here. Got my young'un over a bout of near pneumonia last winter. Doc's an all right guy in my book."

By the time the haircut was over, Spur knew little more about Doc Slocum.

He had missed lunch, so he got a sandwich at a small cafe. He ordered thin sliced roast beef with lots of lettuce and a big dill pickle. The waitress was tired before she got to work. She might also own the small eatery, he couldn't tell. She made the sandwich from homemade bread, slicing the roast beef with a wicked looking, twelve-inch blade.

She reacted to his question about Doc quickly.

"Nope, don't know where he comes from. We got a habit in this town of not prying too much about folks. Don't care where they been. Just care how they act while they here. Might be a good idea for you to do the same. You're a stranger in town. Everybody knows that. They say you're looking to buy a business. That true?"

"Yes, that was my intention. But I want to be sure the town has the basics like a doctor, a good sheriff, law and order, and some good spots to eat."

"We got them," she said with a grin. "Especially the eats, like here. You ever have a better roast beef sandwich?"

"Matter of fact, I can't remember one," Spur said. They chatted about the weather and the town until Spur had finished his sandwich. He paid for it and left feeling vaguely impatient. He wasn't getting anywhere with his investigation. How could he be sure Doc Slocum was the man Washington wanted?

How could he be sure that the Doc was spreading the fake five dollar bills around? He needed some evidence, but that seemed hard to find. No wonder somebody had put a proviso on his orders.

Poker! A good tough game of poker always cleared his mind. Gave him a new perspective on a problem. He walked down the street to the Evangeline and found a seat on a poker table. He bought in with a double eagle, and a half hour later he had about seventy-five dollars worth of chips in front of him.

A new player slid into a chair across from him. Evangeline herself.

He started to get up, but the other three men in the game did not.

She smiled and motioned for him to sit down. It was his deal.

"Five card stud, two cards down, five dollars ante," he said.

Evangeline nodded and put a five dollar chip into the pot from her stack on the table.

"Table stakes, no new money," Spur said. He shuffled the cards, placed the deck flat on the table top and carefully passed out two down cards to each player. There was twenty-five dollars in the pot—a cowboy's wages for a month.

He slid the next card off the top of the deck and placed it face up to the first man, and did so for each player. Evangeline had an ace of hearts, and high. She bet two dollars. Spur had a King showing. He looked at his hole cards, A King and an Ace. Cut down the odds of her having a pair. He raised it five dollars and everyone stayed in.

On the second round he called them as he played the cards face up around the circle.

"A four and a seven. A pair of sixes, Queen and a King possible straight." Evangeline had an Ace and a seven. His own King caught a ten, no help.

"Pair of sixes bets," Spur said.

"Two dollars," the cowboy said.

Everyone stayed in, nobody raised.

Spur dealt the third card face up and called the round.

"Four, seven and a six. Possible straight, ruins the man's three sixes." The second player caught a Queen. "Pair of sixes and a Queen. No help there." The third man got his Jack. "Jack, Queen and King. Possible straight. Now for the lady." He dealt out an Ace. "Pair of Aces for the business woman." he slid his card off and turned it up. "A King, pair of Kings. Pair of Aces high bets."

Evangeline looked at the cards, stared at the possible straight and without changing her expression pushed out two ten dollar chips. Spur was next to her, he met the bet and added a fiver.

"Twenty-five to you, sir," Spur said. The 4-7-6 hand man folded. The pair of sixes and Queen studied his hand, then shook his head and threw his cards face down on the chips.

The last man snorted and threw in his hand.
Evangeline looked at Spur. "Let's see your five, and
add another twenty. How good a gambler are you,
McCoy?"

Spur stared at the pair of Aces. Not good odds
that she could have three Aces with a third one
showing. Two sixes were up so she could not get a
full house. Two pair? Possible but he had his three
Kings, even with one King showing.

Spur pushed in the twenty, he had four dollars
left. "And raise you four, my limit."

Evangeline frowned slightly as she looked at his
cards, then added four one dollar chips to the pot.

"Call," she said softly.

Spur turned over his third King. "Three wise men
from afar," he said.

Evangeline scooped up her cards and threw them
face down on the pot. "Beats me," she said.

Spur pulled in the pot, over a hundred and sixty-
five dollars.

The deal went around and Spur lost twenty
dollars on the next two bad hands. On the third one
he lost fifty on a pair of Aces, but when Evangeline
dealt he had two Queens on a hand of five card draw.
He opened for ten dollars on the Jacks or better rule
and threw away three cards. Everyone knew he had
a pair. He drew the first three cards and sat back not
looking at them. Two of the men looked at their
cards and threw them in. Evidently they were
beaten by his pair.

The third man frowned down a smile and held.
Evangeline took two cards. Was she filling or
bluffing?

Spur looked at his cards close to his chest, edging
one into view at a time. Besides the pair of Queens,
he had a seven, then came a three. Not much help.

The last card was another seven. Two pair.

A weak hand to be betting on. He checked the bet and the man across looked up quickly and bet ten dollars. Evangeline met it and raised him ten.

Twenty to Spur. He took a slow breath folded his cards and laid them face down in front of him. Then he pushed two tens into the pot.

The man across from Spur added a ten.

"Call," he said.

Evangeline laid down three fours. "Is that enough?" she asked. The men dropped their cards face down and she pulled in the pot.

Two hours later, Spur was down to twenty-five dollars. He was five dollars ahead.

"I'm out," Spur said standing up. It was getting toward five o'clock and he was no farther along with his case—either of them. Evangeline stood as well. She walked away and he followed her to the bar.

Spur stopped beside her. "Could I take the big winner out to dinner?" he asked.

She smiled. "Best place in town?" she asked.

He nodded.

"I'll be ready in ten minutes. Don't get lost."

She hurried toward the back stairs.

A half hour later Spur and Evangeline settled down at a table at a small eatery just off Main Street. It featured "Authentic New Orleans Ribs," and was run by a black husband and wife team.

"You didn't blink when I suggested ribs," Evangeline said. "Which means you've had them down south somewhere."

"New Orleans," Spur said, slurring the words together with the accent of the "or" the way the natives say it.

"You do get around. I still wonder why you're

here. You don't seem to be buying a business very fast."

"I'm a cautious man."

"Not the way you play poker you aren't."

"Where I really am conservative is in my choice of women."

She laughed. "Now I know you're bluffing me. I'd raise right now on a pair of Jacks."

"I opened with Jacks but I have an Ace high," he said.

She shook her head. "Not good enough, cowboy. I've got an Ace-King high."

He grinned and their salads came, huge helpings of tossed greenery with strips of carrots and wedges of tomatoes and some potent dressing.

They worked on the salad silently for a few minutes.

"Are you going to stay here in Johnson Corners forever?" he asked.

"Probably. I've got some roots down."

"But no family."

"I'm an only child. Both my parents are dead. I've never been close to any of the rest of my family tree. Two whole limbs have refused to talk to me since I began running the saloon, so I'm not missing much."

"I was thinking about a family of your own, establishing the Evangeline dynasty, and a string of gaming houses across the west, maybe a partnership with the Overland Stage Lines."

She laughed and bit a carrot stick in half.

"No such ambitions. Running one gaming house takes all of my time."

"Delegate responsibility."

"In a saloon that's a license to steal. Have you

ever seen an honest barkeep? There's no way to know how many drinks they pour. How do you keep track?''

"True. I knew a saloon owner in Kansas once. When he tended bar he even stole from himself!''

Their ribs came then, a huge platter filled with pork ribs and lathered with a barbecue sauce that stood up and said hello half way to your mouth.

The light skinned black woman brought the ribs and then tied big white bibs around their necks and gave them two linen napkins each.

"Just so you can enjoy your ribs," she said with a smile that showed gleaming white teeth. "Y'all enjoy your dinner now, y'hear?''

They were black-eyed peas and turnip greens and slabs of thick white bread, fresh salted butter and a covered pot of blackberry jam. The coffee came steaming hot in the cup with a heavy crockery pitcher full on the side.

"Now these are ribs!" Spur said after the first bite. "How come you kept this place a secret from me?''

Evangeline would have answered but she had a six inch rib at her mouth chewing off the delicious pork.

They finished the ribs and Martha was there at once to remove the tray and replace it with ice cold slices of rich red watermelon.

"I must be dead and this is heaven!" Spur said. Martha grinned and left them to their dessert.

Walking back to the Evangeline saloon, he pondered about telling Evangeline exactly what he was trying to do. He decided not to, not yet. He had a few more night watches to make first. He would go to the sheriff and Evangeline and the newspaper man as the last resort. The way things were looking, he just might have to do that soon.

At the Evangeline she ushered him to the foot of the stairs up to her quarters and held out her hand.

"Mr. McCoy, I had a delightful afternoon and evening. We should do this again, one of these days."

"I ate enough to last me a week," Spur said.

"So we'll make it in a week." She smiled. "Unless you get hungry before then."

She took a step upward and turned. She was eye to eye with him. She smiled.

"Mr. McCoy. Would you do me one small favor?"

"Of course, Miss Evangeline."

She leaned toward him her eyes closed and touched his lips to his. He didn't touch her with his hands. She never touched him. Their lips clung together for precious moments, then she eased away from him.

It took a moment for her eyes to come open, and she put out a hand which he caught to steady her.

She crinkled up her nose and the twin dimples popped inward on her cheeks. Her black eyes sparkled.

"Well now, that was nice." She turned abruptly. "Good night, Mr. McCoy. Perhaps we can do this again one of these nights." Then she walked up the steps and did not look back. When she stepped inside the door above, Spur McCoy went out of the saloon and back to his room at the Aspen Hotel. He found it empty, put the chair handle under his locked door and waited until just after midnight. Then he slid out his window to the hitch-roof and down to the ground.

It took him ten minutes to find a good spot to

watch the front door of the newspaper office. Then he settled down and waited. He checked the position of the Big Dipper, and when the movement of the Dipper around the North Star told Spur that it was four a.m. he rose, stiff and sore and walked back to the hotel.

He didn't want to bother climbing in his window, but the door was locked and braced with the chair. He got inside without attracting attention and slept until eight-thirty the next morning.

8

Willard Kleaner walked past the Carson Hotel as he did every morning on his way to work at his uncle's Aspen Hotel. This morning he stopped and stared, then recovered and kept moving so as not to attract attention.

Two desperados reined in at the hitching rack in front of the Carson, dismounted and tied up. Slowly and with seeming pain, they eased their saddlebags off the mounts, took blanket rolls and small crushed carpetbags from their tie down spots behind saddles and limped into the Carson Hotel. They had been on a long, rugged ride, Willard could tell.

Willard knew what they were at once. He could recognize the type anywhere. They definitely were bank robbers who had been on the run for several days, weeks maybe, and were here to hide out, get a hot bath and eat some good food for a change.

It was like in *Ranger Dale and the Robber's Roost*. Ranger Dale hadn't been sure about the robbers at first, but he had tracked them down quickly. This pair looked about as worn out as the outlaws in the book had been. Neither showed any signs of a gunfight wound, but both were heavily bearded—the two week kind, not a three or six months beard. Their hair was shaggy; they were dirty and their clothes worn and torn.

The nags they rode in on looked ready for the glue factory somewhere, Willard decided. He hurried past the Carson, to the Aspen Hotel and asked the room clerk if he'd seen Mr. McCoy come down.

McCoy was in the dining room having breakfast. Willard hurried in and stood there in front of the table, turning his small bill cap in his hands. When McCoy looked up, Willard was ready.

"Sir, you said to come to you again if I saw something . . ."

Spur put a finger across his lips, and Willard stopped.

"But you said . . ."

"Not here. Out in the lobby." Spur put down his napkin on the bones of his breakfast, and they went into the lobby where Spur eased onto a soft couch and Willard sat beside him.

"I saw two of them. They just got into town and went into the Carson Hotel. A mangy, beat up pair of desperados they are, Mr. McCoy."

Spur's eyes twinkled but he tried not to let the boy see it. He listened as Willard gave detailed descriptions of both men, ages, height, weight, and what they wore.

"No sense setting around here, Willard. Let's go and see if we can find them. Chances are they registered at the hotel and left right away heading to the closest bar for something to drink."

Spur and Willard left by the side door, then Spur

checked the saloon across the street from the Carson Hotel. It was closed so early in the morning. Down the street three doors was another saloon with the door standing open. Inside, Spur found the pair at the stand-up bar of rough lumber. Sawdust on the floor absorbed the spilled whiskey, spit and now and again, blood.

The men were precisely as Willard had described. With a jolt, Spur stared at the taller man. "Abe Varner!" Spur whispered. He hadn't seen Varner since he was last in Kansas. Varner had cheated a hangman in a small county seat when three of his friends rode in with guns blazing, killed the sheriff and one deputy and got away clean.

Abe Varner was a bank robber, and had killed half a dozen men in the process. He could have only one purpose for being in Johnson Corners.

Spur did not know the other man, but he was a match for Varner in style and appearance. A two man gang of bank robbers was better than doing it alone. The barkeep stood in front of Spur.

"Yeah, got any Rough Cut chawing tobacco?"

The apron brought out a plug and tossed it on the counter. Spur tossed him a quarter in return and left the saloon. The purchase made him just another customer. Abe Varner would not think it unusual. The killer was smart, clever. That was why he had stayed alive so long.

This assignment might turn out to be more than just a hunt for a missing man after all.

Spur eased outside and motioned to Willard. "You're right, son, at least one of those men is a wanted killer, and a bank robber. They've probably been on the road for a long time. I'll watch them for a while."

Spur grinned and slapped Willard on the back.

"Hey, that was really good, smart thinking to peg these guys. There could be a reward in this. Now get back to work."

Spur leaned against the clothing store front wall and kept the saloon door in sight. He felt uneasy. He should be working on his other two problems, not taking on a new one. Now he had three cases, not one.

At least there was no mystery about Abe Varner. No mistaking him for someone else. A cold blooded killer with no conscience. Spur had to decide if he would take him into custody right now or see what he was up to. There could be four or five more men outside of town letting Varner set it up and then they would all swoop down on the bank.

Spur wandered down the boardwalk and looked across the street at the Concord Bank. Two doors, one in front, one in back and lots of windows. If he were going to rob it he'd want at least four men. He pondered the idea of telling the sheriff and the banker.

Spur decided to tell neither one. He would watch the pair and if the robbers tried to take the bank, he would hit back so hard they wouldn't know what to do.

As he stood across the street from the bank, he saw the pair of robbers coming down the boardwalk on his side. Spur found a chair and leaned back against a storefront.

Varner and his friend passed within six feet of Spur. His hat was pulled down over his eyes, letting him see out, but not offering anyone a look at him.

Both robbers studied the bank as they walked past. They ankled across the street and went by the money pit close up, pausing as if going inside. Spur figured they had the place well reconnoitered already.

He followed them up the street and watched them go into the Carson Hotel. Something about Varner he was trying to remember. Then he had it. Varner liked to attack a bank just before closing time, when the workers and any guards were tired.

He'd take it just before the vault was closed for the night, so he had fewer problems getting to the money. After the hit on the bank he would charge away and could get lost in the darkness. That was the way Spur remembered Varner had worked before. This time he would have some surprises.

Spur sat down on the edge of the boardwalk just down from the Carson hostelry. A year ago a flash flood had poured down through Main Street, gouging out tons of loose dirt. When they got it leveled off again, the street was eighteen inches below the boardwalks in some spots.

Spur checked a grandfather clock in the Johnson Corner jeweler's window. It was only a little after ten in the morning. He figured the pair would eat again soon, then have a sleep and be ready to take the bank at 2:45.

Spur pushed away from the boardwalk and ambled across the street to Moon's General Store. He did not go into Priscilla's store. She could be bothersome.

In the store he picked out a double barreled shotgun and a box of shells with double ought buck loads. The shots were the same size as a .32 pistol slug, from eight to thirteen in each round depending on the length. He took the long ones and distributed the shells in all of his pockets.

Nothing so effective for close in fighting like a

scatter gun and double ought buck. If he ran the army, every army unit in Indian country would arm every second man with a shotgun.

Spur arranged with Bill Moon to let him leave the unloaded shotgun just inside the store door, and meandered down the block. The Concord State Bank was situated in mid block, with only a front and rear door.

He leaned against the barber shop wall and speculated. If he covered the front, they could go in that way and out the back and down the alley. Get away clean. If he tried to cover the back he left the front open.

Spur had to get help or confide to the banker his suspicions and wait inside the bank. He didn't trust the sheriff because he knew nothing about him. Now there wasn't time to find out. He'd go with the banker.

Spur walked into the bank at two o'clock and talked with the president and owner, Barton Concord.

"Ah, Mr. McCoy. How are you finding our small town?"

"Dangerous," Spur said with an edge in his voice. "Could I talk to you privately?"

They went into the banker's office. As soon as the door shut Spur checked out the window. He did not see Varner or his partner.

"I think your bank is going to be robbed today, Mr. Concord. I'm a special lawman from the U.S. government in town looking for a murder suspect. I recognized the two men. If they act the way they have in the past, they will come in just before the bank closes at three and take it over."

"The sheriff! I'll call him."

"No, there isn't time. And if Varner spots anything out of the ordinary, he'll walk on by. Don't even tell your clerks. I'll be here with a shotgun and back both of them down. You can disarm them and then, we'll call the sheriff."

"Don't like guns in my back."

"Maybe you'd rather let them clean out your safe and your teller cages."

"No . . . no. That's what we pay the sheriff for. We should let him know."

"Tell him if you want to, but if you do, I'm going back to my hotel room. I'm trying to do you a favor."

Concord began to sweat. He wiped the moisture from his forehead and looked at the window, then at crossed infantry sabers on the wall.

"I had enough of fighting and killng in the war." At last he shrugged. "All right. If you think it's best. I just don't want any of my people getting hurt. Money can be replaced. My people can't."

Spur nodded. "I'll get my shotgun and come in the back door in five minutes. You have it open for me."

When Spur came up the alley to the bank a few minutes later, the banker stood outside waiting. He unlocked the door and they went inside. Spur unwrapped the new shotgun and pushed two rounds into the barrels.

Inside the bank, Spur looked for a hiding place. There was no spot in front of the cages. He'd have to be behind them, which would be a little awkward. It all depended how many men Varner had. The more he thought of the layout, the more he figured there would be only two men.

At least that's how Spur would do this bank.

Come in at 2:58, pull the door shade, lock it and take over the place. Tie up customers and workers, clean out the cash and leave by the back door.

With Varner you could never tell. He had a reputation of getting into trouble by shooting too much. A "wanted" flyer said the man simply enjoyed killing. That worried Spur. If there were only two men, Spur had a chance.

He found his spot, a small storage closet at the far side of the safe with a door that opened outward. Spur could leave the door ajar a crack and see everything going on. He told Concord who agreed. Spur asked Concord to be in his office with the door shut at closing time.

The clock moved. When it was a quarter of three, Spur pulled the closet door shut to a thin crack and put four shotgun shells in his right pocket where he could get to them quickly.

At five minutes to three the clerk and the two tellers were watching the number of people in the bank. They rushed to get most of them out by the three o'clock closing. None of them knew why Spur was in the closet.

When the clock hit three and struck, the head teller took his ring of keys and went to the door. Just as he reached the key for the lock, strong arms slammed the door open, jolting the teller off his feet.

Two men rushed into the bank, six-guns out. One turned and closed and locked the door. The other waved his gun at the two customers and the other employees.

"No heroes, and nobody gets hurt!" Abe Varner said loudly but in a controlled voice. "Tellers, clear out your money drawer and put it all on the marble in front of you. Do it now!"

The second man left the door and ran around the counter to the vault and saw that the big door was still open. He charged inside and began dumping money into a white flour sack he took from his belt.

Varner scowled at the customers.

"You, old man, lay down on the floor, on your face. Do it, right now." Varner watched as the man slowly knelt and then went to the floor.

"Miss, you too, on your back, next to him." She sat down then lay on the floor and shivered, her eyes frightened.

"You two tellers, or whatever, out here, fast. Get down beside your buddy there. Anybody reach for a hideout and he's dead, y'hear?"

Varner edged toward the counter, scooped up all the money and bills and dropped them into his flour sack, then went around the end of the counter to help his partner in the safe.

Spur McCoy at last had a shot. The muzzle of the shotgun was only an inch out of the closet when Spur pulled the trigger. Half of the .32 caliber sized slugs caught Abe Varner in the chest, churned through his ribs and lungs and blew four inches of his backbone against the far window which shattered and sent shards of glass spraying into the street.

The robber in the vault fired his pistol out the big opening. He peered around the door from floor level, saw the smoke from the shotgun muzzle near the closet and put three rounds into the door as he zigzagged to the protection of the counter, then rushed toward the back door.

Spur stormed out of the closet, triggered the second barrel of the scatter gun down the hallway, but the robber expected the move and had dropped behind a stack of boxes. He leaped up after the shot passed, fired three times with his pistol down the hallway at Spur and charged out the back door.

By the time Spur got to the door, all he saw was the hind quarters of the black horse rounding the end of the alley and heading out of town. Another horse, saddled and provisioned, had been tied to the back yard fence of the house on the other side of the alley.

The bank owner looked out the back door, his face pale and terrified.

"Call the sheriff and the undertaker!" Spur shouted. "I'm going after the other one!"

Spur vaulted into the saddle of the horse Varner had planned to use, pulled the reins loose and pounded the big gray down the alley after the second robber. He had left the shotgun in the hallway. Now all he had was his long barreled .45, and more than twenty useless shotgun shells.

9

Spur McCoy was a quarter of a mile out of town on the Denver Stage Road before he saw the robber again. The Secret Service agent topped a slight rise and looked down hill. The rider on the black had stopped near a large Douglas fir to check his back trail. When he saw Spur he cut into the timber along the trail and vanished.

The Denver Stage Road here followed a gentle downgrade to a valley below where it crossed and climbed upward higher than the community of Johnson Corners which rested at 6,235 feet.

Spur rode forward slowly. The thick fir, lodgepole pine and Engelmann spruce would serve as a perfect blind for bushwhacking. He pulled the gray off the road two hundred yards from where the robber vanished into the woods, and began working ahead at a walk.

He would try to cut the man's trail and track him. It would be simple in the soft footing of the forest floor, where decades of pine needles and leaves from the aspen had created a six-inch deep mulch.

He found the trail ten minutes later. The marks in the mulch showed that the rider was pushing his horse fast. Spur moved out on the trail, slowing when needed, but racing ahead when there was only one logical direction for the rider to take.

A half hour later the trail led across a small stream. Spur rode into the open not thinking about being shot at. Just as his horse stepped in the water a rifle cracked from less than fifty yards away, and the bullet whispered over Spur's head. The last step of the horse into foot deep water had pulled him downward to safety.

Spur jolted off the horse and raced to a pile of boulders on the near side of the stream. Three rifle slugs splattered granite as he ran but the lead missed. He had seen a rifle on board the borrowed horse, but he had no idea if there was a box of rounds for it.

It was no help now as his horse stood hock deep in the creek thirty feet away taking a long drink.

Another rifle round hit the rocks he lay behind. The angry lead ricocheted off into the timber. A bright sun began to slide behind the distant ridges of the Rocky Mountains. It would be dark in two hours.

Spur pulled his long barreled Colt and juked his head around the side of the rock to locate the smoke from the black powder. He saw it drifting from a thicket of brush just down wind from a solid looking aspen. He sighted in waist high to the left to the Aspen and fired.

His round brought two more slugs zinging over the rock. Then there was silence. Spur lifted the top of his low crowned brown hat over the rim of the rocks on the end of his pistol barrel. There was no reaction.

He whistled for his horse, but it had moved another twenty feet away from him to the far bank and grazed on some new grass. Varner had not trained the animal to come on call. So, all he had to do was run to the horse and use her as a cover to get into the timber.

That could be deadly if the robber was still around.

Only one way to find out.

Who wanted to live forever?

As the Indians said: This was a good day to die.

Spur held his Colt ready, surged away from the rocks and raced for the horse which went right on munching.

No shots slammed through the cool, high mountain air at him.

McCoy grabbed the reins, stepped into the saddle and rode hard into the fringe of aspens and small fir bordering the stream.

When he was safely into the woods he stopped and listened. The only thing he could hear was the scream of a large red tailed hawk, and then the wind blowing through the seventy and eighty foot high, old growth conifers.

The outlaw had seen his leader killed, he would understand the rules of the game. His horse had been loaded for a long ride. But would he choose to run or to fight? In another two hours he could escape into darkness without fear of being followed.

Spur would have to wait for morning to pick up his trail and by then he would be forty miles away. The robber had all the advantages: he could fade away in the darkness, he could stand and fight, he could try to bushwhack Spur again, he could ride around in circles until Spur gave up and went back to town.

Somehow Spur felt the man would fight. He had the looks of a fighter. He had seen his partner gunned down and might want revenge. He would shoot from hiding if he could arrange it, and in these mountains and timber it would be easy to do.

Spur cut the trail quickly this time and saw that the horseman was not galloping. The black had been held to a walk and to Spur's surprise the trail turned back toward town. They were less than two miles from Johnson Corners. Why would he go back that way?

As Spur followed the trail, the answer came quickly. The rider crossed a rushing stream that was thirty feet wide and belly deep on the horse, then angled into the upper end of the valley the stream had carved. It was strewn with horse sized boulders.

There was a forest of them, and few trees, as if the boulders had grown here instead of trees. The soil was sandy and thin. No wonder no Douglas firs decided to thrive here.

He paused at the start of the valley of boulders, then saw the glint of sun off metal and dropped off his horse, pulled out the rifle, an 1866 Winchester .44. He had always liked these guns. Varner had picked well.

The weapon was 43 inches long with a tubular magazine that held 12 rim fire cartridges. Loaded the rifle weighed nine pounds. But it could fire 13 rounds without reloading. It was a newer model of the old Henry .44. Spur checked the chamber and there was a round in place. In the saddle bag he found two boxes of the .44 caliber rifle sounds. He dumped a dozen of them in his pocket and tied the horse to a bush.

Then Spur began moving forward through the big rocks toward where he had seen the rifle flash at him in the sun. It was slow going.

Spur kept track of his direction by a twin topped Engelmann spruce near the end of the short valley. Once he scaled a boulder that had a chunk broken out. For two minutes he peered over the top of the granite hoping to see movement, but there was none. He had not seen the man's horse.

He figured the outlaw had tied his horse in the woods at the far end of the valley, and worked back into the rocks to a good spot for a ten yard ambush where he couldn't miss.

That was what Spur feared he might try.

He came around the side of a boulder nearly as big as a house, and twenty feet ahead saw the back of a man vanish around another big rock. Spur waited. The Jasper might backtrack. The Winchester was ready to fire. He sighted in on the boulder and the one past that and waited.

Nothing.

Spur moved again, rushing forward to the next cover, the rock the killer had just left. For the flash of a second Spur heard a noise and looked up. The robber was on top of the rock less than six feet away! Spur lifted the Winchester and fired. The unaimed round skidded off the stone breaking up and splattered some of its hot lead into the robber who dropped out of sight.

"Don't be a fool," Spur called. "You're hurt and I'll kill you if I have to just like I did Varner. You ready to die?"

There was no answer.

The stick of dynamite with a short fuse sailed over the granite boulder and Spur dove away from it, rolling as far as he could toward the open space behind the rock.

The blast went off with a cracking roar.

Dynamite in the open makes a furious sound and concussion, but without shrapnel behind it the effectiveness is minimal. Spur shook his head and lifted up, a fresh round in his Winchester.

He could see no movement.

Slowly he edged around the big boulder, every nerve ending alert and tingling, ready to report any sight, sound or touch of the enemy.

Around the boulder Spur found a few spots of blood and an empty rifle cartridge. That was all.

He looked ahead. More big rocks.

A rifle bullet splattered off the rock just past him, and Spur dove to the side away from the sound of the shot and crouched behind a smaller rock. The robber had angled to the left instead of moving forward. Spur searched for the blue smoke that gave away the gunman's position. He found it but there was no target.

As he watched, the robber lifted up and fired again. Spur had time only to duck before the slug slammed into his protective rock. He reached up and fired his pistol at the position in a purely defensive move.

Then there was silence in the high country.

Spur wished he had made up some small dynamite bombs before he came—except he didn't know he was coming. He had found that by taping roofing nails to a stick of dynamite with a short fuse, he had an effective grenade that he could throw a hundred feet while the fuse burned.

Now he saw the robber move toward the woods. Spur fired twice with the rifle at the retreating figure. Where was he going? Where was his horse?

On foot the man would be much easier to run to ground. He seemed to be working toward the left of the small valley. Spur stopped trying to shoot the man and ran flat out toward the far end of the valley less than a hundred yards away now. He slanted far to the left hoping to come out in the trees well before the robber did.

He heard only one more shot which he figured was defensive, and then he left the last boulder and rushed twenty yards across an open meadow into the brush and aspen and fringes of young fir trees in the open where the sun could nourish them.

He paused a moment, made sure he had a new round in the Winchester, then jogged forward through the edge of the woods. Where had the man left his horse?

Spur heard a nicker, ahead, and edged around a big spruce and saw the horse tied to an aspen. It took him a moment to find the position he wanted. He was ten yards from the mount, and slightly behind it, but with a good field of fire toward the edge of the valley.

Spur lay down beside a huge Douglas fir, sighted in just past he horse and waited.

It was two or three minutes before Spur heard the man coming. He swore softly, and used his rifle as a crutch as he limped around the last boulder, took a long look behind him and then hobbled toward the brush.

Spur tracked him, waited until he entered the woods and turned toward the horse. Spur wanted to take him back alive, to put him on trial. He lowered his sights, aimed at the injured left leg and squeezed off the round.

The crack of the Winchester caught the man totally by surprise. He had no time to move before the heavy .44 caliber slug tore into his left thigh, spun him backward and dumped him into the mulch in plain sight.

"Drop the iron!" Spur bellowed. "Drop it and put up both hands or you're buzzard food in about ten seconds."

Slowly the man's hands came up.

He sat up then, his face a twisted, angry mask of pain.

"Yeah, yeah! Don't shoot no more. I don't want to die. Just get me to a doctor!"

"Throw out your pistol!"

"Right, yes." A six-gun came out of leather slowly and the man tossed it away from him. He pushed the rifle butt first toward Spur so the trigger was well out of his reach.

"Hands high!" Spur demanded. He lifted up, keeping the robber in his sights and moved forward slowly. The wounded man made no try to move.

"I'm bleeding to death!" the robber shouted.

Spur moved quicker then, checked the robber for a hidden derringer, then put down his rifle and examined the thigh wound. It was bleeding too much. Spur took the neckerchief from the robber and pushed it against the back of his leg where the round had exited.

"Hold it there," Spur said. He took his own big red handkerchief and tied it tightly around the leg, pressing the compress in place to stop the flow of blood. The lead splatter wounds in his lower leg were not serious. They had stopped bleeding.

"Nothing broken," Spur said. "You're damn lucky I didn't blow you in half in the bank."

"The way you did Abe?"

"Yes, you were next. What's your name?"

"George Washington."

"Sure. Well, George, I bet the sheriff has a broadside or two on you. Teaming up with Varner means you've got a wanted for you from somewhere. Now, get on your horse, unless you want to walk."

It took them nearly two hours to get back to Johnson Corners. Darkness had fallen, but they rode the last mile on the Stage Road.

Spur tied both horses in front of the Sheriff's Office and found a deputy waiting for him.

"Trouble?" the deputy asked.

"No we were on a picnic and got stung by hornets. Where's the sheriff? Tell him I've got a prisoner for him over at Doc Slocum's."

Spur and his prisoner went on to the doctor's office where the medic checked the wound and at once cut off the robber's pant leg and went to work.

He seemed to know what he was doing. He probed the wound to make sure the bullet all came out. The second probe with a long wire like tool made the robber pass out.

"Easier this way," Doc Slocum said. "I don't hold with that fancy ether stuff that's coming out." He doused all the wounds with carbolic and then wrapped them up with clean white bandages. White tape completed the job.

Sheriff Phillip Gump knocked on the door and came in. He looked at Spur, then at the prisoner.

"This the other bank robber?" the lawman asked.

"Seems to be, what's left of him," Doc Slocum said.

"Can I put him in jail?"

"Sure if the county wants to pay me to change his dressing every two days. There or here."

In his pocket, Spur found a gold one dollar piece smaller than a dime and handed it to the medic.

"On his account," Spur said. Then nodded at the lawman. "Peers I need to talk to you about that other robber. You have a paper for me to sign?"

"Yep. You better come down to the office with this hombre and we'll get it done. Ain't often we have a bank robbery where a stranger knows about it in advance and guns down the robbers."

"Knew Abe Varner from before, Sheriff. Never seen this one though. Says he's George Washington."

The sheriff snorted, picked up the unconscious man, hoisted him over his shoulder and carried him out the door. Spur McCoy followed.

He paused. "Oh, Doc. There's two horses at the rail out front. Used to belong to two bank robbers. I'd think the county will transfer all rights to you for medical services. Livery can probably buy them from you." Spur grinned and left to catch up with the sheriff. He had some explaining to do.

10

Spur sat across the desk from the big lawman and showed him the thin sheet of parchment he took from between pieces of a thick card in his wallet. The letter detailed Spur's position as a member of the U.S. Secret Service, and that he had jurisdiction in all matters local, county, territorial, state, and federal.

The parchment was signed by the President of the United States, U.S. Grant, and William Wood, director of the Agency. A two inch embossed seal took up half the page.

Sheriff Gump handed the parchment back to Spur. He folded it and inserted it between the halves of the heavy cardboard backed picture and put it away in his wallet.

"Nobody but you can know about this, Sheriff," Spur said softly. "I still have a job to do here."

"Yes, fine with me. I always cooperate with the

federal authorities, especially now that we're a state. Anything I can do to help you?"

"My real job here is not as violent as this one turned out to be. If I need help, I'll sure call on you. This other matter is much more delicate."

"I'm always here."

Spur stood. "There is something else, Sheriff. I never would have known either of the robbers were in town if it hadn't been for a young man here. His name is Willard Kleaner."

"He told you about them?"

"Certainly did. Is there any kind of wanted posters on the men? If there are any dead or alive papers, he should be the one to get the reward on Varner."

"I'll look into it."

"Oh, I'd also like to set up a twenty-five dollar good citizen award for Willard, just in case nothing else comes through. It would go with a letter of commendation from you, as sheriff."

The sheriff chuckled. "He's the one who sent me on a wild goose chase once. Guess he was right this time. I'll arrange it."

Spur handed him a gold double eagle and a good five dollar bill.

"Be much obliged, Sheriff. Now, seems to me, I missed supper somewhere along the way."

Spur went back to his room, washed up and changed clothes, then walked downstairs to the dining room and had a steak dinner and two desserts. By the time he finished it was after eight o'clock.

He went back up the stairs wondering if he should go over to the Envangeline for a hand of poker, or if he should watch the printing plant again. That had to be the key, but so far he was at a dead end on the counterfeiting and the right identity of George Slocum was the killer from Washington, D.C.

He came through the lobby and started up the stairs when he saw Priscilla Davis. She smiled at him and he nodded. She went up the steps after he did, and then hurried down the hallway as he opened his door.

"I've been waiting for you, Mr. McCoy," she said softly. "I knew you would come."

She looked up and down the hall, and when she saw no one, she stepped into his room and tugged him inside, then closed the door.

"I couldn't wait to see you again! Spur McCoy you simply set me on fire, do you know that?"

"Miss Davis, I don't think you should be here. Your reputation."

"Oh, poo. I don't give a whit about that. What good is a reputation? It can't keep you warm at night? It can't make love to you." She wore a short jacket over a full skirted dress. She pulled the jacket off and Spur was amazed to see that the top of the dress had been folded down. Nothing covered her breasts.

"You like my titties, you told me you did. Please pet them. Please kiss me!"

She walked toward him slowly. "I don't ask much. Just use me however you want. Strip me or just push up my dress. You don't even have to take your pants off if you want it fast and rough . . ."

Spur held out his hands as she walked toward him. He caught her shoulders and kept her away.

"No, Priscilla. I don't think so. You want too much. What happened to the story about the man who wanted you pregnant?"

"Oh, poo. Did you believe that? I made that up so you would be nice to me, so you would make love to me. Was that so bad? I love to make love. Don't you?"

"Well, yes, but I'm a man."

"So, I'm a woman. I love it as much as you do. More I think, yes, definitely more." She threw the jacket to one side and reached behind her to open some snaps and hooks and then pulled the dress over her head.

Priscilla stood before him naked. Her lovely breasts shook for a moment, and then began a small dance as she walked toward him.

"Priscilla, don't you understand?"

Her hands fumbled at his belt. One massaged the long hard lump forming quickly in back of his fly. "Oh, he likes it! He likes to see my titties and my muff of crotch hair. He wants inside! I just know he wants inside me!"

Spur backed up again, tripped over the chair and fell on the bed on his back. Priscilla was on top of him in the blink of an eye. Suddenly he was laughing.

"You are persistent," he said from his back. He felt her hands rubbing his erection through his pants. Then she began opening the buttons on his fly.

"Am I sexy too?"

"Yes, extremely sexy."

"You want to do it with me?"

"Do what?"

"Make love . . . fuck three or four times."

He watched her. Her hands fought through fabric and closed around his erection.

"Do you want him inside me?"

McCoy groaned. He was only a man, not a saint. The woman had problems, but it wasn't up to him to solve them. Right now he had a rather insistent case of swelling that she could relieve.

"Hey, big cock, you want him inside my warm hole?"

Slowly Spur nodded.

She grinned. Spur rolled her over and spread her legs wide and thrust forward. He knew his pants would chafe her. He knew that he was fully clothed and that it might hurt her. But he found her heartland and stabbed and burst past the tightness, then he slid into a lubricated sheath that accepted him.

At once her legs came up around his waist, then his armpits where she locked them together.

"Darling, make this first one so fast you'll be ready for more!"

Spur grunted and drove forward. He was so on fire he hardly thought about her. He panted and humped her and drove hard and fast and let only his own desires guide him. For a moment he worked it up, then he paused letting the thrill remain, but pushing it slowly away. Then he moved her legs so they rested on top of his shoulders and he arched his back and pounded his hips like a pile driver slamming his cock into her juicy slit.

She took all he could offer and thrust to meet him as he powered higher and higher.

Faster and faster, harder and harder, and Spur pounded his own music, with not even a thought of the woman. Then the dam broke and the surge swept downstream and carried him along as his hips slammed harder and harder, moving him deeper and deeper until at last he exploded with a dozen hard thrusts, each one tougher and deeper than the last.

Then he eased her legs down and fell on top of her spent half dead.

She let him rest for five minutes, then moved and he rolled off her, flat on his back.

She sat up and watched him. "Nice, good. You're good at making love. You have anything up here to drink?"

He took a pint of whiskey from a drawer. He kept the bottle for medicinal purposes, but since neither of them had been shot it was not needed as an antiseptic. He mixed a drink of whiskey with the cool water from the ceramic pitcher and she downed half of it.

"I think I like your place here," she said. "I'll have to come back every night."

"I'd be good for two nights, then you'd have to bury me."

She shook her head. "Your big rod just gets harder and harder the more he's used. I should know. Is it my turn yet?"

"Not until you take my clothes off."

"Hell, I can do that easy."

It took her all of two minutes to strip him naked, then she grinned as she inspected him as he lay on the bed, one foot on his lifted knee, and his hands under his head.

"I know just how I'm going to do it," she said and sat on his stomach.

"Up there?"

"Yes, up here. I've . . . I've never been done this way."

"You have to do most of the doing."

"Good, show me how."

"First there's a basic male requirement before anything very sexy can happen."

"Oh," she said. She scooted down and lifted up and moved until she sat on his legs.

"What a poor little, sad, soft worm."

"That's a whip, lady."

"He's a worm who dreams of being a lance. Can I make him into a lance?"

She could, and did.

A few minutes later, Priscilla squealed as she lowered herself gently on his shaft as she held it upright.

"My god, this even *feels wicked!*" she whispered. "I want to do it all night this way!"

She settled down until her round bottom hit his pelvic bones, then she squealed in delight and looked at him. "Why didn't you tell me there were other ways to make love? I need to know them all. Will you teach me?"

"Sorry, I'm not a qualified teacher. I'm sure you do all right all by yourself." He didn't have to tell her what to do next. She instinctively lifted up and dropped down on him, then she built up a rhythm and slowly angled forward until she was riding him like a pony.

"Lordy but this is wild!" Priscilla crooned. "Whyn't anybody show me this before?"

"Probably didn't know you had the talent for it," Spur said, then he felt the woman start to climax and she fell on top of him shaking and vibrating and spasming like she was having a fit, then she smiled and went through the same series of spasms again before she trailed off and lay still. He was sure she was sleeping.

The one eye opened. "Hell no, I ain't sleeping, big stick. Just loving every second of it. You know I'm thinking of moving to a new town and opening up myself a fancy ladies house. Think I could make a go of it?''

"Just don't steal all the trade away from your girls, Priscilla." Spur gave a pair of grunting strokes and shot his load and rolled her away from him. Spur got up and began dressing.

"Thought you said I could stay all night?"

"I didn't even say you could come inside. Now get dressed or I'll set you in the hall bare assed naked."

"Don't see why you hate me, Spur McCoy."

"I don't hate you, Priscilla. I have some work to get done before the sun comes up. And it doesn't involve a pretty woman. So hustle your bones."

She dressed and was ready when he was.

"You and me make a good team, don't we? I'll be back every night you want me. Or you could come up to my house. I really don't live behind the store. Pa left me a nice place, three bedrooms, we could use all three beds every night!"

Spur grabbed her shoulders and stared at her sternly. "Priscilla. I told you, I have work to do. It's serious work and I don't have time to play sexy games with you every night. I hope you realize that."

"Anything you say, Spur. But you can put that spur of yours in my cunny just anytime you want!"

Spur shook his head and led her to the door. He had strapped on his .45 and took his hat. He checked the hallway and when it was clear he pushed her out and told her to go down the steps. He'd used the back stairs to protect her reputation.

When he was sure she was gone, Spur slid out the door, locked it and went down the back steps.

He walked quickly to the alley behind the newspaper and found a window that would be lighted if anyone worked at the press.

For two hours he sat there watching. Nothing happened. He stood, stretched and walked two blocks to get the kicks out of his legs. Then he leaned against a fence and watched for three more hours before he gave it up. There was nothing going on at the printing plant. That meant Doc had all the bills made up he needed. He could be sliding them into use a few at a time, as he needed them.

Spur walked the three blocks down to Doc Slocum's office. The place was dark. No reason any lights should be on here. He had taken care of the emergency and was probably in bed by now.

Spur went past the Evangeline saloon and found it open. Only a half dozen gamblers played at two tables. Evangeline sat at her elevated table nursing a beer. Spur stopped beside her table and pointed at a chair. She nodded.

"Out kind of late, aren't you for a hero who saved all of our money at the bank. Let me buy our hero a beer."

She signalled the barkeep who brought a bottle of beer. Spur thanked her and pulled at it.

"I thought you might be in for another poker game," she said.

"I got tied up on another project. But I've still got you on my list. I never let a woman beat me at pocker."

"Lots of women are expert gamblers, me for one."

"But I never let a man beat me at poker, either. I'm not prejudiced."

She laughed and sipped at her beer. Then watched him a moment. "Spur McCoy, you're not in town to buy a business. I figured that out the first day you were here. You're not a real businessman. There's an aura about you, a quality, an animal-like tenseness, an alertness like you expect to be shot at the next second or two.

"You try to hide it, to be casual, but I've seen it before. I used to know a gunfighter who was the same way, and a sheriff who could never turn it off.

"When you went after those bank robbers, I finally realized that you're a lawman. Just what kind, I don't know. And I certainly haven't figured what you're after here in town. Fact is, I don't care much, as long as it isn't me."

She smiled at him and lifted her beer.

"How did I do? Am I about right?"

11

Secret Service Agent McCoy watched the small, delicate gambler in the Evangeline gaming house, and a slow smile spread across his face.

"Lady Gambler, you just pushed all of your chips into the pot, are you sure that you've won?"

"I've got a royal flush, I don't see how you can beat me."

Spur reached out and put his big paw over her small hand. "You win, but don't tell anyone. I still have some work to do in town and I need to be incognito."

She laughed softly. "Hey, you can go to cognito if you want to or stay here. I won't tell a soul. You still haven't told me what kind of a lawman you are." Her eyes sparkled and her twin dimples popped inward.

"Probably won't until I get things cleared up. You playing any black jack tonight?"

She took out the cards from the drawer in her

desk. Spur picked them up and checked the sides, then the face. He smiled and put them back.

"Could you tell if the cards had been shaved or marked?"

"Can an unweaned calf find his mamma in a herd of a hundred cows?"

Spur put the four phony five dollar bills on the table and pushed one to the center of the table. She dealt a hand and he won with a twenty to her eighteen. He pulled a five and played again. At the end of twenty minutes Spur had lost the four five dollar bills.

"Take a look at those greenbacks," Spur said softly. She looked at them.

"Are they good currency?"

"I never notice bills much." She shrugged. "Feel good."

"Check the serial numbers."

"Oh, my god! They're all the same. Then they must be counterfeit. All bills are supposed to have different numbers on them, aren't they?"

Spur flipped a twenty dollar gold piece on the table and took the four fake fives back.

"Just don't tell anybody about this either. It's what I'm working on. Don't let on, don't refuse fivers, or tell your aprons to watch for them. I don't want any tip off to the counterfeiter."

She smiled, and reached over and touched his hand. "Thanks for trusting me. I might have a printing press in the back room turning these out myself."

"You don't, I checked."

Evangeline laughed. "You did not."

Spur stood. "Past my bed time. I better move on."

"Thanks for the game, I'm still ahead."

"I'll get even, next time."

"Good, there will be a next time."

Spur nodded at her and then walked out the saloon door. He found few people on the street. Nothing unusual. He went into his hotel, up to the second floor and then looked for the stairs to the roof. He found it at the far end of the hall.

Without much trouble, he picked the lock and went up the dusty stairs to the roof. The stars were out and in this high country they looked close enough to pick and put in a diamond pouch.

He went to the parapet built around the rooftop and leaned on it watching the town. All of the businesses below except two saloons were closed and dark. A few stragglers left the watering holes, then even they closed.

Spur spotted one figure leaving the Johnson Mercantile, it was Priscilla. She went down the street toward some residences and vanished in the gloom of the quarter moon.

A deputy sheriff made his rounds, routinely trying doors on the businesses, walking slowly, sure how many times he would make the circuit before dawn.

Spur saw a flare of light down near Doc Slocum's house, then the rattle of a buggy as one, one-horse rig followed another down the street and out the Denver Stage Road. An emergency this time of night had to mean the imminent birth of a new citizen.

For a moment he thought he saw a flare of light near the newspaper office. Yes, it came again, then the sound of a door closing two blocks down. This might be important. Why would the newsman come

109

back to his office after midnight? Spur left the roof, returned to the ground floor and out the rear door of the Aspen Hotel.

He came to the newspaper office quickly but found it as dark as it had been on his previous patrols.

Something had happened here. He went down the vacant lot beside the news plant and soon found a small shoulder high window. Spur looked inside. No lights showed.

He pushed on the double hung window and it was not locked, the wooden frame sliding upward easily. Spur found a wooden box and stood on it so he could squeeze through the opening and inside. He used a sulphur match to light his way, found a candle and began exploring the back shop of the newspaper.

The Secret Service agent found plenty of printing inks, even some green, but nothing that was suspicious. He explored the whole back shop, checking printing papers, but found none that could be used for making five dollar bills.

Spur checked the back door and saw that it was locked only by a bar across two iron holders. He lifted the bar and peered outside. Where were the telltale clues of the counterfeiter?

The rattling of the front door came through the silent building like a burglar alarm. Spur quickly blew out the candle, but he knew it was too late. Whoever it had been at the door must have seen the candlelight. He hurried to the back door and eased it open, before he could sprint away, a form came running around the corner brandishing a darkly silent pistol.

Spur froze against the inside of the door, counting on the lawman or owner to charge into the darkness of the building interior.

For a moment the man outside hesitated. Then he struck a pair of matches, held them high and stepped inside the print plant.

Spur slashed at the hand with the matches with one fist, and powered his second down on the man's right hand that held the pistol.

The six-gun clattered to the floor and the matches died as Spur rushd past the other man into the alley and pounded fast down the length to Fourth Street and then up it to Main. He stopped running, went through another alley and walked quickly to the rear entrance to the Aspen Hotel.

Two minutes later he was in his hotel room where he locked and braced the door with a chair, then undressed in the dark and crawled into his empty bed.

Close.

At least he still had most of his cover story in place. But he had struck out again on the counterfeiting. If all else failed he would have to go to the bank and see if they could spot any deposit having large numbers of the bills included. One of the retail stores in town would be the best chance as the pipeline into the economy. Surely the doctor was working through someone else. The sawbones made so little in this town he could never circulate many of his counterfeit bills.

Spur rolled over and tried to go to sleep. He couldn't. There had to be something here that he was missing, something right under his nose that would give away the counterfeiter and tie down Doc Slocum's involvement. But what the hell was it?

Spur looked at his Waterbury at two-thirty by lighting a match. He checked again and it was four a.m. He must have slept part of the time, but he couldn't remember. When morning came at five-thirty and he rolled out so his feet hit the cold boards of the floor, he wondered if he had slept at all.

And still he had no idea where the right handles were to pull to find out what he needed to know.

He had a miserable breakfast in the cafe across the street. The waitress and cook were both mad at the world and so was he. When he got to the sheriff's office at eight that morning, the sheriff was cheerful and pleased.

"Worked up a right smart certificate, we did. Betty in the courthouse is good at making them things. Here want to see it?"

Sheriff Gump brought out a roll of stiff paper and spread it flat for Spur to read. It was hand printed with fancy lettering, old English he thought, and lots of scrolls and doo-dads around it. It read:

"Be it hereby known to all persons, that the Sheriff of Forest county, State of Colorado, does hereby applaud and commend one Willard Kleaner, fifteen years of age, for his part in recognizing two wanted felons and then alerting officials of the presence in our community of the two bank robbers.

"Said information by young Kleaner, his alertness and ability to convey such matter to friends and members of this department, did aid and abet and greatly help law officers to prevent the bank robbery and bring the desperados to justice.

"Willard Kleaner is hereby made the first official honorary Deputy Sheriff of Forest County by my order, and is entitled to all of the honors and privileges thereunto.

"The Sheriff's Department of Johnson County hereby awards William Kleaner the sum of twenty-five dollars, to reward him for his good citizenship. Drawn and dated this Seventeenth Day of June in the year of Eighteen hundred and Seventy-seven. By my order and hand . . . Sheriff Phillip Gump."

Spur handed it back. "Beautiful, Sheriff. Willard will treasure this award forever."

"Giving it to him at at little ceremony on the steps of the courthouse at ten this morning. I want you to be there."

"I'll be there, Sheriff. You find any wanted posters on either of the men?"

"Three on Varner, but no big cash reward. One hundred dollar one but I'd have to deliver his body to Tombstone, Arizona. I figure that's too far."

"Need nose plugs this time of year before you got him there. Put him on boot hill."

"Here we call it Culligan Swamp. Same idea. He'll be put down today." The sheriff hesitated. "How. . . how is your other problem coming along?"

"Slow. Too damn slow. But that's why they pay me this tremendous salary. I probably make about half of what you do." Spur walked to the door. "I'll keep you informed if this gets to the legal stage. I'm hoping somehow that it won't."

Spur turned to go out, then stepped back in the office. "Sheriff, you ever have any trouble with the woman who runs the Johnson Mercantile?"

"Priscilla Davis? Now and then. She seems to be settling down nicely to running the store. Quite a shock to her when her father died." He crinkled his brow. "Why?"

"Just a coincidence, I guess. She reminds me of somebody I used to know. Forget it, doesn't mean a thing."

Later that morning at the ceremony at ten o'clock, Zelda and Ronald Lewton stood proudly beside Willard as he was presented the certificate. It had been mounted in a frame that could be hung and had a piece of glass over it to protect it.

Two dozen people gathered around the steps as the sheriff made a little speech. Then the president of the bank, Barton Concord, gave a talk about how the future of the town was in the good hands of young men like Willard, and how proud he was of Willard and that he had opened a savings account at the bank in Willard's name with fifteen dollars already deposited in it.

More cheering followed that. But when the sheriff asked Willard to say something he just held up the frame and smiled. He was too overcome to say a word.

Ron Lewton had to help his wife back to the hotel. She was a bit unsteady on her feet and Spur figured she had some kind of illness. Willard ran ahead and showed the frame to everyone in the hotel, then put it on the wall until he could take it home and hang it in his room.

Spur McCoy stood on Main Street and looked at the newspaper plant and at Doc Slocum. What the hell was he going to do?

12

Willard Kleaner stood in the Aspen Hotel an stared at his certificate in the frame on the wall. It was the most wonderful thing that had ever happened to him. And he had forty dollars in hand! It was more money than he had ever owned . . . or even thought about.

He felt of the two crisp bills in his pocket and asked his uncle if he could take off a few minutes.

"I want to go to the bank, sir, to deposit my reward money in my new savings account."

"You best be paying attention to your work, boy. Not parading around with your money showing. Did you move that broke bed out of 104 and put the new one in?"

"No sir. That's my next project."

"You best be getting to it." Lewton paused. "I could hold that twenty-five dollars for you for safe-keeping."

Willard shook his head. "No sir. Thank you but I

want to keep it myself until I can deposit it. I never had twenty-five dollars before!" He hurried away toward the room on the first floor that needed the new bed. Some drunk had broken it the night before.

The idea grew slowly in Willard's mind as he worked the rest of the morning. At noon he ran all the way to the livery and talked to the man there. His name was Josh and he liked kids. He saw Willard coming and made a sound like a trumpet.

"Our local hero comes!" Josh said grinning.

"None of that," Willard said. "Just doing my . . . my civic duty the way every straight shooter should."

"Anyhow you rope it, cowboy, you done good. What's on your mind?"

"A horse. You got one for sale cheap?"

"How cheap?"

"Twenty dollars, horse, saddle, saddle blanket and bridle."

"You peer to be goin' somewhere?"

"No sir, Josh. I just want a horse of my own I can ride." He paused a moment. "I want to learn how to be a cowboy!"

Josh grinned. "In that case I might even give you some lessons. Come back here and lets look around. Might grub up something." He considered it a minute.

"Fact is, Doc Slocum sold me those two nags the bank robbers rode. The black is a valuable animal, but I could let you have the gray and her gear for twenty dollars."

"I'll take her!" Willard shrieked so delighted and excited that he could hardly talk normally.

Josh grinned. "Better look at her first. I might be pulling a fast one on you."

They examined the gray in a stall and Josh showed Willard the saddle, blanket, saddle bags and the bridle. There was also a lasso and Willard noticed that the saddle had a boot to hold a rifle.

"I think I want to buy her," Willard said. "About how old is she?"

Josh pulled the gray's lips apart and looked at her teeth.

"I'd say maybe eight or nine. Got fifteen good years left in her you take care of her. Oh, you got a place to keep her?"

"Sure have! My uncle has a little barn in back of his house. He keeps a horse there all the time. Plenty of room for two."

Willard held out the twenty dollar greenback. "You'll write me out a receipt won't you, so I have a bill of sale. I don't want to get my neck stretched for horse stealing."

Josh chuckled. "Sounds like you been reading them dime novels. I read one oncet in a while."

He eyed Willard. "You work over at the hotel, right? You come back after work and I'll have her saddled and ready. And with a bill of sale. You keep your greenback until then."

"Yes sir," Willard said. He walked up to the gray and patted her flank, then ran his hand along her back and scratched her ear. The gray turned toward him with big brown eyes.

"She looks like she wants a friend," Willard said.

Josh chuckled. "Guess so. Now she's found one. You come back this evening."

Willard ran back to the hotel. He had all his usual work done and started on the special things Uncle Ronald always had ready. At five-thirty he left and went to the stable. The gray was saddled and ready.

Willard gave Josh the twenty, accepted the bill of sale with his name on it and the date.

"You know how to get up on a horse?"

"Sure. Always the left side. That's the left when you're facing the same way the horse is. They get used to that, I don't know why."

"Right. Willard, you ever ridden before?"

"No sir. But I've read considerable about it."

"Can you get that saddle off?"

"Could you show me how?"

Josh grinned and demonstrated to Willard how to take the saddle off. Then he went through it step by step how to saddle up a mount. When he was through he pulled the saddle off and the blanket.

"Your turn," Josh said.

Willard put the saddle on correctly, and Josh waved him on his way.

The young man from Chicago could hardly believe it. He was on his own horse! He had a saddle and bridle and even saddle bags, and he was riding down the street of a Western town! It was almost more than he could accept. He held the reins loosely in his left hand, the way Billy Ringo did in *The Big Cattle Drive*, and let his right hand rest on his thigh, near where his .44 should be.

Wow! He had his own horse. He had not even thought what his uncle might say about it. Now his mount twisted. He could say whatever he wanted to, Willard knew for sure that he was keeping the gray. She didn't even have a name yet. She looked like a gray lady, a gray ghost. Yes! He would call her Ghost. That was a good name.

He rode down the side street, urged Ghost into a canter and almost shook himself to death. How in the world did you keep your bottom in the saddle when she was bouncing that way? Maybe Josh would give him some riding lessons, too.

Willard stopped Ghost in front of his uncle's house and tied the reins to the lilac bush and went inside.

He found his aunt in the living room, as usual. He watched her for a moment but she didn't even hear the screen door slam. She was too far into her wine bottle. Willard shrugged, went back outside and led Ghost around to the small barn and into the second stall. He gave her a feeding of oats and took off her saddle and bridle. She watched him with her big brown eyes. When she saw the oats she began eating.

Willard stayed there an hour, watching her, brushing her down with his uncle's brush. He didn't know if he did it right, but she liked the attention. When he went into the house it was almost dark.

His uncle was there. Aunt Zelda was not in the living room. Her husband had carried her into the bedroom again. It happened about half the time.

"Where you been, boy?" Ronald Lewton barked.

"Out in the barn feeding my new horse. You want to come see her. I call her . . ."

"Your what?"

"My new horse, Ghost. She's a gray, about the size of yours. I bought her today for twenty dollars."

"We'll take her back to Josh first thing in the morning."

Willard had never stood up to his uncle before. He was a half inch taller than the older man. Now he squared his shoulders and put a frown on his face.

"No. No, Uncle Ronald. I won't take Ghost back. She's mine. I bought her with my own money. You can't make me take her back!"

Ronald made the mistake of trying to hit his nephew. His hand shot out, but Willard pushed up his left hand to block it and his right hand tightened into a fist and he struck back.

His knuckles slammed into his uncle's jaw and staggered him back two steps.

"You hit me! You ungrateful child!"

"You tried to hit me first," Willard said. "And I'm not ungrateful. I just want to keep my horse."

"Who is going to buy feed for the animal?"

"I will. I can pay for it from that twenty dollars a month you get from my estate. The lawyer said it should come directly to me when I'm sixteen. That's in a couple of months."

"You know about . . ." Ronald Lewton felt a wave of loss sweep over him. He had been investing that twenty dollars a month at six percent and making a good return. How did the boy know about the financial . . .

"I'm going to keep Ghost, Uncle Ronald. If you won't let me keep her, I'll move out."

"You can't do that."

"I can. I can get a job at another hotel, or in a store. I'm big enough to work hard. I can earn twice what you pay me."

"Now, Willard. Don't jump to conclusions here. Of course you can keep the horse. Let's go see her. You paid how much for her? You got a saddle and bridle too. Well, well."

Ronald Lewton had never felt worse in his life. His wife was a drunk, his hotel was barely scraping by, and now his nephew was threatening to leave and take his twenty dollars a month with him. He would have to placate the boy somehow. At least until he was sixteen. Lordy, why did Zelda have to drink so much?

Spur McCoy sat and stared at his cards in Evangeline's. So far he had been there two hours after supper. He had lost twenty dollars and needed to get even.

It had been a worthless day. Most of the morning had been taken up with Willard and when he tried to dig into Doc Slocum's background in the afternoon, people clammed up like they had something to hide.

A customer in the general store laid it out for him. "Look, we don't know you. We know Doc. He might not be the best doctor in the world, but he's all we got. We can't live here and take a sick child thirty miles to a doctor. Way I see it, we stick by Doc, least wise until we know for damned sure who you are and what you want."

Others said about the same thing. For the moment he forgot about the counterfeiter. One damn problem at a time. Unless they were the same problem. Spur got an idea what he could do the next day and he felt better.

He concentrated on his poker and a half hour later by playing conservatively and with the odds, he was ten dollars ahead. The barkeep brought him a note and Spur read it quickly.

"Now that you're ahead, come to my table and let me win it back." It was signed only with a capital "E."

Spur bowed out on the next hand and went around the saloon, then slid into the only other chair at the table on the slightly raised platform.

"Good evening, owner, general manager and top game playing lady," McCoy said.

When she looked up at him, Spur sucked in a quick breath. She was more beautiful than ever. Her alabaster complexion was tinted with the touch of a blush and her lips showed the use of a little red brush. Her eyes looked deep ultramarine blue tonight instead of black and they fairly cracked with energy. Her soft brown hair was brushed to a sheen and billowed around her face and shoulders. The only thing missing were the twin dimples.

"Good evening famous man from the east coast. I hope your project is moving along well."

"I'm not talking business, I'm on a winning streak. You want to play some cards or not?"

"My, touchy. You want monte, faro, rouge et noir, Boston, seven up, euchre or maybe some draw poker?"

"Just some twenty-one, less concentration needed."

She smiled. "Why don't you want to concentrate?"

"I knew a beautiful lady gambler once on the Mississippi River boats. She won a pile of money. She figured that she had an advantage. She was an excellent gambler. She could judge other players extremely well, and if all else failed she could flirt so outrageously that the men would lose their concentration."

"And she won?"

"Almost always. She won enough that eventually she bought her own riverboat, married the captain and settled down in St. Louis."

"Shows what can happen to a girl if she isn't careful." They both laughed. Evangeline dealt. Spur was not concentrating. But he never bet more than a dollar on a game, and when he had won fifteen dollars he closed his hands around the cards.

"Enough. Evangeline, you're not concentrating and you sure aren't flirting. What's the matter?"

She watched him for a moment, her dark eyes looking for the smallest hint of how he felt.

"Spur McCoy. I want you to come up to my rooms in back, but I don't know how to ask you. I'm not indicating in any way that I want you to become intimate. But I do want to talk, and to get to know you better, without these damn pasteboards between us."

Spur stood. "I'd be pleased to see you to your door. When we're there you can ask me in, or send me away. That's the time to make the decisions."

She left first, and Spur had one more cold beer at the bar, then went out the front door. He came around to the alley door and she opened it when he knocked. They went up a flight of closed steps to the second floor.

She had moved walls and cut doors and turned the six former cribs into a delightful apartment with kitchen and big sitting room and a large bedroom.

She had not bothered to invite him in, she simply opened the door and walked in and he followed her. She let him light the lamp and she turned up another one and they sat on a sofa in the big room.

"Nice, did you fix it up yourself?"

"Yes." She looked away, then turned back. "Spur McCoy, I'm getting restless. I guess I liked the gambler's life, the moving from town to town. There was always new sights, different kinds of food, fresh faces, vistas and oceans and rivers. Now it's the same day in and day out."

"Take a trip to Europe, you can afford it. Sail across the ocean on one of the steamships."

"Never thought of that. But, no. That doesn't sound good."

"Put in another saloon, make it bigger, fancier."

"Town can't afford one. I would be running a smaller place out of business. I'm not that hungry anymore."

"There's one more route to try."

She looked up, so eager, eyes sparkling, wanting to know.

"What? What else could I try?"

"Take a lover," he said. Spur reached in and let his lips touch hers in a soft, tender kiss.

She pulled back and slapped him.

Spur smiled. He waited, watching her.

Her face twisted into a frown. "Damn, I didn't mean to slap you. Sorry." She moved closer to him, reached up and kissed him. Her arms went around him and the kiss lasted longer than he thought it would.

When she pulled back her eyes came open slowly. Then she caught both of his hands.

"Spur McCoy, I promised myself I wouldn't do that. Damn but I've wanted to. You're such an attractive, such a wonderful man. But that is not saying that I will pretend I'm married to you and jump into bed.

"What I need to do right now is think. You go downstairs and have a beer, and I might come back down. If I don't by the time the beer is gone, my door will be locked and barred."

She pushed toward him again and pressed closely against his chest and kissed him seriously, a lover's kiss. When she pulled away she sighed.

"Oh, glory, but does that bring back memories! Now, Spur McCoy, you be a gentleman and get yourself out of here. On second thought, I'm going to lock and double bar my door as soon as you step out. I've got a lot of thinking to do. And I know that you would not take advantage of me."

Spur bent and kissed the tip of her nose. "You know that a lady never says that unless she is hoping that it will happen." He kissed her lips so softly she barely felt him. But when she opened her eyes he had stood and was near the door.

"Damn, you are leaving."

"When you want me to stay, you'll have the door barred when I'm on the inside," Spur said. He went out the door, down the steps and out the alley to his hotel room.

13

Spur had been in his room at the Aspen Hotel for ten minutes when a soft knock sounded on his door. He had locked it when he came in. He stood at the wash bowl bare to the waist and had just finished scrubbing himself clean.

Spur grabbed his six-gun from his holster hanging on the bed post and moved silently to the door. From the wall beside the opening he paused.

"Yes?" he asked.

"Room service," a woman's voice said.

"What?"

"I've brought up your order from the kitchen," the voice said coming faintly through the panel.

Spur frowned, unlocked the door from the side and holding the pistol ready, swung open the door. Tessie stood there with a covered basket over one arm. She wore a tight blouse, a brown skirt and a big grin.

"Figured it was time I came calling, to welcome a

stranger to our city," she said with a thin smile. Spur remembered her well from the first day he hit town. She was eighteen or a year more, sturdily built with long blonde hair and delicious large breasts. Spur had been in a sexy mood ever since Evangeline had pushed against him in her apartment.

"Can I come in?" Tessie asked. "I've brought you a late night supper, and even a bottle of wine. You like wine?"

Spur chuckled, waved her in and let the hammer down slowly on the Colt. He closed the door and locked it.

"Fact is I am hungry again. What goodies did you bring?"

"Besides me, you mean?" she asked. She put down the basket on the floor and caught his hand and led him to the bed. "First you have to get hungrier." She sat down and he settled beside her.

Her brown eyes glowed with anticipation. Slowly she leaned foward and kissed his lips. Tessie came away slowly. "Oh, yes, yes! You are just as good as I remembered."

Spur unbuttoned the middle of her blouse and pushed his hand inside. There was no other cloth under the blouse and his hand closed around her warm breast.

"Feels so much better when you do that," she said. "I got a sister who's just sixteen and she likes to mess around. We sleep together 'cause we're short on beds. She ain't had a man yet, but some nights we mess around finger fucking each other. She says she likes me better."

"Sixteen? She may change her mind."

"You want to convince her, Spur? You could do it fast."

Spur laughed. "Not if she's sixteen, too young. Give her time." She finished opening the buttons and pulled her blouse off, showing twin mounds, high set with small pink nipples flowering on wide pink areolas.

"If you're really hungry you can chew a while on these," Tessie crooned.

Spur lay on his back and pulled her over him, sucking one breast into his mouth.

"Oh, damn! You know the first time a man did that for me I came right in his face. I mean I exploded and the kid was so surprised he thought he hurt me and ran out of the woods and left me there wanting and with only my own two fingers to push into my burning little pussy. I hope you don't run off and leave me."

Spur changed to her second hanging mound and she groaned in appreciation.

"Oh, yes! Just nothing like a good chew job to get a girl in the mood. Lordy! am I in the mood. I'd guess that you could do me just any way you want to." Her hands stroked his chest, played with the black hair, toyed with his man breast buds.

"Ain't it funny how a woman's tits grow and a man's don't? I wonder why that is? I mean, what good is a man's tits anyway, he don't have no milk. Just kind of a waste."

Spur came away from her and tugged at her skirt. She sat up and stripped off the skirt and wore nothing under it. She pulled at his pants. His boots were already off. When his pants came down he took his underpants with them and she giggled.

"Lordy, I ain't never seen me one any better than

that! Lordy he is big and long and just so delicious!'' She dropped on the bed on her hands and knees. "I saw me two dogs just humping up a hurricane today. Do me that way, Spur. I ain't never been done dog fashion before. Bet it is wild!''

Spur hesitated.

"Come on, Spur. I want it that way.''

Spur moved up behind her and did what she asked, and only a few seconds later she shrieked.

"Oh, God, I'm gonna explode right now!''

Tessie climaxed three times so quickly that they surged over top of one another, and she lost her balance and fell to the bed. Spur was caught by surprise and before he could stop they both had fallen and rolled off the bed.

Tessie howled in delight as she sprawled beside Spur on the floor. Spur sat up and shook his head.

"That is the most ridiculous thing that ever happened to me in bed with a woman," he said.

Tessie's laughter trailed off and she reached in and kissed Spur, then lifted up on her knees.

"Damn, all this sex makes me hungry. You ready?''

They sat on the bed and examined the wicker basket she had brought. Inside were six drumsticks she had filched from the kitchen, a salt shaker, slabs of bread and fresh butter, half of a lemon cream pie, the wine bottle and two glasses, and six fancily decorated cup cakes.

He reached for the pie.

"That's dessert. Chicken first." She said it with a touch of authority. Then she jerked her head and covered her face with one hand.

"Oops, sorry. I was the oldest of eight. I just naturally had to take care of the little ones.''

Spur grabbed a chicken leg, salted it from the shaker and bit into it. To his surprise it was still slightly warm. He made three of the legs vanish and then tried a cup cake.

She watched him, ate nothing herself, and poured the wine. She had no trouble with the cork.

"You like wine?" Tessie asked.

"With good food it goes well sometimes. I'm not one of those people who knows much about the vintages or years or kinds of wine."

"You sure talk fancy. You from back east somewhere? My granddaddy came from Maine."

He told her where he grew up and her eyes widened.

"Really gosh truthful. Is there that many people in one town? A million I heard."

"Could be, I haven't been back there in a few years."

Tessie nodded. "Okay." She reached for Spur's crotch. "Hey, you ever do it while you were eating?"

"What?"

"You know, make love to somebody while you both were eating?"

"No, that would be a first."

"Me too! Let's do it. The pie. We can both be eating the pie and just fucking up a storm!"

Spur laughed, then looked at the pie and fondled her big breasts.

"You are crazy, you know that?"

"Sure, got to be crazy whenever this forest fire gets burning this way between my legs. Only one thing will put out the fire. Come on, let's try!"

She stretched out on the bed holding the half a pie. "You afraid to try it?"

Spur couldn't keep from laughing again. It was so ridiculous it was silly. But he was feeling silly, and as sexy as he ever had.

"A bite of the pie first. I want to be sure it's good." He took the pie from her hand and gouged out a bite, licking his lips when he was done. For an answer he pushed over her and dropped full length on her frame.

Sixty seconds later they were locked together and sharing the pie.

"Bite and stroke," she said and giggled.

By the time the pie was gone, they were both laughing so hard it was difficult to stay sexy. Spur pushed away and sat on the edge of the bed shaking his head.

She stood in front of him putting on her skirt.

"I know just how you feel, Spur McCoy. I was too silly and we lost the serious purpose of sex." Tessie giggled. "But wasn't it a wild party? Can you ever remember having so much fun and laughing so much while you were getting serviced?"

Spur shook his head. "Nothing to compare. You win, hands down." He watched her dress. She came up to him before she buttoned her blouse and let him kiss her breasts goodbye.

"Why do men go crazy over tits? Do you know?"

Spur shook his head.

"I got them with me all the time. Nothing special. But men really get worked up over a tit slipping out of a blouse."

She walked to the door. Tessie had cleaned up the picnic and some of the crumbs. She had the rest of the wine as well.

"Hey, big man. You want a party, you just let me

know. Next one will be totally different. Maybe a drive in the country. You ever made love in the grass?"

She grinned, slipped out the door and closed it.

Spur didn't have any trouble at all going to sleep.

When he woke up the next morning he decided it was time to confront Doc Slocum about the counterfeiting. And he had a good idea how to do it.

After he scrubbed down and shaved, Spur cleaned up the rest of the party from the night before and put on his town clothes, suit pants, a white shirt and string tie and his go-to-meetin' brown doeskin vest. His big six-gun went on his hip tied low.

Spur had a stack of flapjacks and bacon for breakfast, then walked down to Doc Slocum's office and went in. There were two women and a man waiting. He took a chair and a half hour later got in to see the sawbones.

Doc Slocum's cheeks looked pinker this morning, and Spur guessed it was more John Barleycorn than it was sunburn. Doc dropped his 160 pounds into a creaking chair and his brown eyes stared evenly at McCoy.

"Been hearing some strange talk about you, McCoy."

"Do tell. I look strange to you?"

"A mite. Looks don't bother me. Hear you're fancy with that gun of yours, that you know bank robbers and kill them, and that you are something of a poker player."

"Talk does get around."

"You're not here for a medical problem." It was a statement of fact by the doctor.

"That's right. I'm a businessman looking to make a profit."

"I'm just a country doctor . . ."

"That's what most folks hereabouts think. Which is why I'm here. Met a man in Chicago few weeks back. He said you were a good man to know. That you had been in the business before."

Doc scowled, reached in a drawer, then shook his head and shut the drawer. Spur could see the shoulder of a whiskey bottle in the opening.

"Never been to Chicago."

"What he told me. But he said you could help me move some independently produced greenbacks." Doc reacted and Spur hurried on. "Not looking for a big score. You get sixty percent. I've got ten thousand, but I'm willing to give you a thousand worth for just four hundred."

Doc Slocum stared at Spur with anger flashing from his eyes. But his voice was steady when he spoke even though his fingers turned white where his hands gripped the chair.

"Get out of my office! I am not and never have been a counterfeiter. I wouldn't know how to pass your phony bills even if I was tempted. I make a living here, that's all I ask. I even help a few people who are hurting. Now get out of my office."

Spur chuckled and shook his head. "Not a very convincing performance, Doc. The man from Chicago said you'd been away from the trade for a while. Didn't give me a name, but he described you right down to the whiskey cheeks, and brown eyes. He said you were playing at being a doctor here in Johnson Corners."

Doc stood and walked around his desk, stared out the window and then came back and faced Spur.

"I still don't know what you're talking about. I've never been a counterfeiter. I don't want your fake bills. Now please leave. I just heard someone come in who needs me."

"Yeah, right by the script. My friend in Chicago just about called how you would react. He was surprised to know you really was playing doctor, though. The part about the people needing you is good."

Doc Slocum doubled his fists and took a step forward Spur who was still seated, then reconsidered. His face spewed fury.

"My Chicago contact gave me one more persuader. He said I could always go to the local sheriff and ask him to dig up an old wanted poster on you. I think he said the name was Horace Olson. He said you had some major problems in Washington, D.C."

Doc Slocum sat down quickly in his chair. He put his face in his hands for a moment, then recovered. He turned and left the room without another word. Spur followed him but he went to the reception room and asked a lady and a small boy to come into his examining room.

Spur had no chance to push the conversation, or the accusation. Doc would have no hint who Spur was. The friend in Chicago trick must have worked. The more Spur thought about it, the more he was sure that Doc Slocum was not the local funny money maker. If not him, then who could it be?

Spur sat down in the waiting room. A half hour later the woman came out thanking the doctor. The sawbones helped her out the door, then turned and stared at McCoy.

"Come in here, might as well get this over with."

He walked into his office where they had talked before.

When they both sat down, Doc Slocum leaned over his desk.

"Now, let's get it out in the open. What's this about counterfeit money?"

Spur took out four of the five dollar bills with identical serial numbers and laid them side by side on the desk.

"Check the serial numbers. They are about as phony as they get."

Doc looked at them and shrugged. "If you say so. I wouldn't know one from the other. But I do know that each bill is supposed to have a different number. So they are fake, I don't know anything about them."

"Is that the truth, Doc?"

"Damn right! I don't like . . ." He sighed. "All right. I never expected to be able to hide this long. You're right, my real name is Horace Olson, and I came from Washington, D.C. But that was a long time ago. I made a small mistake and I paid a terrible price for it."

"Small mistake? Counterfeiting and murder are not exactly small mistakes."

"Murder? Not me, I was never . . ."

"You were charged by the Washington police with murder and counterfeiting."

"No! If it was Archibald Vincent you're talking about who died, he had a bad heart. I kept warning him. Then one day he got excited and his heart simply gave out on him. That was at the same time the counterfeiting scheme he headed went bad and I ran as far and as fast as I could."

"So you knew about the counterfeiting?"

"Not until the last few days. They used some of my offices, and my people. They even forged my name on some orders. I was the legitimate front for them and they took advantage of me. I knew nothing about the making of fake bills."

Spur watched him. Doc had an honest face. Spur had been watching men try to lie out of problems for years now and he had an uncanny nack for picking out the liars from those telling the truth.

"There's still a warrant out for you in Washington, D.C., Doc. What are we going to do about that?"

Doc's pudgy, pink face reddened even more. Sweat beaded on his forehead.

"Christ, I don't know, McCoy. I've battled this for a long time. Didn't do a damn thing wrong, but knew I'd get burned for it. I should have stayed and cleared it up. Too damn late now. Guess you'll have to decide. But if you arrest me, I'll get a lawyer and fight it from here. You'll have a battle on your hands."

Spur stood up. "Yep, reckoned that I might. I better talk to some more folks around town before I decide. Oh, that counterfeiting here in Johnson Corners. Keep that quiet for now, all right? I want to surprise the culprit."

"Fine by me." Doc stood. "Just remember, the folks in this town got only one doctor. They won't take kindly to losing him, even if it's just me."

14

On the way back toward his hotel from Doc
Slocum's office, Spur passed Priscilla Davis's store.
She stood at the open front door and motioned for
him to come in. He turned on the boardwalk and
moved to the screen door which she held open.

"I really need to talk to you for a few minutes, Mr.
McCoy," she said formally. He nodded and went
inside. No one else seemed to be in the store.

She caught his hand and led him behind the cash
register where the back room started and they were
shielded from the street. Impulsively she reached up
and kissed him, pressing her body firmly against his
from crotch to chest and Spur felt the instant heat
of her flesh.

"Oh, my, that is nice," Priscilla said. She stepped
back. "I know we can't stretch out here on the floor
right now, but I desperately wanted to kiss you
again." She frowned. "Actually I needed to kiss you
and tell you what I've decided. I think it's time the

store has a man to help fun it. Some of the things I don't know much about. Oh, I can get along, but it takes a man's touch."

She watched him closely.

"Spur, I'm offering to sell you half the store for a thousand dollars. Then if things work out right, I want to marry you and turn the whole thing over to you and have six babies with you as their father. Spur, my own true love, I want to have a baby so bad!"

"Priscilla, that just wouldn't work out. My job keeps me moving around a lot. I'm just not ready to settle down to any one town."

"But you could be ready if I helped." She opened her blouse and spread it to show her breasts. Priscilla walked up to him and took his hands and put them on her chest. Then she stroked his crotch and found Spur's stiffening penis.

"See! See! He wants to stay with me! He wants to come inside me right now. I know he does!"

Spur fondled her breasts a moment, then stepped back.

"Priscilla, I never told you I loved you or wanted to stay here. I can't. I have to move on. There is just no chance that we could be married, so forget about that. You told me you just wanted to have a good time."

"No! I always wanted to marry you. I demonstrated that the first time when you attacked me and raped me. I didn't complain. Then in your room I didn't scream when you forced yourself on me again."

Her face clouded and anger sparked from her eyes. "But now, now, Spur McCoy, you are trifling with my affection. You have ruined me, made love to me, maybe even made me pregnant! You will marry me in case I might get pregnant, or I'll get the sheriff after you. I'll charge you with rape, three times, with raping me and now leaving me."

"That's not what happened, Priscilla. I didn't rape you. The whole sexy meeting was your idea, you insisted, you led. If anything, you were the one who seduced me that first time, as you very well know."

Fury built in her. She charged at him, her blouse still open, her breasts bouncing as she tried to scratch his face. He caught her hands.

"Not a chance in hell, woman!" Spur said softly. "You go ahead and play your games, but with somebody else. When you do get pregnant you'll have to move to another town or try to figure out who got you in a family way."

He threw her hands down and she slumped against the wall.

"Now forget it. The sheriff probably already knows about your open blouse policy, how you throw yourself at men. From now on we'll just steer clear of each other!"

"No! I'll die if you don't marry me!"

Spur laughed. "You must have been an actress, but this performance isn't that good. For your own good, just stay away from me."

Spur marched back to the front door, turned and scowled at Priscilla who still hadn't closed her blouse. He shrugged and went out the door to the boardwalk.

He was about to step off the walk into the street when he saw a gray horse coming toward him.

Astride the mount sat Willard Kleaner.

Spur waved at him and Willard pulled the gray to a stop next to Spur.

"Seen my new horse yet, Mr. McCoy?" Willard asked, his eyes glowing with pride.

"Not close up, Willard. A fine a looking gray as I've seen in a long time. Is she yours?"

"Yes sir. Bought her with my own money. Now I need to learn how to ride better and to rope. Can you . . ." Willard hesitated. "Mr. McCoy, can you use a rope?"

"Tolerable, Willard. I've earned my keep on a cattle drive or two."

"Could you teach me? I got a rope along with my outfit."

"Right now?"

"Why not? I got time before I got to work."

Spur put his hands on his hips and frowned at the boy. Then he grinned. "A half hour, if you'll practice tonight for an hour."

Willard promised that he'd practice and they went down the alley until they came to a fence and Spur took the lariat. It was a good cowboy's rope. He set a loop and swung it around his head once and pitched the open hoop over a fence post and snaked the rope tight.

"Easy once you get the hang of it," Spur explained. "The important thing is to keep your loop open so it can catch what you're throwing at. You ever see a roundup or a branding on one of the ranches round here?"

"Golly, no, Mr. McCoy."

"Should ride out to a ranch and watch one some time. Do you good. When they brand range cattle one cowboy ropes the front two legs of the steer, then the other man ropes the back two. That's the hard part. First you just learn how to catch that fence post."

Spur showed him how to hold the rope, how to set the loop and hold it, then swing it around his head. The first time Willard threw the rope he forgot to hold on to the loose end. By the fifth throw Willard roped the fence post.

"It's harder to do when you're on a horse because you're at a different angle and you're moving, but then so might be your target. You learn to rope the posts for a while. That'll keep you busy."

Willard moved forward and back, and then began walking past the post. On almost every turn he caught the post. At the end of fifteen minutes Spur held up his hands.

"Enough for one day. Didn't you say you had to get to the hotel to work?"

"Yeah. Wish I didn't." His young jaw set in a hard line. "One of these days I'll get good enough with my rope and horse so I can go get a job on a ranch as a real cowboy."

Not a lot of that work up this high in the mountains," Spur said. "But you keep working at it."

Willard took something from his saddlebag and brought it over to Spur.

"Look what I got me just today!" Willard said with a bucket just running over with pride.

He unwrapped an old, and well worn .44 six-gun.

Spur looked at it with surprise. He picked it up, hefted it, tried the action and spun the cylinder. It was empty. Most of the bluing had worn off it. One walnut hand grip was missing. Spur handed the weapon back holding the barrel.

"No need for you to get a six-gun," Spur said. "I

kind of wish you hadn't. Most cowboys wear six-guns only to shoot at rattlesnakes. Most of them miss."

"But all the cowboy books say that every range hand has a six-gun and a rifle and can use them!"

"Dime store novels don't picture the West how it really is, Willard. They write how they think it is. Most of those writers never ventured west of the Mississippi river."

Willard looked shocked. He wrapped up the weapon in a greasy cloth and stared at Spur.

"Mr. McCoy, I can't rightly believe that. I don't aim to get no bullets for it. Not yet."

"Willard, keep it wrapped up in the barn somewhere. Don't take it out on the street. A piece like that could get you in big trouble. You understand?"

"Yes, I understand, Mr. McCoy. I promise to keep it put away, for a while at least."

They walked back to the hotel and Willard tied his gray to the hitching rail in front of the hostelry and stared up the steps.

Ronald Lewton, the hotel owner, stood on the top step waiting for him.

Spur walked up with Willard and watched Lewton. The smaller man nodded at Spur then turned to Willard.

"You're ten minutes late. What are you trying to do, make me angry? You know what your responsibilities are.'

"Yes sir. I was just . . ." He stopped. "I won't be late again, I promise." He hurried into the hotel.

Spur stared hard at Lewton.

"Kind of hard on the boy, aren't you?"

"That's my business, sir. No, I don't want to sell my hotel. That completes our business."

Spur shook his head. "Not really, Lewton. I hear the boy has quite an inheritance coming to him. You keep treating him this way and he'll hate you by the time he gets his money. Is that what you want?"

Lewton jerked his head back in surprise. "No, no of course not. I'm just trying to do what's best for Willard. Lost both his parents."

"I heard. Also understand there's twenty dollars a month that you get to help raise the boy."

Lewton stiffened. "Which is absolutely no business of yours, sir!"

"You're right. But it might be some interest to the boy. Best you think about that sometime. Relax a little. He's a good kid, and he's going to be a man in two or three years."

Lewton turned and stalked into the hotel without looking back. Spur shrugged. He had tried. He'd seen it happen before. Spur walked down the steps to the first set of chairs outside the front of a store and sat in one and leaned back against the wall. He tilted his hat down over his eyes and put his mind to work on the problem.

Point one: Doc Slocum probably wasn't guilty of anything more than choosing the wrong friends in Washington, D.C. But Spur still had to take him in —or come up with some mighty convincing evidence for his superiors.

Point two: He still had a counterfeiter at large in the small village he had to find. He was near certain now that the man was not Doc Slocum. The sawbones had been totally surprised by the evidence Spur had shown him.

So who? One of the bigger gambling palaces? They could finance their whole operation that way, lose for a while and then win it all back with a big stack of chips bought with bogus money.

The only trouble with that theory was that Evangeline's was the biggest, richest saloon-gaming house in town. He'd lay high odds that Evangeline was not the fake money producer. She wasn't the type.

So who did he have left? Just a few merchants who seemed to be scratching to pay the rent or the mortgage to the bank every month.

The newsman? Highly unlikely. His establishment was not flush with money. The very nature of most newsmen was honesty to the core.

Spur went over the alternatives again in his mind, then dropped the front legs of the chair to the board-walk with a thumb and stood. He knew where he might find some answers. There was one place, and one person in the average small Western town where the most was known about the area and its people. He hoped that Johnson Corners had a good reliable representative of the profession.

Spur grinned and turned up the street in the direction of the Palace, Johnson Corners' only whore-house.

15

The only fancy lady house in town was a former residence a block off Main Street just one street down from the bank. It was fancy, with gingerbread work around the windows, cupolas, big windows on all three floors, and three chimneys for the fire-places.

Spur had heard about Princess Hanshoe the first day he was in town. She ran the local house and the sheriff made sure she had no competition as long as she kept the price reasonable, the girls as clean as possible and at least one who was somewhat pretty.

Spur started to knock, but a small neatly painted sign on the door said: "You made it this far, Come On IN!"

He turned a silver knob and let himself in. It was an entrance hall, the kind many homes in the East had where you could take off heavy wraps, and put down umbrellas and overshoes.

A small bell rang when he opened the door. Now

he heard a mumble of voices from somewhere in the house.

"It's only ten-thirty in the morning for god's sake!" one piercing voice protested.

Spur grinned. The ladies must have had a long night of work. As he waited he looked at the decorations. There were oil paintings on three of the four walls, two of them quite good showing a seascape in one and a landscape in the other. Both were unsigned.

He was admiring the brush work on the seascape when footsteps sounded behind him. He did not turn.

"Fascinated by the delicate work on that one?" a husky voice asked behind him. It was female but just barely.

"As a matter of fact I am," Spur said. "It's good. There's no signature. Is it a local artist?" He turned and smiled down at a short, slightly plump woman in her forties. She wore a bathrobe and had a kerchief hiding her hair.

The woman looked as if she had just woke up. Large blue eyes stared out at him from a slightly puffy face that had no other color at all. She frowned.

"Damn right it's by a local artist, me. I used to know how to do that." She squinted at him. "Oh, yeah. You're the new man in town. Trying to buy a business, you wanted us to think. Most figure you're some kind of a lawman, that is after the way you brought in them two bank robbers. Thanks for saving my money in the bank."

Spur grinned. "You're welcome. Spur McCoy is the name, and you're right. I don't want to buy your house."

"Damn, probably the only chance I'll ever have. You ain't here to get serviced, that's for damn certain. Good looker like you won't never have to pay for love."

"Just need to talk. You had your morning coffee yet?"

She laughed. "You can call me Princess. Fact is I ain't had coffee nor the potty or nothing yet. Usual we don't get woke up this time of day."

"I'll make the fire if you'll get the coffee pot," Spur said.

"Damn, didn't think they made them like you any more. Follow me to the coffee pot."

She led the way to the kitchen where Spur got the fire going from cut kindling and branches, then added some split fir and soon the fire heated through the iron grate and into the coffee water. They sat at a cheerful kitchen table and looked out on a back yard that sported a fence to fence garden that already had rows of growing vegetables.

"What I hate most about this country is the short growing season. Now down in Tennessee we had a season that lasts three times as long as we have here."

"You have a good knack with a garden."

"Like to try. You said you wanted to talk."

Spur told her about the phony money, laid out the four five dollar bills.

"Figured you was the law, never guessed from Washington, D.C. Wow." She put in the coffee and let it boil. "No sir, them bills would fool me. Probably got some now with that same serial number. What do I do with them?"

"Keep them, for now. My job is to find out who is running his own printing press."

"Somebody here in town?"

"Probably. At least someone here must be passing the money. Who would have that chance? Who could do it?" He paused while she frowned, thinking. "There could even be a hint, a bit of talk in the heat of passion, bragging by some man who wanted to impress a lady . . ."

"Not a chance. Professional secrets."

"This counterfeiter could ruin the town. If word gets out it could make people accept only gold coins. Cause one hell of a mess. You wouldn't want that to happen, Princess."

"And you could get nasty about my business, I know. Well, let me think."

She stood, moved to the stove and slid the coffee back off the heat to let it settle, then poured two cups and provided Spur with sugar and milk, but he used neither.

"I'm thinking, don't rush me."

A door to one side opened and a girl walked in. She wore a man's pants cut off at the knees and nothing else. Her long red hair was mussed, her face still sleepy. She had large breasts, heavily nippled, that swayed as she walked. She saw Spur and stopped for a moment.

Then she shrugged, went to the stove and poured a cup of coffee and without a word sat down at the table across from Spur. She didn't say a thing, simply drank her coffee and stared at Spur.

Princess began to nod. "Yeah, something is coming. Somebody said something about having a way to get rich, but he wasn't going to. Instead he was going to help the whole town. Said he had a regular money machine."

Spur tried to concentrate on Princess but his gaze

kept wandering back to the girl's breasts. She was smiling at him now waking up gradually. She moved and her breasts bounced.

"Vivian, stop that! He's not a customer."

"Might be if I shake them just right. I wouldn't mind, right now. Right here on the table. Hell, I'll give him a pop for free. Ain't he pretty?"

Princess shook her head. "It's hard as hell to get good help these days, Spur. This one for instance. Good tits, but no sense of business."

Spur laughed and looked back at Princess. "That sounds like my man, the one who wanted to help the whole town. Can you remember who he was?"

Princess shook her head. "He was drunk at the time, and I just ignored what he said. Lots of men get a little drunk and before they come. I can't remember who he was. A regular. I usually don't work, but we were really busy that night."

"Sounds like the newspaper guy," Vivian said.

"No, not him. He don't come in much." Princess shook her head and then closed her eyes thinking.

Vivian cupped her breasts and lifted them for Spur's benefit, then stood and leaned over making them swing down showing their true size.

"Vivian, get another cup of coffee and get your big tits out of here," Princess said. "I'm trying to think."

Vivian grinned, leaned in and kissed Spur on the cheek, then filled her coffee cup and swayed out the door.

Princess shook her head. "No use. I can't think of his name right now. But I will. Might take me some time. Where you staying? I'll send a note to you when I get the name." Spur told her. She stood up.

"Now to more interesting things." Princess

grinned. "One nice thing about this business. Your basic stock is always there and it don't wear out or get used up. You want Vivian? A free one to show my appreciation to the folks in Washington."

Spur stood and shook his head. "She's not really my type, Princess. And right now I'm on duty, so I can't. You understand."

"Sure, if she don't get you a hard-on, she don't. The matter is closed. I'll come up with the name in a day or two. Damn sure I will. Got me a good memory."

"Just one caution, Princess. What we talked about can't leave this room. It has to be in the strictest confidence. I need to surprise the counterfeiter. If he gets wind I'm here on his trail, he'll vanish or destroy the evidence and I'll never get this worked out."

"You bet. I don't tell tales out of school."

Spur finished his coffee, thanked the madam and went out the front door. Two spinster types met him on the sidewalk and sniffed self righteously as they passed him.

Spur was tempted to ask them if they lived at the house, but merely chuckled to himself and went down to Main Street.

Spur walked back to his hotel room where he washed up and changed his shirt, then had an early noon meal in the hotel dining room. He winked at Tessie in the hallway. She motioned him into the room she was cleaning, but he grinned and walked the other way.

He got to Doc Slocum's office just before he closed for dinner. There was only one other patient in the waiting room when Spur arrived and the medico took care of her quickly. He let her out and locked the outer door, then stared at Spur.

"I suppose you're here to argue with me."

"Not at all. But we do need to talk. I've got this warrant with both your names on it, and a boss in Washington who is hounding me to bring your body back to the capital for a trial. What the hell am I supposed to do?"

Doc Slocum sat on the white painted wooden bench along one wall of the waiting room and rubbed his face with his hands. His fat cheeks looked redder today.

"I had studied two years to be a doctor in Washington before I ran out of money and had to quit, did you know that? Then I got into business but I never got back to medicine. When everything blew up I left my wife and baby girl and ran. Yes, I'm a coward, too.

"I wasn't strong enough to face the public scandal, even though I knew I'd win. It was too much for me."

"So you came West."

"To a small town where they didn't have a doctor. I still had all my medical books, and I got some more. I put in six hours every night after my office closed for two years going through the last of the medical learning I needed. So nobody can say I'm not a trained physician. That much about me is honest and straight."

"Requirements for physicians are not really set up yet here," Spur said. "We have no argument with you on that score."

"You know I'm the only doctor for thirty, thirty-five mile ride in any direction? What these folks going to do for a doctor if you haul me out of here?"

"Worries me a lot, Doc. Convince me you should stay."

"Told you, Archibald Vincent died of a heart

attack. He wasn't shot or stabbed or strangled. How did the police say he died?"

"They didn't. My report just says he was killed."

"So straighten them out on it. He died a natural death, and nobody is a murderer. I laid it out for you about the counterfeiting. They used me. They used my small firm and my connection with the printing company and did things in my name I never authorized. I was duped."

"Might be hard to prove now one way or another," Spur said with a long puzzled look.

"McCoy, you'd be wasting tax payers money to haul me back to the capital for a trial. I'll get a good lawyer and he can prove in a minute that I'm not guilty of anything. You won't even be able to bring charges before they're thrown out of court. I know that much about the law."

"I'm starting to agree with you. Let me think it over. You can help your case by helping me on this other problem, the local counterfeiting."

"I told you, I wouldn't know how to start."

"But you know this town. Who in town is smart enough and has enough connections in Denver, probably, to get plates made and print off all this fake money?"

"Sure it's here in town?"

"No, but it's a good bet. Who could do it?"

"Take some thinking. I could come up with two or three right off. We have a lawyer by the name of Nevin Nelson. He's smart enough. He has a good practice, could float a lot of fake money. And he goes to Denver once a month at least. Has some clients there I understand."

"Sounds promising. Who else?"

"Josh, the livery man. He might not look it, but

he's the second richest man in town next to our banker. He owns about half of Main Street. Bought the land early, and put up the stores as he had money and kept renting them. He don't have to work if he don't want to. Likes to keep his hand in. Reckon he could hire somebody to do the Denver part. Trouble is, Josh has more money now than he can ever spend. Why would he make fake money? It just doesn't figure."

"Good point. But for some men, there never is enough money. Maybe Josh wants to own all of the town, including the bank. How well do you know him?"

"Not a chance he could do that. Those are the only two names I can come up with right off. Let me do some thinking." He watched Spur.

"Are you satisfied that I have nothing to do with the counterfeiting here in town?"

"Coming around that way. You don't take in enough cold cash to pass more than about fifty dollars a year." Spur paused. "Oh, Doc, you ever remarry?"

"Course not, I'm still married. Can't get me on that one. I do have a woman. We pretended to get married. Living in sin, but I'm no bigamist. And yes, I send money to my wife every month. She must know it comes from me. I send it through a Denver bank so my name or address is never used."

"I'm sorry about all this, Doc."

"Yeah, you look just sorry as hell. Now I need to get something to eat before folks start coming in again. You mind if I go have some dinner?"

Spur stood and walked to the door, unlatched it and looked back. "Doc, we nail down that counterfeiter, then we'll decide just what to do about you, fair enough? It's going to take some tall convincing."

"I could hire somebody to gun you down in some alley, McCoy," Doc said.

"Could, Doc, but you won't. I've seen too many killers. You just aren't one of them." Spur turned his back on the doctor and offered his back as a target as he walked out the door, closing it softly behind him.

16

Spur left the medical offices and walked two blocks back toward the center of the small town. He was not sure what to do about the doctor. It might take a couple of days to sort it all out. From the vague nature of his orders, he realized now there was some confusion in Washington about the case as well.

He slowed as he passed the alley next to the saddle shop. As he did a six-gun thundered from the narrow space and Spur felt a rush of air as a bullet slammed past his chest and dug into the street beyond him.

Spur lunged forward out of the alley and to the boardwalk next to the saddle shop, and drew his own weapon as he peered around the corner. Another slug tore into the wood just over his head and he jerked back out of sight.

For a fleeting moment he wondered if he had misjudged Doc Slocum. Then he shook his head. Impossible. The medic just wasn't the killing type. He bellied down on the boardwalk and peeked around the corner of the store from ground level. All he saw was a shadowy figure vanishing around the far end of the alley into the next street.

Spur leaped up and raced down the alley, paused at the end of it and looked out into the street. There were only two businesses here and a pair of houses. A man sat on a horse across the street watching Spur.

The man walked the mount across and grinned. "Guess you're after that person who came out of the alley just a minute ago. She was running right scared. Didn't get a good look at her but she had on a dark blue dress and a blue bonnet. She went into that second store down there, the feed store."

"A woman?"

"Right sure of that, mister. Pretty one, too."

Spur thanked him and walked quickly to the Corners Feed Store and went inside.

At once he was assaulted by the meal-like smell of crushed oats, ground corn and cracked wheat. The store front was backed by a small elevator and a feed grinding mill.

There was no one in the store. Spur went through the open door in back into the mill section. A man stood sacking grain from a hopper. He looked up and waved. The falling grain made so much noise speaking was of little use.

Spur looked around the milling area quickly and found the woman in a blue dress and blue bonnet standing behind sacks of grain.

"Well, Priscilla Davis. I should have known. I'm glad you're not a better shot." This far from the hopper they could talk and be understood.

She frowned, drew back. "I don't know what

you're talking about. I came in here for feed for my horse."

"Of course you did. But that was after you took two shots at me up on Main Street."

Spur moved quickly, jerked her reticule from her hands and opened it. Inside he found a weapon. He pulled it out and sniffed the barrel. It had been fired recently. He looked at it closer. It was a .38 caliber center fire weapon made only the year before, a Remington New Line Revolver #3. It was light with no trigger guard but used a rod ejector. A woman's gun.

He pushed the weapon in his belt and led her back into the store and then outside to the dusty street.

"I should take you down to the sheriff and charge you with attempted murder."

"You can't prove anything, Spur McCoy. Lots of people want to shoot you. I've heard you're here to take our doctor away. A lot of the woman are talking about it. They plan on stopping you. If I shot at you, I had a much better reason than that."

"You did try to kill me. Why?"

"Because you're supposed to marry me, and now you're backing out of it. I hate you!"

"Probably, but that's all your own doing. You better just forget about me and run your store, and find some nice quiet way to trap a man into marrying you. For you, getting pregnant might be the best idea after all."

Priscilla shouted something at him in fury and marched away through the inch-deep dust of the street toward her store.

Spur watched her go. She would be more trouble for him, he knew. The woman was not at all stable. He was surprised she had survived this long. There was a type of man who would love to move in on her, marry her, loot the store and house and ride off with the profits. So far she had been lucky.

Spur touched the long barreled Colt in his holster and walked toward the newspaper office. He had been headed there when Priscilla bushwhacked him. He wanted to lay his cards on the table for the newsman and see what help he could be. Spur was near-certain now that Hans Walker was not the counterfeiter.

However, Walker could be a good source of information about who the counterfeiter might be.

When Spur walked in the shop, Hans had his editor's hat on. He was furiously working at the front desk writing with a stub pencil on a pad of paper.

"Sorry, can't talk now, have to get this story done so it can be in this week's edition."

"You publish every week?"

"Well, no. Usually we wait until we have enough news and enough ads to make it worth while. You a newsman?"

"No. I'm a lawman, and I want to give you the biggest story you've ever had."

"The bank robbery is the one, I bet. Tell me how you knew about it going to happen. Is it true that you knew that dead man before, what was his name?"

"Abe Varner. Yes, I knew him before. Chased him before."

"Figured from what the sheriff said."

"I don't want to talk about the robbery. I want to talk about these." Spur handed the newspaperman the four five dollar bills."

"Is that genuine U.S. currency?"

Hans turned the bills over, felt of them, then nodded. "Sure seem good to me. Course I don't handle that much money every day. Our banker would know."

"He didn't. Check them again."

"Well, if you're so keen on them, at least one of them must be a bad bill, but I swear I can't tell which one."

"Look at the serial numbers."

"Land sakes! They all have the same number. So they all are counterfeit?"

"Right. My job is to find out who made and passed them."

"And since I have a printing press, I'm a suspect?"

"No. I've ruled you out. Not much goes on here nights, and you were surprised by the fake bills. Besides, you have no good way to pass the money."

"So you're giving me a story about the counterfeiting?"

"No, this is all confidential. What I want from you is help. Some suggestions about who in town might be prone to this sort of scheme and would have the contacts to do it."

"My first choice would be our banker, Bart Concord. But if you know him the idea is ludicrous. He isn't living high, he doesn't go to Denver every week to spend his money. His house is no better than mine and he dresses like everyone else. If he did it he didn't make a cent from the operation.

"So I'd have to go on to our bigshot lawyer who moved here from Denver after some family scandal."

"That would be Nevin Nelson?"

"Exactly. Never could find out what happened in

Denver, but the rumor is that he got his sister-in-law pregnant. Her husband, his brother, was sterile, and suddenly she starts to get a swelled belly, and all hell broke loose. Word is that he'd been bedding her for two years."

"So he'd have the connections for an engraver and printer in Denver and the morals to do the job?"

"About what I'm saying, McCoy. When can I print the story?"

"When I arrest someone. Not a word before, otherwise the culprit will take off scotfree."

"Understood. Not let me fill in some blanks I have on this robbery story. You killed Varner while he was threatening others in the bank. How many shots did you fire?"

"One."

Spur spent another fifteen minutes answering questions for the newsman, then thanked him and went out to the boardwalk. It took him five minutes to find the lawyer's office. It was upstairs over the barbershop. Spur knocked on the outer door and went in.

The office was well furnished, better than most of the houses in town, Spur decided. Carefully crafted oak furniture, some with thick upholstery, filled the room. A large oak desk sat in one corner and behind it a tall, broad shouldered man sat with a thin cigar in a long holder. He looked up, curious.

"Yes?"

"Mr. Nelson?"

"Yes. How can I help you?"

"I need some professional advice about a piece of property. I'm willing to pay."

"I charge two dollars an hour."

"That much? A working man earns little more

than a dollar a day, maybe thirty dollars a month."

"My fee is two dollars an hour for professional advice."

Spur shrugged. "All right. I want to know what the legal status is of the store owned and run by Priscilla Davies. Also about what the market value of the store is and if the building and land go with it."

"She wants to sell?" Nelson asked.

"That's not what I'm paying you for. I want to know the legal status of the property and business."

"Yes, of course. I can have that information for you by tomorrow."

Spur had not sat down. He took a twenty dollar double gold eagle from his pocket and handed it to the lawyer. "I prefer to pay in advance, will four dollars cover the bill?"

"Probably." The lawyer took out a purse and extracted a single and three five dollar bills. He gave them to Spur who folded them and put them in his pocket.

"I'll be by at noon tomorrow for the information. I just hope you have the answers I want." He walked out without saying goodbye.

Down the steps, Spur leaned against the wall and examined the five dollar bills. All the serial numbers were different, all had numbers not on the counterfeit bills. At least the lawyer wasn't passing them brazenly himself. It meant nothing. Spur had to find out more about this lawyer.

Spur turned back toward the Aspen Hotel. It was hot and he wanted a bath before dinner. He didn't care if Tessie came and scrubbed his back or not. He felt grimy.

He was half a block away from the hotel when he

saw a commotion in front of the hostelry. Two dozen women were milling about. Most of them had children in tow. They completely blocked the steps up to the hotel.

He frowned and continued forward out of curiosity. Something had the women all excited. It could be the vote. They didn't have it here yet.

He was at the edge of the group of women angling for the side of the steps when one of the women shouted.

"That's him! That's Spur McCoy, the federal lawman who wants to steal our doctor away from us!"

The women pushed their children ahead of them, held hands with the other women and before he knew it, had circled him and trapped him in their midst.

"You can't take our doctor away!" one woman shouted.

"I have four children who need Doc Slocum. You take him away and you kill one of my children!"

Spur held up his hands but they kept shouting. They hit the same theme over and over again. When Spur tried to push through the circle, two small boys grabbed his legs and hung on. The women shoved him back into the circle.

At last all of them quieted but one, who seemed to be the spokesman. She moved inside the circle and stared at Spur.

"Mr. McCoy. We realize that you are a federal lawman and that you've come to town for a purpose. We know you have a duty to do here. All we want to do is consider all the facts. We don't believe that Doctor George Slocum committed any foul deed in the East.

"Further we believe that even if he had, the good

works, the humanitarian efforts, the Christian charity the man has shown since he's been our doctor here, overbalance by a hundred fold any misdemeanor he may have committed.

"Without Doc Slocum this town would be in continual danger. There is no doctor for thirty-five to forty miles in any direction. We are isolated here and need a resident medical expert.

"Will you agree to let our doctor stay in town?"

The women were quiet. A horse whinnied down the street. Somewhere a leather whip cracked over the back of a stubborn mule.

"Ladies, I share your concern for Johnson Corners. I am still gathering evidence. What you have to say will have a bearing on whether Doc Slocum stays or leaves this community. However this is a matter for the law, not for a mob. Violence and mob action will not be tolerated. I have jurisdiction here and anyone who participates in a mob will be punished, whether that person is a man or a woman."

"Let us keep our doctor! He saved my baby's life when he was only three weeks old!" someone shouted.

"Without him this town could dry up and be eaten by the squirrels. Save our doctor!"

"Temper your justice with some mercy!" another shrilled.

"Save our doctor!" someone screamed.

The group picked it up as a chant and repeated it over and over again. Wagons stopped in the street. Riders reined in and soon the street in front of the hotel was clogged with buggies, wagons and the stage coach which came rolling in.

Spur edged toward the ring of women. They held

fast. He caught the wrists of two women in his powerful hands.

"I'm going to pull your hands apart. I don't want to hurt you. Why don't you just let go by yourself?"

Neither woman would look at him and held on tightly. Spur tugged a moment, then pulled harder and their hands came apart. He hurried up the steps and into the hotel before the women could stop him.

He continued upstairs to his outside room and watched from behind the closed curtains. The women remained in the street and on the steps for an hour. Spur did not get a bath, and he was late getting down to supper that evening. He was sure of one thing. If Doc Slocum did stay in Johnson Corners he would be more appreciated than ever. Now all Secret Agent Spur had to do was decide whether to take Doc Slocum back for trial or not.

17

That evening Spur wandered into the Evangeline
Saloon and Gaming House and played some faro but
lost twenty dollars quickly and gave it up. He saw
Evangeline supervising the whole operation from
her raised table and walked over to her.

"Just the man I want to see," she said sternly.
"You have some explaining to do. I hear that you
were serenaded tonight by some of our unhappy
women."

"True, are you going to join the chorus?"

"I sing only solo . . . or perhaps sometimes in
duet."

Spur slumped in the chair. "I've got a hell of a
problem. Any suggestions?"

"Not a one. Out of my area of concern." She
brightened and both dimples popped inward. "Want
to play some twenty-one?"

"Not really. I'm on a losing streak."

"How about some poker, that's the thinking man's game."

Spur wrinkled his brow and shook his head slowly. "Too many distractions down here."

He watched her. She looked up and saw him. Her dimples vanished, her smile faded. For a moment she was totally serious.

"Do you want to come upstairs and play?"

He touched her hand and was surprised when she jumped.

"Yes, Evangeline. I would like to come upstairs with you."

"And play poker," she added quickly.

"Yes, and play poker."

He left first, went out the front door and waited ten minutes, then went around to the saloon's private back door. It was unlocked. He went in, locked it behind him and walked quietly up the steep wooden stairs to the apartment over the saloon.

She met him at the door, stood on tip toes and kissed his lips quickly, then scurried away.

"Coffee, tea, wine or whiskey?"

"Coffee is too much trouble. How about a light whiskey and branch water."

"Make that two," she said softly and smiled at his surprise. "Remember a good gambler has to be able to hold her whiskey. I lost a big game only once because I couldn't drink as much as the men in the game. Never happened again."

They sat at a small table and she brought out the whiskey bottle, two glasses and a pitcher of cold water.

"All the comforts of the bar," he said.

She let him fix the drinks as she dealt a hand of

five card draw poker. They had no chips. There was no talk of any stakes.

They played two games and were on their second whiskey when she frowned.

"McCoy, there is no incentive to play well, to win. We need some stakes."

"Chips, matches, double eagles?"

She shook her head. She bent in and kissed him again and let her lips linger on his. Evangeline sighed, and watched him from so close she couldn't focus on his face. She edged back until he cleared and she smiled.

"Mr. McCoy. This is going to take some doing, and some getting used to for me, but I have decided that I am going to seduce you before the night is over. But that means I'm going to need some encouragement, some incentive."

Evangeline giggled and Spur saw the whiskey at work.

"Which means I think we should play strip poker!"

Spur laughed softly, reached in and kissed her cheek, then her lips quickly. "Good idea. Body stakes, whatever we're wearing is all we can bet."

She nodded and dealt a hand of seven card stud. It took more betting.

"A shoe to ante," Evangeline said. She slid off one of her shoes and put it on the table. Spur bent and unlaced his boot, then pulled it off and put it beside the shoe.

Spur won with a full house, Aces up.

A half hour later, Spur won a pot of two shoes, two socks, a blouse and a shirt.

'House rule," Evangeline said. "Once . . . once a

person takes off an item of clothing, it can't be put back on."

Spur nodded. He sat wearing only his pants. She had on a skirt and her chemise which covered her but outlined clearly her thrusting breasts.

The next hand was draw poker. Spur had most of the clothes they had taken off. Evangeline had only what she wore and two socks.

The game was seven card stud and Spur dealt. She bet a sock each time as the second and third cards came face up. Spur was high with a pair of deuces and he bet a sock.

Evangeline motioned to him. "Kiss me," she said softly. He leaned in and kissed her lips and was surprised how they fluttered open for a moment, then closed. When they parted she lifted the chemise over her head and put it in the pot.

Her breasts were small and firm, with bright red nipples over nearly colorless areolas.

"Beautiful!" Spur whispered.

"Then kiss me and then them," Evangeline said.

When he kissed her, her mouth was open and she stood slowly and broke off the kiss and led him toward the bedroom.

"I'm tired of playing cards," she said with a sly smile. "Can you think of any other game we could play?"

"I'll do my best," Spur said.

They settled down on the edge of the bed and she reached for his pants and quickly unbuttoned the fly.

"I want to see the good stuff!" she said. She pulled down his pants and short underwear together until his erection slanted upward.

"Oh, sweet mother, look at that!" She turned to

him and took a deep breath. "He's so beautiful you should never hide him!" She pulled his pants off the rest of the way and threw them on the floor. Then she pushed to the middle of the bed.

"You haven't kissed my bouncers yet."

Spur did, working around each breast, capping the journey by kissing, licking and then tenderly nibbling at her nipples.

"Sweet Mother! I've never had such a beautiful build up as this before. Not even my late husband." She giggled. "No, especially not my late husband."

He touched her skirt but the caught his hand and pulled it away. "Not yet, sweetheart."

It was ten minutes more before he got her skirt off and then she wouldn't let him touch the silk drawers she wore.

"I'm not ready," she protested.

Spur rolled on top of her, spread her legs and lay on her crotch, humping slowly with his hips until her hips began to beat in rhythm with his. Then he unbuttoned the drawers, slid them down and she kicked them off her feet.

"Oh, yes!" she said. "Now I'm ready!"

He entered her gently, felt her hot response and they raced together to their first climax quickly.

As they lay in each other's arms in the afterglow, Evangeline kissed him and sighed, "At least a dozen more times!" she said. "Now that I'm in the mood I want to stay that way all night. Promise me you won't get tired and run out on me."

Spur promised.

"Let's talk about Doc. You have to let him stay here. The town needs him. I've been going to him once a month or so. What would any of us do without him?"

They talked about Doc for a half hour. Spur brought up all of the legal problems he had, and how Doc should go back just to clear his name.

"But he's got an excellent reputation right here in his new life. Why would he want to go back there? His wife and family are here. Three kids already. He's respected, loved, needed, right here in Johnson Corners."

Spur fixed them new drinks and changed the subject. "Since you're so good solving my problems, who is the counterfeiter here in town?"

"Who? Only one man could do it all, that's Bart Concord, our banker. Who else could spread fake money around so easily?"

"Could, is the right word, here. He could. But from what I've seen of him and what other people tell me, he isn't the kind of man who would do something like that. This little bundle of five dollar bills could put half the town into bankruptcy, make twenty families flat broke and out in the street."

Evangeline nibbled his ear. "So don't believe me. Are you rested up enough?"

"Rested enough for what?"

She hit him in the shoulder. "Another way, let's try it another way."

By midnight they had made love four times. Evangeline fixed them a midnight breakfast of hashbrowns, over easy eggs, toast and jam and lots of coffee.

Neither of them had bothered to dress. They ate over the small table and when the last of the food and coffee were gone Spur led her back to the bedroom.

"This time I want to be on top," Evangeline said. Spur grinned.

"Anywhere, anytime," he said. Spur knew he should be working on the case, somehow. He pushed it out of his mind. Tomorrow would be time enough. He felt the womanly soft body lowering on him and he jolted upward in delight.

They woke up a little after seven the next morning and Evangeline looked at Spur in surprise for a moment. Then a brilliant smile transformed her face into a feast of pleasures as she reached over and kissed Spur's chest.

He was up in a second, holding her on the bed.

"Hey, you got breakfast last night, my turn this morning. Let me prowl your ice box and your cupboard."

A half hour later he had breakfast ready, a stack of hotcakes, with hot syrup, half a dozen strips of bacon and two sunny side up eggs on top of the cakes. A big cup of coffee completed the meal.

For a small lady, Evangeline had a good appetite. He made two more flapjacks for her and then they settled down on the edge of the bed, still undressed, watching each other.

"That was the best night of lovemaking I've ever had, including my honeymoon!" Evangeline said. She laughed. "Do you have time for a couple more?"

Spur stroked her breasts, then kissed them before he shook his head. "I'd be a stretcher case before noon. And I do have some work to do. First a change of clothes, and then another talk with Doc, probably. Were you serious about picking the banker for the counterfeiter?"

"Absolutely. He's the only one in town I can think of who has the outlets for passing the bills. He simply puts in half bad fives when we ask for change or cash checks, or get a loan. It's perfect."

"Too perfect, that's why I don't believe it."

"If I'm right, you owe me a week's camping trip up the Little Blue River."

"Camping? You like to camp?"

"My favorite hobby. I go every summer. I have all the equipment."

"You're on. And if I win, you have to let me run the roulette wheel for a night downstairs, and keep all of my winnings."

"Deal."

Spur got dressed. She watched him, lying on the bed in a series of provocative and sexy poses, but she couldn't entice him into taking off his clothes.

"Business calls," he said. He left the dishes for her to wash and a messy kitchen, but kissed her long and with feeling when he was ready to go down the steps.

"Will I see you tonight, here, for supper?"

"Who will run the store?"

"Freddie, my number one man downstairs. He manages for me and is honest. First honest manager I've ever found. But I pay him well."

"Deal." Spur went out the door and down the steps. It was a little after nine when he walked into the hotel and found a note in his key box. He took it upstairs and was about to order bath water when he read the note. It was signed by "Princess."

"Mr. McCoy. I remembered the man. He doesn't come in a lot but for special occasions and he always wants me and sometimes I make an exception. This time was about three months ago, and he kept telling me how he had a money tree. Then he paid me with six five dollar bills. I didn't think anything of it. He is a good tipper.

"Now I see how he could afford it. The man is our banker, Bart Concord. He has to be the counter-feiter."

"I'll be damned," Spur McCoy said out loud.

18

Spur stared at the note from the madam and snorted. So the counterfeiter was the banker after all, if Princess's memory was right. He figured it was. So he had misread Concord. The country bumpkin had outjuggled him. He'd take care of that oversight as soon as the bank opened. No sense going in early and let him get suspicious.

Spur washed up, shaved and changed clothes. Things were starting to come together. But could Concord have done the whole thing by himself? He wondered.

He still had to decide about Doc Slocum. Doc should go back and face the charges and prove them wrong. But that would involve his first wife and child and his whole old way of life. He was settled here, was loved and needed. What more could a man ask for?

Still, the law said he had to go back.

Spur McCoy was the law out here. What he said,

what he did was the only law some of these folks saw in years.

He went down to the street and walked out of town on the Denver road. It was little more than a wagon track, but the stages maneuvered over it. Eventually there would have to be country road work done. But not for a few years.

Doc, what the hell was he going to do about Doc?

He walked out for half an hour trying to sort out everything he knew about the case, then turned and came back. He was on the outskirts of town when he saw a gray horse tied to a tree near some rocks. He heard a shot from behind the rocks and when he came closer he realized it was Willard Kleaner's mount.

Spur started to walk toward the horse when he heard another shot and then a scream. He ran for the rocks. Behind them he found Willard sprawled on the ground, a six-gun in the dirt and blood gushing from the boy's right upper thigh.

Spur pulled the boy's kerchief from around his throat and folded it into a compress and pushed it against the spurting blood. He stripped off his belt and cinched it up around the leg to hold the cloth in place over the wound.

"What happened?" Spur asked as he worked.

"Practicing my draw," Willard said through his pain. "I got mixed up and I guess I shot myself."

"I thought you agreed . . ." Spur stopped. The kid looked so chagrined, so hurting that Spur didn't have the heart to scold him.

Spur stuffed the boy's six-gun in his belt, picked him up carefully, protested the right thigh and began walking the quarter mile into town.

"I can ride," Willard said through gritted teeth.

"You ride six feet and that thigh will bust open again, then nobody could stop it. A man don't have to lose much blood to come up dead. Saw it happen too many times in the big war."

At the edge of town someone saw them and ran to bring Doc Slocum. A block from the medic's office the compress came off and blood spurted from the wound again.

"You must have hit a big artery in there, Willard," Spur said. He put the strapping youth on a patch of green grass on a lawn in front of a house and fumbled with the compress.

"Let me do that," a voice said over Spur's shoulder.

Doc Slocum knelt down beside Spur and his knowing hands began to examine the wound. He put on a fresh compress and held it in place slowing the blood flow. He put some white sticky tape over the compress to hold it.

"I can't do it here. That might hold until we get him to my office. Where's a cart?"

"Too slow," Spur said. "I'll carry him. You watch the wound."

Spur picked up Willard and carried him again. He took long swinging strides, almost running but keeping it smooth so Willard didn't jolt. A dozen people on the sidewalks watched as they hurried down Main Street to the doctor's office and inside.

The compress came off again and a spurt of blood shot out hitting Spur in the chest.

"Damnit!" Doc spouted. "We got to hurry!" He quickly cut a hole in a large piece of white cloth and put it over Willard with the hole over the wound. Then he used a fresh compress and held it with his hand. He had Spur hold the compress in place and wrapped his belt around Willard's thigh and twisted it tight until it almost cut off the blood flow. Then he examined the wound again.

He repaired what damage he could, then stitched the sides of the bullet hole back together. Halfway through Willard sighed and passed out.

Doc finished, put a tight bandage over the wound after he had coated it with some salve, then put a second bandage over the first. He sat back and wiped the sweat off his forehead.

Spur sagged into a chair across the room.

"Damn good thing you came, Doc. He was bleeding like a throat-slit steer."

"Just routine. I get my share of gunshots. This one was strange, like it came from above, slanted down through the thigh and out almost at once."

"Accident, Doc. Willard shot himself learning how to draw."

"Damn fool kid."

"He never would have made it without you, Doc. I've seen too many men die of gunshot wounds not that bad. I couldn't get the bleeding stopped."

"Takes a little know-how is all." Doc looked embarrassed. "Help me get Willard into the recovery room, could you? He's grown half a hand since he got to town."

When Willard was safely tucked into bed in the next room, and a small woman brought in to watch him, Doc and Spur went into the doctor's office.

"Take off that shirt or it's ruined," Doc said. That was the first time Spur noticed the blood. Doc rinsed out the blood from the shirt in cold water, then used a little soap to get the last of the stain clean. He wrung out the wet shirt and hung it over a chair.

"I didn't know you did laundry, too, Doc."

"When a man's fighting for his life, McCoy, anything that helps, helps. You decided what to do about me yet?"

"Frankly . . . no. Like today, without you Willard would be dead by now. That helps. I'll decide soon."

Twenty minutes later Spur's light shirt was dry and he put it on. Doc Slocum was with a patient. Spur slipped out the side door and checked his vest. No blood on it. It hid most of the wrinkles in the just dry shirt.

A man ahead stared at Spur as he walked along the boardwalk. He turned and Spur tensed, his hand near his six-gun, but the man only rubbed his face.

"Say, are you that U.S. Marshal guy?"

"Close enough," Spur said.

"You just can't take away Doc Slocum. He done saved my right arm last winter. No doc here I'd have lost it sure. I was in a logging accident and Doc came out to the camp and stitched me back together again. Told me what to do and all. I'd be a one armed man by now if it warn't for him."

"Yes, thank you, I understand." Spur went past him and toward the hotel. He was stopped three more times on the street by men and women all urging him to let Doc stay in town.

At the hotel, a circle of a dozen women silently walked around the front steps. Each carried a stick with a sign on it. They all said, "Save our Doctor!" Spur saw them well down the street and circled the block and went in the back door and up to his room. He changed his shirt and checked his six-gun, then he went out the side door to see the banker. It was after ten by that time and the doors would be open.

Spur walked into the bank, saw the president's office door was open and went in. He closed the door behind him and stood in front of the modest desk, staring hard at Bart Concord.

"It's over, Concord. I'm from the United States Secret Service and I'm arresting you for counterfeiting five dollar bills and distributing them."

Concord leaned back in his chair. Surprise flooded his face, then slowly it crumpled. His shoulders sagged and he shook his head. "I told him it wouldn't last forever. Figured we'd get caught sometime. I was even starting to pull back some."

Spur sat down. "Tell me about it."

"Well it started about two years ago. This man I know said he could get an engraved plate for a five dollar bill. He knew I had a printing press. It's a hobby of mine. I print up all the forms for the bank, and my own stationery, things like that. At first I told him not a chance. I'm a banker, the honesty of the currency is a vital factor in my business. Counterfeit could ruin me.

"Then he pointed out that it might help, too. I could start making loans at low interest and without the usual collateral, so we could help out some struggling business firms. We could help people buy houses. All of this because we'd be using about half counterfeit for the actual cash we advanced.

"It took me several months to come around. In that time two businesses went broke that I could have saved. One man lost his house and shot himself leaving a wife and two children. At last I figured I'd do it. I would not make any profit from it, and it would be for the good of the town.

"By then this other man said he could get the plate, but I'd have to print up ten thousand dollars worth of the fives for him, and he would circulate them in Denver.

"By that time I was trapped. He said he'd go to the sheriff if I tried to back out. So, a month later I began experimenting with the press. My partner brought the paper from Denver. He said it was almost exactly the same kind the Treasury Department used to print the bills."

"Just who is this partner of yours, Concord."

The banker got up and walked to a closet, then came back. "I don't think I should tell you. He'd kill me for sure. He's told me as much."

"We'll get to that later. What happened next?"

"I got the press set right and the ink exactly the shade I needed and I printed off fifty. Just for fun I began passing them around town. Nobody knew the difference. I even checked with my two tellers who handle money all day. They couldn't tell the difference.

"Of course I never let them see two of the bills together. The serial numbers are a dead giveaway. My partner took fifty of them to Denver and passed them with no problems. People tend to trust a fiver more than they would a ten or a twenty. A twenty dollar bill is half a month's pay for most working men.

"After that I printed off five thousand worth for my partner and then two thousand for me. I began using it for special loans, I'd make. I kept two businesses afloat with those loans, and now they are solid and making money. I'm proud of that, McCoy, even if it might not have been entirely legal."

"Let's see the press, Concord."

The banker took him into a double locked back room where the platen printing press stood next to a window. There was a type case with six drawers of different fonts of hand set type of several sizes. A table held stacks of paper, and half a dozen bank forms were stacked on another table.

Spur looked at the forms. "You do good press work. Where is the plate?"

"It's not mine. My partner . . ."

"Who is this partner? You're going to have to tell me sometime. I guarantee that I'll protect you from him whoever he is."

"I realize that you'll try. He's a most forceful individual and quite frankly he frightens me."

"You should be more scared of me, Concord. I can put you into a federal prison for twenty years."

Concord wiped at moisture on his forehead. "I know that. This could hurt a lot of people. But . . . it doesn't have to. I've had a plan to pick up the bad money as it came into the bank in deposits. Most of the bills would be laundered out of the local system in about a year."

"The plate, Concord."

The banker sighed, went to the wall and pushed back a hidden panel and then lifted out a two-foot square section of the wall. Behind it was a safe. He twirled the knob, opened the door and took out a small package wrapped in a dozen layers of newspaper.

Inside was the metal engraved printing plate. Spur took it to the window and checked it against one of the fake bills. There was no doubt, it was the right plate. A small imperfection on the lower edge of the figure five, showed on both plate and bill.

Spur held the plate by both ends and slammed it against the edge of the window sill. The zinc plate broke neatly in half.

"Oh, God! I'm a dead man! He's going to kill me for sure now!"

"Who, Nevin Nelson?"

"Yes . . . how did you know?"

"I've been in town a while. So Nelson is the partner. He had the contacts in Denver, right?"

"Yes. Then once it got going he threatened to expose me to the sheriff, ruin me, close down my bank. I couldn't let that happen. All these good people *depend on me.*"

"Too bad their trust wasn't better placed. Concord, do you have any idea how many of the counterfeit bills you circulated in town?"

"Oh, yes, exactly. I keep records. So far the total is just a little over eight thousand four hundred. I haven't made any loans from the fake money for several months now."

"That's a lot of bills, Concord. How much have you printed for Nelson to take to Denver?"

"He kept pressuring me. He said he had to pay three thousand for the plate. So far it's up to a little over twelve thousand."

"It's over, you realize that?"

Concord slumped in a chair. "Yes, the printing is over. But I've had a plan all along to bring the bills back in. To go through the cash receipts every day and take out the bad bills and replace them with genuine ones."

Spur looked at him in surprise. He'd never caught a counterfeiter before who had any plans to make good on his bad bills. He was interested.

"Just how would that work, Concord?"

"Like I said. After the tellers went home, I'd go through their cash drawers and the receipts and deposits for the day and simply replace the bad bills with good ones from my private account."

"How long would it take?"

"To get them all? Never could. Some of them go out of town on the stage with visitors. Somebody might send a fiver in a letter home. But I figure I can capture about 95 percent of the bad bills in a little over a year."

Spur rubbed his jaw. It just might be worth it. It certainly would be better than jailing Concord and letting that eight thousand in counterfeit keep circulating or be called in and bankrupt some of the citizens.

"What would your partner say about this plan?"

"He'd kill me to save his own skin. Right now I think he suspects you're more than you told him."

"So my next move is to go see your good friend, Nevin Nelson the lawyer from Denver with the unsavory past."

"You heard about that?"

"Everyone has. First, do you have any more of the bad money printed?"

"Yes. I keep some on hand."

"How much?"

"About five thousand. That's a thousand bills. I keep them wrapped in ten stacks of a hundred each."

"Get them."

Concord went back to the safe and brought out the bundles of bills. Spur checked them. The serial numbers were identical.

"Damn fine engraving work, and printing. Too bad it was all illegal. You have a stove in here?"

Five minutes later they fed the last of the bills into the pot bellied heating stove in the storage room and Concord shook his head.

"Damn sad way to see my printing work come to its end this way."

"Better than stoking the furnace at the federal prison in Denver."

Spur made his decision quickly. "Concord, I'll trust you to do what you say you will. Tonight you begin laundering out the bad money. You have enough to cover it all?"

"I'll sell one building I own and that should cover what I'm short. You mean you'll really let me do it this way?"

"I don't see any value in ruining a lot of other folks lives for the mistakes you made. In the meantime you'll have a fine to pay to Uncle Sam and a lot of community service work to do here in town. I'll be through town from time to time to check up on you. I find any more funny money, your ass gets burned right into the nearest federal lockup!"

"No chance of that, Mr. McCoy. My only worry now is Nelson. How can you convince him to go along with this?"

"That's my problem, and it is a problem. That's my next visit. I'd suggest you stay in the bank and rest of the morning. You get set to clean up the five dollar population around Johnson Corners." Spur walked out of the bank. He had ten of the bad bills and the broken plate for evidence if he ever needed it. He hadn't decided if he'd even report this to his superiors.

19

Spur McCoy walked from the bank with a dozen thoughts churning through his head. He figured that Nevin Nelson was not the kind of man to take being arrested peacefully. He would come out fighting and clawing. The man might already be out of town running for his life.

No, Nelson was also the kind of man who would not run until he had to. So he would be here, in his office, waiting for Spur to call back on him for the estimate of the legal position of the Priscilla Davis property. And he was suspicious of Spur's motives.

Spur would find out soon enough where Nelson was.

Spur put his foot on the first wooden step leading upward toward the lawyer's office. He checked his .45 in its leather, and found it loose and ready. Spur walked up the steps and touched the lawyer's door. It was unlatched and swung open.

"Come in, McCoy," Nelson's voice said from

beyond the door. "Unlatched it just special for you."

Spur pushed open the door and stared at the business end of a sawed off shotgun, double barreled. The black muzzles gazed at him from just over the top of the lawyer's desk.

"Thought you'd be in to see me after your long talk with my little fat friend. Did he vomit up everything he knew? You are a lawman, right?"

McCoy watched the man's eyes, they were always the clue to a man with a gun. Nelson's were steady, hard, determined. He'd pull the trigger at the slightest movement of Spur's right hand toward his gun. Slowly McCoy lifted both hands until they were even with his head.

"Just came in to get that report I paid you for."

"Sure you did. Put your hands down slowly, then cross your arms in front. You move sudden and you're dead with buckshot. Now answer my question. You are a lawman or not?"

"You know I am or you wouldn't have that widow-maker in your hands. I'm here to pick up that thirteen thousand dollars in bogus five dollar bills you owe the U.S. Government."

"Figured as how. Now we have problem, you and I. How do I kill you so nobody knows it was me? At least nobody except fat Concord can know and he don't matter a tinker's damn."

Nelson scowled at Spur for a moment, then lifted from the chair slowly, keeping the shotgun centered at the lawman's chest.

"Not an inch. I don't want to see any part of you move more than a quarter of an inch or you'll get blown in half with both barrels. Ever seen a man shot this close with a scattergun? Not pretty, but that wouldn't bother you. You'd already be in hell stoking the furnaces.''

As he talked, Nelson moved slowly around the desk, to the side of Spur, then behind him. The Secret Service Agent saw it all, including the six-gun in Nelson's belt.

There was simply no chance, no way to try to draw against the aimed and cocked shotgun. He'd be dead before his hand touched iron.

So he waited.

As Nelson edged sideways behind Spur and out of sight, the lawman figured what was coming. It came quicker than he expected, the stunning, blow to the back of his head by the butt of the pistol, setting off a dozen brilliant flashes in his head. He tried to swing around to defend himself somehow.

But it was too late, the signal wires controlling his shoulders and arms shorted out and then his legs went and he tried to catch himself as he fell forward, missing the desk but slamming his forehead into the wooden floor with a jolt.

By that time Spur never felt the fall. He was unconscious.

Over him, Nelson grinned.

"Not such a big shot government agent now, are you, Spur McCoy? Only problem is what to do with you. Has to be the back way. Damn, wish I had one of those new steamer trunks. I could carry you down the back stairs, but you're a big one.''

Spur had fallen on his six-gun. Nelson used his foot to roll him over, then pulled out the long barreled weapon and snorted. He put it in a desk drawer, then used strong twine and tied Spur's hands behind him, then his ankles together.

"Time to call in a few favors," Nelson said softly.

He went out his front door and down two offices to the third one and talked for a moment with a big man behind a desk. The man had a thick beard and hair longer than the fashion. He belched, nodded and followed Nelson back to his office.

"He'd be a heap easier to move if he was already dead," the shaggy man said. "I could use my knife right now."

"No, for God's sakes, man, use your head. That would leave blood stains all over the place. You should be that smart. We untie him and both of us help him down the back steps and into a buggy. Then when he's out of sight we tie him up again and take him for a nice long ride he won't come back from. Even you should be able to understand that, Quint."

"Yeah, sure I can. Let's move him."

They dragged him by the shoulders to the back door, then Nelson looked up. There was a small porch-like passage along the three offices to the steps at the far end.

"Untie him now," Nelson said. They cut the twine and lifted Spur upright. He was a dead weight.

"We'll put him between us, arms over our shoulders. We can carry him that way and it'll look like he's drunk."

Nelson went back for Spur's hat and jammed it down low on his head half covering his face. "That helps."

They positioned Spur between them and opened the door. Someone was going down the last of the steps. They waited. When he left they moved out on the passage. Spur's feet dragged along. They talked to each other, looked at Spur, pretending he was drunk. Nobody paid attention to them.

One woman looked out a back window and then quickly away. At the stairs they were so narrow one man had to go first, so the three of them were sideways on the steps.

"Damn this is hard," Quint said. He was the man above Spur.

"Shut up and get it done," Nelson whispered. "And be sure you remember how to use that Colt in your belt when you get outside of town a ways. I don't want him found for a long time, you understand that?"

Before Quint could respond, Spur came alive in their arms. He lashed out with his left foot, jamming it in Nelson's side and ramming him down the last six steps so he landed in a heap at the bottom. Spur swung his free right hand, jolting his fist into the surprised Quint's jaw. He was driven back a step. Spur's left hand came free of Quint and he slammed his left fist deep into the unprotected belly before him. Quint yelled and sat down on the steps, his eyes glassy.

Spur powered one more right fist into Quint's face, sending him into dream land. Quickly Spur grabbed the six-gun from Quint's belt and spun. He saw Nelson pawing for the gun at his belt as he ran around the corner of the building heading down the short end of the alley.

Spur leaped down the remaining steps and ran after Nelson. McCoy's slashed at blood that ran into his right eye from the wound on his forehead. He got around the building and listened to a slug crash into the wall beside him.

Missed.

Thirty yards ahead. Nelson had stopped to take aim, now he sprinted on down the alley. Spur ran after him. He turned at the end of the alley toward Main. That meant more people, less chance for a good shot.

Spur took the corner around the hardware store at the alley mouth wide, felt the whisper of hot lead lancing through the air just over his head, and surged ahead as Nelson darted across Main and vanished into a haberdashery.

A woman looked at the blood pouring down Spur's face and fainted in front of the grocery. Spur dashed across the street to the men's clothing store and paused at the door. He heard nothing inside so darted in, exposing himself for a second in the light of the door.

A pistol round exploded sharply in the confines of the small store, but the slug ripped through only fabric as it cut a double hole in Spur's pants leg.

McCoy came with his borrowed gun up, cocked and ready but he found only a frightened store owner flat on the floor behind a counter pointing at the rear of the store.

Spur pushed open the door slowly from a crouch, let one shot sing through the opening, then he rushed in. The back door was ajar. He ran to it and looked out. He saw Nelson running away but getting tired. Spur threw two shots at the figure and saw one round hit his shoulder. Nelson staggered, turned and fired two more rounds from his weapon, then it clicked on empty.

He carried it as he ran across the alley into a back yard and on through it.

Spur pushed three more rounds from the loops in his gun belt into his borrowed .45 as he ran. It gave him six shots if he had the chance.

Nelson was wounded and kept running. That meant the chase would be a long one. Spur knew he had to keep the man off a horse. The house on this side of the street had no shed, but the two on the other side of the street did.

Horses!

Spur ran faster, wiped some of the blood off his face and cleaned his left hand on his pants leg. He heard a horse nicker, and then saw Nelson in the other yard, trying to mount a horse.

Spur sent a shot over his head.

"Hold it, right there, Nelson. No way you can get past me."

"Dead or alive, I'm going to try."

A woman came out of the back of the house, saw Nelson on the horse, then Spur with the gun. She lifted a shotgun wavering between aiming at Spur and Nelson who had mounted now.

"Put down that six-gun, mister, or I'll dust you off with birdshot. You on my Bessie, get down nice and easy."

Nelson ignored her, dug his heels into the horse and slammed forward, the only way he could go, directly at Spur.

The woman lifted the barrel and fired the first round over her horse's head, then turned and aimed at Spur. He dove for the ground behind the end of a low rock wall just as the buckshot peppered the rocks and the ground around him.

A half a second later the bay horse leaped over the wall directly over Spur and galloped away to the south. Spur jumped up but the pair was already out of pistol range.

"Ma'am, I'm a law officer, I'd like to borrow a horse to chase this outlaw. You have another one saddled?"

"You that McCoy guy?"

"Yes, ma'am and a wanted outlaw is getting away."

"Why didn't you say so? Philip is saddled and ready." She ran to the shed and brought out a big black. "Philip will outrun Bessie any day. Here. You want the scatter gun?"

Spur mounted, then took the shotgun and ten shells she had in her apron pocket.

"Much obliged. I'll bring back both your horses."

Spur kicked the black in the flanks and he jolted forward, then settled down to a steady cantor until Spur urged him into a gallop toward the fast vanishing bay ahead of them.

An hour later Spur settled down to playing a game of cat and mouse with Nelson. He knew the territory. He had led Spur into a series of small valleys and ridges, hiding now and then, but having to show himself to cross the next narrow opening.

The man running had the advantage. At every bit of cover there were always two directions he could take. The hunter had to wait to see which direction his quarry went before he could follow.

Then Spur saw something ahead that gave him hope. Nelson had made the turn that meant soon he would wind into a box canyon. It ended in a sheer rock wall of no more than twenty feet, but impossible to ride out of. Nelson might be able to climb out, but at least it would hold him up.

Spur cut across country, losing sight of Nelson for a few minutes, cutting off two valleys, and coming into a position where his man would have to come out of the last ridge and plunge across a hundred yard wide valley.

The cleared area was knee deep in waving green grass fed by the winter snows and its spring melt off. Spur waited under a fully leafed aspen that hid him entirely.

Five minutes later, Nelson came out of the edge of the cover on the far side. He looked behind, then rode hard across the open stretch.

He came within ten yards of where Spur figured he would dash back into cover, hoping this time not to have been seen. As Nelson came into the darkness from the light he was momentarily blinded.

Spur was ready. Nelson stopped five yards into the woods to let his eyes adjust. Spur had the pistol up with a two handed grip and aimed at Nelson's chest. The round went wide, smashed into Nelson's good shoulder, slamming him off the horse and screaming on the ground.

Spur rode up quickly, but Nelson was gone. The Secret Agent quieted his horse and listened. A boot broke a twig to the left. Spur moved his horse that way and found Nelson behind a two foot thick lodgepole pine.

He held up his pistol and aimed it at Spur.

"You're out of rounds, remember?"

"I had a pocket full. I planned ahead. Get down from your horse and take off your boots."

Spur fired a round between the man's feet. He jumped back.

"I'm not fooling. I have six shots left. You're a dead man."

Spur could see in the chambers of the weapon now. There was no dull reflection of lead inside any of them. Chances were the one under the hammer was also empty.

"So shoot. I'm waiting."

Blood stained Nelson's left arm. His right wrist seemed broken the way he held it. He stared at Spur a moment, then threw the empty weapon at him and ran into the thick brush.

For five minutes Spur herded a tired Nelson, moving him back toward his horse. Once Spur fired the shotgun over Nelson's head.

"Go ahead, kill me!" he raved. "I'm not going to any goddamn jail. That would be worse than dead."

They were in an open stretch where Nelson had nothing to hide behind. He picked up a four foot branch and swinging it as a club, charged Spur on the black.

Spur skittered the black backward out of reach.

"Put down the club, Nelson."

The man charged again, whacking the horse on the forelegs but there was little force in the blow. The horse screamed and ran off ten yards before Spur got him under control.

Spur moved back to the counterfeiter.

"Drop it or I'll shoot," Spur said. Nelson charged. Spur fired at his legs. The second slug hit one leg, but Nelson kept coming. The next round triggered before Spur could stop it found Nelson falling from the first hit.

The second slug hit him squarely in the face, just left of his right eye. He was dead by the time he hit the forest floor and rolled over on his back.

An hour later, Spur had dumped Nelson's body off the bay in front of the sheriff's office, then returned the two horses to the woman who owned them along with the shotgun and nine shells.

Back at the Sheriff's Office he told the sheriff he had wanted to question Nelson in connection with a counterfeiting case. The victim had drawn down on him, slugged him and was in the process of trying to kill him when he escaped and knocked out a man called Quint, and pursued the victim who refused to surrender.

The sheriff wrote down Spur's statement, had him sign it and then shook his head.

"We had a right nice and quiet town before you arrived. Are there going to be any more bodies dumped around here in the near future?"

"Won't be my doing if there are," Spur said. "My business here is almost finished."

"You got your man?"

"Yes, indeed, Sheriff. I got him."

"What about Doc Slocum?"

"That I'll let you know about tomorrow. First I have to go over to the doctor's office and get some minor surgery done on my scalp."

"Good luck. Doc might just decide to stitch up your mouth while he's at it!"

20

Ronald Lewton had been pacing in front of the sheriff's office for ten minutes when Spur came out. His anger had been building all the time and when he saw the Secret Service Agent, he flew at him with his arms waving.

"Why in the world did you encourage the boy to buy the gun? You should be ashamed of yourself! You almost got him killed. Then what would you have done? I know, I saw you teaching him with the rope. You undoubtedly suggested he buy the gun that he shot himself with."

Spur held up his hands but when that did no good he shouted.

"Hold it! Stop, right now! It's a little late for you to start showing some concern for the boy. You work him eight hours a day without paying him, you take his monthly stipend from his estate, and you treat him like poor relation.

"What in hell is the matter with you?"

Lewton dropped his hands. His face worked and tears seeped from his eyes. His shoulders sagged and all at once he was crying. Tears flowed down his cheeks. He sobbed and then furiously tried to stop.

"I . . . I . . . I guess I'm angry at myself. You're right. I've not appreciated the boy. He's smart and bright, he's a good boy. I'm sorry I accused you about the gun."

"I saw it. He showed it to me. I told him to put it away. He said he would. It must have been too much of a temptation. You know he's safe now. Doc Slocum saved his life."

"I'd guess you did too, carrying him into town that way."

"Had to be done. Now I need to let the sawbones take care of my head."

"Oh, land sakes, McCoy! Didn't notice. That's quite a gouge out of your forehead. It's bleeding again. You best get that fixed up right soon."

"On my way." Spur continued down the boardwalk toward the medical office. He was just past Priscilla Davis's store when he heard someone behind him. He turned and saw Priscilla there running toward him. She had a frown on her face and when she came closer he saw she was terribly upset.

He stopped and turned toward her. Priscilla was only four feet away when she lifted her right hand and he saw the gun. Before he could move she fired three times.

Spur dove to the left, rolled into the alley and pressed against the side of the building. He should be dead. The muzzle had been centered on his chest when she fired all three times.

Priscilla screamed and raced into the alley after him. She looked at the wrong side first and Spur leaped across the opening and caught her from behind and slapped the weapon from her hand. He spun her away and picked up the gun from the dust.

A minute later Sheriff Phillip Gump ran into the alley. Spur had broken open the weapon, an Adams Pocket Revolver. The fancy little .32 caliber weapon had gold inlay on the barrel, cylinder and body.

"McCoy, you all right?" Sheriff Gump asked.

"Guess so. Don't seem to be bleeding anywhere now."

"Look at the rounds."

Spur did as the sheriff suggested. They were blanks. Regular cartridges but with rounds of cardboard stuffed in where the lead slug should be and sealed with wax.

"You know about Priscilla?"

"Nearly everybody in town does. Too bad nobody told you. She's usually harmless enough. When she takes a fancy to a man and he doesn't return the affection, she gets downright unhappy and dangerous."

"I know. The first time her pistol had rounds with lead slugs in them. She barely missed me."

"Sorry, McCoy. I usually check her guns once a week and put in blanks. She doesn't remember. Guess I slipped up."

McCoy laughed. "Sheriff, I'm just glad she got this Adams with the blanks. Otherwise you'd be setting up a funeral right now. Who taught this lady to shoot?"

"Don't know. Her daddy, probably. She kind of went to pieces after he died. Some people say she and her father had what we call an unnatural relationship. At least he kept her satisfied sexually and in line. Last four or five years have been right lively when Priscilla gets her dander up.''

Spur looked at the woman. She leaned against the wall in the alley, staring into the street. She paid no attention to them. A moment later she lifted her skirts delicately to keep them out of the dust and dirt, walked daintily to the boardwalk and vanished down the block.

"She don't even remember what happened," Sheriff Gump said. "Sad case. She's such a pretty woman. No man around here will go anywhere near her. Not even with that gold mine of a store she owns thrown in."

Spur handed the fancy little gun to the sheriff. "Better reload this one and put it back where she keeps her weapons. Hope the next guy in town has a warning."

"Guess I could meet each stage and tell folks, but somehow I don't have the time, and it seems a little cruel. She hasn't even wounded anyone so far."

"Glad I didn't break her record. Now I better get down to Doc Slocum's before my head starts bleeding again."

"Have you decided . . ."

"No, Sheriff Gump. When I decide what to do about Doc, everyone will know." He turned and walked down to the boards and on toward the medical office.

He made one stop at the Moon General Store and asked if they had magazines and books. They had a few in the back corner. Spur made his purchase and left with it in a brown wrapper.

Doc Slocum snorted when he saw him.

"Wouldn't let me fix you up when you was here,

would you? Contrary cuss if I ever saw one. Now sit down and be quiet so I can get the blood off you and then maybe you'll stop scaring our little old ladies. Hear you made one faint already today and got shot full of cardboard by another one."

"You knew about Priscilla? Why didn't you tell me?"

"Didn't know you were sinning with her. Man's got a right to some privacy."

"In this case privacy could have got me killed."

"Couldn't have happened to a more deserving gent."

"Don't be mad just because you never made the wanted posters, Doc. I could solve that for you by sending a telegram to Washington. They'd print me up a good one. Make the reward two dollars. If you were in good health."

"Quiet while I spread some whiskey over your head."

"Usually I take it internally."

"Not this time."

"You're still mad at me. Furious, I'd guess. Sheriff Gump said you might stitch my mouth shut."

"Damn fine idea."

He used a cloth and washed off the gash in Spur's forehead, then splashed it with alcohol from a bottle.

Spur jolted sideways. "Damn! I like it better in my mouth."

"Later."

"Hear you have three kids, Doc."

"True. Roots. People like roots."

"What in hell am I going to tell Washington?"

"Lie. They won't believe the truth."

Doc put some salve on the wound, which wasn't as

deep as it looked, and taped it together. He put a bandage over it and washed his hands.

"You'll be good as new in a year or two. I tried to leave it so you'll have a big scar."

"Thanks, Doc. Now where is Will? I've got something for him."

"Right where we put him, second door down. He's got visitors."

When Spur opened the door he saw Ron Lewton and his wife sitting by Willard's bed. They looked up as he came in.

"Hi, Cowboy," Spur said. "Won't take up much of your time."

"Hi, Mr. McCoy. I got lots of time. Doc says I got to stay here for two more days, then at home for a week again before I start walking much. Something about part of me growing back together."

"Good, keep you out of trouble. Oh, brought you something to make the time go by." Spur handed him the small sack and stepped back.

Willard eagerly opened the paper and took out three Western dime novels. His eyes glowed as he looked at them.

"Wow, look at this Aunt Zelda! The latest ones! *Kid Rodeo and the Silver Moon*, and another one, *Sharpshooters at Rimrock Ranch*, and this one, *Rustlers on the Circle K*. Wow! I'll have enough to keep me reading for more than two days. Thanks Mr. McCoy!"

"It's going to cost you."

"Easy, I can pay for them. Uncle Ronald says I get to keep the twenty dollars a month from my inheritance."

"That's fine, Will, but this is a different kind of cost. You have to put that six-gun away in your uncle's hotel safe and leave it there until you're eighteen. You have no need for a pistol and it can only get you in more trouble."

"Yeah, I guess you're right. But in *Six-Guns and Rustlers*, this fifteen year old kid . . ." He stopped and grinned. "Yeah, that's just a story written by some guy in Chicago or New York who has never been west of the Mississippi."

They all laughed.

Zelda brought up a package and pushed it on the bed.

"I brought you some of your things, Willard," she said softly. She hadn't had a drink all morning.

Willard opened the sack and grinned. "Four of my Western novels! Great. Now I can compare them. Thanks!" He reached out and hugged his aunt who was slightly embarrassed.

Spur waved. "I have one more job to do. Don't like it, but I have to do it. You get well now and concentrate on your riding and roping. That's what a cowboy needs to do. When you get good enough, I bet your uncle could arrange for you to stay on one of the ranches for a couple of months next summer and learn to be a real cowhand."

When Spur left, Willard and his uncle were talking about the possibilities.

Spur took a deep breath, felt the blood pounding in his wounded forehead and went to the street. He heard the noise before he opened the outer door. It sounded like a marching band.

Just outside the office door he stopped short. There were a hundred people there standing silently. Now they all looked at him. The sounds had come from an undermanned German Oom Pah band. A man in the front of the crowd held up his hand and the band stopped its brassy sound.

"Spur McCoy. This delegation is here to make damn sure that you don't take away our only doctor. Don't know how much of a Western man you are. A good doctor is one reason most folks stayed here in Johnson Corners. Means the town is going to survive and grow and a place we can put down roots and establish a family and a good life.

"Ain't a big town, yet. But Doc Slocum is helping it grow, helping us stay healthy, and takes care of us when we get sick or hurt. Hear that young Will wouldn't have made it if Doc hadn't been here ready.

"Lots of others would be six feet under right now, except for Doc. We know you think he done wrong back East. We don't give a tinker's damn about back East. We are here and Doc is here and we want him to stay.

"We think you got the wrong charges or the wrong man. Anyway, anything he might have done has been more than paid for by all the good he's done out here.

"Oh, one last thing. We believe in law and order, but sometimes it takes a local militia to settle matters. We got about fifty guns here right now, all legally deputized by Sheriff Gump to form a posse. We don't aim to let anybody take Doc Slocum out of town. Not even you.

"That's it, McCoy. That's where we stand."

Spur pushed his low crowned brown hat back on his head. The sun glinted off the Mexican silver pesos on the headband.

"Good people of Johnson Corners. Let me make

one thing clear. Fifty guns, or a thousand guns, wouldn't persuade me to leave Doc Slocum here." There was a rumble of anger from the crowd. Spur hurried on.

"**Ten thousand guns wouldn't do the job**, not if I knew he should be taken back to Washington, D.C. to face charges. However, I have investigated the case completely, and have determined that this man is not guilty of anything more than being afraid. And I ask, are there any of us who haven't been afraid of something at one time or another?"

"What I'm saying is that I'm not going to take Doc Slocum away. As far as I'm concerned, he's a free man!"

There were shouts of joy. The German band struck up and a dozen people began a square dance in the street. Bells rang, a dozen men fired pistols into the air and there was a swarm of people on the boardwalk to shake Spur's hand. As soon as he could, he slipped away through the throng and worked his way to the Evangeline Saloon and Gaming House. He went through the front door and took a cold bottle of beer that Evangeline held out for him.

She took his hand and led him to her table. The saloon was just open and only two card players were there. She put her small white hand over his large browner one.

"Thanks, McCoy. Thanks for letting Doc Slocum stay in town.,"

"No thanks needed, but you're welcome. Like I said, he was innocent. Why disrupt the lives of six or eight people so he can prove it? I'll dream up something to put the whole case to rest."

"That's after our camping trip."

"Oh, damn."

"I did win our bet didn't I? I bet that the counter-feiter was our banker Bart Concord. He's the one, right?"

"Oh, damn."

"You said that. Isn't he the bogus bills man?"

"Yes. He's the one."

"Good, you did lose the bet. We go camping up the Little Blue River for a week. I told you I have enough gear for two."

"Won't people talk?"

"They do now. Saloon owner is the same as saloon girl which is the same as *puta*, whore, prostitute, fancy lady. I've already been painted that way, I guess it's about time I start getting some of the good stuff that goes along with the name."

"You're not a naughty lady."

"Thanks for the support. What am I, a loose woman?"

"A wonderful woman, and as I remember, excitingly tight!"

Her glance came up quickly and she grinned. "A gentleman wouldn't have said that."

"Sometimes it's no fun to be a gentleman." He sipped his beer.

"I bet you haven't had dinner yet. It's almost noon. Let's go upstairs and I'll show you I can cook."

She took his hand and led him past the bar to the rear door and up the stairs to her apartment.

"I don't care who is watching," she whispered.

In the kitchen he turned a straight backed chair around and sat on it as he watched her.

"This camping trip, could we work in some fishing and a little hunting?"

"Might, if you cooperate."

"Oh. I'm good at that. I'm wondering about the accommodations. This equipment you have, does it include blanket rolls?"

"Of course. You won't have to sleep under fir boughs to stay warm."

"Good, good. The blanket rolls. Are they for one or made for two people?"

She finished slicing potatoes into a skillet and grinned. "I'd say that also depends on how you play your cards."

"Oh. I'd think I could play them just about anyway the dealer wanted them played."

"Good. Now, you never did tell me the details about our banker friend. I know you had a long talk with him this morning. My guess is that he confessed. Right?"

He told her what happened and how it was extremely important to keep it quiet.

"Concord will pick up all of the five dollar bill forgeries gradually, and the general public will know nothing about it. The only people in town who know have promised to keep it quiet so there won't be a panic, and so nobody will go bankrupt or lose his house or savings."

Twenty minutes later they sat down to a meal of fresh fried potatoes and onions and cheese, fresh peas and hot buttered sweet corn on the cob.

"I hope your camp cooking is this good," he said.

"Depends what the hunter and fisherman brings me to cook," she said. Then she stood. "Now there's something else I want to talk to you about that we didn't quite get to last night. It's in the bedroom."

"I have a headache," Spur said.

"Good. I have just the right kind of intense physical exercise to cure it."

"You're sure?"

"Positive."

"I may need more than one treatment."

"We have a week to see if the cure will work."

Spur McCoy smiled. "Sounds fair to me," he said and they hurried into the bedroom.

TEXAS TEASE

1

A rifle snarled to Spur McCoy's left and in the same
instant a bullet sang by his head sending the U.S.
Secret Service agent diving off his mount and
twisting to hit the ground on his hands and feet. He
had been moving through a small patch of black oak
and mesquite along a little dry stream bed. He
hadn't noticed any other rider nearby.

His right fist raked the six-gun from his holster.
Another shot came, higher this time, far over his
head into the branches of an ancient cottonwood
above.

Spur's horse ran on for a dozen yards and stopped,
head down grazing on the new spring grass that still
showed green through the weeds and leafmold.

Spur looked around. He was in at the edge of the
fringe of trees that had sucked enough nourishment
to flourish along this little stream that ran full in the
fall when the rains came. He had not seen nor heard
anyone since he rode in out of the hot sun a few
minutes before.

He crawled forward toward a foot-thick black
walnut tree and looked around it from ground level

in the direction of the rifle report. Through the light brush and a few oak branches he saw a partially hidden rider on a white horse. The mount moved toward Spur cautiously.

Spur's six-gun came up when he saw a rifle aimed in his general direction. Brush and cottonwood leaves covered most of the rider and horse. He pondered shooting through the light cover. No, the smallest twig or branch could deflect a pistol bullet. He had to wait and be sure.

His trigger finger tightened to half-pull as he tracked the rider past a small oak and into the open beyond the low brush.

When McCoy saw the rider plainly, he swore. The rifleman was a woman. She hadn't noticed him or his horse although she could easily see the mount grazing twenty yards away. Instead she concentrated on the branches of a tree just in front of him. She lifted the rifle and shot again. Spur saw that it was a small bore weapon.

"Oh, damn I missed!" she wailed, then looked around as if to see if anyone had heard her swear and giggled. Quickly she ejected the round and pushed another one in the single shot weapon. At least it was new enough to use solid cartridges.

Spur stood up behind the tree and stepped into the open. She sat her horse astride like a man, not twenty feet away. She wore a soft green blouse, a small cap over brown hair and a brown skirt.

"I won't shoot if you don't," Spur called.

She started from surprise, triggered the weapon and sent the bullet slamming into the ground a dozen feet in front of Spur. Then she looked at him and her surprise turned into a smile.

A big jackrabbit leaped from high grass near where the rifle bullet struck. Its long ears laid back as it took three running hops and vanished behind some brush.

"Oh, dear, Daddy would scold me for sure. I'm terribly sorry, I really didn't mean to fire at all. You frightened me, and I jumped and nearly fell off Prince here and then my finger just . . ." She paused and watched him closer. "Good, I think you're smiling."

"That's the second time you've shot at me. The first time you missed by a good six inches."

"Oh, dear. Did I really?" She swung down from the horse with a practiced move. She wore a divided skirt to facilitate her riding.

She walked the white mount toward him.

"I didn't intend to shoot near you, I thought I was alone out here. I often come hunting squirrels—not to hit them, just to see how close I can come. And you? You're a stranger around Johnson Creek."

She waved her hand toward the start of the little town that could be seen across the flat Texas panhandle perhaps half a mile to the north.

"Yes, a stranger and I'm just coming to town. If you promise not to shoot at me anymore, I'll risk catching my mount and riding on."

"I promise. I'm going back to town, too, may I ride along with you?"

McCoy nodded and they walked toward his horse where it kept munching on the tender young grass. He watched her for a moment. She was a mite of a thing, barely five feet tall, with rich brown hair that fell out of the cap and down over her shoulders. He guessed her eyes were brown too. She was slender, even in the riding skirt, and showed small breasts under the blouse.

Her sweet smile snared his attention. She had a delightful, innocent, remarkably pretty face. Her eyes sparkled as she watched him. He guessed she must be nineteen or twenty.

"Really, I won't shoot at you again. I won't even load the rifle. My daddy gave it to me on my tenth birthday and taught me to use it. I'm a whole lot better at target practice then I am at hunting. I don't like to kill animals.

"You haven't told me your name. I'm Beth Johnson, and my grandfather started the town. Yes, *those Johnsons.* Do you have a name?"

McCoy laughed. He told her his name and that he was going to the little town on business.

She put one hand on her chin, sizing him up. "Let's see, about six feet and two inches tall and two hundred pounds. Reddish brown hair, a thick, full moustache and mutton chop sideburns. A rugged, outdoor face with dangerous green eyes. Your hands aren't tough enough for you to be a cowboy, no rope burns. You're too nice to be an outlaw, and I know all of the U.S. Marshals up here in the panhandle. No sample cases so you can't be a drummer."

Beth lifted her left foot into high stirrup and swung into the saddle on the white mare. She scowled at him for a minute as he caught the reins of his mare and settled into the leather.

"I give up. You're Spur McCoy, but I don't know what line of work you are in." She grinned. "I'm just naturally curious, that's all." She whipped the white mount around and galloped for a hundred yards toward town, then turned and waited for him as Spur walked his bay up to her.

"You don't like racing. Maybe you're a gambler?" She shook her head. "Nope, your vest isn't fancy enough. I give up."

They rode along in silence for a while. She kept glancing at him. At last a slow smile began to grow. "Oh, yes, I have it! You're the new man who is coming to run the hardware store. You look like a reliable merchant type."

"Sorry, Beth. I wouldn't know a twenty penny nail from a come-along."

"Oh."

"But I do have business in town. I've heard of a Harry Johnson. Are you any relation to him?"

"Yes, he was my father. He died, was murdered, two weeks ago."

"Murdered? Harry Johnson?"

"Yes somebody shot him five times, while he lay in his bed. I heard the shots, and by the time I got there . . ." Beth looked away and rubbed at her eyes.

"I'm sorry, Beth. He was the one I was coming to see, but don't tell anyone I said so. You ride on ahead. I'll come see you later today."

She wiped her eyes, nodded. "Only if you'll help me find out who killed him. I must know. The town marshal here is worse than useless." Her face was composed now, and took on a serious stern strength that caught him by surprise.

"Of course, that's part of my job now, to find out who killed your father."

"Come see me at the bank."

"Which one?" he asked.

"The only one, the Johnson Bank. It's mine now. I'm the banker for most of the county." She kicked the white horse with her heels and it lunged forward and raced the last hundred yards into town.

Spur McCoy came in a quarter of a mile around by a different road. The first thing he wanted was a cold beer.

Johnson Creek, Texas was about as he had guessed from the size and location. One main street where all of the town's businesses were located. The commercial section was almost two blocks long with a good-sized Catholic church at the far end. There were clapboard houses, mostly one-story tall, spreading back on right angled streets from Main. A few more than four hundred souls called this place home.

He found the town's one hotel, Johnson House, a three-story affair painted a soft brown, with a stoop and a porch big enough for three all-weather captains' chairs on each side. He tied up at the hitching rail out front, stepped up six inches to the boardwalk and went up the steps with his small carpetbag in his left hand.

Spur McCoy had learned to walk like a mountain cat, always alert, ready to move any direction at any time, observing everything that went on around him. Immediately aware of any danger. He felt none now. Nobody knew he was coming to town. Still the man he had come to see had been viciously murdered with five rounds.

It was not a good way to start a case.

He signed in under his own name at the desk, and asked for a second floor room with a window on Main Street. That way he could keep track of what happened. As he signed his name, the clerk craned his neck to read it. He was jittery, so nervous his hand almost shook. After he read Spur's name he calmed down enough to take money for the room.

Spur paid three dollars and fifty cents for the room, for seven nights. At fifty cents a night he knew this was not Houston. The room was barely worth fifty cents. The bed springs sagged under the lumpy mattress, the mirror over the small wash stand was cracked, and so was the china washbowl.

The room may have been ten feet square, but he doubted it. A small dresser and one chair completed the furniture. But the window did open on Main Street. He stood there a moment looking out. He saw the young woman, Beth Johnson, whom he had met outside of town, leave one building, cross the street and go into another store.

The second business was the bank, a solid looking structure of brick, two stories, set on a corner.

Yes, the rich young girl with the rifle. He dug into his carpetbag and shook out a clean shirt, stripped off his dirty one and his kerchief and gave himself a half bath in the cold water of the wash basin.

Then he shaved, combed his hair, put on the clean shirt and his second vest of brown doeskin, and perched the low crowned brown hat on his head. The hat had a string of Mexican silver coins around the crown. One of them had a bullet hole in it.

Across the street in the Lucky Horseshoe saloon, he tilted a cold bottle of beer and grinned at the apron.

"Settles the trail dust," Spur said.

The barkeep was big, heavy and surely worked as the bouncer when needed. He nodded at Spur's comment. "Figured you was new in town."

He felt it again, an undercurrent, a tension. It was as though half the folks in the town were holding their breath waiting for something ugly to happen. He'd noticed it in the room clerk. As he had walked across the street one woman gave him a wide berth and two men stared at him hard, almost in confrontation. He had passed the incidents off as his being a stranger in town. Now he wondered.

A man got a beer from the barkeep and slid a dozen feet down the bar away from Spur.

"Friend, this doesn't seem to be a particularly neighborly kind of town," Spur said.

"Some say."

"People seem like they got some bad tasting grub in their craw and they can't spit it out."

"Been known to happen. You want another beer?"

Spur shook his head and the apron moved away. McCoy spotted a poker game at the side of the saloon. Poker players were a good test of a community.

He walked back to the game, saw a vacant chair and stood behind it. "Mind if I sit in for a few hands?" McCoy asked. "New money into the game."

For a moment no one replied. Three men at the table looked at the fourth, a rangy man with sunburned face and rope scarred hands. He shook his head. "Sorry, this is our last game."

Spur nodded as he eased away from the table and went back to the bar. He ordered another of the stubby beers. When the apron set up the drink, Spur's gaze held him.

"What's happening in this town? Every person but one I've met so far is wound up spring tight about to explode."

"Town's got some troubles, but me, I try to stay out of them. Lost one eye at The Wilderness, don't aim to fight anybody else's fight from here on. Got me enough trouble with the dam deadbeats cadging drinks."

"Fair enough. The Wilderness, that wasn't trouble, that was disaster for both sides. Where can I find the sheriff?"

"No sheriff here, he's at the county seat. We got a town marshal, such as he is. Down Main Street a block and a half. Next to the stage office. Can't miss it."

Spur finished the short beer and went out the door with a wandering step. Nobody in this Texas high plains country seemed to be moving any faster than required.

He watched the people as he moved along the boardwalk. Most were quiet, reserved, smiled if they noticed his big grin. But no one stopped to chat, ask about the news from wherever he came from. They were only worried faces staring back at him.

He passed two general stores, a small freight office, then a meat market with a half a beef hanging in the window. Next to it was the Centennial Barbershop and a saddle maker. A saddle in the small display window looked like an excellent example of a real craftsman at work.

He passed a well stocked drug store, and then came to the stage office and the small sign over the next doorway that said simply, "Johnson Creek Jail." He went in and found a counter across most of the ten foot wide room. Behind it stood a man six inches shorter than Spur. He wore a black hat, vest and jacket and a Colt .44 hung in a belt holster that was hitched up so high it would be awkward to draw.

"Looking for the marshal," Spur said.

"You found him. I'm Marshal Ludlow."

"I just rode into town on business, and I can't figure out what is going on out there. The whole town seems ready to blow apart. There's a tension in the air that's almost like lightning."

"Local problem, none of your concern."

"What's the problem?"

"None of your affair."

"Marshal, it is my affair. I'm about ready to get my head blown off by some hothead with a hogsleg and you say it doesn't concern me?"

Marshal Ludlow paced slowly around his small office in back of the counter. Spur saw a door that led to some jail cells in back. When Ludlow stopped moving he lifted his hands palms up.

"The war's only been over for four years. Feelings are still running high in the South. Now we get this Bagger in town and he brings with him fifty voting citizens, everyone of them black. He gets himself voted in as town mayor. He's a Carpetbagger of the worst kind. Lots of southern towns and cities are having trouble with Carpetbaggers from the north. We'll deal with him eventually, in our own fashion.''

"That explains part of it. Baggers, I've heard plenty about them." He also had a sheaf of papers detailing how he, as a federal law officer and enforcement agent, had to bend over backwards to be sure that the Carpetbagger northerners and their black associates were given total protection under the new laws.

Ludlow watched him.

Spur shrugged. "Fine, at least I know. I don't want to get in no trouble here. Came on business, do my business and move on, or stay."

"What kind of business you have to do here?"

"Retail. Hear there's a hardware store for sale here."

The lawman snorted. "You don't look like a store man. Not with that tan and sunwhipped face. Besides, you wear your six-gun too low on your thigh. Only one reason, for a quick draw. I've seen a few like you. Don't like fast guns around here. Best if you do your business fast and get out of town."

"An order, Marshal?"

The smaller man watched Spur for a moment, then his glance fell and he turned away, looking smaller. "Mostly I make suggestions. Mostly they get followed. Up to you." But his voice had lost its snap. His lack of self confidence showed plainly. But a coward's backshooting a man makes him just as dead Spur knew.

"Thanks, Marshal. I'm not at all opposed to taking suggestions. Now, one more thing. Where can I find a gent named Harry Johnson? I'm a long-time friend of Harry's. He invited me up this way to see his town and his daughter and his bank."

"You don't know?"

"Know what, Marshal?"

"Harry Johnson died about two weeks ago. Tragic really. He'll be missed around this town."

Spur watched Ludlow critically, but there was no hint that he knew more than he was saying.

"From what Doctor Greenly said, he had some stomach problems and then something ruptured. Died in just a few minutes in the middle of the night."

"I'll have to visit the family. Is there a widow?"

"No, just his daughter Beth. She's probably at the bank this time of day."

Spur thanked him, strode out of the office, and marched down the street toward the bank. He was headed there but he saw the office of the local newspaper across the street. That would be his next stop. Why had the local doctor covered up the murder? Was it really murder or had Beth Johnson been making up little girl stories? There was one quick way to find out.

2

Spur angled across the dirt street to the *Johnson Creek Record*. The newspaper office was narrow, squeezed in between the barbershop and the Habberman Meat Market. The sign on the outside looked new, but it wasn't, just well painted.

Inside he found the usual counter across the room that was only fifteen feet to the wall. A double door led into the backshop and pressroom. Nobody was in the front office but he heard activity.

"Back here," a voice shouted from the rear.

Spur went around the counter and through the open door. The newspaper plant smelled as they all do, slightly musty, and overpowering with the unmistakable odor of newsprint, paper stock and printer's ink.

The back shop was slightly less stocked than many he had seen, but it was adequate, with a one-sheet flat bed press that was hand cranked.

Standing next to the type case was a man in his late forties, blond, with a plain, open face behind wire rimmed spectacles, a big nose and slightly protruding teeth.

"Breaking down last week's front page. What can I do for you, stranger?"

As he spoke the man pulled solid rule slugs from the wooden form that held the type and headlines for last week's front page of the *Record*. Then he picked up a handful of the small metal pieces that each had one letter formed on the top. Automatically he read the letter and dropped it in a designated bin in a type case in front of him.

"You must have a good memory where each letter goes," Spur said.

The man's expression never changed. "Nope. Just habit and practice. Rote really. Been casing type for twenty years. They tell me I did the whole front page one night while I was sleeping."

Spur grinned. "Two jobs at once. My name is McCoy, and I'm wondering if I could take a look at last week's paper to catch up on what's happening in town."

"That's why I print it. I'm Hans Runner. Cost you a nickel for the paper."

Spur found a dime in his pocket and laid it on the edge of the front page form.

"Keep the change. I'll get a paper out front. Mind if I read it here?"

"Help yourself." The man hesitated. "We don't get many strangers around here. Is there a story for the paper why you're in town? Maybe interested in the closed up hardware store? We sure could use that place being open."

"Might be, looking around a bit. Is it a good store? Why is it closed?"

"Right good little hardware. It's got things nobody else carries in town. We ain't a big town and a hardware store is one we need. Closed? Oh, old

Charley took sick last winter, lingered on for a while, finally got pneumonia and died overnight. No kin that we know of."

"I'll look it over." Spur went back to the front of the office, found the stack of this week's paper and scanned the front page. There was no death story about Harry Johnson. He looked around, found a rack that held previous editions. They were neatly punched with three holes and held between half inch thick sticks that bound them together.

He took off the current one and checked the front page for the previous edition. It had been two weeks since the paper came out. The story was the lead with a banner across the top of the page.

"Harry Johnson Dies at 52. Son of Town's founder succumbed last night to a sudden stomach malady that took him quickly according to Dr. Greenly. The physician said he was summoned about midnight, and by the time he got there, Mr. Johnson was bleeding internally and there was no possible way to save his life."

Spur read the rest of the story. Nothing was said about any violence, or shots being fired. The town marshal was not mentioned. A simple, unexplained, sudden death of a man in his prime.

Another item on that front page caught his eye: "Mayor White Defends Position." The story under the headline said: "Major Don White today denied that he is an opportunist from the North, who came to Texas to take advantage of the reconstruction laws. He said he is here for the long term, that he loves this town and is fighting to make it better in every way.

"He pointed out that he has already established a free public library, that he is considering gas lights for some of the Main Street areas, and that he will strictly control gambling, and all saloons and that the town will not tolerate fancy women.

"Critics say that White is little more than a Carpetbagger, here to fill his own pockets at the city's expense. They point out that he had himself voted a $200 monthly salary, when the previous mayor served for nothing. White said a professional manager for the city is needed and must be paid for.

"Dr. Greenly, one of Mr. White's continuing critics, says that everyone knows that Mr. White won the election because he brought in fifty Negro men and registered them to vote under the new federal reconstruction laws. Before the fifty men arrived in town from the Houston area, Dr. Greenly says there were only eighty-three men registered to vote in the city.

"Twenty local men, mostly drifters, who had never voted before and could not read nor write, were scooped up by Mr. White and registered, then paid to vote the way he told them, Dr. Greenly charged. This gave Mr. White an unbeatable total of seventy sure votes.

"Since many men were out of town on election day or ill or failed to vote, the total vote in five previous elections had been an average of 56. Last election a total of 114 voted. The mayor won election over his opponent 82 to 32.

"Dr. Greenly said he is investigating the state law on election fraud, and may call for a new election if he can prove that the votes were obtained under ' incentive or duress.' "

Spur read the rest of the story quickly. "Baggers," he said softly. Carpetbaggers from the North. Hundreds of them swept down on the South to use the new reconstruction voting rights of the newly franchised Negro voters and virtually take over whole cities and counties. Carpetbaggers had produced more hard feelings than anything since the war ended.

He turned back to the current paper and saw a story on the front page. "Man Shot Dead, Riot Ensues." The story told how a black man had been shot while trying to steal a bottle of whiskey from a local saloon. The head shot killed him and he was laid out on a door outside the saloon with a warning: *Baggers who steal get kilt dead. Go home Baggers or Else!*"

The mayor and a dozen of his black friends protested to the town marshal. Marshal Ludlow looked over the situation and said it was his opinion that the man had been shot while committing a felony, the barman was not charged since the body was on private property, he could not remove it without the consent of the property owner.

A short time later the story said, thirty enraged and armed black men stormed into Main Street, recovered the body of the dead man and took him to the cemetery for a funeral.

Spur read the rest of the paper closely. There were two more incidents of robbery that were laid to the new blacks in town, but there had been no charges brought. The mayor had intervened in each case and repaid the loss.

Now Spur understood the tenor of the town. There was a real crisis building here. The townspeople had suffered about all they would under the Carpetbagger. Even now the fuse might be lit and burning somewhere. Spur went back to talk to the newsman.

"These Baggers been around for a while?"

"Too damned long, but we haven't figured out a way to get rid of them yet without a lot of bloodshed. Right now things are heating up.

Wouldn't wonder that the top might blow off in a week or so. Just sort of feels that way.''

"You lived here long?'' Spur asked.

"I know this town. Been here for ten years or more now. Thought the town would grow more than it has. I'm just scratching to hang on. Now city taxes went up again.''

"Mayor White's doing?''

"Damn right. He got four new city councilmen elected. All blacks, and all do exactly what he tells them. Three of the four can't read nor write. But they can talk.''

"White controls the vote?''

"Every time. He said we needed something called Public Welfare. Says a person who is blind or deaf and can't support himself, should get help from the town. Says if a man can't find work to feed his family, the town taxes should help him.

"Now he's got 45 of those 50 blacks on this Public Welfare. Us taxpayers handing out a dole to them blacks every day so they can sit on their asses and make jokes about us. Ain't the American way!

"Don't mind feeding Mrs. Giersbach, cause she's blind and got no kin, but to dole out good money and food to folks to sit around and play poker all day for matches, just ain't right. Folks around here about had a bellyful.

"You can feel the tension out there on the street. Blacks don't even come down town much anymore. And the good blacks we had here before, now don't know what to do.''

"This whole thing must be bad for business,'' Spur ventured.

"Damn right! My ad space fell off twenty percent in the last six months since White's been here. And I didn't have that much more to start with. Taxes are just too high. One store closed down, mostly because of taxes.''

Runner put down a handful of rule slugs in a tray at one side of the type case and wiped his forehead leaving a smudge of black ink. He pulled out a new font drawer of larger sized type and went to work casing the headline letters and numbers.

"Ain't right, what he's doing. Sure we lost the war, and we paid for it. Hell we pay every day. I just don't think Abe Lincoln wanted us to pay this way. His getting shot probably was the worst thing that ever happened for the South, next to losing the war, of course.''

Spur folded the paper and put it under his arm. "Doesn't sound like a favorable climate to open a new business in, does it, Mr. Runner?''

"No sir, Mr. McCoy, much as I hate to say it, sure don't seem like it. I could sure'n hell use your advertising and printing work, too.'' He pied a column of type and began casing the individual letters. "Hell, maybe it'll work itself out. I'm staying right here, I damn well know that!''

Spur thanked him and walked back on the street, glad to know a little more about this powder keg of a town. He just hoped that he would be around in the right place to stamp out the fuse if it started burning.

He went up the street to the brick bank building and stepped inside. It had two teller windows protected with iron cages and a long counter separating the bankers from the customers.

A door to one side led into an office he guessed would be that of the president . . . Beth Johnson.

He walked to one of the cages and asked to see Miss Johnson. The teller took his name and asked him to wait. A moment later Beth flew out of her office smiling at him. She wore a conservative loose fitting blue dress that covered her from chin to wrist to toes.

"Mr. McCoy! I was hoping you would stop by. We have a lot of things to talk about. Please, come into my office."

Inside the large room she closed the door and softly threw a bolt locking them in. When she turned her smiled had bloomed even larger.

"Why didn't you tell me about the Carpetbaggers?" he asked sharply.

She lifted her head defensively, brown eyes taking on a hurt look. Then she shot up her brows and shook her head. "I didn't think it mattered that much. Besides, with too much trouble here, you might have wanted to leave town. I need you to stay. The whole town of Johnson Creek needs you to stay."

"First I have to know who is lying here. You tell me your father was shot five times. The marshal, the doctor and the newspaper say he died of a stomach problem. Are you lying, or are they?"

"They are. Doctor Greenly got here just a few minutes after the shooting, and he said there was nothing could be done for Daddy. Then he carefully explained to me that since Daddy was trying to get the Carpetbaggers and the townspeople together on this big conflict, that we needed to be careful.

"If we said Daddy was murdered, each side would accuse the other of doing it. And the whole thing could flare up into a war. I don't want anyone else to be hurt. Daddy tried to work out the problems between the sides. He just couldn't."

Spur walked around the office, looked at some of her father's pictures and mementos on the wall she hadn't yet got around to removing. He looked at a heavily curtained window. Then he came back to where Beth stood behind the big desk.

"All right I believe you. There is a cover-up, but we don't know why. The reasons the doctor gave are ridiculous. Why did he really want it hushed up?"

"It could have been a hot head from either side who did it. I don't see why there were five shots, but maybe he just wanted to make sure."

Tears seeped from her eyes. She walked slowly to him and put her arms around his back and pressed tightly against his chest. Her head barely came to his chin.

"Spur McCoy, I need you desperately here. The whole town needs you. I . . . I'm willing to do anything you want me to do, if you'll only stay and help me find out who killed my father."

She stepped back and began unbuttoning the fasteners of her dress.

"Beth, you don't . . ."

She stopped him by reaching up and kissing his lips. For a moment her tongue washed his lips through her open mouth, then she came away. Quickly she opened the buttons and pulled the dress apart. She lifted the chemise showing her small, round breasts with light pink areolas and small pink buds of nipples.

"Spur McCoy, I'll make love to you right now, right here, anyway you want me to. Don't you understand? I desperately need you to find my father's killer!"

She caught his head and pulled it down so his mouth touched her right breast. Spur kissed the orb, moved to the other one and kissed it, then lifted up and kissed her lips softly.

He pulled her chemise down to cover her, then adjusted her dress and buttoned it.

"I'm staying. Don't think you can bribe me with your delicious, sexy body. It looks like I have a lot of work to do here, and I need to get started. I want you to help me, but not by laying on your back. I need your memory, your knowledge of the town and its people."

"Yes, yes, I'll help." She turned away and stamped her foot on the floor. "Damn!" She looked up and smiled. "Damn, it wouldn't have been that big a sacrifice for me. Did it ever occur to you that I might have *wanted* to make love to you, just for the pure, wild, sexy pleasure of it?"

Beth turned at once and went behind her desk.

"Mr. McCoy, would you sit down right here and we'll start to work on our problem. Ask me anything you want to know about this town, I've lived here all my life. I know everything there is to know about Johnson Creek."

Spur stood watching her. He went around the desk, lifted her up and kissed her hard and demanding, his hand covering one of her breasts and massaging it gently. He let the kiss last a long time, then he broke it off and went back to the front of the desk.

"That's a small sample, something we can look forward to sometime in the future. Right now, we do have a lot of work to do."

For a moment Beth was in a soft, wonderful world that she didn't want to leave. Then she blinked and saw Spur across her desk. She remembered his kiss, his caress of her breast. Yes, it would be something to look forward to.

She smiled, blinked again. Then she leaned toward him. "Mr. McCoy, I will look with delight every day to the future. Now, I believe you said we had some work to do. What is it you need to know about Johnson Creek and its people?

3

Beth Johnson looked at Spur McCoy for a moment and smiled softly. He had said later. Good.

"Now, about our town. Seven months ago Don White came into Johnson Creek with his fifty Negroes. He registered them to vote, registered himself and legally put up four of his people for city council seats and himself for mayor.

"For a month he went around town registering every drifter and no-account he could find who would vote the way he was told to for five dollars. He found plenty.

"When the election came he won by a paid for landslide. Every one of his people voted. We've been trying to do something about it ever since with no luck. He's made changes, increased taxes twice and as you know has all his blacks either on the city payroll or on a dole from the city.

"Dr. Greenly said if White works the way other Carpetbaggers around here do it, he'll try for some big contract or cash award and abscond with all the city money he can grab, leaving his coloreds in the lurch."

"Does it look like he'll do that?" Spur asked.

"I'd think so. Everything points that way. But he's slick. Butter won't melt in his mouth."

"His four city councilmen, do they count?"

"Only to vote. Only one of them can read or write. They do what he tells them, nothing more."

"Any hope on the city council?"

"Only Zed Hiatt is left from the old town council. Five votes on the council. Zed isn't a brilliant man. He's a widower and a jeweler. Quite good at designing jewelry, but no push, no starch in his backbone. He never fights the majority, simply votes no and they charge forward."

Spur scowled, paced the room and watched her.

"The town marshal. I take it he's hired or fired by the city. So he must be working closely with Don White."

"Not really. He was marshal before White came to town. White let him stay on, nobody is sure why. Public opinion, maybe. White tells Ludlow what to do and usually he does it. If he didn't that would be cause for firing him.

"Garth keeps to himself a lot. He was away for a while in the war and then came back, wounded. Lost an eye, I think. He does the job. It isn't that hard in Johnson Creek."

"Deputies?"

"Usually he has one man on nights. The night man sleeps in the jail, so can handle most of the problems. Not much doing here after about ten o'clock. That's when the saloons have to close. New law by the new mayor."

"Who else should I know?"

"June. You have to meet June. I bet not even you could walk away from June Black. June is a seamstress here in town. Twenty-one, maybe

29

twenty-five, nobody knows. She's a breed, but not the usual kind. June had a black mother and a Kiowa Indian father.

"A pretty girl, sultry, and . . . Well, you'll see. She knows everything about both sides in town. She's also the nearest thing to a fancy lady we have. She accepts some special male visitors now and then, but on an exclusive basis. Expensive, too, I've heard."

"Would she know much about White?"

"Not from that angle, he's got a little black chitty of his own. She looks like she's about thirteen, but she could be fourteen. Her body is at least twenty-five!"

"June is a social outcast then, but still makes dresses for the uppity women in town who can afford it?"

"Right. And she's a good seamstress. Let's see, who else. You said you've met Hans Runner. He's a character. Has a wife, but nobody sees much of her. He runs the best paper we've had here in years."

She paused and looked out the window. She had opened the drapes so the sun would shine in.

"You should know about our whiskey priest. The Catholic bosses somewhere sent us a priest who couldn't be tolerated anywhere else. He uses more Communion wine than any other churchman in history, but prefers his drink to be much stronger.

"The story is that Father Desmond was chased out of his last parish after one of the women in the church told the bishop that the priest had accosted her, had his way with her when she went to his quarters for special guidance."

Beth walked around the room, her hips working smoothly under the blue dress. Spur did not miss her subtle way of showing off her best features.

"That's about the best gossip on the people I think might be able to help you. They all know more than most about what goes on in town. Do you want me to go along with you, introduce you to them?"

"Why don't you introduce me to the priest, after that I'll be on my own."

She smiled. "Sounds safe enough. Right about now he should be in his quarters or in the chapel. Let's go."

They went out the front door, and she held his arm as they negotiated the dirt of the street, angling around a fresh pile of horse droppings. Dirt and manure in the street were common factors in every Western town, and Spur had grown accustomed to them.

They stepped up a foot to the boardwalk on the far side in front of a closed store, when a woman came screaming out the front door.

She shrilled at the top of her voice. Her dress was half ripped off, one large breast sagged from her bodice and blood showed on her face. Spur grabbed the woman, Beth pulled her dress around to cover her and Beth nodded toward the bakery next door.

They hurried the woman inside and the baker motioned them into the back room where there was a chair. Beth took over, helping the woman sit down, blotting perspiration from her forehead, all the time talking calmly to her.

She had stopped screaming as soon as Beth put her arm around her and helped her into the bakery. Now tears came, huge gasping sobs that shook her.

Beth asked her gently what happened.

"They raped me! Two of them black baggers. They caught me in the alley, dragged me inside and . . . and did it. Twice, both of them twice!" She began crying again. The baker had been listening.

He took a six-gun from a drawer in the bakery and hurried out the door.

Too late, Spur realized what he was up to and he nodded to Beth and went after the baker. He was far too late. The baker must have shouted the news as soon as he hit the street.

Everywhere men grabbed at weapons, women and children darted off the street into the first store they could find.

More than two dozen men, all armed with pistols, rifles and shotguns prowled Main Street.

Spur ran for the jail. The marshal met him on the way out.

"I know, I know. Something like this is hard to stop." He ran up the street and fired his six-gun five times into the air.

"There will be no violence here!" he shouted. "The guilty men will be found and punished. Now go back to work, back to your homes, all of you."

Three men ran around the corner from Second Street. They had in tow two blacks. Ropes were around the colored men's necks and they were naked to the waist.

"Got them, by Jesus!" one of the white men yelled. "Drunk as skunks, both of them. Found them hiding in the old store where they done it. One didn't even have his pants back on yet."

Marshal Ludlow looked at the three men, solid citizens all of them. He stared at the two blacks.

"You do that white woman? You raped her in the old store?"

Both stared at him and wouldn't reply.

"Lynch the black bastards!" one man roared.

Spur's six-gun blasted into the air. "Enough of that kind of talk. We've got laws here."

"Wanta see Mista White," one of the Negroes said.

"You can talk to him in jail," the marshal said. Neither of you has denied that you raped that woman. You're both under arrest."

Someone in the crowd cheered. Another man yelled for a hanging.

Spur watched the crowd of more than forty men now. He motioned for Ludlow to take the prisoners away. Spur walked behind them, facing the crowd. His Remmington .44 drawn and covering them.

"The first man who gets any ideas about gun play is a dead hombre," Spur said. The crowd slowed.

Ludlow pushed the two black men through the jail door, slammed and locked it. Spur watched as he closed the two-inch thick inside shutters on the window. Then he looked at the crowd.

"It's a matter for the law now. Break it up here. Get back to your jobs or wherever you were. The excitement is all over. Move out, now!"

They scattered but slowly, watching the jail.

Somebody at the far end of the crowd yelled for a hanging, but Spur couldn't tell who it was.

Before they had walked fifty yards up the street, they heard a volley of shots coming from a half block farther on. Spur and the rest of them ran up to the corner of third, but found nothing.

Too late, Spur realized his mistake. A diversion! As he turned there came four spaced shots from behind them, near the jail. They raced back that way and found the two Negroes on the boardwalk in front of the jail. Both had been shot twice in the head from close range and were dead.

Inside the jail, Marshal Ludlow lay on the floor, still unconscious from a blow to the back of the head. The rear door into the jail and the door to the alley were both open. Someone had surprised the marshal.

By the time Spur brought the marshal back to consciousness, Don White stormed into the jail.

"Stop them! For God's sake, stop them! The ghouls are parading up and down Main Street with the bodies of those two boys. Get out there and stop them Marshal Ludlow, or turn in your badge!"

Garth Ludlow blinked as he looked up at White. Then he rose slowly to his feet, weaved as he tried to get his balance. Then he tore the badge off his shirt and slapped it into the mayor's face.

"Take your goddamned job, and your badge. I quit." He walked out the front door and Spur followed him. Spur looked toward the yelling and shouting up the street. The parade turned and the wagon hauling the bodies came down Main Street toward Spur.

Two men led the horses and the cheering. Spur put one shot into the air, then twenty feet away shouted into the sudden stillness.

"Hold it, right there, if you want to move another step, you're doing it over my body." Slowly he holstered his gun and stared at both men.

"You both have iron, let's see if you can use it. Right now, both of you draw and fire, or get the hell out of the street."

The two men were from a ranch. The only thing they had ever shot at were jackrabbits and rattlesnakes. They backed down and hurried into the crowd.

"Get the undertaker!" Spur bellowed. "The rest of you have thirty seconds to get off the street or I'm hauling you in to jail. Vamoose!"

Before the undertaker got there, a black man

hurried in from the side street. Mayor White talked with him a moment, and then both got on the wagon and drove down the side street and out toward the cemetery.

The curious, the angry, the ordinary citizens came out of the stores and talked in low tones. They had no idea who this gunman was who took over and stopped the violence, but some cheered him silently. Maybe he was the one who could save the town from the Carpetbaggers.

The mayor came back and called to Spur.

"Mr. McCoy, I'm told you've called. I want to thank you for stopping this thing. It could have become ugly."

"I'd say two rapes and two murders was already ugly, Mayor. What are you going to do about it?"

"What can I do?"

"You could give this town you stole back to the citizens and go return to wherever you came from. You're an opportunist of the worst kind, White. I'm surprised that you don't slit your own throat one of these mornings when you're shaving. How can you live with yourself? How can you stand to look into the black soul of that man in the mirror every morning?"

Spur spun on his heel and strode away. He heard more shooting and charged up the street into the scene. A black man had just been shot coming out of a store. Before anyone could move, a white couple coming down the street in a carriage was shot dead by a rifle.

Spur grabbed a rifle from a man standing on the sidewalk and blasted four shots into the air.

"Now listen to this!" he bellowed. Every head turned and the three blocks of Main Street were suddenly quiet.

"My name is Spur McCoy. I'm a United States Secret Service Agent from Washington D.C. I'm taking over the law enforcement of this town as of now. There will be no more gunplay in Johnson Creek starting now. Anyone carrying a weapon will be arrested. No guns are permitted in public view. The next person who fires a weapon will be arrested."

He stalked to the boardwalk and caught the man who he heard bragging that he had killed the Negro. He slammed the rifle out of his hands, twisted one arm behind his back and marched him to the middle of the street.

"This man is under arrest for murder. Anyone else who fires a weapon in town will also be arrested. Now get about your peaceful business."

Spur turned his back on the majority of the people and marched his prisoner to the jail. There he found the deputy who heard about the marshal resigning. Spur ordered him to stay on duty and to find a second deputy for the night shift.

Spur stood outside the small jail a moment. Things were not going well. How could he find out who killed Harry Thompson in the middle of a damn riot? He shrugged. Maybe the whiskey priest could help him calm the people. That was his next stop.

4

Spur McCoy scowled as he saw the luxury of the Catholic church in this dirt poor town. The faithful suffered in this life so the church could have a real gold dome and an altar that was worth as much as half the town. The grounds were watered and well tended, undoubtedly by many volunteers.

He pasted a smile on his face and approached one of the dark robed sisters who showed him where Father Desmond was. He was in his quarters at the back of the complex. The only priest in the parish had a six or seven room apartment attached to the small parochial school.

Spur knocked on the door and waited. A few moments later the heavy panel opened and a short man on the heavy side stood there in clerical collar and shirt, but no black jacket.

Father Desmond was fifty-two, had a tick that bothered his left eye, and a flat Gaelic face, and soft blue, watery eyes. His face was sallow white, with a liver spot on his right cheek. He had not shaved that morning and dark stubble patterned his jaw.

"Yes, you're the new man in town. Maybe you can

do something about this bunch of Godless Carpetbaggers we have." He held out his hand. "I'm
Father Desmond. I understand you want to talk to
me."

"Fact is, I do, Pastor. If you have the time?"

"Now is a good time, come in, my son."

Spur was on the verge of flaring up, declaring that
he was not Catholic and he was not the man's son;
instead he stepped inside the pleasantly cool and
well furnished room.

Father Desmond closed the door and motioned for
Spur to sit on one of the sofas in the big room.

"Now, I hear you've been talking with our
marshal, the newspaperman and pretty little Beth
Johnson. This must be about the Carpetbaggers,
right?"

"Partly. I understand you know just about everything that goes on in Johnson Creek. That's why I
wanted to come and see you."

The priest laughed lightly and in the gush of air,
Spur smelled the tinge of whiskey breath.

"You flatter me, Mr. Spur. Through the confessional, I do have an ear to much of the communtiy,
but that is shared only with God. However, there is
much else in town that I am aware of, and that I
hear about."

"Pastor Desmond, I'm a peace officer, a U.S.
Secret Service Agent working for the Federal
Government. There are some problems in this town
that local authorities can't solve. We were called in
to help. I'd appreciate all of the cooperation I can
get from you."

"Anything I can do, Mr. McCoy, to help the
people of Johnson Creek, I feel it is my duty to do.
What are you concerned about besides the way the
Carpetbaggers are looting our town?"

"First the baggers. Do you have any influence with the town council?"

"No, absolutely none. Not a one of them is Catholic. Zed Hiatt was a shirtsleeve Catholic, but fell by the wayside years ago. The black men are Baptists, I think, and Don White is an atheist. I can't be of much help there."

"All right, Pastor. The other problem is Harry Johnson. He wrote me a letter. Said he had something that he wanted to confess. Now I'm not sure how Johnson died. The marshal and the doctor say he died of stomach problems. But a witness says there were shots heard. Just how reliable are the doctor and the marshal? Could they be covering up something?"

Father Desmond had reached for a wine bottle on a small table near the sofa. He paused and frowned. When he picked up the glasses they jiggled together. Slowly he poured wine into the two glasses and handed one to Spur.

"A good, robust port wine is good for digestion. Now, about how reliable those two men are. I've never had any cause to doubt the word of either one. I know them only casually, but they seem like reasonable, steady men."

Spur sipped the wine. He was no expert, but this was not a bargain bottle off a shelf. He watched the priest. The blue, watery eyes held steady.

"All right, Pastor Desmond. You know why I'm here. If you hear of anything that I should know that will help on either case, you'll be doing the whole town a favor by telling me."

Spur sipped the wine again, set down the glass and stood.

"Now, I better be moving. I have a lot of people to talk to today."

The priest stood as well and led the way to the door.

"If I discover anything that seems important, I'll be sure to contact you."

Spur eased his hat on at the door, touched the brim and walked out into the sunshine.

Behind him, the priest closed the door slowly, then he locked it. He moved with a sudden tiredness as he headed for his big bedroom at the end of the hall. There he stepped inside and his face broke into a smile.

Calida stood by the bed. She had just finished making it up. She wore only a short petticoat of cotton covering her slender young form, her rich black hair fell to her waist. She looked at Father Desmond and love and devotion bled from her eyes.

Calida's face was round, small, her eyes jet black, her nose sculptured and pert in a pretty face. Now her smile was dazzling.

"Should I stay?" she asked. Her English was good. She had been orphaned and raised by the sisters since she was two. She had grown straight and true and developed breasts the nuns had been surprised by. Now they thrust against the thin petticoat, her nipples already hard and pulsating.

"Yes, I need you now more than ever."

She sat on the bed waiting. He tugged at his clerical collar. She sprang up to help him.

He began talking then, talking to her, to a congregation, to his bishop, to the Pope. Even talking to God.

"Calida, I am a sinner, you know that. You know my vices, my weaknesses. Probably the whole town does. I know they call me a whiskey priest. Still I can say Mass. The bishop sent me here to get me out of his way, so I wouldn't embarrass him or the church.''

As he talked she slipped off his shirt, then worked at his belt and the buttons on his fly.

"God knows I have tried!" he shouted the words. Her hands fell away from him for a moment. "I have tried to serve God! There were just so many other desires. Oh, sweet God . . . desires! I have had so many. I have been sorely tempted so often, and fell just as often.

"I can't refuse a lovely woman, one of the first ones? Ah, when I was younger and much stronger. It was my first parish, and she was the wife of a man who traveled a great deal. She came to confession and pleaded with me to absolve her of wicked thoughts, of a fantasy that she had been making love to a neighbor.

"After the confession, I walked in the church garden. It was a large church and I was only one of several priests. I realized that she always came to confession when I was in the box. She found me in the garden and took me behind some hanging vines and we made a secret place and she kissed me. Then I kissed her and she told me I must make love to her or she would explode. She opened her bodice and put my hands on her warm breasts, and then I couldn't stop.''

Calida had taken the rest of his clothes off. She sat beside him still in the petticoat waiting. Gently he reached for her, kissed her sweet lips, then lifted the petticoat over her head.

He gasped in pleasure at her beauty. Her body was that of a young goddess: perfect legs, a tiny waist, surging upward thrust breasts so young and proud and heavily tipped with soft pink nipples that quivered as he stroked them.

"Ever since that first time, Calida, I have been a sinner in the eyes of God and man. In San Antonio I even defiled a young nun. She became pregnant and left the order quietly. We both knew she was not destined to be a nun.

"But was I to be a priest? I wrestled with that problem for years. Oh, I said Mass, I gave the sacraments, but was I worthy to be a priest?"

"I was here during the war as you were growing up."

He fondled her breasts, then lay down on the bed and she lay close beside him. He kissed her breasts.

"Near the end of the war something happened which I had trouble even then explaining, and now it is a misty, uncertain nightmare for me."

She kissed him, pushed him on his back and rolled on top of him as she had done so often before. Her breasts hung delightfully over his face.

"Then, Calida, two weeks ago, the whole ugly, terrible nightmare rose up again, and again some stranger took control of my body and made my hand do a terrible thing, and I will never be the same again!"

Calida lowered a breast to his mouth.

"Father, don't talk that way. You frighten me when you talk like that. For a while you used to do that, then you stopped. No more."

He was quiet for a moment, then he kissed her breast and sucked it into his mouth.

"Yes! Father! I will make you feel good again. Please let me make you feel better!"

Without waiting she found his erection and lifted and shifted her young hips as she had done so often before and lowered onto him. Then she moved slowly at first, then faster and faster, riding him like a pony, bringing him quickly to a climax.

When his panting and quivering and thrusting were over, he pushed her away and sat on the edge of the bed.

Father Desmond began to cry. Soundlessly at first, then with racking sobs and gasps as he let the pain and the anger and the shame flow out of him.

She held him as he quieted, his tear streaked face looked at her, and he began sobbing again.

"I had no right to defile you, too!" he whined through his tears. "No right. I am evil. I don't deserve to live."

A knock sounded on his door.

"Yes?" he said.

"Father, Mrs. Ortega. She needs you. Her husband says it is time for the last rites."

"Yes, Sister. I will be there shortly."

"She is dying, Father, you must go," Calida said softly.

"Soon, soon." He looked at his Calida again, so young, so pure, so beautiful! He touched her breasts and felt them burning with her desire. He bent and kissed them and then he forgot everything as he made love to Calida again on his bed, even as Mrs. Ortega came closer and closer to death.

He stared at the wall. He had sinned again, the sins of a priest! He was sure now that he did not deserve to live.

He lifted away from Calida, kissed her sweaty forehead and told her to rest. Quickly he dressed and slipped out the door. Sister M. Wanda led him down the corridor.

"Mrs. Ortega is still failing. She is waiting for you to come before she dies."

Father Desmond nodded and hurried through the back gate of the church grounds and over two streets to the small Ortega house. It had only a wooden box for a table and two chairs in the first room, and a makeshift bed in the second.

Mrs. Ortega saw him and she smiled. Quickly he gave her the last rites and she smiled again, reached for his hand and kissed it. Then she looked at her husband, smiled again, and died.

Her husband shook his hand and thanked him. Father Desmond left the house quickly. How could anyone have such faith? Long ago he had argued with himself that the entire idea of religion was a myth, the creation of the mind of man. That all religions around the world were based on fear . . . fear of death. He had laboriously traced them back to their foundings, and each one carried the same theme, magic and myth, fear of death and the search for a reason for life.

Little by little he had come to the conclusion that there was no reason for life. All the trappings and grandeur, all of the organization and platitudes and rituals and traditions of the Catholic church were simply another means for deceiving the poor and the ignorant.

Where did that leave him? He was either a cynical manipulator of the innocent, a monster deceiver and a charlatan or he was so ignorant and stupid that he couldn't recognize the truth about religion when it slapped him in the face.

Father Desmond walked slowly back to the church.

He was not stupid or ignorant. His teachers had told him that. They doubted sometimes his dedication, his "call." Lies, all lies! The Catholic church was truly a huge monolith perpetuating itself. A monster of a religious business reaching all the way to Rome!

How had he lived with himself being such a pious hypocrite all these years?

Calida had made it possible lately. Before there had been others willing to lay with him. Some thought they defiled him, others were sure they were piling up credits in heaven that would show up at the pearly gates in St. Peter's log book. What a surprise for them when they died and never woke up! When they knew for sure that dead is dead. That there is nothing else to life but life itself. When it was over . . . it's over!

He laughed. How simple, how stupid people were! How like little children!

How terrible his transgressions against humanity! He had not transgressed against God, since gods were figments of man's imagination. Like the Romans. We scoff at the idea of a thousand Roman gods.

We laugh at the animism gods of the primitives in many lands. But five thousand years from now, will not the intelligent men of that day, howl with glee at the ridiculous mythology of Christianity that millions of people believed in, and many died for?

Father Desmond walked slowly to the rear gate of the church yard. So many volunteers kept the gardens beautiful. A labor of love. He too had a labor of love.

He went into his quarters, told Calida that he was feeling tired and could not say the five P.M. Mass. He wanted to be alone this evening. He kissed her cheek and told her to go and read a good book.

Father Desmond walked slowly into his large bedroom, locked both doors, took out a bottle of whiskey and a pitcher of water and proceeded to drink himself insensible as he lay on his big bed, alternately laughing at the stupidity of man, and crying for the lost love of God.

5

When Spur McCoy left the Catholic church and Father Desmond, he headed for the building he had seen marked as the city offices. It had to contain the mayor's office. It was time Spur had it out with the duly elected mayor.

Spur McCoy walked confidently. He was as Beth had estimated a little over six feet two and about two hundred pounds. He was a crack shot with pistol or rifle, an expert hand to hand fighter with fists, knife or staff.

His outdoor work kept him constantly on the go and tip top physical condition.

After Congress established the Secret Service in 1865 to protect the currency, Spur had applied and become one of its first agents. Before that, he had served the last two years of the war in Washington D.C. as an aide to long time senator Arthur B. Walton of New York.

Spur walked another block down Main and saw the city offices.

He had not always been in the West. Spur was born in New York City where his father was a wealthy merchant and importer. Spur went to Harvard and graduated when he was twenty-four years old. After that he worked for his father for two years in some of his businesses, then took a commission in the Army during the war.

He served six months in the Secret Service's Washington D.C. office before he was assigned as chief of the Western division of the service, with an office in St. Louis. His responsibility was everything west of the Mississippi.

With such a big area, he was constantly on the move. At first the Secret Service was the only federal agency that could enforce Federal laws. Which meant the service quickly expanded from its role of hunting counterfeiters, to working on any type of federal crime.

Spur walked into the city offices and asked to see the mayor. A small, black-haired woman with her hair in a severe bun on the back of her head asked his name and announced him.

Don White looked up from his desk and a stack of papers Spur guessed had just been put there for effect.

"Ah, Agent McCoy. I never had a chance to thank you for the excellent work you did this morning in controlling what could have been a full scale riot. The city thanks you."

"White, I didn't come here for any thanks. I want to know how soon you can be out of town?"

A huge black man Spur had not seen sitting in the corner of the room leaped to his feet, his hands holding a double barreled shotgun that had been sawed off.

"No," White said sharply. "Willy here gets nervous when anyone uses that tone of voice with me, Mr. McCoy. As you know, I am entirely and perfectly legal here. I was voted into office by a majority of my constituents. The new Federal election laws specify that all Negroes be allowed the right of the vote without any exclusions.

"I for one, intend to see that those laws are carried out, and that my Negro brothers get to use their vote franchise."

"White, you know damn well you don't care a bit about all that. You're here for power and money. But most Carpetbaggers head for bigger towns. How is there much for anybody to steal here in Johnson Creek? That's what I can't figure out."

"Don't try, it'll strain your small brain. All you have to do, Federal lawman, is make sure that the newly enfranchised voters who are with me and those long time residents of this small town, maintain their right to vote. That's your job, lawman." White grinned at Spur.

"Now if you don't have some official business, I'm going to ask Willy here to help you leave."

"Willy might wind up with a broken face if he tries," Spur said evenly, so softly that Willy couldn't hear.

White snorted. "He'd make kindling out of you. Just walk out and don't break up any furniture."

"Where's the big money, White? That I can't figure. It's easy to see how you stir up the people, let your Negroes run wild in town without their women. That figures. But it's the money, your payoff for all this work, that I can't figure out where it's coming from."

Spur walked toward the door. "Where you from, White?"

"I'm from Johnson Creek."

"Before that, New York, Baltimore?"

White laughed. "Chicago."

"That figures, too. You were a nothing in the big city. So you heard about the Carpetbaggers and you decided to get in on it before it was worn out. You're almost too late, White."

Spur heard the snap as a shotgun meshed barrel and stock as it was ready to fire. He turned and looked at the armed guard.

Willy grinned at him.

"Double ought buck," Willy said. "From here with both barrels, I can damn near cut you in half."

"No, Willy," White said. "We'd have a dozen Federal agents down here within a week. We don't need that."

Willy lifted the shotgun, disappointed that he wasn't going to get to use it.

"Walk carefully, Mayor White," Spur said. Then he turned his back on both of them and marched out the door and to the street.

As Spur moved he filed away what he had seen. There were four black men sitting at desks in the city offices. White must have moved some of his men in those jobs. He wondered if they got done, or done right.

He cut across the street, sidestepped a prancing black pulling a fancy buggy, and went up the wooden steps to the Johnson House Hotel. When he asked for his key at the desk, there was a note under it. The clerk gave him both and turned away.

Spur read the note. It was from Beth:

"Spur McCoy. I insist on your coming to my house tonight for a small dinner party I'm giving. The address is 124 South First Street. Casual dress will be fine. I'll expect you promptly at 6:30 so cook will not be angry. If for any reason (except death of course) you can't attend, I shall be forever angry and furious and disappointed. See you at 6:30 . . . Beth Johnson."

He looked again at the note, then drew his pocket watch from his trousers and checked the time. Already it was past three. He had missed his noon meal somewhere along the way. He wasn't worried. He could miss any two meals a day and function at top efficiency.

Spur went up to his room and sat by the window staring down at Main Street. Why had Harry Johnson sent that letter to Washington? What was it he wanted to confess that he could not trust to the local government? He wondered if the Carpetbaggers were the cause of that distrust, or was there some deeper, more serious problem?

Could the whole thing have anything to do with the just finished Civil War? The fighting had been over scarcely four years. Old angers, old hatreds were fading slowly from that titanic struggle, and would never die out until the participants themselves were buried. There was little actual war action in this section of Texas. A few border raiders perhaps.

The raiders were not a proud part of the war for either side. Most of them had regular Army leadership, but they gathered their forces from the rabble of those times. Many of the raiders on both sides were little better than outlaws and killers who pirated most of the booty for their own uses, and little of the supposed gain actually reached the participating armies.

Raiders, he would remember that possibility.

Spur lay on the bed fully clothed and pondered his problem. The priest had been no help. He probably knew nothing, and was more wrapped up in his own problems and hanging on to his play acting role as a religious leader.

The marshal, now the ex-marshal, had not indicated in any way that shots had been fired into Harry Johnson. There was a chance he didn't know it, if the doctor had taken the body directly to the undertaker.

It was after four when he went to the bank. It was closed. He went on to the Johnson place and rang the bell. A slightly flustered Beth Johnson answered the door.

"You're early," she said. Her brown hair was mussed, she wore a long robe and a frown.

"We need to talk. I want to know exactly what Dr. Greenly said to you the night your father died. We can do it now before the dinner."

She held the door open and waved him inside. "First you sit and read some of father's books, while I finish dressing. You are very naughty coming so early before a lady has a chance to get herself ready."

"You look fine."

"Oh, damn! I don't want to look just fine, I want to look gorgeous! Now stay in the library until I put myself together."

Spur found himself in the man's room, a combination library and den, with two walls filled with books. All had been filed alphabetically according to the author.

He found some classics, some Shakespeare, some poems by a man named Longfellow, and some from a new writer by the name of Mark Twain. On another shelf were books by Walt Whitman, and more poems from Emily Dickinson. Harry Johnson had a wide interest in his reading. Spur picked up a volume by Bret Harte, a collection of some of his short stories.

Spur settled down to the opening story, *The Outcasts of Poker Flat.*

"As Mr. John Oakhurst, gambler, stepped into the main street of Poker Flat on the morning of the 23rd of November, 1850, he was conscious of a change in its moral atmosphere since the preceding night. Two or three men, conversing earnestly together, ceased as he approached and exchanged significant glances . . ."

Fully a half hour later, Beth Johnson appeared in the den doorway. The gown she wore was expensive, finely tailored and cut low in front not so much revealing her bosom, but displaying the fact that there was little there to reveal. Her hair had been lifted up on her head and pinned in place with a few ringlets around her ears and on her forehead.

"What a marvelous transformation!" Spur said, dropping Bret Harte, eager to get on with his questions for Beth.

Beth blushed. She curtsied, then looked up at him. "It is just a dress I got a while back, and . . . I wanted to look . . . nice for you." She came in and sat down in an upholstered chair near the short sofa where he sat.

"You had some questions?"

"Tell me everything that happened the night your father died."

"Everything . . . well. It was a normal evening. We had dinner, then I played the piano for a while and father read. We both went to bed early and that's the last I remember until later that night when I woke. I have no idea what time it was.

"Voices. I heard three or four different voices.

They seemed to be arguing, and they came from down the second floor hallway where my father's room was. At first I thought I was dreaming and tried to go back to sleep. But I heard them again.

"I decided to get up. As I hunted for my robe I heard the shots. A number of them. I wasn't sure how many. Then there was nothing but silence.

"By the time I got my robe on and hurried down the hall, I found my father's room door open and his lamp burning. Inside Daddy lay across the bed on his back. I could see the blood on his face and his hands, and then on the sheets under him."

She stopped and covered her face. "It was horrible. I knew that Father was dead. All that blood. But I hurried downstairs and roused our cook and told her to get dressed and rush over and get Doctor Greenly. She was back in a short time, saying she had found the doctor on the boardwalk as she passed Main Street."

"It was maybe five minutes after she left the house that Dr. Greenly was here. He took over. Made me leave the room, examined Daddy, then came out and told me."

"How did he tell you, Beth?"

"First he said Daddy had died. There was nothing he could do to help him. I cried and cried, and when I stopped, Dr. Greenly said he had Daddy taken to the undertaker. It would be best that way.

"That's when I asked him who shot my father. He said what shots? So I told him earlier in the evening I had heard some men arguing, and then later some shots three or four, I wasn't sure."

Beth stood and paced up and down in front of the sofa, looking at Spur now and then.

"So, Dr. Greenly said he didn't want to tell me, but my father had been shot, murdered. He didn't want to worry me. And he said it would be better not to tell anyone right now. He said with all the anger in town over the Carpetbaggers, it would be best.

"Daddy was trying to get both sides together to try to work out the problems. Dr. Greenly said a hot head from either side could have killed Daddy. He said if we made an announcement about it, each side would blame the other and the whole thing could blow up, like I told you before.

"I fought the whole idea, but I was tired, and drained, and he convinced me not to say a word about it. Not just yet."

"Did the newsman, Hans Runner, say anything about your father being murdered rather than dying of natural causes?"

"No. I'm not sure that he knew. Dr. Greenly might have told him what he wanted him to know for the story in the *Record* the next week."

She looked out the window. "The day of the funeral a strange thing happened. The undertaker took me aside and said he knew the doctor said natural causes, but he found five bullets in my father's chest and stomach. He dug them out. Two were .44's or .45's and one a .32 and one a .38 and the last one an old minnie ball. He said it was none of his concern, but he wanted me to know."

Spur sat up straighter. "Five bullets, which could have come from at least four and probably five guns. Did five men shoot your father that night?"

"I just don't know what to think. I haven't said anything yet, but I was about ready to when I shot at you in the brush."

Now it was Spur's turn to get up and walk around the room. "Why would five people shoot one man?

It doesn't make sense. One shot or two will usually kill a person. Why five?''

"That's what I've been trying to figure out ever since.''

There was a knock on the door.

"Dinner is ready, Mr. McCoy. May I take your arm?''

"Just don't go too far with it.''

"What. Oh, a joke. Yes. I'll only take it to the dinner table.''

They went down the hall to a dining room and at once he saw that the table had been set for only two.

"When you say a little dinner party, you do mean it is going to be small and exclusive, don't you?''

"I'm a selfish person. I don't believe in sharing. And tonight I want you all to myself.''

"I think that is taken care of. Now, some more questions. Did you hear any words or sentences when the men were arguing? Even a single word might be important.''

She frowned as he sat her at the luxuriously laid out table. He sat across from her. She shook her head.

"Nothing. I figured at the time it was a dream, so I didn't bother remembering any of it.''

"All right. Now, did your father have any enemies, the kind who might kill him?''

"No! That's why this is so grotesque. Certainly not five men who wanted him dead so badly that they would all shoot him. There is simply no one!''

"Wrong, Beth. There are five out there in this town. Make me a list of what your father did for recreation. Did he play softball on Saturdays, go fishing, ride horses, build fancy buggies or practice shooting pistols in his back yard. I want a list of everything he did, every organization he belonged to, what committees and groups he worked with. Let's do that right now.''

Hilda, the cook came in the door with the first course, a green salad with an interesting dressing.

"Let's wait on the list. First I want to stuff you with fine food.''

The meal was outstanding, and as they had ice cream and cookies for dessert, Beth made out the list of her father's groups and organizations. It was short.

"The Board of Trustees at the Congregational church, City Election Board, the County Planning Commission, and the Home Guard, but that was disbanded just after the war.''

"Hobbies?''

"Pitched a mean game of horseshoe, liked to ride, do those fancy show horse things. He was on the Merchant's Association Board and a member of the Road Commission. For a while he used to play poker once a month, but I'm not sure they kept up the game. That's about it.''

"You're sure.''

"There might have been a State Banker's Group, I'm not certain there.'' She paused. "Let's go into the living room. I love a fire in the fireplace. And it's still cool enough out nights to make it feel good.''

Spur hestitated and Beth groaned.

"Damn! Won't I ever learn? This is one man who will not be rushed. So don't rush him. Just be nice and look pretty and don't let him know that you'd die for a good night kiss . . . even.''

Spur laughed. "Hey, sometimes rushing can be fun. But right now I've got a million things to check out. I am supposed to be working you know. Anybody else I should see on your list of locals who know the town?''

"Yes, Big Paul Smith, our saddlemaker. He knows everyone, is a friend to all, and is the best leather man in six counties. He usually works late. Stop by now and see if he's open. He's just down from the jewelry store the other side of the bank.''

At the door Spur touched her shoulders, then picked her up and kissed her gently on the mouth and put her down. For a moment she didn't move.

"Could we try that again when I'm ready for it?''

Spur grinned and bent down and kissed her again. This time her arms came around him and the kiss was one of fire and meaning.

When she let him go, she leaned against the wall and smiled.

"Oh, boy, now I'm sorry I didn't try to rush you. Don't stay away long.''

Spur grinned, kissed her forehead and went out the door and down the front walk to the street. He had a late date with a saddlemaker. The questions kept bothering him. Why would five men shoot the same man and why did the doctor try to cover it up? The doctor's logic for the cover up was laughable. But it wouldn't be if the doctor was one of the men who shot Harry Johnson.

6

The Secret Agent strode down the middle of the dusty, dark Johnson Creek street. There was little moon, just a slice. He looked up, checking for the Big Dipper and North Star. The Dipper was hanging sideways to the left of the North Star. The handle was almost overhead with the pointer stars angled in from about where the eleven number was on his watch.

That would make it somewhere around eight P.M. By four A.M. the dipper would be rotated almost to the bottom point where the six hand was on a watch. The dipper swung around the North Star once every twenty-four hours. Cowboys doing nightriding on a herd of cattle called the Big Dipper their star time Waterbury.

Spur checked the boardwalks. There were half a dozen men loafing or walking along past the closed stores. Most of them moved from one saloon and gambling hall to the next.

Spur saw the bank and headed toward it across the street. He passed the Silver Dollar saloon and as a shaft of yellow light shone on him from one of the big windows. When the light bathed him, a shot snarled into the Texas night air.

Spur dodged to the side and dove behind a big rain barrel at the near corner of the saloon. Two more shots flared from the edge of the alley. Both rounds struck the barrel and penetrated the side, but died in the water inside.

Spur came up firing his Remmington .44, blasting three shots at the mouth of the alley, then charging toward it along the protection of the front of the saloon.

He sent a drunk sprawling as they collided outside the swinging doors to the saloon. Spur kept his own feet and flattened against the corner of the saloon. He peered around into the darkness of the alley.

Someone ran the other way.

Spur jolted around the corner of the saloon and plunged into the inky depths of the darkness. He paused, his heart racing, his breath coming in quick gasps. Through it he heard more steps ahead, slower this time.

He thumbed the three spent rounds from his revolver and pushed in four new ones . . . he had six shots now. He fired twice at the footsteps, then surged to the other side of the alley as he charged forward.

Again he paused, listening. A baby cried somewhere. A woman shouted something at a man who laughed.

He moved forward on cougar paws, not disturbing a rock or clod, not even moving the air before him. Twenty feet down the dark alley, he heard something. Two deep buildings came all the way to the alley, but a short one allowed a thirty foot hole between them.

In that dark place someone moved again. Spur

held his Remmington as far to the right as he could reach and fired into the black place between the longer buildings. As soon as he blasted one shot he jumped to his left to put him well away from his own gun's flare.

Three shots in quick succession blasted from the black hole between the longer buildings. The lead was all ticketed for Spur's muzzle flash, where the bushwacker thought his victim still stood.

That was what Spur was waiting for. He returned the fire with his last three shots, bracketing the attacker's muzzle flash.

When the sound of the gunfire trailed off, Spur could hear a man's low scream of desperation. He waited. The man could be faking him into a trap.

Then Spur heard a death rattle, the last surge of air from dead lungs. Nobody could fake the deadly sound. Still he moved forward slowly. Then in the slice of moonlight he found the man pitched backwards, face up, one hand holding his chest where blood had seeped but was now stopped.

Somebody came out of the rear door of the business.

"What in tarnation is going on back here?" a man asked.

"Bring a light," Spur said. "I think a man just died."

The store owner brought the light and the undertaker. Spur had never seen the dead man before. He was white, about thirty and had the rope scarred hands of a cowboy.

The merchant nodded. "Yep, seen him around. Think he works for one of the small cattle outfits, not sure."

"He tried to bushwhack me," Spur said. " You know any reason he'd try that?"

The merchant squinted at Spur in the poor light of the coal oil lantern.

"You that Federal lawman." He shook his head. "Nope, don't know how he would be on either side in the city problems. Maybe he just don't like lawmen."

"Happens," Spur said. He stood and walked into the darkness leaving the dead man where he fell.

The saddlemaker was still working when Spur knocked on the locked front door. He sat on a chair beside a high table. Then Spur lost him. When the door opened Spur could still not see the Big Paul Smith he was looking for.

"Down here," Smith said. "Not everybody can be six-six."

Spur looked down and saw a perfectly formed small man, a midget no more than thirty-six inches tall. He stifled an urge to squat down to shake hands.

"Evening, Mr. Smith. My name is McCoy. Could we talk for a few minutes?"

Even in the dim light, Spur could see the man's eyes twinkle.

"Always glad to accommodate the United States Secret Service. I've been wondering how it can be secret if you told us who you are?"

"That seems to be the way with secrets. I'd like to talk to you for a few minutes if I could. Beth Johnson said I should come and see you."

"Beautiful Beth! Yes, a fine friend. Please come in." He closed the door and went back to his work bench, jumping up to a stool where he worked on a half done saddle.

Paul Smith was a true midget, his proportions were normal, he was simply a small man. His dark eyes showed an uncommon strength and understanding.

"Yes, the death of Harry Johnson. How does a perfectly healthy man one day, have stomach problems, and die overnight? It is an interesting question, and one I hope you are considering."

"Considering, yes. That's part of the reason I'm here. Do you have any special knowledge about this particular death?"

Smith punched a series of holes in a thick slab of leather, then began threading rawhide decoration through them. He shook his head slowly.

"Nothing in particular. But it does leave itself open to the question of foul play. Why or who, I would have no ideas."

"But you know the town."

"True, as well as anyone. I have more time to watch people, to assess them, to speculate, to evaluate. I'm an recalcitrant people watcher."

"And a well educated one."

"Mr. McCoy, I read a great deal."

"Who could cover up foul play in such a death?"

"You would need the doctor, the marshal and probably the undertaker."

"Let's start with the marshal. Why would he cover up a killing of a prominent, rich man?"

"I've thought about that. The why must be money, lots of money either now or in the future. Harry Johnson was the richest man in town. His father owned all the town at one time. He decided he wanted a community here and put up stores, and rented them, then sold them.

"Right now Beth Johnson owns about sixty percent of all the real estate property in Johnson Creek."

"And pays at least sixty percent of the taxes."

"True. I've eliminated all other reasons for homicide in Mr. Johnson's case. There is no woman involved, no power struggle, no public image to maintain or shatter, no ambition to prove. That leaves only money for a motive. Find the money and you find the killer."

"If he was killed."

Paul Smith formed a piece of leather around the right side of the saddle and cut it to fit. "Mr. McCoy, we both know that Harry Johnson was murdered. We just don't know why." He smiled for a moment and then looked up.

"You see, I'm a good friend of the only undertaker in town. He told me certain curious facts that I'm sure Beth Johnson also knows. So we move on to motive and the 'who.' "

"Any ideas?"

"None whatsoever. First the motive, the money."

"What do you know about our ex-marshal?"

"A lot. Most of it not applicable to the current discussion. He went to war early, and came back quickly, wounded. In those days he was a strong willed man but weak in body. Now he has regained his physical strength, but he is a weak man, afraid of something. He's whole, but weak. I'm not sure why."

Spur watched the small man's strong hands tool a piece of leather, working in a pattern with awl, filed nail heads, and small hand tools.

"What's your views on the Carpetbaggers, Mr. Smith?"

"Opportunists, pure and simple. Half the people in town knows what the mayor's trying to do, they just don't know how to stop him."

"What is he trying, Mr. Smith?"

The small man smiled and his eyes went wide.

"To sack the city treasury. To rob Johnson Creek of every dollar he can get, then vanish to the north and leave the Negroes in the lurch without a friend, a dollar, a job, or a dole."

"Just the way it has happened time and time again across the South since the Reconstruction laws," the Secret Service agent said. "The problem here is the timing. I'd need to catch him directly in the act."

"Timing is not a real problem for you, Mr. Secret Service man. Most money comes into a government entity when it levies taxes and those taxes are called due."

"True." Spur laughed softly. "So tomorrow I can find out when the taxes assessments are due on city property."

"You don't have to wait. I have my statement, and I'll pay it on the last day. All taxes are due and payable in two days."

"Two days?"

"Day after tomorrow at 4 P.M. is the last moment to pay without a penalty. At least 95 percent of the taxes will have been paid by that last day."

"Mr. Smith, you don't give a man much time."

"Time is always on the side of the law," Smith said. He watched McCoy. "you're an educated man, college probably. Am I right?"

"Harvard. Economics."

Paul Smith put down his tools. "Well, well. This calls for an ivy hall celebration. I'm a Yale man. Do you have time for a serious meeting with a really good bottle of wine? It's from France and I've been saving it for a special occasion."

Spur grinned. "I'd be delighted, even to drink with a Yale man. Lead on McDuff!"

Smith lived in back of the wonderful leather smells of his shop. He led the way and Spur found himself in a finely decorated, and neatly kept living room. The furniture was half size, to accommodate Smith.

The small man waved Spur to a couch which was large enough for him. Smith pulled a bottle of wine from a wall rack and brushed dust off the label.

"Yes, yes! Almost fifteen years old! A rosé that I think you'll like." He pulled out the cork and sniffed it, then gave it to Spur.

"Aroma. One third of the test of a good wine. Body and taste, as I remember. But I usually only talk about wine when I'm drinking it, which may account for my fuzzy memory of wine and wines."

He poured two long stemmed wine glasses and passed the first to Spur. The Secret Service Agent had learned to like wine. They never had it at home in New York.

"A rosé, you say. I don't think I've tried it before."

"A man must try many things in his life to know what he likes. Like the winsome, beautiful Beth." He looked up sharply. "Don't laugh or I'll put you out of my house." For a moment he chuckled. "It might be a hard thing for me to do, even with a shotgun, but never mind. I was talking about the sweetest rose of any I know, Miss Johnson."

"You've had your eye on her for a time?"

"Aye, I have. And even in four years she has grown away from me. Once we were the same size." He took a deep breath that came as a sigh of resignation. "Some things just can't be helped. I would have given everything I own if she would have stopped growing when she was thirty-five inches tall."

"Yes, my friend, but remember the man who said: 'There is no wisdom in useless and hopeless sorrow.' "

"Games, I love games! Let's see, useless and hopeless sorrow. Sounds like Shakespeare, but it isn't. No . . . I almost had it. Yes . . . I have it, the letters. The letters of Samuel Johnson."

Spur laughed and clapped in appreciation. "Sir, not one man in ten thousand would know that quotation, least of all who had written it first. How come you do?"

Paul Smith smiled, sniffed of the wine, then drained the glass.

"Yes, the glories of praise. 'Man is wont for praise.' Who said that?"

"Shakespeare, Milton, perhaps Ben Franklin?"

"Wrong on all counts. That statement is by one Paul Smith, Esquire. At your service. How did I know the Sam Johnson quote? I was a master in English at Yale. I graduated second in my class secure knowing that I had a teaching position in a small private college in the East. We contacted each other by letter. My letters of recommendation were laudatory, and I was given assurances I had the position as lecturer in English Literature."

He filled his glass again. "Then as you suspect, I arrived on the campus. I was there for approximately twenty minutes before I was sent packing. It seems they had no place for a small man."

"A small man with a large mind was what frightened them," Spur said. "I shall never send any of my children to that school!"

"Nor I!" Paul shouted, then laughed. "And since neither of us have any children, at least any to speak of, 'tis an easy task, Horatio!"

Spur held up his wine glass and Paul filled it.

"Now to the rub. How now you and Shakespeare? Did this lout, this commoner, this toiler in the stable, this handyman around a theatre, really write the works attributed to one William S. or perchance was it the honorable Lord, the highborn and higher yet educated Sir Francis Bacon?''

"You fault me sir!" Paul cried. Then fell into a spate of laughing. "Must we continue to speak in Shakespearian quotes? Me thinks not!" He laughed again.

"While at Yale I made a close study of both men. And at last I came to one conclusion. Bacon was three years older than Willy. And Bacon lived about ten years longer than Shakespeare. While Bacon seemed the more logical man to write the Shakespearian plays with their wit and wisdom and their high tone and such a *feeling* of the English highborn, the man himself, Bacon, was not mentally capable of doing the task. Nor did Bacon know that much about theatre."

Spur raised the usual counter argument and settled down to an evening he hadn't enjoyed since leaving the ivy halls. It would be a good four hours before the argument, still long from resolved, was given up for the time, and Spur headed for his room at the hotel.

7

Don White had brooded about his situation ever since that lawman, that Spur McCoy, had left the City Hall. For a while he had retreated into his private quarters. Then he went out and ate the biggest steak dinner the hotel could offer. He felt somewhat better. Back in his room he yelled at the four Negroes who were his private guard force, told them to move about, to do something.

The four guards, all armed with sawed off double barreled shotguns, occupied a room just behind White's. He had built in four bunks for them, and kept two on duty with him around the clock on twelve hour shifts. Waking or sleeping, he was protected.

The City Hall had once been a store. He had refitted it, moved in the city jobs from several locations, and built himself quarters in back, all rent free of course, courtesy of the city.

His bedroom was large, eighteen feet square, with a big bed in one corner. It had been specially made for him and was twice as wide as most double beds. The bathtub in the other corner was special too, a lay down kind, with fancy claw legs.

He walked into the big room now and took off the jacket which he always wore. It separated him from the common folks in this hick town.

There was one other person in the room, a slender black girl with firm, full breasts and short hair. She now sat cross-legged on the big bed. She wore a skirt but nothing above her waist. She smiled and shook her shoulders so her breasts did a fancy and practiced little dance.

Her name was Ruth, and she had been a dance hall girl in Houston before he rescued her. She wouldn't say for sure, but he guessed that she was about twenty.

"Hey, our mayor is here! Your Honor, sir. You have a good supper?"

He stood in front of her staring down.

"Damn good. I deserved it. I'm keeping your belly full, ain't I?"

"Right now I'd rather you filled something else. You wanting? You ready? I can get you ready quick."

White ignored her, went to the back door and told one of the guards to move to the front door, outside it, and kept one man on the rear. There was no window in the big room. He called it his maximum secure position.

When the men were situated, he went back to the bed and sat down. Ruth curled around him from the back. She had slipped off her skirt and was naked black. She snaked under his arms, then up his chest and nibbled at his lips. Her breasts massaged his chest as she moved slowly from side to side, then lifted higher, pushing one breast then the other into his mouth.

White bit the morsels, teased her erect black

nipples, then roughly pushed her away. She landed on the bed, bounced and came up to her knees at once and walked toward him.

"Something different," he said. "Make it damn different. You used to be more fun."

Ruth sensed the threat. She knew she was temporary and could be replaced at any time. She came up behind him again, stripped off his shirt, then took down his pants and pulled his half boots off so he was naked white.

On the hard floor in front of where White sat on the bed, Ruth did a dance. It was basic and sexy. She had learned it from a black whore in New Orleans when she was sixteen. Ruth had never known the dance to fail to bring the man danced for into heat.

It began slow, her whole body not a foot in front of White, gyrating and swaying in motion to an African beat. Ruth heard the dance was a fertility rite and she had no doubts. It got her as worked up as it did the man.

She kept her body gyrating, moved her big breasts so they swayed and jiggled half an inch from his face. Then moving in so they brushed his lips and then away.

With each half a minute the beat quickened. Her hips swung and her black crotch hair glistened from her sweat. She came toward him again, her legs spread, jumping in little steps toward him, her crotch open, exposed, offered.

She nudged him with her shoulders and with her hands, eased him back on the bed. Ruth went to her knees on each side of his torso and slowly humping and grinding her hips, worked up higher and higher toward his face.

She saw the glints in his eyes, heard his breathing

surge faster. His long stick was hard and ready. She moved higher on his chest, closer, higher yet.

At last her hips reached a surging, grinding speed that brought a wail from White.

Her hips slowed and she positioned them directly over his face. A wet stream seeped down her right leg. Her outer lips were swollen and oozing.

Slowly she lowered herself over him. He cried out again in need and she let her labia settle over his face.

White jammed his tongue upward. For a minute he drank in her juices, then he slammed her to the bed, lifted her to her hands and knees and spread her legs. He bellowed in satisfaction as he took her from the rear.

She yelped in surprise and fulfillment as he slammed into her again and again.

"Take that you little black slut!" he roared. "You asked for it! Christ, how did you learn to fuck so good, so many ways? You must have had a damned good teacher."

Then he lost control and jolted against her so hard she crumpled to the bed as his one hundred and seventy pounds hit her with all the force he could manage.

A minute later he rolled to one side and lay on his stomach, his breath coming like fissures in a giant steam vent.

Ruth sat beside him combing her hair. She snorted softly and looked over at him.

"Was that different enough for you, Big Stud? You man enough to take that three times a day? You think you'll ever find a mama who can do you better? Not a chance. I'm your woman for now and for as long as time, or until I get knocked up. But that ain't ever gonna happen cause I know how to stop it. So you just rest up and when you're ready, I'll show you another way, something so wild you might just be knocked on your tail for a whole week!''

She laughed softly, went to the bathtub and poured in two buckets of hot water and had a luxurious bath, while Don White slept, trying to gain back some of his strength.

He came upright an hour later. The working day was not over yet in the city clerk's office outside. White dressed, ignored Ruth's naked black form, and went back into the City Hall section of the building.

One of the store owners stood before Victor, paying his taxes.

"Too damn much," the merchant said. "Just barely able to make a living as it is."

"Yeah, don't complain so much or I'll raise your taxes to double, you got that?" Victor said. The merchant gave him thirty-six dollars, took a receipt and stalked out of the room.

White had come in quietly, and stood in back of Victor, as the small Negro counted the money. He divided it in half, put half of it in the small strong box under his desk, and the rest in his pants pocket.

White didn't say a word. He opened the door into his quarters silently, then closed it smartly and walked toward Victor.

"Yes suh, Mistah White. We doing good business today. Take in one hell of a lot of money. You wanta count it?"

"Later, Victor. Time to close up. I'll help. Don't want you hurting your back carrying all that money." White picked up the portable strong box and motioned for Victor to follow him, and walked back to his private quarters.

He put the strong box on the bed, and nodded at it and then Ruth. She had not dressed. She posed for Victor who grinned and reached for her breasts. She edged away out of reach.

"Back here, Victor," White said. They went through the back guard room where two men slept and into an unused section of the old store behind that. Light came through a sky window.

White held out his hand. "Saw you shorting the county up there, Victor. Your black ass is in trouble."

"No suh, Mistah White! I just making it easier to count." His eyes went wide, then he backed up as White's big fist hit him in the side of the face. A bone broke, and Victor screamed. He jolted to one side and ran for the back door, but White beat him there.

White thundered a stiff right fist into Victor's unprotected belly. The black man bent over and White rammed his knee upward, slamming Victor's head high, disorienting him. He nearly fell, then staggered.

White took his time now, first his right fist, then his left smashed into Victor's battered face. When he bent low enough, White powered his knee upward into Victor's jaw. At last he fell down and couldn't get up.

White knelt beside him, picked up Victor's arm and held it.

"Victor, you just got fired. I never want to see your ugly black face again, you hear? I see you again, I'll have one of the guns put both barrels of double ought buck through your guts. You get out of town fast or you're dead meat!"

White slapped Victor's face gently.

"You understand, boy?"

Victor's head nodded slowly.

White caught the black arm again, held the wrist in one hand and Victor's elbow in the other. Then he slammed the forearm down across White's knee.

Victor screamed as both forearm bones broke and jagged bone daggered through the flesh becoming white streaks in the bloody red field.

White went through the unconscious man's pockets, took out a wad of greenbacks and ten double gold eagles. He put the money in his pants and kicked Victor in the ribs. Then picked up the still unconscious Victor and threw him out the back door into the alley.

Back in his bedroom he soaked his hand in a pan of cold water and scowled at Ruth.

"Get your damn clothes on. I don't want you running around here bare assed unless I tell you to. And keep your tits covered up too. This ain't some damn whore house. You want to peddle tail you wait until I'm through with you." He lifted his hand to slap at her rump, but she wiggled it out of his reach.

She dressed slowly, where he could watch.

"Just one more, it's early."

"Shut up, I got problems. I just had to send Victor on vacation. Now I need a new city clerk."

"I could to that. I can read and write and add."

"You'd have to leave your clothes on. Wouldn't work. I'll get somebody for tomorrow."

He opened the strong box on the bed, and Ruth jumped on top of the money.

"Glory! Look at all that cash money! I love it!"

He back handed her along the rump pushing her off the money. Quickly he separated the bills into denominations and counted them, then the double eagles. They had taken in a thousand, two hundred and twenty-seven dollars that day.

"That makes nearly five thousand, here and in the bank," White said as if thinking out loud.

"When we leaving, Big Stud? Tonight? Just you and me and the money the way you promised? We ditch these shit pitching blacks and let them make out the best they can?"

White looked at her, caught her arm and pulled her toward him. He played with her breasts through the fabric of her thin blouse.

"Not tonight. We can make another thousand dollars tomorrow. You know how much I worked for in Chicago? Twenty-five dollars a month! A thousand dollars is more than three years of pay for what I was doing! Three god damned years! You don't even know how much money a thousand is."

"Yes I do, honey. And I want me a diamond necklace just as soon as we hit Houston. You promised me. Remember, swore a fucking oath and you promised."

White sat there looking at her. He was seeing Emma Lou Fisher, back in Chicago. The sweet little girl who had let him touch her breasts just once, then told him if he wanted to do that again he had to marry her. She had been a tease, but he wanted her so damn bad.

He'd go back with his five thousand and he'd take her everywhere and buy her presents and clothes and show her off and get her so hot that she'd pull off her dress and the rest of her clothes the first time he asked her to. She was going to be a great new bedmate.

Yeah! This would all be worth it to see the expression on her face when he slammed his ten inches deep into her slot! She would love it, and with five thousand . . . he could set himself up in business. Just one more day. One more day!

8

Spur McCoy had been up and moving for three hours when the Needlecraft and Stitchery shop opened on Main Street. This small place, with its living quarters in back, was the workplace of June Black, the best seamstress in this half of Texas.

When she lifted the roll blind on the door, Spur McCoy crossed the street from the leaned back chair he had been holding down in front of the hardware, and went inside.

He wasn't ready for the attractive woman who looked up at him. She was black and she wasn't. She was Indian but something more. It was a delightful combination that Spur McCoy found immediately appealing.

"Good morning, and what can I do for you, Mr. Spur McCoy?"

White teeth flashed as she grinned, her dark eyes doing a little dance as she saw his surprise. Her face was oval, not round, with a firm jaw and high cheekbones. June's skin was a soft brownish shade, her hair jet black and cropped close around her head. Full eyebrows and dark bangs cut straight over her eyes, gave her a slightly wild look.

"One of the nice things about a small town," Spur said slowly. "Everyone knows everyone else, especially a stranger. You must be Miss June Black, the best seamstress in Texas."

June smiled, looked down at the seam she was stitching. Then she glanced up. "I probably am, but damn few will admit it. How about a pair of hand tailored dress shirts, or a new suit? I'm good at men's clothes, too."

"I would think you are. No, my wardrobe isn't that important in this job. But I could use some advice. Mind if I sit and jawbone a while as you work?"

"I'd be pleased, honored that a U.S. Secret Service agent thinks I have any secrets." She laughed. "Besides *those* secrets, I mean."

She stood and went to a bolt of cloth. Spur McCoy sucked in a quick breath. Her figure was outstanding. High, full breasts, with a tiny waist and solid woman hips. She was only an inch or two over five feet, but it was the most interesting sixty-two inches of body Spur McCoy could remember ever seeing.

She cut a length of cloth off the bolt with scissors and returned to her cutting board.

"So, secrets," she said staring at him honestly. "You've probably got a secret or two yourself. You ask the questions, and I'll try to answer. Oh, somebody probably told you that I'm a talker. I do talk, so don't expect yes or no answers."

"Suits me fine. I don't have any yes-no questions."

"First, so you won't be too embarrassed to ask, but want to know. It was my mother who was a Negro and my father who was the Indian, a rampaging Kiowa brave who my mother never saw again after he took her by force three times one night. That was outside of Amarillo a ways. My ma died when I was ten and I've made my own way since then."

"I'd say you got the best features from both your parents. You're a beautiful woman, dazzling. I'm impressed."

Her smile brightened and her eyes thanked him. He went on.

"First, any comments on the Bagger here in town?"

"A few hundred. This man White is using my people for his own ends. We all know that, but so far there's no legal way to stop him, and this is a small town where we don't just up and shoot down somebody just because he might be doing bad.

"And those poor blacks he brought in from Houston? They nothing but cotton pickers. Not one in fifty of them can read or write. They vote the way White tells them. They mostly sit around and drink and chase the white women and play cards.

"You know them boys get a handout from the city? For doing nothing. Human welfare, or something like that White calls it. I never heard of no such thing in my life.

"Damn! I work ten, twelve hours a day and I hardly take in as much as they get for doing nothing. Then one or two of them comes around at night wanting me to haul their ashes for the pleasure of doing a real black man!"

"Any ideas how the Carpetbagger episode here is going to end, June?"

"Yes, the way they all end. The Bagger takes off some day just before he's about to get shot. He grabs whatever he can, or he plans it and gets out of town with everydime in the city treasury. But it's hard because you can't arrest a man for what he's going to do. Then after he does it, he's out of the county before you know he's even gone."

"June, you almost sound like a policeman." Spur smiled at her and she looked up from her stitching and smiled back. Then Spur found himself watching the line of cleavage that showed just over her blouse, and the surging breasts the cloth covered. He could see her nipples clearly pushing out the fabric farther.

She caught him looking at her breasts and laughed. "Spur, I don't mind you checking out my tits. You wouldn't be a normal man if you didn't." She nodded. "Lands sakes, I don't see a man as handsome and as well put together as you but once in an old possum's age. You look, I don't mind."

It was Spur's turn to laugh to cover up his embarrassment.

"I didn't mean to be rude, but the whole package is just fantastic. Now, back to work. You must have known Harry Johnson. What can you tell me about his death? Did you hear anything? What about rumors around town? Anyone bragging about killing him?"

"Land sakes, Spur McCoy, you know I can't tell you nothing like that I heard. I'm kind of like a doctor or a priest, privileged information. Anyway the paper says Harry died of natural causes. Stomach ulcer or something."

Spur stood and bent over her cutting board. He put his hands on the surface and stared at her hard.

"June Black, this is the United States Government asking you a question. I can get a court order if I have to. If you know anything about Harry Johnson's death, you are required to tell me right now."

"Oh, Lordy, but you are sexy when you get so angry and demanding." She stood and walked to the shelf of bolts of cloth, fingered one for a moment and came back.

"All right. I guess you're right. Nothing legal in my not talking, but just didn't seem right." She stopped and frowned. "Yes, it was after Harry died. One of the men I see . . . talk to now and then . . . is Zed Hiatt, our councilman." She laughed softly. "The stories I could tell you about him. His wife died about three years ago, and he came in the back way one night so nervous he acted like a forty-five year old virgin."

She got up and went to a small pot bellied wood burning stove at the side of the room.

"You want some tea? I usually have some tea about is time of day. Long as it don't get too hot to have a fire." She built a quick fire and put a pot on with precisely two cups of water, then stepped back and made sure the fire was burning.

"Zed is one of those 'needing' kind of men. He needs to crack his gonads every couple of weeks, but more important he needs to feel a little domination over someone or something. He's not vicious or mean. But sex seems to give him a dose of normal aggressiveness. I used to know a professor in Houston who told me all of these things. He was an interesting man."

She went back to the stove, checked the fire, then the hot water and put the tea strainer in the pot. Two minutes later she poured tea into two cups.

"You take anything in your tea?" she asked. When he shook his head she came back with the cups.

"One night he came in, maybe a week ago, and was so excited he could hardly wait to get undressed. He told me that he had actually had a climax without me. He had told me that after his wife died he tried to masturbate, but couldn't ever make it.

"At first he said he couldn't tell me about his lost load, but I teased him and played with him and said I wouldn't do any more unless he told me. At last he did.

"Zed, gentle, quiet, inept little Zed told me that he had cum in his pants one night. It took me an hour to get it out of him, and finally he whispered to me. He said he had shot a man, and the excitement, the thrill of it had made him shoot his cum all over his pants."

She sipped at the tea watching him over the cup's rim. "As soon as he told me that I dropped the subject. I don't want to get involved in somebody getting killed. But as I thought back, the only person in town who had died recently had been Harry Johnson. But since he died of natural causes . . ."

"He didn't. This is confidential, June. Tell no one. Harry Johnson was shot five times, by five different guns."

She frowned, took the needle and began stitching on a dress sleeve again.

"Shot five times? But with five different guns? Why for goodness sakes? If a man is dead . . ."

"That's what I'm trying to find out, June. Anything you can tell me might help."

"You think . . . then it's possible . . . I can't believe that soft little Zed would ever . . ." She stood and went to the front window. "He was excited, even telling me about it. I guess it's possible that Zed could have been one of the men who shot Harry. But I don't have any idea why."

"Beth heard an argument by a number of voices just before the shots. By the time she got there everyone was gone and her father was dead."

"Oh, my God! That poor girl! She's always been one of my favorites in town. I do dresses for her. Of course we're not what you'd call social equals. Zed . . . my God! It's hard to believe."

She came back and sat behind her cutting table again.

"June, with this as a foundation, is there anything else that you've heard or heard about, that might tie in with Harry Johnson's murder? Anything at all, no matter how slight?"

She stitched on the sleeve for a minute, then her black eyes looked up at him.

"My God! It could be . . ." She shook her head. "But that just couldn't be. Ain't reasonable." She frowned and at last looked at him again.

"Two nights ago Garth Ludlow stopped by to collect his 'license fee.' He figures I owe him something. He was busting to talk. Some men get that way when they get worked up. Anyway he talked for an hour and then he said he had something he really wanted to tell me that I wouldn't believe. He said I'd be amazed at the four other men in on the little affair. Four others. Five men. I don't know. It could have been a poker game, or a target practice bet. I don't know."

"But he was more excited about this than usual?"

"Oh, yes. Lots of times he drops in, and wham bang and he's out of here. He was in the war. Gets afraid sometimes over almost nothing. He's not a real strong man, emotionally. Never saw why he wanted to be town marshal. Course nothing much happens up here."

Spur turned his low crowned brown hat around

and around in his hands.

"Four other men . . . that would make five of them. Five shot Harry. Circumstantial evidence. But it's a pointing. I thought at first that the town marshal would have to be in on the cover-up. I never figured he could be one of the killers."

"Wouldn't Doc Greenly have to be one of them?"

"On the cover-up, maybe on the murder too. Going to be damn hard to prove unless we can get somebody to confess. From what you've said, Zed is probably the weakest of the three. I'll have to have a confidential talk with the jeweler. My watch has been running a little slow lately anyway."

June stood and caught his hand. "That is all I can help you with on the Harry Johnson problem. Nothing else fits. Now, I have a problem of my own I want you to help me with."

She went to the front door, locked it and put a closed sign on it, and led Spur into the back part of the store. It had been converted into living quarters. There was a small cooking stove, a heater, a single bed and dresser and a table and two chairs.

"Home," she said. She turned toward him, put her arms around him and stretched up and kissed his lips. She held the kiss for a long time and pushed her body firmly against his. When her lips escaped from his she sighed.

"Spur McCoy, I have this wild, furious itch to know what you look like naked."

Spur moved his hand down until it held one of her big breasts and he grinned at her. "June, I've been wondering the same thing about you. If you've got the time, I've got some scratching that should take care of your itch."

She smiled and unbuttoned his shirt and ran her hands over his chest, playing with the thatch of black hair there.

"I kill for a man with hair on his chest." She eased off his leather vest, then took his shirt off.

As she did, he was busy with the blouse that covered up her twin points of interest. Under the blouse was a soft cotton chemise and under that a binder that made her bosom look somewhat smaller than it actually was.

As the binder came off, Spur's eyes widened in awe. Twin mounds surged away from the restricting cloth. Heavy, thumb sized nipples were already gorged with hot blood and he could almost see them pulsating. Palm sized areolas, a shade of pink lighter than the dark pink nipples crowned the surging breasts.

"Fantastic!" Spur said with a note of reverence. He bent and kissed each nipple, then licked and kissed one breast, then the other one.

June had closed her eyes and stood with her feet well apart so she wouldn't topple over. She smiled with her eyes still shut. "Spur McCoy, you are a man who knows how to treat a woman right. I love that. Most men just think of themselves and their own urgent need."

"I like to enjoy myself on the way there," Spur said. "I always figure that you might want the same kind of pleasure."

She caught his hand and pulled him toward the bed. "I have the rest of the morning. The first time you can do me hard and fast. Don't even take your pants or your boots off!"

She dropped on the bed on her back, lifted her knees and the skirt fell around her waist.

"Get me out of those damned drawers, quick!"

Spur found the buttons and snaps, and soon had the cotton drawers with small pink ribbons on them loose enough to pull down. She urged him on and slid the garment off her feet. Her legs lifted again and parted.

"Now! Spur sweetheart, do me now!"

By the time Spur opened his fly her legs were resting on his shoulders. She was open and wanting. He moved in closer, then positioned himself and drove in with a hard thrust.

"Oh, Damn!" June shrieked. "Wonderful! Wonderful! So good!" Her hips pounded up at him. "Harder, sweetheart! I love it! You're so good! More, more!"

For just a moment, Spur marveled at this small sex machine, then he concentrated on his work and three strokes later he felt the woman under him coil and explode. Her whole body rattled and shook. She screamed, her voice rising to a high pitch and then trailing off into a wail and a long series that lasted three or four minutes.

Her passion excited Spur and he jolted faster until he could no longer hold the floodgates and he erupted into his own climax that tore the last breath from him and stiffened his whole body as he planted the seeds of the race deep inside this writhing body below him.

Slowly they both tapered off and after ten minutes they lay in each other's arms, side by side, still connected.

Her eyes came open lazily and she stared at him.

"In ten years, I've never made love so marvelously!"

"It was wonderful."

Her gaze held his. "I want you to stay right here all day. Can you do that? I want to make love to you all day and then all night. I want to get you so worn out you won't be able to lift off the bed to put your clothes on!"

"Fourteen times," Spur said.

"What?"

"Fourteen times, my record. Can you stand it that many times?"

June grinned and rubbed her breasts against his chest. "My own personal record is twenty-seven. But I don't really talk about it. I was young and crazy then."

"How old are you now?"

For a moment she frowned at him, then shrugged. "Twenty-four, is that too old?"

"Of course not."

"I started making my living on my back when I was thirteen. I mean it was the only way I had to survive." She kissed him. "Now this is just a kind of hobby. I missed it at first, the human contact, the compliments. Now I'm selective. Hell, I even get political. I'm nice to the men who can protect me and help me in my business."

"You prefer dressmaking?"

"Of course! I'm an artist with a needle and shears. My big tits don't help me a whit there. If I cut the pattern wrong, or stitch the seam crooked, it shows, no matter how good my tail meets up with yours."

She pulled away from him, leaned in and kissed his nose. "You hungry? It's getting on toward mid-morning. They say the young ones get hungry afterwards, and the older men get sleepy."

"I'm hungry," Spur said and laughed.

She made pan fried potatoes and onions for him. Slices of fresh potatoes fried in bacon grease and the onions put in the last two minutes. She had made bread the day before. It was sturdy and high without holes. June took fresh butter from a small square wooden box in one corner of the room.

"Look at this," she said. "The hardware store

man sold it to me. It's called an ice refrigerator, and I have ice brought in twice a week from the ice house. I can keep milk and meat and butter for three or four days without them spoiling."

"What won't they think of next?"

"I hear in New York a man is working on a horseless carriage."

"I've seen lots of those. The trouble is they can't move."

"This one can. It has a little motor on it, an engine of some kind, not steam, but something that runs on coal oil or such and chugs right down the road."

"I'll believe it when I see it," Spur said and dug into another helping of fried potatoes and onions. This time June added three fried eggs sunnyside up and some strawberry jam for the bread. She said she had made the jam herself.

It was just before noon when Spur dressed and walked to the rear door of the dress shop. June reached up and kissed his lips then stepped back.

"You stay away from me now, Spur McCoy. You'll ruin me for these local boys. It was a marvelous party." She frowned. "If I hear anything else about shootings that might tie to Harry, I'll certainly let you know about it."

She stepped back, then came forward and kissed him again.

"Oh, damn, what am I doing letting you get away?" She lifted her brows. "Being smart, that's what. I could never rope and hold a critter like you, Spur McCoy. Just don't forget me." She pushed him out the door and he heard her throw the bolt behind him.

Then she laughed softly, "Good bye, Spur McCoy, the best one ever!"

9

Spur walked down Main Street with a near martial
beat as he headed for the jewelry store. He checked
his pockets and found that his watch was not in its
usual spot. He would have to go back to the hotel to
pick it up before he went to see Zed Hiatt. The call
had to at least appear to be legitimate.

He reversed himself for a block, and went up the
hotel steps. The town was about the same, people
still nervous, unhappy, now angry about the new
tax increase.

Spur went into the Johnson House Hotel and
asked at the small desk for his key. There was a
note. Spur read it and looked around the small
lobby. A woman on the far side facing the desk rose
slowly and came toward him.

She was sturdy, with proper shoes, a skirt that
brushed the floor and a proper jacket and hat even
though the temperature was climbing into the
eighties.

The note said simply: "Mr. McCoy. My name is
Mrs. Walter Trembolt. Could I have a word with
you over here? I'm a respectable woman. My

husband runs the blacksmith shop and we are both good Baptists.''

Spur smiled as the woman walked up to him.

"Mrs. Trembolt, I would guess.''

She nodded curtly. "Yes, we must talk.''

"We can talk right here in the lobby if that would be all right. Won't you sit down?''

She sat across from him in an upholstered chair. She was a woman of about forty, her face pinched as if from constant frowning. She carried herself stiffly erect and cold blue eyes now stared at him.

"Mr. McCoy, I understand you're a Secret Service agent from the Washington D.C. government. I don't know exactly what that is or what you're supposed to do, but you must help us.''

"That's what I'm here for, Ma'am.''

"This Mr. White from Chicago is an agent of the devil. You must drive him out of town and let us get back to our proper ways and go about our business of spreading the Good News about Jesus Christ our Lord.''

"Mrs. Trembolt. I've been making certain inquiries about Mr. White. So far your local people have been able to find nothing he has done which is illegal. According to the Reconstruction Laws, there are certain changes that must come to the state of Texas. It's simply the law.''

"The man is Lucifer incarnate! He is the devil himself and he is ruining our small community. I keep praying for God almighty to strike Don White dead, but I must not be praying hard enough.''

"I'm sorry, Mrs. Trembolt, prayer isn't my line of work. What I deal with are legal facts showing that Mr. White has violated the law, any law. That way he can be tried, convicted and removed from office. Do you have any evidence I can use to do this?''

"Oh, no. I'm not one to go to the law. I'm a Christian. This man is violating our Christian principles and I want him removed from office."

"Mrs. Trembolt, I'm sure you're a dedicated Christian woman, but what we must have are facts, evidence."

The woman sitting across from him stiffened even more if that were possible. She sniffed.

"Mr. McCoy. I'll have you know I am the mother of four sons and three daughters. That is how *dedicated a Christian I am!* I'm doing my bit to populate this God-forsaken, wicked country with good Christian folks. I also try to do what is best for the community and the church.

"Surely this man can be reasoned with. No matter how anti-Christ, he must have some decency."

"Yes, Mrs. Trembolt it is possible. Why don't you go over to City Hall right now and reason with Mr. White? I'm sure he would be pleased to see you and have a long talk. I spoke with him only yesterday."

"Don't patronize me, Mr. McCoy. I am a responsible citizen, a loyal American, and I hate what this riffraff, this white trash from Chicago is doing to Johnson Creek!" She stood quickly, started to leave, then remembering her manners and turned back. Spur had stood as she did, she seemed surprised to see him standing. "Oh, well, good bye, Mr. McCoy. We must all work in our own ways for the glory of the Lord." She turned and began to walk away.

"Good bye, Mrs. Trembolt. I wish you every success," Spur said as she turned.

He watched her go with a small shake of his head. If only it were that easy. He was on his way up to his room when he was handed another note by the desk clerk.

"Sorry, Mr. McCoy, this one came earlier and I forgot it."

He opened the second note. It was from Beth: "Spur. Please come to my house for dinner and to stay here while you are in Johnson Corner. I have a large house as you know, and you can pick a room with a lock on the inside! I promise not to attack you. Hope to see you for supper tonight."

He smiled and pushed the note into his pocket, picked up his railroad type pocket watch from his room and headed toward the jewelry store. The doctor's office came into view first, so he made a short detour across the street.

Doctor Greenly had a modest practice. He was the only doctor in town and for fifteen miles on all sides. He lived in a house beside the converted store where he had his offices. The building had been painted white with a soft blue trim, and even looked clean on the outside.

He went in the door marked "Office" and was met by a smiling young woman who asked his name and what he wanted to see the doctor about.

"Miss, it's personal," Spur said after signing the sheet of paper pasted to a piece of cardboard.

The girl smiled. She seemed to be seventeen or eighteen.

"Mr. McCoy," she said glancing at the sheet. "Most medical work is highly personal. Is this medically personal or something else?"

"It's about a gunshot wound."

The girl glanced at him quickly. "You have a gunshot wound?"

"No."

"Oh!" She frowned and left the small waiting room at once. Spur saw two others in the room, one a woman with a baby, and the second an old man with one eye. McCoy sat on a wooden chair that had been painted the same light blue of the exterior trim. Must have had some paint left over.

A moment later the young girl came up to Spur. "Dr. Greenly will see you now," she said. "This way, please."

She led him into the next room, through it and down a hall to an office with a desk, two chairs, books and a framed medical degree on the wall.

Dr. Horace Greenly sat behind the desk looking at a yellow pad and a medical book, going from one to the other. He mumbled something, made a penciled note on the yellow sheet and frowned. When he looked up at Spur, the same frown was in place. The girl had left and closed the door.

"Gunshot wound?" he said staring at Spur. The doctor was in his late forties, short even for 1869 at five feet four inches. He had a full head of red hair which had lost none of its carrot color. His eyes were an emerald shade of green, and his face was pale, with bags under his eyes and a touch of whiteness creeping over the lens of his eyes. The "white blindness" could overwhelm him within ten years and he was fighting it.

He shook his head. "I'm afraid I don't understand. Who are you, and what's this about a gunshot?"

"My name is Spur McCoy, Dr. Greenly. The man who was shot is Harry Johnson. Harry was shot five times, by five different guns. How come you covered up a murder?"

Dr. Greenly was not surprised or shaken. He picked up his pencil and began making marks on the yellow papaer.

"As soon as I got there I knew Harry had been killed. Didn't see any sense in letting this town blow apart. I told his daughter, Beth, that the Carpet-baggers would blame the towners, and the towners would blame the Baggers. They'd start shooting up the town, we'd have the Civil War all over again. I didn't think it was worth it."

"So you lied."

"For a good reason. I reported it to the town marshal as a death by gunshot wounds by person unknown. We can open the investigation anytime when the town is quieted down."

"When is that going to be, Doctor Greenly?"

"I don't know, not for a while yet. Feelings still running high. You've been on the street."

'Do you have any ideas about who the killers could be?"

"None at all. I know there were five bullet wounds in and around the chest and heart. Beyond that it's out of my area. I'm a doctor, not a Pinkerton detective." He paused. "You are, though. Not Pinkerton, but with the U.S. Secret Service. This why you're in town, to look into a murder?"

"Partly. We received a letter from Harry Johnson saying he had something he wanted to tell us. He said he could tell the local authorities, but he didn't trust them."

"He was right about that. Bunch of damn Carpet-bagging bastards!"

"Well, Doctor, I'm glad to see that you're so calm and collected about this governmental problem the town has. I still am not satisfied with why you covered up a murder. Especially one that must involve five people."

"I told you my reasons. So arrest me. I told the lawman, so I don't think I broke any law."

"How about conspiracy to commit a felony? That's what covering up a murder is."

"Wouldn't make it to court in our county."

"It would in the Federal Court in Houston."

"We're a long way from Houston."

"Which of the five bullets killed Harry?"

"Can't say unless you can tell me which one was fired first through fifth. Two hit his heart, three in his lungs. Either of the heart shots would have done it. The lung punctures would have killed him, too, but slower."

"Dr. Greenly, I'm not at all pleased with your medical ethics in this case. Legally you're still liable to be arrested. If you discover anything else, anything at all, that touches on this death, you better look me up and tell me before the sun goes down on that day."

"Don't rightly know what that might be, McCoy."

Spur stood, his hat in his left hand. The doctor made no move to get up.

"Greenly, I hope your medical knowledge and skills are a lot better than your ethics." He walked out of the room without saying goodbye.

Outside in the street, Spur stared back at the neatly painted doctor's office. Something was still wrong here, but he had no idea what it was.

So the town marshal knew about the five bullets. Two people knew and did nothing. What would the marshal have to gain? The water was getting danker and murkier by the moment.

He turned and walked on toward the jeweler. The front door was open and he went in. The usual glass topped case showed fancy pocket watches, pendant watches and a collection of wedding rings and a few special pearl and diamond rings, bracelets and necklaces.

A tall, heavy man lifted a jeweler's glass from his eye and looked at Spur. He had to wait a moment for his eyes to readjust, then his smile seemed to slip off his face.

"Yes sir, how may I help you?" Zed Hiatt asked.

"Mr. Hiatt?" Spur asked.

"The same."

"Good, they tell me you're the best man in town on a good pocket watch. Mine seems to be running a mite slow lately."

"Probably needs cleaning."

"Don't have that much time. That takes a couple of days, doesn't it?"

"Would now, I have some ahead of you."

"Oh! Could you adjust it to run just a little faster? Isn't there an adjustment inside somewhere?"

"Yep, I can do that." Zed looked up at him. "You're that Secret Service man I heard was in town?"

"The same. I hear you're on the city council now."

"True, for all the good it does. Get outvoted three to one on every issue. Try to do things need doing. The coloreds only want to talk about money, the damn dole!"

"That upsets you, Mr. Hiatt?"

"Like it does every other white man in town. We should be thinking about gas lights for the streets, maybe some cobblestone or paving of some kind for Main Street. We don't, not now."

"Mr. Hiatt, what do you know about the murder of Harry Johnson?"

Zed had been opening the back of Spur's pocket watch. He dropped it on the workbench. His hands shook so hard he could not even hold the small jeweler's tool. Sweat beaded rapidly on his forehead. He looked up and fear oozed from his eyes.

"M . . . Murder? Heard he died of stomach problems."

"True, Zed, five lead slugs fired at close range from five different pistols, probably by five different people."

"The paper said . . . Murder? I don't understand." His voice had changed. It vibrated, he coughed once, his eyes watered. "I . . . He was a good friend. Known Harry a long time. Didn't know what you said. Five? Why would five people shoot . . . Oh, God! You sure you're right?"

"Positively. I'm in town to dig out the killers. Right now everyone in Johnson Creek is a suspect. Where were you that night about two weeks ago when Harry Johnson was murdered in cold blood?"

"Where? Two weeks ago? What night? Most likely I was home reading. I do lots of reading since Etta died." He started to get up, then changed his mind and almost fell off the chair as he eased back down.

"What the hell! I was probably home. How can a person prove he was home alone reading?"

"Tough thing to prove, Zed. Just wondered. You put some thought on it and try to come up with some witnesses. Maybe you played poker or went out for a drink, or had company. You think on it and I'll stop by later on this week. I have a lot of people to talk to."

Spur stood there for a moment.

"My watch?"

Zed seemed to come alive again. "Oh, yes." He picked up the watch, made a small adjustment on the inside and pressed the parts back together. "That should speed it up just a mite."

"How much do I owe you?"

"Never make charges for adjustments." He shook

his head. "Old Harry murdered. Just can't believe it."

"Going to surprise a lot of folks. Thanks for your help." Spur walked out and across the street where he went into the Overbay General Store and from the darker interior, watched the jeweler's office.

Spur had investigated a pair of fine leather riding gloves for only a moment when Zed came out of his shop, locked his door and walked quickly up the street. Spur waited until he was half a block ahead, then followed on the other side of the street.

Another half block down, Zed turned into the *Johnson Creek Record* office. Spur stepped into a saloon and bought a beer and watched through the front window. Curious. Had he frightened the big man? He had been surprised when Spur used the word, murder. Dropped Spur's watch and his tool.

An over reaction even for a friend of Harry's. Yes, this and what June had told him seemed to point to Zed Hiatt as one of the five killers. But why? He could see nothing in common for the three men he suspected so far. They all lived in the same town, that was about it.

Scare a calf and it ran for its mother. Frighten a child and it often ran home or to a parent. Scare a killer, wouldn't he run for support to someone else who had also been in on the plot? That could mean that Hans Runner, the newspaperman was also in on the plot. He certainly didn't tell the right story in his paper.

June said that Garth Ludlow had been excited about something a week ago, but changed his mind and wouldn't tell her. It could tie in. He would be a more sure fourth suspect now. He knew about the five slugs in the dead man, but had not mentioned it. Was he the fourth man who pulled a trigger that night? Maybe he was painting Dr. Greenly with the wrong brush. Perhaps he *was concerned* about the town. He might not be involved.

But why had five men who knew Harry Johnson murdered him?

He needed to have some idea why these men banded together in the first place. What held three or four such different types together? He could not figure out anything they had in common.

After a half hour had passed and Zed had not left the printing plant, Spur walked over and tried the door. Locked. He saw a note on the front door. It said "Out . . . Be Back SOON."

Spur pondered that a moment as he walked away. Two killers could be going to talk to the other three. He would be especially careful with his back from now on. No open windows, no dark alleys, no light in his room.

There were five men in town with each one thinking he was a killer. In this case Spur hoped that thinking did not make it so . . . again with him as the victim.

10

Spur had walked only half a block away from the newspaper office when he heard a shot. His hand darted to his hogleg and came up with iron.

A buggy had just turned the corner a hundred feet ahead of him and headed away from him down Main Street. He could see four black men in the rig, each with a rifle, shotgun or pistol. They shouted and screamed and fired their weapons at second story windows as the horse and buggy raced down Main.

Spur was too far away to stop it. He could only watch as the rig tore along Main, scattering horses, other rigs and pedestrians as the Negroes blasted windows. Half the glass in the second and third floor of the Johnson House fell to the onslaught.

As quickly as it began the shooting stopped and the rig turned off Main and was gone. Half a dozen men jumped on horses and spurred after the four men. It was doubtful they would ever find the right ones.

Spur walked toward the small marshal's office. Were the shootings the result of a plan, or was it just four liquored up men with nothing to do?

Three stores ahead of him more firing sounded. Two shots blasted into the Texas afternoon. Spur raced forward, saw two cowboys duck and run away from an empty store next to the freight office. Another shot blazed into the stillness. Now Spur knew it came from the empty store.

Inside the store someone screamed, then Milicent Trembolt staggered out of the unused store. Her skirt was half ripped off and bloody. Her blouse hung on her shoulders in shreds where it had been sliced twenty times by a sharp knife. Both her breasts showed plainly through the tatters. Blood stained one breast.

She held a six-gun in both hands, swung around and fired it again into the store. A Negro man tumbled out of the doorway, his shirt off, one hand holding his bloody shoulder.

Before anyone could move, Mrs. Trembolt lifted the weapon and fired from six feet away, hitting the black man in the face, slamming him backward into a quick death.

Mrs. Trembolt screamed and dropped the gun. Two women rushed forward and caught her just before she fell. The women quickly covered her and helped her walk slowly into the drug store next to the freight office on the other side.

Doc Greenly hurried up the boardwalk and into the store. Spur checked the body of the colored. He was dead. There were signs of a struggle and blood in the old store.

Spur stood in the doorway of the drug store. Doc had the woman sitting up and he was talking to her. A moment later he urged her to stand and they went out through the alley toward the doctor's office.

Spur looked up as someone screamed as he ran forward. The sound came from a large man with a bare chest and arms like oak branches. He waved a double barreled shotgun in his right hand.

"Oh, God! Here comes Walt!" someone said.

"He finds out what happened to his wife he'll gun down every black man he can find!" another voice said.

Spur stood on the boardwalk between the raging man and the store where his wife had been. Walt charged forward, started to brush past Spur. Too late he saw the foot out. Spur tripped Walt and grabbed the shotgun as Walt stumbled past him and then sprawled in the dust.

Spur broke open the weapon, let both shells fall into his hand and closed it again.

Walt began to get up.

"Hold it, Walt!" Spur commanded in his best parade ground voice. The talk around the boardwalk stopped. Walt looked up, his face a furious mask of hatred.

"Black bastards hurt my wife! I got a right to kill them!"

"Which ones, Walt? How you going to know which ones? You kill anybody, Walt, and I'll throw you in your own iron jail. You want that?"

Walt roared with rage and crawled to his hands and knees. Spur kicked him in the stomach just hard enough to roll him over and knock half the wind out of him.

"Stay down, Walt, or I'll have to lock you up. Do you want that?"

Walt sat up sucking in air. When he could talk he shook his head. "Where's my wife?"

"Over at Doc Greenly's," Spur said. "Why don't you walk on over there and help her? She needs you now."

Walt stood slowly, nodded at Spur and reached

for his long gun.

"I'll keep it for a while, Walt. It'll be down at the marshal's office. Pick it up tomorrow."

Walt nodded and walked off toward the doctor's office.

Spur turned and strode across the street toward City Hall. The Secret Agent pushed open the door and walked inside, saw the mayor's office door closed and marched up to it. He turned the knob and rammed the door open so hard it hit the wall.

Mayor White had his feet up on the desk as he worked out some final plans. He sat up quickly when Spur leaned over his desk.

"Take it easy, McCoy. We've had enough problems around here for one day. I know, I know. I heard all about it. None of my doings. Those men are citizens, free to get in trouble or not just like any other citizen."

"Bullshit!" Spur McCoy roared. "We both know what those men are, and how you got elected. You've got an hour to get out of here, to take your black voters out of town, at least two or three miles and set up a camp."

"Not likely. You've got no authority."

Spur drew the .44 off his hip so fast White suddenly was staring down the black muzzle of death. Spur pressed the iron's cold barrel against White's forehead.

"As I was saying, Mayor White. You get your men out of here within an hour. This is a forced evacuation for the public good and you will obey. If you don't, half of them could be shot down in a blood bath. If you thought the town was on edge before, you haven't even started to know what it's like out there now.

"You get out the back way with your people, NOW!"

"Impossible, McCoy."

Spur holstered the weapon in one smooth move, caught White by the shirt front and one arm and threw him against the wall. White hit and sagged, slumping to the floor, total surprise washing over his face.

"Right now, damnit!" Spur thundered. "Do you get the picture? Do you finally understand the danger?"

"Yes, yes. All right. I'll get things started. This is just temporary."

Spur spun around and ran back to the street.

Garth Ludlow stood there moving people past the death scene. He wore his marshal's badge again. He waved Spur over.

"Figured it was about time I came back to work. Looks like the town can use me."

"That's for damn sure."

"Oh, Father Desmond is looking for you. Any idea what he wants?"

"Personal, Marshal. Something personal." Just then the priest came through the crowd and called to Spur. The Secret Agent walked to meet the priest in his black habit.

"Mr. McCoy, I'd like to talk to you. There's something I need to tell you."

"Father it will have to wait. Right now we have a near riot shaping up. I'd appreciate it if you could stay visible here on the street and try to calm down the people you have some influence with. It would be a help."

"Yes, of course. I'll be glad to help. Could we set up a meeting first thing in the morning? Things should be settled down by then.''

"That will be fine, Father. About nine o'clock.''

Spur heard screams up the street and he moved that way. By the time he got there things had quieted down. He was afraid the rest of the afternoon was going to be like that.

It was. People grouped on the street talking about what to do to the coloreds. Then word came through that the Negroes had all moved out, they went south somewhere.

"Hail, I don't know if they coming back or not," one cowboy said. "I saw a whole bunch of them riding and walking down the Amarillo road, about an hour ago.''

"Let's go after them!'' Somebody shouted.

Spur fired the borrowed shotgun into the air and quickly broke up the budding riot.

Twice more before dark he used the shotgun to get the attention of troublemakers. It was a miracle that nobody got killed.

He slipped up the steps to his second floor hotel room and found it was one of those that had had windows blasted out. A light burned in his room when he got there and he pushed the door open with the muzzle of his .44.

Beth Johnson sat on the bed playing solitaire with a new deck of cards. She had swept up the glass and shaken it all out of the bedding.

"Hi," Beth said. "You've been busy.''

"Just another day as a glamorous Secret Service agent," Spur said slipping the lock on the door and pushing a chair under the handle. He dropped his gunbelt over the bedpost and sat down beside her.

"You get my note?''

"Yes. Been busy.''

"So I've heard. Are we worth it?''

"Some of you."

"Good. I figured you were not going to come up to my house so I decided to come to yours. You haven't had dinner yet so we have fried chicken, biscuits and gravy, mashed potatoes, three vegetables and sliced peaches for dessert. Hungry?"

He ate everything she brought. It was long past dark when he finished the last of the food and the two bottles of warm beer. She explained they had been cold when she brought them.

"Any progress on my father's five killers?" Beth asked.

"I think I may know who four of them are, but I still have no idea why, or what binds these men together in this kind of an execution plot."

She sat on the edge of the bed, her pretty face in a frown, brown hair sweeping over her shoulders. "I know Daddy went to play poker once a month or so. Would that help? He never liked to play much but said it was a get together for old times sake."

"Who did he play with?"

"I don't know. He never said. I never thought it was important enough to ask. I don't even know where he played."

"Not at one of the saloons?"

"No, it must have been at somebody's house. He mentioned once or twice that the man's wife really had a good snack for them after the game."

"One more question. Does the city have an account at your bank?"

"Yes, three or four of them. Why?"

"Make some excuse and don't let them take out any money from any of the accounts. Special bank examiner is coming or something."

"Why? It's city money."

"But the wrong people may draw it out and keep

it, like stealing, like Carpetbaggers."

"Oh. I don't know, it might be worth it to let him take the money and leave. Then most of the coloreds would leave too, because the dole would end fast. Maybe a few of the good workers would stay."

"Tomorrow, he'll try to make his run tomorrow. I made him get all of his blacks out of town so they wouldn't get massacred." Spur slid down on the bed and closed his eyes.

"Hey, you can't go to sleep. I know I promised not to seduce you, but that doesn't mean you can't at least kiss me once, or twice, or a dozen or more."

Spur laughed and pulled her down beside him. He kissed her and she snuggled against him.

"That's better. I hate a man who is a hard loser."

"Who lost? I thought I was winning. I have this winsome wench in my bed and the door's locked. I've just had a great meal she brought and she has no one to protect her honor."

Beth giggled. "Now we're starting to get somewhere."

"Be quiet and kiss me."

She rolled over on top of him and giggled.

"What's so funny?" he asked.

"I was just wishing that I had huge tits like June has so I could pop one out about now and slowly lower the dangling beauty into your mouth."

"Size isn't everything. Let me show you what I mean." He opened the buttons on her dress, pulled up her chemise and lowered her right breast into his mouth. He kissed the breast, then licked the nipple until she squealed, then sucked her whole breast into his mouth.

"Yes, yes! I think you might have a wonderful idea there. Who needs cow tits!"

Beth moaned softly. "My God but that makes me

hot! How do you get me worked up so fast!" She reached for his crotch and found a growing lump there. Eagerly she massaged it and it grew in size.

He shifted to her other breast.

"I feel so warm all over, so soft and wanting. I feel like my breasts are on fire and my . . . my down there . . . is all soft and wet!"

She pulled her breast from his mouth and sat up. Quickly she opened his belt and then his fly and tugged his pants and short drawers down. His manhood leaped up eager for combat.

"Oh my! He's so huge! I didn't know they ever got that big. I mean the only other time . . . well he was just a kid really. My God, look at him!"

Her hands closed around his shaft and held him tenderly. She touched the purple head and moaned softly. Then her hands lifted his heavy scrotum and played with his balls.

When she leaned over him there were tears in her eyes.

"Spur I want you to take me so much, but it wouldn't work. It hurt the first time, and I know . . . I just know that nothing that huge would ever fit inside me. If it did it would hurt so much I'd die!"

"All your big talk was just talk, wasn't it? There isn't a man's prick made that won't fit in any grown woman. It just takes some warming up, some getting ready. I promise it won't hurt. Christ you've got me so wanting you now . . ."

"Won't hurt?"

"It will feel so good you'll die of pleasure."

As he talked he massaged her breasts. He saw the small nipples rise and fill with blood. Then he ran his hand down her stomach to the top of the skirt.

"I really shouldn't."

"But you want to."

"Yes, so much, and with you! Only with you forever!"

"That's a hell of a long time."

"Good."

He slid his hand under the waist of her skirt and she caught it for a moment. He kissed her lips and she sighed and released his hand.

"I . . . I guess maybe . . ."

His hands found the fasteners at the side and he opened them, then pushed her skirt down. She wore two petticoats. He pushed them down too, then pulled her skirt and petticoats off over her feet.

Gently he took off her shoes and began massaging her feet.

"What are you doing?"

"Part of that getting ready. Do you like this?"

"Yes, it's relaxing."

His hands left her feet and worked up her gently curved legs. He marveled how fresh and pure they were, unmarked by bruise or cut or age.

When he came to her undergarment, it was a short kind of frilly silk he hadn't seen before. It had elastic around the waist and around each leg. Gently he pushed his hand under the elastic and down her tender, flat belly.

"Oh, no!" she said sharply. Her hands pressed on his hand through the fabric.

Again he kissed her, forcing his tongue between her teeth and into her mouth. Beth sighed softly, her hand came away and he moved it lower as the kiss continued.

He found the thatch of soft hair and stroked it. She murmured something, then sighed and he felt her legs drifting apart.

Quickly he bent and put his head to her crotch and before she noticed, he chewed a hole through the soft silk fabric. She half sat up and watched him fascinated.

"That's the most outrageous, the sexiest thing I've ever heard of!" she said half in awe, half in desire.

"Now, sweet Spur! Do me now! Push him into me!"

But Spur wasn't ready. His hand went to the hole in the silk and he stroked her outer lips, rubbed her tiny clit again and again until she screamed in joy and jolted in a gyrating, bouncing climax that left Spur in stark wonder. When she quieted she looked up at him.

"Maybe now, I'm ready?"

He nodded. She smiled, grabbed his penis and pulled it toward her crotch.

Spur lowered and nudged her slit. The lips parted and juices flowed and a second later he slid into her depths without a flicker of fear or pain from Beth.

"It's . . . it's . . . indescribable!" she said at last.

He made it last, coming almost to his climax, then pausing and backing away. Three more times Beth climaxed as he carried her along. Then in one tremendous rush they both came at the same time and lay there panting, her slender flanks heaving, his chest pounding to gain more air.

Her arms wrapped around him like a barbed wire fence.

"Now I'll never let you go," she said. "Anybody else would be a let down."

"Almost every man and woman is good in bed."

"Not like this. I have an idea. I have plenty of money. Why don't we get married and we can . . . can fuck this way every night for a hundred years!"

Spur shook his head and kissed her nose. "I'm not the marrying kind, at least not right now."

"Then don't marry me, we'll live in sin and we can make love this way every night for fifty years!"

"Fifty years is a long, long time."

Beth pouted for a minute. Her brown eyes shadowed with petulance. She swung her hair around so it covered his face.

"At least you can stay here and do it to me every night for two years, or until I get so sore I can't even spread my legs!"

He kissed her again.

"We'll talk about it," he said and a short time later they both went to sleep.

She woke him before morning and had him ready. They made love again. It had been the greatest night of her life and Beth didn't want to let it end. But her eyes turned heavy and she gave in at last and slept.

11

When Father Desmond talked to the Secret Service Agent Spur McCoy, he had made up his mind what he must do. He had to tell someone about the whole thing. He had struggled with the burden for too long. It had been a lark for him at first, a kind of rebellion, a release perhaps.

Then after the first shots had been fired, a course was set that no one, not even God could change. He thought about that for a moment and quickly changed 'could' to 'would.' All of the death, the screaming, and then . . . the find.

Father Desmond shook his head. He stayed on the street for an hour, talking to people, trying to calm them down. He decided he had been at least partly successful. There were no more shootings and very few squabbles.

He had urged all his Catholics to go home and leave the situation to the authorities. He had done little enough. Even if he had helped save one person's life this afternoon, he was still far, far from making up for that terrible night four years ago.

Pushing it all far away into the back alleys of his

mind, he headed toward the church and his quarters. He slipped in without Calida hearing him, went straight to the small chapel he had built in one of the rooms, and prayed on his knees for half an hour. Then he prostrated himself on the floor in front of the crucified Christ and prayed without ceasing for an hour.

Only then could he get to his feet and go into the living room, where Calida waited for him. She was such a pure vessel, so uncomplicated, uneducated, and trusting. Tonight he told the cook to go to her relatives house for a visit. Then he and Calida made their own supper in the big kitchen.

He had exactly what he wanted: a vegetable stew with just a few pieces of browned beef thrown in to give it flavor. He seasoned it with a whole bay leaf and let it cook its flavor through the mixture. He added enough water so there would be a juicy gravy to cover the potatoes when mashed on his plate.

For years, cooking had been one of his vices. He gave it up one year for Lent as he remembered, and somehow never found the time again.

Calida smiled at him as they worked on the food. She unbuttoned the simple white blouse she wore saying that it was too warm. She wore nothing under it, and the open blouse offered many quick glimpses of her breasts. Father Desmond was stirred, sexually, as he had been so many times lately.

After the meal, they left the dishes for the cook to wash the next day and retreated into his study and bedroom. Once inside Calida locked the door and stripped off her blouse.

She walked slowly to him, her arms out, her breasts swaying delightfully.

Father Desmond cursed himself silently. He had

hoped to be strong enough this one last time, but there was no chance. She needed him! He nearly laughed out loud at his justification. A thirteen year old girl does not need sexual gratification. She hardly understood his passion, and so far had shown none of her own.

He caught her hand and pulled her to the floor. Slowly he kissed her body from the top of her head down to her toes, casting aside any shielding clothing in the process. She lay on the bare floor looking at him, her eyes trusting, her lips curved in a sweet smile.

How had he come to this point? How had a man of God become a whiskey priest and a priestly seducer?

Even as he thought of it, he wasn't sure. His very first sexual experience had been with another altar boy. The other boy had been nearly thirteen and he asked Desmond if he'd ever jerked off. Desmond was twelve and he had heard the words, and knew what they meant, but hadn't tried it.

Once when climbing a tree he had strained to get to a limb and he felt his penis harden and something jet out of it. But he had never tried to make it happen.

They sat down behind the altar after everyone had left and pulled down their pants. The other boy's penis was hard and he helped Desmond, then became so excited he did it for the younger boy, climaxing himself when Desmond did.

That had been so many years ago. Father Desmond stroked the sleek, bountiful body of Calida. A year later he had found out about girls. A cousin of his on a picnic had teased him and ran into the woods. He followed and when he found her she had her blouse open and showed him her growing breasts. She had been fourteen and well developed.

She quickly opened his pants, and played with him, but before she could get her skirt and drawers off, he had ejaculated and she hit him in the eye and ran off just mad as hell.

After that he pumped off his pud, as he called it, twice a week. But it wasn't until he was fifteen that he actually had intercourse. She had been fifteen, too, that summer, as curious about boys as he was about girls.

They had piano lessons right after each other, and that Saturday afternoon walking home after the lessons, they stopped in a small park. She had kissed him first, "just for fun," she had told him. That led to more kisses and exploring and then a panting, passionate joining of their bodies both with all of their clothes still on.

She had been disappointed and never let him touch her again. He had been thrilled and started looking for "that kind of girl" who liked sex as much as he did.

Then he went to study for the priesthood and discovered that girls were not the only means for sexual relief. But he broke from that mold as soon as he could.

The first time he made love after he became an ordained priest, he was in abject misery for a week. At his confession that week he told his senior paster of his sin, and the older priest counseled him.

He said quite simply that before a priest is a priest, he must be a man. Man is a sexual being, he can't live normally without some sexual feelings. The senior priest told Desmond to be careful, to beat down those feelings whenever he could. If he occasionally fell from grace, his confessor, and

114

surely God himself who made man a sexual creature, would understand.

The bishop did not understand. Nor did the husband of one of the biggest givers to the church.

Father Desmond began a round of singularly unpopular, poor and hard to serve parishes.

Now he smiled as he watched Calida. So innocent. She must be kept that way. Innocent in all ways except sexually. She had gladly provided him with every type of sexual gratification he asked of her. But still a child.

She looked up and smiled. "Father, may I have the honor of undressing you?" she asked.

He nodded. One last time.

As she took off his priestly habit, he watched her, noted her every movement, every smile, each crease in her beautiful face when she smiled. Small wrinkles on her forehead as she frowned. Soft, dark eyes, thin, yet sensuous lips.

Mostly he watched the movement of her breasts as she undressed him. So perfect, so beautiful! Woman was breasts! So delicately formed, so useful, so marvelously picturesque! If he were a poet he would write a sonnet to breasts.

When she had stripped off all his clothes, he contrasted his starkly white skin with her golden brown. Her skin was beautiful. His pathetic. At five six he was not a big man, but he had stayed in passable shape. Sometimes this was because he ate nothing but whiskey for three days at a time.

He smiled. He had been slightly drunk in Houston. It had caused the bishop to vow his vengeance. The woman involved had known of Father Desmond's weakness. She had reason to work in the church office now and then, and had heard stories.

He was sure she had set out to trap him. She had a tantalizing way of showing up when he was alone, and then telling him how much she admired him. Six times she had seen him when they were alone, in the garden, the church library, once in the confessional. Each time she moved closer to showing him that she would not mind his advances.

But this time he had held true! He had resisted. The final blow came when he received a note from a messenger. The woman needed him at her home at once. An emergency! He hurried there thinking something had happened to her.

She let him in, looking worried. She wore a heavy robe and hurried ahead of him up the stairs and into the master bedroom. She had locked the door behind them, waved him forward into the bathroom, where a large tub had been specially built into the end of the room.

Calmly she dropped the robe and was naked.

"Father Desmond, I want you to take a bath with me, and any other interesting games we might figure out to play." She had smiled and kissed him, then undressed him and led him into the tub filled with warm water and bubbles.

He had fallen from Grace, deep and hard. The third time they left the water and used the big bed. That was when her husband walked into the bedroom. She had planned it all along. She didn't mind getting caught, as long as she could take him down. The bishop transferred him immediately.

Father Desmond caressed Calida's young body and then gently they made love. He had never felt more satisfaction, more at peace. How had he fallen so far that he could find peace when defying the church, breaking his vows?

He held her in his arms. She was one woman who

wanted nothing from him, who wanted only to give to him, perhaps in return for some love and tenderness. She was too good for him, but he refused to share her with anyone.

Slowly he eased her to the bed, sat up at his small desk and wrote a letter. He started it a second time, then had it the way he wanted it. He dated and signed it. Then he sealed it in an envelope, wrote a name on the outside and went back to the bed.

She must not know, he must keep her pure and clean and innocent before God. He sat beside her on the bed, stroked her, petted her marvelous young form.

"Calida, put your head in my lap and close your eyes," he told her gently. He bent and kissed her cheek. "I'll always love you, small one," he said softly.

Then with a knife he had brought with him from the desk, he slit her precious throat, slicing through the big artery on the side of her neck. For a moment she struggled. He held her. In ten seconds she was dead, her blood gushed out of her carotid artery, soaking his legs and the bed.

Swiftly he gave her the last rites. He was crying then, softly with many tears. He prayed again, purifying her soul, then clasped his bloody hands and asked for his own forgiveness.

He bent again and kissed her bloody cheek, then slit his own throat and fell on top of her in death as swift as hers.

12

McCoy was up and moving with the sun the next morning. He left Beth tangled in the sheet after kissing her cheek. He had a quick breakfast and then walked the streets. Everything was calm. He saw a few people, but nowhere were there any black faces.

The men he saw were grim and tight lipped.

Marshal Garth Ludlow was also out patrolling.

"Looks quiet," Ludlow said.

"So far. I booted the mayor and his coloreds out of town until things cool down. Don't know how long I can keep them out."

"Blood will flow in the street if they come back today," Ludlow said.

"Probably." Spur looked toward the store front that served as City Hall. "Got me a feeling things are going to come to a head here soon. Maybe today. Is this the last day to pay city taxes?"

"Yep, without a penalty."

"You've raised a posse before, Marshal Ludlow?"

"One or two."

"Don't forget how. I'm hoping we won't have the

need. Got me a gut feeling.''

"You think White will make a run for it?"

"Don't the Baggers always do that?"

"True. We watch the son of a bitch!"

"We watch everybody."

They nodded and went their ways around the waking town.

After making the rounds for another hour, Spur walked up to the Catholic church. It was quiet. No early Mass yet. He remembered his meeting with the priest and checked his pocket watch. Not quite eight. He was supposed to be here at nine. What's an hour early?

He walked in through the gate in the six-foot church wall around the garden. He knew the way to the priest's quarters. The parsonage had been set to one side, with an outside door through the wall. Spur had come in the long way. He saw a sister walking into the church and nodded.

He knocked on the front door and waited. There was no response. After a moment he knocked again. When there was no answer the second time he tried the door. It was unlocked. He eased it open and stepped inside.

Maybe the priest was at Mass after all, or confession. He waited a moment in the coolness of the room. It was nicely furnished with heavily built furniture and had a fireplace at the far end.

"Father Desmond?" he called softly. No answer. He tried again. Unusual. The priest should be up and about by now. A tension gripped him and he knew something was wrong. It happened sometimes.

Quickly he began to search the parsonage. At the end of the hall he found a locked door. Gently he tested the lock, then used the point of his pocket knife between the door and casing and forced the bolt back until the door unlocked and swung open.

It was a bedroom and at once he saw the huddled bodies on the bed. Dried blood had made a deep red stain over part of the sheet and on the naked bodies. More blood had splashed and splattered on the floor.

He touched the priest's arm. It was cold, stiff. Both had been dead for ten hours or more. He wanted someone else to find the bodies. Spur wasn't sure why. He looked around the room, saw the envelope on a small desk and to his surprise it had his name on it. Suicide note? He picked it up, folded it and pushed it in his pocket, then hurried to the bedroom door and stepped into the hall.

He made sure the door was set to lock behind him, then closed it and went to the far door. He was right. It opened on the street. When no one was looking, he stepped through the door and into the street. He walked rapidly away and back to Main Street.

He had seen death before, but never a priest and a young girl in such an obviously wicked and sinful situation. Murder and suicide, it had to be. He leaned against the wall of a store and took out the envelope.

It was sealed. Inside he found a piece of white paper with the priest's name printed in the upper left hand corner.

The writing was clear, bold and easy to read. A practiced hand.

"My Dear Agent McCoy:

"I take pen in hand this evening to confess to you and to Almighty God my thousands of sins and transgressions. I am not worthy to be a priest, a vessel of God.

"I have violated this marvelous child

called Calida. I have carnal knowledge of her, and have sinned repeatedly—yet she is my joy and my sanity in an insane world. Calida is as pure as new snow, as innocent as a newborn babe.

"I am a victim of my own excesses. I have loved John Barleycorn more than God. I have adored the gentle hand, the womanly caresses and ministrations of Calida more than I have loved and served Jesus Christ our Lord.

"Some years ago I was also involved in the deaths of twelve men. I have never confessed this sin to any priest, and now I do so to you hoping for absolution. It was a mistake that began as a lark, as a patriotic duty, and wound up in a furious battle that was to stain and cripple my priesthood ever after.

"Ever since it happened, I have regretted that act, and another recently when I was a factor in the untimely death of Harry Johnson. I am eternally damned, and eternally sorry for this monstrous and most grievous sin, for which I plead for forgiveness so I might dwell in the house of the Lord forever and ever.

"Now soon it will be over. I can't go on living with so much sin and violence and seductions and my repeated violations and corruption of this wonderful girl child, Calida.

"The time is here. It will be quick for her. She will not suffer. She will not even know what is to happen. She is soft and pure, an innocent in the eyes of God. May she live in heaven forever.

"Tell my new friends goodbye for me. Tell them that I lived as I wanted to, and now I die as I wish. Farewell. s/Father Ambrose Desmond."

* * *

Spur read the note again, looking for any nuances he had missed. Two items sparked his interest.

"Some years ago," the priest said he had been involved in the death of twelve men. How many years ago? Where? Here in Johnson Creek? Spur had no way of knowing. If only he could have asked the priest some questions.

He had the chance last night and turned the man away. By now Harry Johnson's death might have been cleared up. The priest said he was somehow involved in Harry's death.

"Damnit!" Spur said out loud.

A passing woman looked at him in shocked surprise and walked quickly away.

Spur snorted and refolded the letter and put it in his pocket. He was right in slipping away from the death scene. He wanted someone else to find them. There was a chance whoever was second in command at the church might want to make some changes before the law was called in.

The priest would account for the fifth gun that killed Harry Johnson, if all of Spur's theories and suspicious held together. Father Desmond was clearly despondent over his inability to live up to his priestly duties and code of conduct. Evidently he at last had taken his vows seriously and could not live knowing what he had done, how he had sinned.

If only Spur had talked to him last night!

He turned and walked down the street past the saddle shop. For a moment he wanted to go in and talk with the midget. He changed his mind. He would see June first. Priests had been known to use fancy ladies before, to keep everything simple and secret.

At June's shop the blinds were drawn with a note

pinned to them: "In fitting session. Closed for now. Please call again."

Spur spun around and went to see Beth at the bank. She was in. She closed the door to her new office and he saw that the two hunting prize mounted heads had been taken down from the wall and that a beautiful oil painting of an ocean scene now served as decoration in their place.

He eased into a chair across from her big desk that now was perfectly clean on top except for a pad of paper and a pencil. He watched the small, pretty girl with the deep brown eyes and smiled.

"Beth, that was quite a meeting we had last night," he said.

She smiled, her whole face seemed to glow, her large brown eyes sparkled with enthusiasm and for a moment a hot flash of desire boiled there.

"The most wonderful night of my life! How else can I describe it. Just marvelous. Tonight I want you at my house for dinner and then we can . . . talk after dinner."

"We'll see. Things are happening. I might have found the fifth man in the five gun mystery. What I want to ask now is for you to think again about any groups your father might have been in that had five other men, or more."

"Groups, groups." She stood and walked around the office, came up behind him and kissed his cheek, then moved away, her face serious, concentrating.

"For about five years he was on the Board of Trustees at church. There were six or seven of them. Yes, he was on the school board for a four year term, but that was five or six years ago. What else?"

Spur turned to look at her staring out her window at Main Street. "None of those groups seems quite like the type of men we're hunting. Although I suppose they might be. If we don't know who we're looking for, it could be anybody. That's McCoy's law."

"Last time I mentioned the poker club he was in for the past four or five years. Then I think he went riding with a friend or two for a while, a kind of trail club, where they went on rides through the country just for fun. The cowboys thought they were crazy."

"Riding club. Who was in it?"

"Not sure. I didn't pay any attention. Oh, wait, yes Walt Trembolt the blacksmith was one of them."

"I've met Mr. Trembolt. He seems like a man who gets excited quickly. That may be a start."

She paced again. "There was a group at church called the Sociables. They met once a month for outings, picnics, pot luck suppers, church kind of socials. Mostly couples in it from young to middle aged."

"Not likely our people. The poker club. Do you remember anyone who was involved in it."

"He never talked about that one. Maybe once or twice." She turned and stared at him, her eyes wide, surprise and worry tingeing her features.

"Yes! I remember one name. He remarked two or three times what a good cherry pie that Mrs. Runner always served every time they had the game at the Runner's home!"

"Hans Runner, one of the men we think might be in on the cover-up of your father's death." Spur stood up quickly. "Let me talk to some other people. Some of the card players might know about such a game, especially if it was a regular thing and had a closed group who played. Most real gamblers dream about getting in a continuing game like that."

Spur reached into an inside shirt pocket and took

out a much folded letter that had traveled from Johnson Creek to Washington D.C. and now he had brought it back where it began.

"We're making progress, Beth. Now, I want to show you the letter your father wrote to us. Read it and see if you can help us fill in any of the empty spots."

He handed her the letter and she read:

"Gentlemen. My name is Harry Johnson from Johnson Creek, Texas. I need your help. Some years ago I was involved in an act that I considered at the time to be legal and patriotic, but which it turned out was neither.

"Now I want to clear my conscience and return to the Federal Government something it has lost. I have no trust in our current Carpetbagger local government, and little more trust in the county or state governments.

"I wish to deal directly with a respresentative of some U.S. law enforcement agency, such as a U.S. Marshal. I am sure that you will not be disappointed if you send someone to talk to me. This would have to be categorized as a confession, and as such I am ready to stand trial and accept any punishment that the court feels justified to levy.

"I hope this can be taken care of quickly, since I am not the only person involved in this situation. Your every consideration to my request will be greatly appreciated. Yours truly, Harry Johnson, President of the Johnson Bank of Johnson Creek, Texas."

Beth lowered the paper. Tears seeped from her eyes. She made no move to dry them. Her voice was so soft he could hardly hear her when she spoke.

"I can't believe it. But I know that is Daddy's writing. He must have been roped into something not knowing what it was. Or maybe they made him help them. Whoever they are. Maybe Hans Runner and the others forced him to ride with them."

Spur put his arms around her and she cried on his chest for a moment, then leaned back.

"I'd . . . I'd like to keep this letter."

"Of course. What I'm thinking now, is that the other five found out about this letter. Maybe your father even told them. They decided they couldn't let him confess and involve the rest of them."

"Damn them all!" Beth said savagely. Her tone surprised Spur.

"Beth, I don't want you looking for vengeance. Leave this to me. I'll find the men who shot your father and they will be punished. Promise me you won't go wild and do something that will get both of us in trouble."

He still held her. She looked up and now wiped the tears away. She nodded.

Gently she pushed away from him and went back to her desk. She sat down, wiped her eyes with a small white handkerchief, then looked up at him.

"Oh, Don White came in today. He said he needed twenty-five hundred dollars to pay county bills. He explained to me that the council has set a new policy of cash payments."

"I hope you didn't give any money to him."

"No, I stalled as you directed me to. I told him it would take me two or three days to get that much cash money for him. He went crazy mad, threatened to start a run on the bank and ruin me. He swore that he had to have the cash by today at closing time, or at least by five o'clock.

"Don't give him a dime. He's getting ready to run, so he needs cash. Has he made any deposits of the tax money? He must be taking in thousands at the city office."

"He made one deposit three days ago, but none since then." She paused. "Is he really getting ready to abscond with our money?"

"Looks like it. But that's my problem. Today is the last day to pay taxes. He'll be gone tonight . . . if he can."

He stood and went around the desk.

"Sorry I had to show you that letter, but I wanted the air to be clear, and everything straight between us. No secrets. Now, I need to talk to June again." He grinned. "You sure were right about her figure. I don't think I've ever seen such big . . ."

Beth's hand went quickly over his mouth.

"Sir. It's not polite to praise another woman about her big cow breasts when you're standing toe to toe with the smallest tits in town." Beth laughed, her good humor had returned. "You just be sure to keep your hands off her. I'll take care of any of your wild sexy needs tonight."

He kissed her lips gently, and hurried out the door. Beth Johnson was quite a little bundle of woman.

June was in and free. He sat in a chair near her cutting table and watched her work on a flat piece of cloth. She gave him a cold bottle of Zang's beer.

"June, I'm making progress, but I need some more help."

"In back with our clothes off, or out here?" she said with a quick grin.

"Unfortunately, out here. Do you remember something strange and illegal happening three or four

Dirk Fletcher

years ago? Something that was hushed up or not even known to most of the people in town? It probably involved Harry Johnson and some of the biggest men in the community."

She cut on the cloth, concentrating for a few moments. When she finished she looked up and lifted her brows.

"I guess confidences aren't important to Harry anymore. Yeah, there was something. His wife has been dead for some time, and maybe once or twice a year he'd send me a note and come over late at night. This time he was a little drunk and he drank more after he arrived and as I remember, he couldn't even get his pants off.

"He wanted to talk, mostly. So we talked for two hours and then he paid me ten dollars. He said once years before he got drunk with some other men and they started bragging and the first thing he knew they were armed and riding north. He and the others shot up some men in a camp.

"He never said much more about who they were or what happened, but evidently the men in the woods all died. He said they all thought it was going to be one harassing attack against the enemy. Now I remember. He said it was to be one last angry strike at the Yankees, even though they knew the South had almost lost the war."

Spur nodded. "So, just near the end of the war. Some raid. Maybe he was one of a defense force here in town, something like that. I'll do some research. Harry ever mention this again?"

"He never came back. Maybe he wasn't quite as drunk as he pretended to be and just had to tell somebody. The way Catholics go to confession."

Spur agreed. "Thanks, June. You've been a big help."

She grinned. "Spur McCoy, for you my door is always open. And by that I mean my bedroom door. Anytime."

Spur smiled, touched her shoulder and hurried out to the boardwalk, eager to make his next call.

13

Spur saw the midget working away on a saddle, his back to the door. McCoy eased inside, closed the door silently, sat in the chair and laid his feet gently on the edge of a small, cold stove.

Without turning around, the small man, Big Paul Smith, spoke. "Not bad for a Secret Agent. But you got to remember that your left boot squeaks when you walk and you drop your right shoulder just a tad like you're getting ready to draw."

He turned around and grinned. "Hi, McCoy. I still say that Sir Frances Bacon was the most brilliant man of his day."

Spur laughed. "How in hell did you know it was me? Nobody is that good. Heard someone, maybe, but how did you know?"

"Look over there by that rolled leather. What do you see?"

Spur looked where the small man pointed. A four-inch square mirror had been fixed to the leather bin. When Spur looked in it he saw Big Paul Smith grinning at him.

"You cheated," Spur said.

"Another one over there," Smith said waving at the other side of his shop. I got you covered two ways."

"No contest," Spur said. He lifted his hat and let it settle down over his eyes. "Get back to work, Paul, you can't make any money mouth-jawing with an out of work drifter."

"So true you are, Secret Agent McCoy. How goes the investigation?" Smith slid back onto his stool and went to work on the saddle.

"It's slow. These Carpetbaggers don't help any. What I need is some history. How long you been playing with leather around this town?"

"Little over ten years, man and boy."

"All man. Do you remember when the war was almost over, say about four years ago?"

"Yep. Remember it like it was yesterday. We had a few raids by irregulars. Might have been Northerners, or Southerners, we never knew. A month before the surrender a batch went through one night. Killed two men, raped three or four women, we were never sure, and took a wagon load of food out of the general store."

"Things were a bit touchy here then I'd guess."

"True as blue. We had sort of a home guard. Couple of dozen of the older men who couldn't go to war, and a few of the younger ones who went and came back. Young Garth Ludlow headed the outfit. He was a wounded veteran, and after the last raid they had regular meetings, practiced with their rifles, the whole thing. As I remember they called themselves the Mounted Home Guard."

"You knew the war was going badly for the South?"

"Hell yes. Everybody knew. We was just sort of sitting here wondering after it was over what would happen and when it was going to happen. We expected northern troops to be all over the place as an occupation force."

"How did the men take the coming loss?"

"Damn mad, most of them. Ones who didn't go to war wished to hell they had. Them that were sent home, wished they had stayed on and helped. Frustrated, the whole town was mad as hell and frustrated.

"One day I heard about an offensive raid the Home Guard was going to make. Kind of a last hurrah, one more sting at the hated Bluebellies. Never did hear what happened. Come to think of it, Garth was talking it up like crazy one day, and it seemed like they were going out that night or the next."

The small man put down a leather tool and scratched his nose. "Damn, after that I don't remember Garth saying a word about it. Don't know if they even went or not. Then we heard the war was over. Guess it was all settled a week or two before we knew about it."

Big Paul Smith scratched his thinning brown hair. "Damn, come to think of it, don't remember anybody mentioning that proposed 'raid' again."

"Who were in the Home Guard, you remember any of them?"

"It broke up, of course when the war was over. But I sure as the English Bard himself can't think of any others. One, yeah, I remember one more. Harry Johnson was in it. Told me once he signed up just so he could get in on the riding. Harry did love to fork a horse. He was planning on buying himself a little spread and raise a few beef. He never got around to it."

"It's too late for him to be starting now," Spur

said dropping his feet off the stove. He sat up. "Any more names in that Home Guard you can remember?"

"Jess Holloway. But he moved to California a year or so back. They had twelve or fifteen for one parade, but it went up and down. One night I saw them drilling with only four men."

Spur stood, watched the small man working on the tooling of the leather for a minute. "I'm glad you're not an engraver and that isn't a plate for a twenty dollar bill."

"Tried that once, but I kept putting my own picture on the fifty dollar bill!"

"Should have worked. Thanks for the history lesson. Never know what's going to fit in."

"Welcome. And the next time you need a good saddle . . ."

"I'll stop back."

Spur walked into the morning sunlight. He had most of the pieces. But why would a Home Guard charge into a twelve man patrol of some sort? And was it U.S. Army, or some irregulars, or some border bandits that roamed the line between the North and the South in those terrible days?

He walked part way down the block when he saw Marshal Ludlow striding quickly toward him. Garth looked up and motioned.

"Better come with me, McCoy. We have new trouble. Seems like somebody has killed the priest, Father Desmond."

A few minutes later the two lawmen looked over the priest's bedroom. The large red stain still showed on the rumpled sheets and dried blood coated part of the floor below his figure. Father Desmond lay crumpled on the side of the bed where he had been before. He wore a simple white nightgown.

The young naked girl Spur had seen lying in his lap had been taken away.

Marshal Ludlow bent and looked at the body, tried to move an arm.

"Damn! He's stiff already. Been dead for hours. Why in hell would someone want to murder a priest in his bed?"

A nun came forward. She wore a long black robe and white collar and headpiece that covered all her hair and allowed only a circle of face to show.

"Marshal, I'm Mother Superior Mary Angeles. I found him this way. It looks like someone robbed him. We found the side door open. The lock had been forced from the outside. We suggest that someone broke in, waited for Father Desmond to return, assaulted him sometime last night, and then the intruder took his time lookng for valuables."

Marshal Ludlow nodded. "Seems reasonable. Is anything missing?"

"Oh, yes. We had over twenty dollars in the Altar Fund, and about fifty dollars from our poor box collections. Father Desmond liked to keep the money on hand so he could spend it as we needed to. A gold crucifix is missing as well as three rings Father treasured. One had been blessed by the Pope."

Ludlow made some quick notes on a pad of paper he had brought.

"Any value on the rings, Mother Superior?"

"Sentimental value on one. Father Desmond told me the others were given to him by his parents when he was ordained. Both were worth over a hundred dollars."

"So we can say the robber took the valuables and cash worth three hundred and seventy dollars."

"Begging your pardon, Marshal," Mother

Superior Angeles said. "The killer also took something much more valuable. A loyal servant of God. He took the life of Father Desmond."

"Was anyone else hurt?" Spur asked gently.

Mother Superior's head lifted and she looked quickly at Spur. Too quickly.

"No. No one. We didn't know he was . . . was dead until his housekeeper came in this morning. He usually doesn't sleep in mornings. But she decided he was taking a nap since his inside bedroom door was locked. An hour later she went around and found the street door open. She hurried and told me and I went in and found him. I didn't want the others to see this."

"We understand, Mother Superior," Spur said. "I think we have enough here, don't you, Marshal?"

Ludlow stared at the bloody, waxy figure on the bed and nodded. "Enough to last me for some time."

Outside Marshal Ludlow took off his high crowned brown hat and scratched his hair. "Don't rightly know, McCoy. But to me it looked like too damn much blood around there for just one body to lose. Especially when his throat was slit. Man dies in just a few seconds when that side artery is cut. When the heart stops pumping, the blood stops gushing out. Too damn much blood back there."

"Maybe a priest bleeds more than other men," Spur said.

"Maybe." They walked in silence for a while. "Now that Mother Superior. She was hard as a hickory fence post. She never batted an eyebrow. Tough, efficient. Looks like the kind of person who can get things done."

"Yep, I agree. She can get things done. You figure it was one of the blacks who cut the priest?"

"One of the coloreds? Could have been. One of

them could have been eyeing that priest, slipped back into town last night after dark, slit him and took the loot."

"Possible." Spur looked over at the shorter man. "I hear you used to have a Mounted Home Guard in town during the war. Was Harry Johnson in it?"

"Don't rightly know. I remember hearing about it."

"You did that. In fact you started it after you got back from fighting in the gray uniform. Was Harry in it, too?"

Marshal Ludlow stopped and scratched his chin. "Yeah, I think so, toward the last. It was a tough time. We got raided three or four times by Yankee irregulars. Lost three men the last time, so we decided to put up a fight after that."

"Did you?"

"Hell no. Never got raided again and then the war was over, and we forgot all about the Home Guard. Had enough new problems with Reconstruction and the damn Baggers."

"Life does get complicated."

"You heard from Don White today?" Garth asked. "What in hell is he planning on doing? You know?"

"Probably planning on leaving town. But he won't go without all the money he can steal. That's your job. Watch City Hall and hire a deputy to watch that grove of trees two miles south along that little creek. That's where I took White and his in-the-pocket voters yesterday."

"I'll keep him covered."

"Keep him away from the bank. There's three thousand worth of city money in there he wants."

"I'll let him go in, but I'll be right behind him. He must be ready to run."

"Today is the last day to pay city taxes. This is the most money the city will have in its till all year. Tonight has to be his time, or perhaps tomorrow. The bank is the key. He needs the cash in there."

"Don't worry, it's covered."

Spur watched Ludlow. "I'm still interested in this Home Guard. You must remember some of the other men who were in it. I'd like to talk to some of them. I'm a student of the Civil War. It was a classic struggle, but I've never understood the border states position very well."

"Some of them died, three or four moved on. Harry was in it, I remember now, and Walt the blacksmith. I don't think the hardware man was in . . . but then he left town anyway. Went busted I hear."

"Did you have any medical men? Doc Greenly. Was he in town then?"

"Think he moved here after the war. It all gets kind of fuzzy back there, trying to remember."

"You remember, Ludlow. I want a list of every man you can think of who was in the Home Guard. I'll pick it up tomorrow."

Ludlow looked at up Spur and for a moment hatred flared there, then it faded. The town marshal nodded and walked off toward the bank.

14

Don White woke up that morning feeling gritty, with a bad taste in his mouth and a screaming headache. One more goddamn day! He had to get it done today and be gone with the darkness. It had worked before in Georgia, it would work here.

He was in the house he had rented with city money at the edge of town. Despite the Secret Agent's warning, he had sneaked back into the house from the grove as soon as it was dark. He had to run the city office for one more day. Yesterday he had hired a white woman to accept tax payments.

He made sure he found an honest one, a Baptist, a good churchgoer, Mrs. Hemphil. There was no worry there. He just had to be sure he got there before she tried to deposit the money in the bank. He had no idea what was wrong at the bank. Just his luck to run into some kind of an internal bank problem.

He sat up in his short underwear and wished he had a bath. He couldn't risk starting a fire to heat water. He called in one of the blacks.

"Willy, bring me a bucket of water from that

pump out in the woodshed. Be sure nobody sees you or hears you, or you could be one dead darkie. You understand?"

The big colored man nodded and hurried out for a bucket.

White took a whore's bath in the bucket of cold water and thought over his haul. He had two thousand in cash in a valise hidden in the cupboard. There was over a thousand in checks for taxes some of the merchants had written for him before he made it a rule of cash only.

He had to get to the bank and cash those. There could be no problem there. He would go in just before the bank closed at three. There would be plenty of time after that.

Then there was more than two thousand in the city account deposited in the bank. He had to figure out a way to withdraw that without attracting any suspicion.

He stretched out on the bed in his shirt and clean white pants. "Damn, but this is going to be a good one!" he said softly, then chuckled.

So they told him in Chicago he would never amount to anything. What the hell did they know? He was soon to be a rich man with over five thousand dollars, cash money, in his poke!

Not a one of those fancy Dans in Chicago would have a fifth that much, right now.

It just took some brains, a little bit of luck, and the guts to put it to the damn Southerners.

Ruth came in wearing that little red French nightie he bought for her in Houston. It barely covered her crotch and left both her breasts swinging and bouncing free. On her it looked great.

She dropped down beside him on the bed and leaned over him letting her breasts swing out above him like a pair of upside down ice cream cones.

"Kiss my ladies good morning, handsome prince," she said. He did, licking the nipples, but then pushing her away.

"Get your pussy out of here, Ruth. Right now I got some thinking to do. Today has got to go just right."

"We getting ready to run out on the bastards?"

"We're not running out, we're starting our advance on Houston. Whoever gets left behind, gets left. My buggy will only carry three."

"Hey, I'm glad that I'm one of the three."

He smiled at her and went back to planning. First the bank, get the money on deposit if he had to rob the damn bank, then move out in the buggy to the grove south of town and trade the buggy for the fastest horses he could find. They were saddled, fed and watered and would be ready to go at six o'clock.

There would be room enough for the money in his saddlebags. No one else was going to have a look at the cash. He called to Ruth and stroked her sleek young breasts. She said she was seventeen but he didn't believe her.

She had been the best thing about this little episode. What a delightful young body, and such good tits! Yes, she was a sex machine that never got tired and never was out of the mood. He'd found her in a fancy woman house in New Orleans and rescued her from twenty tricks a day. She was grateful. And she was getting to be a bore.

He pushed her away again. Another state, another bunch of suckers and another woman. Would he go back to Chicago? Not yet. Not when he could make five thousand in six or seven months. It could take a year depending on the next election time. He'd move until he found the right spot—preferably one that had not been swindled by another Carpetbagger from up north.

Christ but these assholes were stupid. Didn't they know what he was going to do? It had been in all the big papers. The farther out in the sticks the better. They *trusted* their elected officials.

He had come south on a whim, a fluke almost. He'd been drinking with this tall queer guy who was buying him drinks and trying to get him to come up to his apartment and play pull a prick with him.

White knew his capacity for beer. He figured he'd take the asshole for six beers, then push him off his stool and walk out of the bar. The queer said he had just come back from Mississippi where he had played Carpetbagger. White had urged him to talk about it.

For two hours the queer had told him exactly how to do it. How to scoop up enough coloreds and promise to pay them, and get them to vote you into office, mayor preferably, or supervisor or director, whatever the county administrator was called. He said he had stripped the treasury of this little county of almost ten thousand dollars.

White had gone willingly when the asshole invited him up to his flat to look at the newspaper clippings about him being elected director of the county.

By that time the queer had White's pants off and was playing around with him. It took him another ten minutes before White had all the information he could glean from the tall queer. Then White punched him out, tied him up and put his own pants back on. He tore the place apart until he found a stash of money, over a thousand dollars in cash!

White set the queer on his own window ledge and told him to tell him where the rest of the money was. He nodded that he would, but when White took the gag out, he screamed. White pushed him out of the fifth floor window and he bellowed all the way to the concrete below.

That same night, White left for the south and had been there ever since. Two years now.

And now another pay day.

Ruth had dressed and watched him.

"I wanna go to the store and buy some perfume," she said. Her voice was starting to irritate him.

"You go downtown and some white hothead will blow your guts out with a shotgun. Ain't you got any sense?"

"Still wanna buy some perfume and a new dress."

"We'll get both for you in Houston. Now sit down and shut up your big mouth, woman!"

For a moment she flared in anger, then she remembered how he had beat her the first week, and the anger turned to a smile.

"You always tell me my cunt is bigger than my mouth." She walked toward him unbuttoning her thin blouse. "Maybe my man would like a nice fast mouth job about now. Just go on doing whatever you're doing, don't mind me. All you have to do is sit up. I'll do the rest."

He had been thinking about tonight and leafing through a magazine. White grinned, shook his head and sat up. At once she was in front of him kneeling on the bedroom floor. She spread his legs and opened his pants fly and pulled them down.

She gave a little cry when she saw that he was stiff already.

"Now just relax, sir. This won't hurt a bit. It shouldn't take too long. Try to relax and let yourself go."

She slid his erection into her mouth, her hands busy with his scrotum.

"Easy on my balls! Oh, damn, where did you learn to eat cock so good!" She pointed at him and he laughed as she sucked his whole prick into her mouth and began bouncing up and down.

He couldn't concentrate on the magazine. At last he swore softly and tossed the reading matter aside. His hips began to counter her forward motion and she gagged once, then adapted and after ten more strokes he started to sweat.

"Christ but you are good with the mouth, Ruthie! Never seen a whore or any cunt who was as good with the mouth as you are. You bite me and I'll tear your tits off!"

She laughed and she sucked and it was more than he could stand. He humped straight up and she sagged, then swallowed and moved slightly but stayed with him until he shot his last load and collapsed on the bed.

She snaked up beside him, kissing his man breasts and tweaking his small nipples.

"Now, Big Daddy, wasn't that worth the price of the ticket?"

He grabbed both her breasts and squeezed.

"Nice, nice!" she wailed.

"Hey, don't get started again. I can't be worn out for the big push this afternoon."

"Whatever you say. I always do exactly what you tell me to do. That's why we make such a good team. You and me, babe."

"Yeah, yeah. You and me. Now I've got to go downtown and get the rest of the cash. You pack that little bag of yours and be ready to travel light. I'll be back here about five this afternoon with the buggy."

She leaned over top of him where he still lay on his back. He hadn't even buttoned up his fly. A sharp pointed knife caressed his throat.

"Tell me again, Big Daddy, that you're taking me with you to Houston. Taking me all the way. I don't care what you tell them blacks out there. It's you and me, right?"

"I told you, damnit. Move that blade."

"Tell me again, Babe. I want to hear you say it again."

"Ruthie, baby, you know I couldn't get along without them big tits of yours and that sweet, dancing pussy. Damn right you go with me. So pack and be ready."

She nicked his throat with the blade, then reached up and kissed it.

"Just a reminder, sweetheart. Nobody runs out on Ruthie. One man tried it. I killed him. Had to go across three states but I found him and put this same knife dead center into his black heart. So I'm glad to hear it's just you and me."

She leaped off the bed and held the knife in front of her. White had never seen it before.

"You got to learn to trust people, Ruthie. I said you was going, so you're going. Now get packed."

He buttoned his fly and walked out of the room. On the other side of the door he stopped and a deadly fury filled his face. He started to go back in, then shook his head and went on to the small back porch and woodshed. From there he could get into the alley.

He needed to check City Hall, see how the money was coming in, and collect it two or three times, so the new white lady clerk did not become upset about having all that cash around.

As he stood in the woodshed one of the men came up to him. He was Fred Washington. The Washington was new, the Fred was also new with his new freedom. He was a hulking field hand, who would never learn to do anything else.

Among the colored voters, White had named him as the enforcer. If anyone got out of line, they had to answer to Fred. Few went against the rules more than once.

In Houston Fred had a few too many beers one night, and nearly tore an arm off a longshoreman on the docks. Two of his buddies stormed up to help and he shattered one's arm and broke the second man's neck.

Fred got away just before the police came, but nobody who saw it had the nerve to turn in Fred for the killing.

Now he watched Don White.

"You say we're going soon," Fred asked.

"Don't worry about it. I said I was going to go to City Hall. Don't try to start thinking at this point, Fred. Just keep Ruth in the house and all three of you stay out of sight. Where is Willy?"

"Sleeping. He saw Ruthie all naked and he jerked off in his hand again."

"Let him sleep. Don't worry about a thing, Fred. Haven't I been taking care of you, and paying you?"

Fred nodded.

"Sure I have. And I always will, Fred. You'll never have to worry about trying to find a job again."

Fred nodded and went back in the house. White let out a long pent up breath and wiped some sweat off his forehead with the back of his hand. That big ape could break him in half with his bare hands. In twelve hours he'd be rid of them, all of them. He snorted. Even Fred, and Ruthie. Especially Ruthie.

Five minutes later, Fred slipped into the alley that led to the City Hall back doors. He found one unlocked as it was always supposed to be, and went inside. This was the back of an old feed store, and still smelled like alfalfa hay, oats and cracked corn.

He went through the door into the finished front section and looked out a second door at Mrs. Hemphil who sat behind the desk marked "Pay City Taxes Here."

Two people stood in line.

White walked out casually, approached Mrs. Hemphil when she had finished with one of those waiting.

"How are we doing this morning, Mrs. Hemphil?"

She was flustered for a moment, then she recovered. "Oh, well, yes. Things are going smoothly. Some people complain because the taxes went up, but I tell them I didn't do it, they should talk to their city council."

"Absolutely correct, Mrs. Hemphil. Let me take your cash box out for deposit. We don't want to tempt anyone here, do we?"

She smiled and slid the cash drawer to him. He carried it quickly to the back room, emptied out the drawer of all but a few ones and two fives and a ten and put the bills into his pocket. There must be three or four hundred!

He took the cash drawer back to Mrs. Hemphil, told her what a good job she was doing, and went to his small office. Inside he opened a cabinet and looked at a sheaf of checks. A paper clip on top of them pinned a paper to the checks. It had a figure, One thousand, three hundred and seventy-two dollars.

That presented a problem. The bankers seemed all upset and nervous about something. Even Beth Johnson was acting funny. He decided to try to cash the checks around noon, when there were more people in the bank. They might want to rush him through so a line wouldn't form.

Yes, he would try that. He put the checks in an envelope. Each check had been endorsed by the city in the person of Mrs. Hemphil, acting city clerk. They were ready for cashing. He put the envelope in his inside jacket pocket.

What was the girl's name in Chicago? He could hardly remember. He would never go back there, he was certain now. With five thousand dollars he could afford to buy more voters, hit a bigger town or county where he would need to produce maybe two hundred votes to swing an election.

Now he'd have the money to finance it. Give each of the blacks a dollar to sign on with him and two dollars a week. Or get some Human Welfare program started to let the county or city pay them.

What was the girl's name in Chicago? She wasn't built half as well as Ruthie. She probably had never been touched. Ruthie could fuck rings around that girl.

He put his hands behind his head and leaned back in the chair. Yes, Houston for a few weeks, living it up, eating the best food he could find. Maybe a quick trip over to New Orleans for some tremendous food and entertainment.

Yeah! He'd heard if you have enough money in New Orleans you can buy a woman who will do anything. He even heard you could absolutely fuck yourself to death over there. Now that would be a damn nice way to go. If you wanted to go. Don White wasn't ready yet for any kind of thinking. But he did have a hankering to be in New Orleans when he could afford to sample any of its pleasures that he wanted.

He grinned, then put his business face on and got up and headed for the Johnson Bank.

15

As he walked, Spur McCoy watched the townspeople. They were still jittery, on edge, half
expecting the fifty Negroes to charge into town with
guns blazing, looting and raping. They had every
right to be afraid. Worse things had happened by
the newly freed Negroes in some parts of the South
after the war.

But this was Texas. There was a sputtering of
vigilante movement, but from what Spur could
guess, no real leader to take over and organize it.
That was one big problem he didn't have to worry
about.

When he got to the bank it was nearly noon.
Inside, he went to Beth's private office and walked
through the open door. She wore a patterned brown
dress with a little jacket and looked almost
businesslike. Spur could not get used to this twig of
a girl sitting behind the president's desk of the
town's bank.

"Good morning, I'd like to borrow a hundred
thousand dollars," Spur said before she looked up.

She laughed and went on writing on a paper.

"Fine, leave your wife and first born as collateral, and I'll draw up the papers at once," she said. Beth looked up and a wonderful smiled transformed her face.

"I'm glad to see you." Then she frowned. "The new city clerk tried to cash six checks this morning. I turned her down, saying there had been a hold put on that account by the Federal Government." She stood and watched Spur closely. "Was that all right? I didn't know what else to say. I'm afraid Don White will storm over here shouting and screaming."

"If he does call me and I'll throw him out."

"You might be busy."

"Let's shelve that problem for a while. I'll take you out for a bite of dinner."

"Oh good!" She looked down and blushed softly. "My . . . my feet still haven't quite come to the ground yet . . . after last night. That was the most wonderful . . ."

One of the tellers came in with some papers. She looked at them, signed the bottom of one and he left.

Spur grinned. "It was wonderful for me too. Now, some food. Then we can worry about White."

At the Demorest Family restaurant they had big bowls of vegetable soup and slabs of fresh baked bread and home made jam. As they ate, Spur told her what he had found out about her father.

"So the jist of it seems to be that your father was a member of the Mounted Guard back near the end of the war. Something happened back there that evidently involved these six men. Now somehow that old event has caused some problems, including your father's death. I'm still digging into it."

Beth sat still for a moment, then nodded. "Yes, I remember the Mounted Home Guards. Daddy was so pleased that he joined. He loved to ride his horse Prince, a big gelding that could outrun anything in town." A tear ran down her cheek.

"I . . . I still miss him so. I guess I'm an orphan now, right?"

"Absolutely, and the only orphan I know of who owns her own bank and about half of the town."

"Oh, that. I'd rather have Daddy back."

"I'd evict three widows and their kids if it would bring him back, Beth. So we do the next best thing. You run the bank the same thoughtful, friendly way your father did. And I'll find out who killed him."

They finished the soup and each had another half a slice of the still warm bread.

"Isn't it terrible about Father Desmond? I don't understand how anybody could kill a priest."

Spur nodded, wondering if he should tell her. He decided against it. When he knew everything about the Home Guard and what happened so long ago, he might tell her. Not now.

"Well, I couldn't eat another bite," Spur said. "Let's go back to the bank and wait for Don White. He's probably mad enough by now to come storming in."

As soon as they walked into the bank, Don White marched up to them.

"What's this about a Federal order to put a hold on the city's bank account?" he asked, his voice only barely pleasant with an undercurrent of fury. "You know the town can't operate without funds from its account."

"Mr. White. You've caused a lot of problems in this town. Some fine people have been hurt badly, and all because of you. From now on I'm doing everything I can to drive you out of office. It's my bank. Legally I can freeze your account if I want to.

Try and find a law that says I can't.

"Now, if you have any problems with that, you go find a good lawyer and sue me. The circuit judge will be around in about two months, I'll talk to you in court then."

He stared at her, his anger rising by the second. He tightened both hands into fists, then looked at Spur who stood directly behind Beth staring hard at White.

He tried to talk, but his anger had forced his voice into a rumble. He shook his head, tried to relax his hands, then at last got the words out.

"I want to close out the city account. Everything in cash right now."

"No. That account has been frozen pending an investigation by Federal authorities. Please leave my bank, now, Mr. White, or you will be forcibly ejected."

White's face turned red. His eyelids lifted showing the whites of his eyes and Spur thought he might have a stroke. He trembled, his hands fisted again but he never stepped toward Beth. Slowly he turned and walked woodenly toward the door. As he opened the heavy door, he looked back, and Spur could not remember seeing a face showing more hatred. Then he was gone.

Beth leaned back against Spur and gave a big sigh.

"I've never been so frightened!" she whispered to him.

"You were great, Beth. You stopped him in his tracks and sent him running." Spur scowled for a moment. "How much money in the city account?"

"I checked this morning. A little over two thousand dollars."

"By now he thinks it's his money. He swindled it

fair and square. The next time he comes back to the bank it'll be with guns. Do you have a bank guard?''

"No, we've never needed one."

"You do now. See if you can hire a man with a good shotgun for the job. Do it quietly. Get him on the job in half an hour or so. Do you have any idea who you can get?''

"Yes. An ex-army man. I'll send a note to him."

Spur watched White out the window. He walked across the street and stared back at the bank. Then walked slowly toward City Hall.

As Spur observed him, he became aware of someone following White. He recognized the person as Mrs. Trembolt. She carried a large reticule and walked quickly after White. But he moved faster and faster and soon outdistanced Milicent Trembolt even though he didn't know he was in a race.

Spur frowned watching her. She evidently had recovered quickly from the rape or attempted rape he had never found out for sure. He did know there had been no charges filed against her for the death of the Negro.

"Spur, what do you think Don White will do next?'' Beth asked.

"What would you do in his place?''

She thought a minute. "I'd come back and rob the bank just before I left town with the rest of the city money.''

"Right. Me too. And that's probably what White is planning right now. He should hit you at least by tomorrow afternoon just before your closing time. When is that?''

"Three o'clock.''

"I'll try to be around, too." He smiled at Beth. "How old are you, Miss Bank President?''

"Almost twenty. The judge said I could take over

control because I was the only survivor. He gave me some kind of a legal paper I have in the safe."

"Good. I'm glad it's all legal. From what everyone says, you're doing just fine."

She smiled and came closer to him and spoke softly. "Was I fine last night? That's important to me."

"You were better than fine, you were great. Now get that guard and think about where you could hide some of the cash you have. Not in the vault, somewhere else. Maybe a desk drawer."

"Good idea."

"I've got another call to make. Watch for White, but don't try to shoot it out with him. You'll just get your people killed. Except the guard, I mean." He grinned and walked out the front door.

Five minutes later he sat in a small room in the side of the school at the Catholic Church and talked with the Mother Superior.

"How long have you been in charge here, Mother Superior?"

"About six years."

"That goes back to the hard times during the war. You were here then when Father Desmond was assigned to this parish?"

"That's right."

"I'm investigating a problem here in town during the end of the war. I hope you can help me."

"I'll do whatever I can, Mr. McCoy."

"You must remember a defense force raised here called the Mounted Home Guard. Marshal Ludlow organized it and it had as many as twelve to fourteen men in it."

"Yes, I remember them drilling, riding. I think once we even heard them doing target practice outside of town."

"Good. Now this next question may be difficult, but I want a truthful answer. Do you remember Father Desmond being a part of this paramilitary group?"

"That would be impossible. A priest could never . . . ."

Spur held up his hand stopping her. "Mother Superior, I don't need a lecture on priestly duties and vows. Was Father Desmond in the Mounted Home Guard? Yes or no."

"No, it would violate his vows."

"Mother Superior, you and I know that Father Desmond had a habit of violating his vows. He was a whiskey priest, a drunk. He also violated his vow of chastity."

"That is not true. I know for a . . ."

Again Spur silenced her.

"Have you made funeral arrangements for Father Desmond?"

"Yes, tomorrow."

"What about arrangements for the girl, Calida?"

Mother Superior looked up sharply, she gasped, then her eyes closed slightly. "So it was you. Sister Evangeline saw someone going toward Father Desmond's quarters early this morning."

She sighed. "This is not an easy task, Mr. McCoy. I do what I think is best for the Church and for my order. What good would it have done to let the marshal see them both that way? It could only have caused hurt and evil."

"I've heard of cases like this before, Mother Superior. I thought you might take care of it, which is why I left so quickly. Father Desmond left a note. Would you like to read it?"

She shook her head. "No. Then I would have more to confess, more to try to forget. But to answer your other question, Calida was returned to her people well to the south. They were told she was attacked by a pack of dogs. They will ask no questions."

"My first question about Father Desmond, Sister?"

"Yes. Father Desmond slipped off from time to time to ride with the men. He enjoyed it. I liked to see him happy at least once in a while. He had so much sadness in his life."

"Do you know if the Guard ever attacked another group of men during the closing days of the war?"

"Attacked?"

"Yes. A final jab at the Yankees. One last protesting raid to vent their frustration at losing the war?"

"Oh, I understand. Lots of the town talk I never hear. But this particular one . . . yes, I do remember. Marshal Ludlow was quite open about it. He wanted to strike one last blow at the enemy."

"And did it happen, Mother Superior?"

"I don't know. Father was gone for a time one night. I remember him coming back very late, it was almost dawn. I was up for my five A.M. prayers. He was tired and *dirty*. He looked worn out. I've never seen him that way before."

"Did he give any explanations, say anything?"

"Curious, he did. I thought nothing of it at the time. It's a phrase we use with each other when we're feeling low or are having problems. He said, 'Pray for me, Sister.'"

"That was all?"

"That was enough."

"Thank you Mother Superior. I assure you that none of this will go any farther. We shall let Father Desmond rest in whatever kind of peace he was hoping to find."

"Bless you, Mr. McCoy."

"I'm not here to destroy, or for retribution. But in this case there has been a great wrong done and I am determined to set it right."

"Right can be both powerful and at the same time destroy."

Spur nodded. "Pray for me, Sister," he said then walked out of the room and into the afternoon Texas sunshine.

Marshal Ludlow fell into step beside Spur as he walked down the street.

"You wondering about the priest, too?"

"What do you mean?"

"Why else you jawing with the Mother Superior in there?"

"Maybe I'm Catholic."

"Maybe pigs can fly. What I figure is the old boy slit his own throat and she covered it up, make out like a burglary. Just to keep his reputation."

"I hear he was a whiskey priest," Spur said. "Why would she worry about his rep?"

"She's a woman, I guess. Maybe she had the wants for his privates. I hear whiskey priests get a woman now and then."

"Probably happens. You have any evidence on this priest that points that way?"

"Nope. Not yet. Probably could find some, if I wanted to dig a bit."

"Why not let it be? So if he did kill himself. What good would it do to bring it out with a big story in the paper?"

"Yeah, what the hell."

"You get anywhere on Harry Johnson's killing?"

"Nope. Dead end. Man had no enemies."

"Keep looking, his daughter is unhappy not knowing what happened."

"I can understand that."

"You working on those names for me on the Mounted Home Guard members?"

"Yep. Thought of one more—Bill Jorerdan down at the livery. He trained with us for about two months."

"Keep thinking, I'll be in touch."

Garth Ludlow said he would and watched the Secret Service Agent walk off toward the hotel. He snorted softly. Be a cold day in hell, Spur McCoy when I give you the important names. He paused for a moment, then turned down the alley. He had five minutes to get to the newspaper office for a special meeting.

16

Marshal Garth Ludlow knocked twice on the alley door of the *Record* newspaper office and waited. A moment later someone looked out a small bored hole in the door and then the door opened.

"Garth," Hans said softly. "Damn glad you could come. I think we got trouble."

"I know we damn well got big trouble," Garth said. "That fucking Government agent has been prodding at me, digging into the Guard. We got to do something."

"The others are over here," Hans said. Leading Garth through the unlighted and un-windowed rear shop of the news plant. They wound past a press, and stacks of boxed paper in the two-page newsprint size, and into a small room built in the larger space at one side.

There were four chairs around a table. Two decks of cards and a bottle of whiskey sat in the center of the table.

Zed Hiatt waved at Garth and wiped sweat off his forehead. Beside him Dr. Greenly had just poured himself a shot of whiskey.

"I thought we settled this a few weeks back," Greenly said. "Why is everyone so itchy?" The medical man downed the shot of whiskey and coughed once, then shook his head. "Hans, you've got to get better booze in this place."

"Just because this government busybody is snooping around is no reason to lose our heads. He asked me some questions about Harry. I told him telling the truth right then would have opened up a civil war in town all over again, white versus the blacks. Thought I convinced him."

Ludlow stood at the head of the table as the others looked up at him from where they sat.

"You probably did. Then he talked to some other people in town, lots of people. He's a bastard once he gets a scent. But I don't think it's as bad as it seems. Still we do have a decison to make. Harry got us into this mess by writing that damn letter. I wish I could see it to know exactly how much he told. Not knowing that, we have to strike out a little blind.

"I should have known that Desmond couldn't take the gaff. Any whiskey priest with a twelve year old for his private fucking has got to be unstable."

"We don't know for sure he was dicking her," Hans said.

"Hell, he as much as told me he was," Zed said. "One night he was skunk drunk and he was bragging how many women he'd had. He liked them young thirteen to fifteen, he said. Know for a fact he brought her in from south somewhere. Wasn't even a local Mex."

"So he's gone and no big loss," Dr. Greenly said. "One less share. We're down to four. We've got no worry about Beth. She's set up for life with the bank."

"Are you men thinking it's about time to cash

in?" Ludlow asked.

"Past time, far as I'm concerned," Dr. Greenly said, "Especially with the bloodhound watching our every move."

"Hell, yes, let's do it," Hans added.

"I'm ready to retire right now," Zed Hiatt said.

"Fine with me, gents." Ludlow looked at them closely. "The problem now is when? Any suggestions?"

"Tonight," Hans said.

The others agreed.

Ludlow nodded. "Sounds soon enough. Remember to bring a shovel, a rifle and a six-gun. We don't want anyone sneaking up on us. We'll have out two guards at all times, and two men working. Damn, we're going to need a wagon."

Ludlow looked around the men. "Who can drive out a wagon?"

Hans waved a hand. "Hell, I rent one now and then to move stuff. I'll get one this afternoon and have it ready."

"Anyone thought what we do after the wagon is loaded?" Ludlow asked. "We don't just split it four ways and drive back into town and unload."

"Christ, more problems," Dr. Greenly said.

"Not problems, just points to be settled before they get to be problems. Planning always pays off." Ludlow stared at the doctor for a moment.

Ludlow shrugged. "I've got that little spread about three miles out of town I own. We'll take it there and then each one of you can move your share wherever you want to."

"What about using it?" Hans asked.

"Just don't try to do anything nearby," Ludlow suggested. "Dallas is as close as I'm going to work any of it."

"Sounds reasonable," Zed said.

They looked at each other. "Meet just north of town at midnight," Ludlow said. "We'll take it from there." Excitement had crept into his voice. "Damn, this is finally going to be over. About goddamned time!"

Zed poured the four shot glasses full of whiskey and they all stood and lifted their glasses.

"To the four of us, to wealth and happiness," they all said in unison. Then they downed the whiskey and looked at each other.

"Damn, I think it's going to happen!" Zed Hiatt said.

Slowly the three men drifted out the back door and went about the rest of their normal day's activities.

At five minutes before three o'clock, Don White and two Negro men slipped into the Johnson Bank. Beth tried to signal to Jim the guard she had hired. He simply nodded to White who he knew was the mayor and turned back to the chair he had been sitting in.

Don White drew a revolver and shot Jim in the back, killing him instantly.

"Nobody move!" White roared. There were three customers in the bank. "You three out here, lay down on your backs on the floor, right now. You have any weapons?"

The two women and one man shook their heads.

"You do and you're dead." One of the black men locked the outside door. The other kept a six-gun trained on the customers. White and the other Negro man jumped the counter. The black cleaned out the teller cages of ready money.

"You tellers, lay down on the floor, now! Beth,

you lay down on that desk. Don't move, any of you or you're dead!''

The teller had finished taking all the paper money from the cages. He stuffed it in a pillowcase he carried and kept his six-gun on the bankers.

White vanished inside the safe and laughed. He found more money than he figured. Quickly he stripped it out of the wooden drawers and dumped the bound packets of tens, fives and twenties into a pillow case he carried.

He passed up the gold. It would be too heavy to carry. He found two more drawers filled with old bills and he swept them into his bag as well. Then he found only empty drawers. He swore, and lifted the sack and laughed, then left the bank vault.

"Nobody move. Don't lift an eyelash." He went up to Beth where she lay on her back on the desk top. For a minute he laughed, then he reached down and fondled her breasts.

"Not a word, woman!" he spat. His hand went lower to her crotch. He spread her legs, then leaned down and lay on her as he kissed her lips. She struggled.

He lifted up, laughed and motioned the Negroes toward the back door. They went down a hall ahead of him. Beth sat up.

"Down!" he thundered lifting his six-gun and turning toward her. She lay down quickly. "Nobody move for five minutes. I got two men with rifles aimed at the front door. Anybody go out there for ten minutes and he's one dead man."

White ran down the hall to the rear of the bank. It was on the corner of the block and the back door was near the street. One of his black men had the door opened. White ran up and pushed him forward.

"Outside, stupid. Let's get away from here!"

The first Negro ran out the door into the alley followed closely by the second. Both had their guns up and ready. White let them get twenty feet ahead. He sent one .44 slug up the hallway into the front of the bank, then reached the door and stepped inside.

A woman jumped around the corner and aimed a double barreled shotgun. She blasted the first round at the Negro who was less than fifteen feet from him.

The double ought buck caught him in the chest and drove him back three feet, blasting six of his ribs into his heart, other slugs chopping his heart and lungs into a mass of spurting blood, shattered bone fragments and splattering tissue.

Without pausing the woman shifted her aim to the second Negro who had lifted his pistol when the second blast of the shotgun caught him. It tore the iron from his hand, shattered his hand and arm and continued forward and almost tore his head off his shoulders. He slammed to the ground six feet from the bank door.

The door had already closed behind Don White. There was nowhere to go but forward. The woman did not take time to reload. She threw the shotgun aside and pulled a foot long butcher knife and charged White.

He had time only to lift his .44 and shoot once. The bullet hit her in the chest, staggered her but she powered forward, the long knife slashing.

White had no time for a second shot before she was on him. The first swipe of the knife severed the arteries and muscles on his right wrist. Fingers relaxed and the White six-gun fell into the dust.

Before White could focus his eyes on the blood spurting wrist, the deadly knife swung again, its razor sharp blade slicing through Don White's neck on the left side. The gush of blood from the carotid artery drenched his shirt and pants as he crumpled to the ground.

The woman fell to her knees, stabbing White, slashing his neck and face, then stabbing again and again in the bloody shirt where his heart should be.

She shuddered and then gasped.

Two men ran into the alley. One of them rushed out to bring the marshal. The other man walked forward looking at the four bleeding and dead bodies.

The woman lifted the knife again, her strength fading quickly now. She swung the knife again, and sliced Don White's nose off his face.

Then she wailed in agony, slumped forward and fell on Don White's silent chest.

Spur McCoy heard the shots. He had been in a store across the street and did not see White or his men slip into the bank. He charged around the corner and into the alley. In one quick glance he knew the two blacks were dead.

Slowly he advanced on the second pair of bodies. He saw the woman and surprise washed over his face. He had seen that dress before today.

He knelt beside the bloody pair and lifted the woman's head. Milicent Trembolt. She had been following White for a reason. She may have followed him all day, figured out what he was going to do, saw him go into the bank and figured White would come out the back way.

Both she and White were dead.

He stood and waved at the crowd. "All right, move back. We can't help these four in any way. Move it back. Did someone go for the marshal?"

One man said the marshal was coming.

Spur pointed at him. "You and you, keep these

people back until the marshal gets here. I need to get into the bank." He checked the two blood splattered pillow cases. When he saw money in them both, he picked them up and carried them into the bank.

He called from the back door.

"Beth. Beth, it's all over. Are you all right in there?"

"Yes! Yes! Most of us are fine."

She flew down the hallway and hugged him. She wouldn't let go. They walked back to the front of the bank.

"Most of us are fine. Jim, the guard, is dead. White shot him in the back without any warning!"

"Sounds like White. He won't hurt anyone ever again."

"You shot him, Spur?"

"No, Milicent Trembolt did. She either shot him or killed him with a butcher knife."

"Oh, dear God!"

"I'm afraid Mrs. Trembolt is dead, too."

"I liked her." Beth wiped sudden tears away. "Will someone come and get Jim?"

"I'll arrange it. I want to get out to that house White had at the edge of town. He must have been ready to run away." Spur kissed her cheek and ran out the back door. The marshal and undertaker were there. He found three horses at the back of the bank. Nobody claimed them. He figured they were White's. He mounted one and rode quickly to the house someone told him the mayor had used.

Just as he came up he saw a small black girl riding away fast on the bay. He let her go.

There was no one else in the house. Spur found the satchel with the city's money in it. There was a blanket roll and a small carpetbag all packed.

Spur picked up the money, searched the house but found no other valuables, and rode back to the bank. He set the satchel on Beth's desk.

"City money, I'd imagine. You'll have to send one of your bookkeepers over to City Hall and check the tax payment records. I'd guess most of this is from the current taxes paid."

"I'd think so."

The bank was quiet. The workers had gone home. The undertaker had carried Jim the guard out and washed the blood off the bank floor. The bodies in back were gone, too. There would be lots of funerals in town the next few days.

"Is it over, Spur?"

"The Carpetbaggers part is over. I'm sure most of the city's money is there. The girl might have taken some of it. Without their dole, the Negroes will drift on to other towns."

"I hope so." She paused. "Now, what about Daddy? Will we ever know?"

"I hope we do. Now I have only one group to watch. The death of Father Desmond may stir these men into action. I'll be watching them."

"What about dinner at my house?"

"Not tonight, Beth. I'm going to be watching every move that Hans Runner and Doc Greenly make."

"I could help. Hard to be in two places at once."

She was right. "You're hired. You watch Doc Greenly. You have a horse and riding clothes?"

"I could ride before I could crawl."

Spur grinned. "Okay, you win. You take Dr. Greenly. Don't let him see you, but don't let him get out the back door or the front without you following him. Can the doctor ride a horse?"

"He can. Told me once he likes to ride. Strange, these men like to ride who don't have to."

"Tonight they may have to."

She reached up and kissed his lips. "I'm going home and dig out my riding clothes. Oh, if the doctor goes somewhere, how do I find you to tell you?"

"If I'm right he'll go the same place that Hans goes. Then we'll find each other." She waved and they went their separate ways from in front of the bank.

17

After the other three men left the back of the newspaper office that afternoon, Hans Runner sat in his big office chair and stared at the wall. It had been a wild, crazy, unpredictable time, the big war. Things had changed, an upheaval had taken place, and for the most part their small town had been passed by this far up in Texas, even by the border raiders.

Then the third raid came by the force of twenty Yankees. They had swept into town, killed three men and scared the rest of the able bodied who could pull a trigger. They had three or four women, used them all night, then raided the general store and the butcher shop and tore off with a wagon full of food and a string of ten stolen horses.

That was the spark that set them off. The very next day a dozen of the men in town got together and demanded that they form some kind of defensive force. Garth Ludlow had been the only man to fight back the night before. He had wounded two of the Yankees before they routed him from the hayloft and chased him ten miles down river. He escaped from the Yankees and rode back into town something of a local hero.

Now they voted him the head of the new Johnson Creek defensive force. He had been at The Wilderness, a classic battle of victory that looked like defeat. He knew what he was doing. A week later he had formed the Mounted Home Guard. Every volunteer had a rifle, a pistol and a good horse. They had trained every day for a week, then once a week after that.

Half the men in town who could ride a horse wanted to be in the Home Guard. At last Garth had tested each man with a rifle. Those who could shoot straight enough qualified for the Home Guard.

They had twenty-five at the time. They were ready. A series of shots, three, then three more was the signal to assemble prepared to fight.

The signal never came.

Hans went to the room at the side of the press and poured himself a shot of whiskey, threw it down and leaned back in his chair.

The Yankee far-ranger patrols evidently pulled back, or moved on. The Mounted Home Guard at Johnson Creek didn't see a Yankee for more than three months. The war was grinding down. More reports of deaths of men in the county. Then two more wounded men came home.

Things were going bad for the Confederacy. When Captain Jones came back home to Johnson Creek wounded in the chest and with just one leg, he said the South had lost the war. It was only a matter of a few months now.

A month later, the news that a detachment of twelve Yankee soldiers had been spotted just north of town caused quite a stir. There was talk of raising the Mounted Home Guard and challenging them, running them out of the county.

Garth had done a lot of fancy talking in the saloons and on the boardwalk. He was all for charging into the damn Yankees. Then that night he got together some of the best men he had behind the livery and did some plain talking.

"Men, I'm sick to death of this damn war, and looks like it's about over. We got us twelve Yankees not five miles from here. I say we pay them a social call. We been training for three months with nothing to shoot at. Who is with me on a little hunting practice?"

Six men stayed. Three went home and Garth made them swear to forget all about it. Garth let the three return home and then turned and stared hard at the five men who stayed with him and were ready to fight.

"This won't be a classic battle, men, and it might wind up being nothing. But by God, we're going to poke them damn Yankees in the ass and let them see how it feels!"

Garth inspected every man. Pistol and rifle and sixty rounds for each. He nodded.

"Let's move out!"

They rode single file, with Garth in the lead. He found the squad of Cavalrymen just where they had been reported, near the well at the old burned out Johnson place.

Garth ordered his men to dismount a quarter of a mile away in a little bunch of cottonwoods. They moved up cautiously and watched the small camp for half an hour.

Garth grinned. One man on guard, and he even had a fire! He must be pretty cocky. Expecting no trouble. He wouldn't even feel the trouble he was getting. Garth waved at the men and they all moved up beside him silently.

"One guard. I'll take him out, them move forward on my hand signal. I'll be in the edge of the firelight. Come in fast but quiet. Got it?"

Garth looked at Father Desmond. He had been surprised when the priest chose to come. "Father, does this bother you? Does it go against your vows?"

"You said I could be your chaplain. If any of you get wounded, I can help."

"Father, if things get tight, I'll need that rifle of yours. You can use it as good as any of the other men here. If it comes down to kill or get killed yourself, you got to decide which one you gonna do."

Hans Runner, Harry Johnson, Dr. Greenly and Zed Hiatt agreed with Garth in a quiet endorsement.

"We'll just see what happens," the priest said.

Garth left them, slipping up on quiet feet toward the well house, then around it to where the guard stood, half in the light, half out. Garth saw the wagon, a big heavy one, with a canvas top and extra wide metal wheels. He wondered what the cargo was.

The squad seemed to be moving it somewhere. Were they its escort and guard, or was it simply supplies for their trip? He would know soon.

He went into a crouch behind the well itself as the guard turned. The Yankee Bluebelly sighed, slung his rifle over his shoulder on the strap and walked to the far side of the camp, then back.

He came within six feet of where Garth crouched. The trained infantryman had out a five-inch skinning-sharp knife and when the Yankee turned his back, Garth sprang forward, took three steps

171

and his left arm whipped around the Yankee throat, half strangling him, cutting off any sound.

Garth's right hand drove the heavy blade down into the Bluebelly's chest, felt the knife slant off a bone and then drive in deep. Twice more he stabbed the soldier, then the man sagged like a limp sack against Garth. He let the body down to the ground quietly and checked. The damn Yankee was dead!

Garth looked over the camp. There were eleven blankets with blue uniforms huddled in them even though it was a warm night.

He signalled the men and they came up quietly. Two went directly to the wagon, cut away bindings inside and some of the canvas which covered everything inside.

Dr. Greenly came back to Garth with a story that made his eyes widen and his pulse race.

"Dr. Greenly, are you sure?" Garth said, his voice breaking with emotion.

"Dead sure. I don't know how much, but more than enough for all six of us."

Garth pulled his men back. Quietly he told them what was on the wagon. They stared at him in amazement.

"Spoils of war, I'd say," Harry Johnson advised.

"Looks like them that takes, keeps," Zed Hiatt said. The other men quietly said about the same thing.

"So we do it," Garth said. He assigned three men to hit each side of the camp where the men were spread.

He cautioned them. "Nobody gets away. We gonna take the wagon and we got to make sure none of these Yankees lives to tell about it. We take them before they can get off a shot. Tough way to go, but as you men know, there's a damn bloody civil war on and in a war men tend to get themselves hurt."

They were told not to fire until Garth did. He gave them plenty of time to get in position. When he saw the faint wave of Harry Johnson, he killed the closest Yankee with a shot to the heart.

The little ranch yard rang with the sound of Sharps and Spencers and a few pistol shots.

"Oh my God!" one Yankee voice screamed. A pistol shot sounded quickly and then all was quiet.

Garth walked up to the fire and built it higher. The other men slowly moved up to the fire. For a time nobody said a word. Their faces showed their sudden baptism by fire in a real war. They were now blooded veterans.

Harry Johnson's face was still white. He said nothing and stared into space for a while then turned his face away from the fire.

Garth had killed enough men that two or three more by his hand made no difference.

Father Desmond looked at Garth and shook his head sadly. Garth did not know if the priest had fired his weapons or not, and he certainly wasn't going to ask him.

Hans Runner grinned at Garth and winked. Hans would be all right. Zed Hiatt looked into the fire. Tears ran down his cheeks and he didn't try to stop them. "My God! Do you men realize we just slaughtered twelve human beings! How can we ever justify this? How can we live with such a crime!"

"It's no crime, Zed," Garth said sharply. "You are a soldier, and this is war. Those men are the enemy. Remember that."

Dr. Greenly came up a moment later.

"All of them are dead, medically, absolutely. What the hell do we do next?"

"Bury them," Garth said. "Deep where they

won't be found for a hundred years."

They at last settled for a common grave six feet deep in a nearby cornfield. Someone suggested the well, but when the ranch was built back, the well would be cleaned and the bodies would be found.

The digging was easy. They found two spades in the half burned barn. Garth would permit no riffling of pockets of the Yankees.

"They were soldiers, who died in battle. Give them the decency of a plain burial."

While two men dug the grave, the other four worked on the wagon. They hitched up the horses and drove the wagon over to the half burned barn. It took an hour to pull up the floorboards on the front unburned section of the barn. Then they dug a shallow hole under the floor and moved the cargo from the wagon to the hole.

They were done about the time the grave was filled.

With aching backs and sore arms, they put the barn floor boards back in place, then scattered hay and dirt over it.

"The wagon," Garth said. "It's Yankee army from end to end. We have to get rid of it somehow."

"Burn it," Hans suggested.

"Too damn slow," Garth said. "That's heavy wood. It would burn for a day and a half."

After ten minutes of wrangling, they drove the big wagon to a bluff a half mile away, unhitched the horses and pushed the heavy rig off the eighty foot drop. It smashed into pieces on the rocks below.

The four draft horses were unharnessed and turned loose. They would find a home at a ranch nearby quickly enough.

With bone weary bodies, the six men rode back to Johnson Creek, arriving just before sunrise. All six slept the clock around, but nobody seemed to notice it.

The day after that a rider came into town and shouted the news. The war was over! The South had lost. The surrender had taken place almost three weeks before.

That night the six members of the Mounted Home Guard who had killed the Yankees gathered in a side room in back of the newspaper office.

"We shot down those men in their sleep three weeks after the war was over!" Harry Johnson shouted. "We're no better than murderers! We killed them for what they carried."

"We didn't know the war was over!" Garth shouted back. "Nobody knew it. The war was still on for us. It was a wartime fight, pure and simple."

For three hours they argued, came close to blows, and at last Dr. Greenly had the final word.

"Right or wrong, it's done. None of us wants to hang for doing what we thought was a patriotic act. I say we just let it sit. We do absolutely nothing. We act as if nothing had happened and in five, maybe ten years, we get together and settle the matter of the goods on that wagon."

An hour after that they had it worked out. They would watch and wait, but they would also have a poker game on the first Saturday night of every month. It had served as a way of keeping in touch with each other, and to support one if he was starting to break.

They had missed on Harry Johnson. Hans knew they should have seen it coming. None of them had. Father Desmond had been the weak link all along. Hans had been with him. The priest had not fired at the Yankees. Hans had not expected him to. The priest had a lot of other problems besides the Home

Guard attack on that Yankee detail.

Harry Johnson's letter had been another matter. Garth said they had to kill him before he talked. Reluctantly they all agreed. Harry had refused to come to the last poker game. They went to see him instead. All had fired into Harry's body. Hans could not remember who fired the first shot.

By all firing, each one could be labeled the killer, and all would be bound by the pledge not to inform on the others, since he then would be informing on himself.

This time Father Desmond had fired. They had held his hand on the gun and forced him to pull the trigger.

Hans Runner put his feet down and poured another shot from the whiskey bottle on the table. Now almost four years after that murderous night, they would finish it. After tonight it would all be over. The alliance of six men so different yet bound together by a deadly secret, would be ended. They could go their separate ways. Now the four survivors would divide the cargo, and their lives would be changed forever.

Hans stared at the newspaper office again, had one more shot of whiskey and went back to setting type for the next edition of the newspaper.

He heard the story about the bank robbery soon after it happened, and hurried over. He'd have a new lead story for the front page. The big story would happen tonight, and he wasn't going to use it. For just a moment his journalistic ethics reared up and bothered him. He thought of that glorious cargo they had buried four years ago, and told his conscious to take his ethics and get lost in whirlwind somewhere.

18

Marshal Garth Ludlow had arrived at the scene of the five killings shortly before Spur had ridden away. He took care of it systematically. Got statements from Beth, called the undertaker, made a sketch of the position of the bodies and what evidently had happened. Then he told the undertaker to remove the bodies.

Five of them inside of about ten minutes. That was a record for Johnson Creek . . . especially with one of the dead being a woman.

At least there was no killer he had to charge out of town to chase down with a posse. He settled in his chair in the jail and let his hat come down over his eyes. The Carpetbagger problem was over. It had been coming to a head for weeks. If any of the transient blacks were still around next week, he'd run them out of town. Most of them were no accounts anyway.

Then there was tonight.

For a moment he hardly believed that it was finally going to end. The adventure that started almost four years ago was almost over. And he would never have to work another day for as long as he lived!

Garth smiled. He could even find a woman, not just a woman, a beauty! One with a pretty face, and a sleek little figure and big tits! All his life he had lusted after women with big knockers. He always picked the whore with the biggest tits no matter what the rest of her was like.

Yeah, and he'd get a beauty who liked to crawl into bed and make love in the wildest ways. He could teach her that. He would be a good teacher. Houston maybe, or on to New Orleans.

It would take some time, but hell, he was a young man, he had plenty of time. After tonight time would be one more thing that he had plenty of. Money and time, what a great combination and what he was going to do!

He had worked hard all his life just trying to find enough to eat and keep a roof over his head. The war had helped him that way. Before he went to war he had been a kid. He was only eighteen when he killed his first man with a blue uniform. That helped a boy turn into a man fast.

His old daddy had died when Garth was ten. He remembered it. The long black carriage and the singing and wailing. They made him look at the box in the ground and told him his daddy was in there. He didn't believe it. His daddy never liked small places. Nobody could make him climb into that little box. Anyway he figured his ma was lying to him, she had lied to him before.

She ran off the next year. He was eleven and stayed with some shirttail cousins for a spell. Only the uncle had ten kids of his own and there never was enough to eat. When he was twelve he ran off and worked on a ranch for a while. Then he took off from there again and wound up in Johnson Creek.

He was a swamper for a couple of saloons. By the time he was fourteen he was big enough to do cattle work, and he signed on at the Lazy L, only they lost all their cattle in the drought and he moved on to a new outfit, then came back to Johnson Creek about when the war started.

He returned a hero to Johnson Creek after the war when he fought the Yankee raiders and got himself named town marshal. Hell, he'd done as good a job as the next town marshal. Had a girl for a while, but she married somebody else, a guy with a small ranch. He saw her now and then. She had four kids and another one on the way. Not at all pretty any more.

Big tits! The pretty woman he married had to have big ones he could play with and swing around. Damn! but he liked big tits. Like June had. Yeah. He should see June tonight before they went out to the old ranch.

He changed his mind in an instant.

No! Instead of humping June, what he had to do was kill Spur McCoy!

The damned Government Agent was getting too close. He had figured out most of it. If he kept going he was bound to make one of the last four men crack and tell the whole thing. Zed Hiatt most likely.

Today, or just after dark. He had to put the Sharps slug through Spur McCoy's heart. By the time the government heard about it and sent somebody to investigate, ex-Town Marshal Garth Ludlow would be in Houston!

How to do it? A rifle would be safest. Ludlow prided himself on keeping his long gun eye sharp. He could drive a ten penny nail at fifty yards.

Ludlow dropped his feet off his desk and headed

for the door. Automatically he adjusted the hog leg at his side, and made sure the iron would not stick in the leather.

Then he moved outside to the boardwalk and started searching for Spur McCoy. He'd find him and track him. He had to know where he would be this afternoon.

The bank. If he went after the rest of the city money in the ex-mayor's house, he would bring it back to the bank.

Garth Ludlow was half a block from the bank when he saw Beth Johnson and McCoy come out the front door of the Johnson Bank. She locked the door, talked a moment to McCoy, then each went in a different direction.

Ludlow kept half a block behind the federal lawman. McCoy never looked behind him. He wandered down the street, stopping in a small restaurant across from the newspaper office. He took a seat near the front window, and Ludlow saw McCoy evidently watching the *Record* front door as he ate.

Ludlow slipped into the alley and ran to the back of the store beside the newspaper. It was a harness shop. He talked to the owner, Sam Wilkinson, and then said he needed to watch out the front window without being seen.

Sam told him to go ahead. From well back from the window, Ludlow could watch McCoy in the restaurant. Spur noticed each time someone went in or out of the newspaper office.

A half hour later, Spur finished his meal quickly, got up and hurried to the door. Then he came out casually and walked down the street toward the center of town.

Ludlow followed Spur who evidently was trailing

Hans Runner. Strange, Ludlow thought. How had McCoy tied Hans into the group? By the cover-up on Harry's death? Maybe.

If McCoy kept trailing Hans until tonight, the whole project could be in serious trouble.

Ludlow did not have his Sharps, or even a Spencer repeating rifle. He might have to rely on his six-gun. Which would mean a closer confrontation.

Or a closer bushwhacking.

Where was Hans going? He had to get a team and wagon from the livery for them to use tonight. Yes! Ludlow turned down the next alley, and ran down it to the street, turned toward the livery. He could be a half block from the livery before either of the men. There was a six foot high board fence along a vacant area they would have to pass.

If he worked it right, he could let Hans pass, then shoot Spur McCoy at nearly point blank range as he passed.

Ludlow was sweating by the time he trotted to the edge of the board fence. He looked around it. Hans had stopped to talk with someone near the general store. Spur would be killing time behind him.

Ludlow picked out the ideal spot. Half a board was missing on the fence about a third of the way down. He could let Spur pass and still have plenty of room for a killing shot, two or three if he needed them.

Marshal Ludlow risked a peek out the broken board hole and saw Hans walking quickly toward him. Thirty yards behind him, McCoy had just passed the General Store and came forward.

Ludlow paced nervously. He drew his revolver and checked the loads. Yes, five and the empty chamber under the hammer. He wiped sweat off his forehead. He'd never been this nervous before. It would be simple. He had his escape route all figured. Across the vacant lot to the next street, past the old burned out hotel, back to Main Street where he would discard his brown leather vest and throw away his hat, and walk back to the jail and put on new ones of different colors. Simple.

He heard the footsteps as Hans came striding forward. There was a blur as Hans passed the half-board hole in the fence. Then a dozen seconds later, he caught the sound of Spur's boots on the hard packed earth outside the fence. They came closer.

Ludlow moved up to within a foot of the hole in the fence. Now it was time!

McCoy walked past the hole. Ludlow lifted his weapon. He had not cocked it! He thumbed back the hammer to put it on half cock. The click sounded as loud as a lightning bolt in the suddenly quiet street.

At once Ludlow pulled the trigger. As he did he saw McCoy dive for the dirt and vanish from view through the hole. Ludlow's six-gun fired. He knew he had missed. He wanted to go to the hole and fire again and again.

A hot slug slammed through the half inch fence and splintered wood at Ludlow. Then another .44 size chunk of hot lead and another forming a pattern around the hole in the fence.

Ludlow ducked and ran for the other side of the lot. He was almost there forty yards away when he heard the next shot from behind him. It kicked up dust at his feet and he slashed around the edge of the burned out hotel and down to Main Street. Quickly he slid out of his vest, pulled the personal items from the fob pockets and tossed the vest in a burn barrel.

Two minutes later he was sitting behind his desk, slipping into a fresh vest, this one of doeskin, a light fawn color, the best one he owned. He pushed out the spent round and slid another one into the weapon.

He wiped sweat from his forehead and shivered. How the hell had he forgotten to halfcock his six-gun? He shook his head and sat in his chair. He should tell Hans about McCoy following him. He would go up there later on.

Ludlow shivered again and ran past the back door to the outhouse. He was too late. He walked back into the jail stiff legged and gingerly cleaned himself and changed into a fresh pair of jeans.

Damn! This was not getting off to a good start for the day that was going to make him rich!

Spur McCoy heard the metallic click of a six-gun cocking just as he passed a gap in the board fence, and instinctively he dove to the ground and drew his new model Army Remmington at the same time.

The round fired at him missed, splattered dirt into his face and sang away. He fired three shots around the deadly hole in the fence and jumped to his feet. His right boot hit an inch high rock and his ankle turned over painfully. All he could do was hop back toward the fence. He saw a flash of a figure running across the vacant lot.

When he got to the hole he saw only a man of average height in blue jeans and wearing a brown leather vest, blue shirt and brown hat vanishing around the old hotel.

There was no chance Spur could catch him with his ankle hurting. The only description he had would fit half the men in Johnson Creek.

Walk it out, he told himself. He walked forward and then back, and soon the ankle responded. It had been only a slight turn and not a dangerous sprain.

He could still walk and ride.

But he had lost track of Hans Runner. The newsman had been heading somewhere. Spur walked on down the extension of second street but saw nothing ahead but the Livery.

Time enough to check that later. He went to the livery and rented a horse and saddle, rode the animal around a few blocks to get used to the gelding, then rode back to the Livery and asked about Hans Runner.

"Yep, he was in. Said he had some equipment to move and took out a heavy wagon. Don't know what he had that he'd need anything that heavy, but he said it would do. Two horses and a wagon." The livery man looked up.

"Yeah, I know who you are, McCoy. That's why I'm talking to you so plain. Don't want no trouble with the law. Hans hired a wagon now and then. Nothing unusual. Said he'd be done with it sometime tomorrow."

Spur thanked him and rode away. Back at the Johnson House Hotel he tied the bay to the hitching rack out front and went to find himself a rifle. He bought one at the General Store, a good used Spencer that probably came home from the war. He got twenty rounds, and then twenty more and another box of forty rounds for his .44. He might be having a war all of his own before the night was over.

Spur rode his horse down Main Street until he was half a block from the newspaper office and tied him to a rail. He found a chair next to the Overbay General Store and leaned back in it, watching the newspaper office.

Nothing stirred inside or outside. After an hour he got back on his horse and rode around the block.

Behind the paper's back door he found a heavy wagon parked, and two plow horses still in the traces. Runner was going to do something tonight it seemed, or in the morning.

Spur found another vantage point nearly a block away where he could keep out of sight. He put his horse in the stall of an empty shed, and sat near a small clump of native mesquite. It was big enough to hide him and still let him see through.

He wasn't sure why, but Spur figured the wagon would be going anywhere that Hans Runner went. He hoped that the men who killed Harry Johnson had been scared enough to take some action. There had to be some kind of a secret they were hiding. Somehow it involved Harry Johnson and his death.

Spur squirmed on the ground. He might have a long wait. He wished he'd brought along some coffee, or a canteen. A nice cold beer would go good about now. He shook his head. Later. He'd put it down as one he owed himself. When this was all over he had in mind a nice quiet week of nothing to do but sit in the shade and maybe do some fishing. Not much fishing around Johnson Creek.

For a moment he thought of Beth Johnson. Maybe he would just move into her big house and relax for a while.

Beth would have some entertainment and recreation ideas. McCoy grinned just thinking about the sweet little package of woman.

Then he sat up straight. Hans Runner walked out of the rear door of his printing plant and headed for the team and the big heavy freight wagon.

19

Spur watched the newspaperman lift a cardboard box and put it in the wagon, then go back into the printing plant.

What the hell? Spur wondered. Not a big load for the wagon. What was the printer/newsman up to?

Spur watched for another hour and nothing happened. He was tired and sore from sitting on the ground. He walked around the block and saw that the blind was down on the front door of the news office. That usually meant that the place was closed. He checked his Waterbury. It was just past five o'clock. Hans could be having supper somewhere.

He found the newsman in the third restaurant he checked. Spur did it without the man seeing him. He went across the street to the Demorest eatery and had a quick medium rare steak and all the side dishes. He was surprised when they charged him sixty cents for it. Mrs. Demorest explained it was the biggest steak she had and she figured he'd want it.

Spur checked again, and Hans was still eating. When Hans finished, he carried a sack with him as he went directly back to his newspaper plant.

By the time Spur had run around the block to his hiding spot, he saw Hans putting the paper sack in the wagon, then heading back inside his place of business.

Spur settled down for a long wait. He had no idea if they would move tonight, or a week from tonight. The men were getting nervous, he knew that. He wondered if Beth was having any luck watching the doctor.

Four hours later Spur still lay there, sprawled now on the dirt of the alley, half awake half asleep, but aware of every cricket, every door slam, every horse whinny for a block around.

He checked the Big Dipper. It's pointer stars were almost due west of the North Star. That made it about ten P.M. Maybe tonight wasn't the night.

As he thought it, the back door of the news office opened and a man came out carrying a lantern. He lifted it at the door, evidently locking it from the outside, then walked to the team, checked them and climbed up on the driver's seat.

Spur grinned. Maybe tonight after all!

When the man slapped the reins against the big heavy horses' backs, Spur slid onto his own saddle and watched as the rig moved out slowly down the alley. He waited until it turned the corner, then rode out the alley the other way. The wagon would not be hard to find.

He rode slowly down Main Street and saw the rig turn onto Main a block ahead. He kept that interval as the heavy wagon rolled through the mostly deserted town. Only the saloons and gambling houses were showing lights. Three blocks out Main it turned into residential, and there a few of the homes had yellow lights, but most of the hard working folks of Johnson Creek were fast asleep in bed.

Spur let the wagon get farther ahead and when it angled for the north trail toward Indian Territory, he hung back more. They were a half mile north of town when Spur heard horses behind him coming up fast. There were two of them coming hard. He turned and looked through the blackness of the night, and saw the first wink of a pistol shot before he heard the sound, he leaned low on the neck of the bay and spurred him hard.

The big animal surged forward, and Spur angled him off the trail into a copse of cottonwoods and big boulders. He jumped down from the horse and dove behind a boulder as another volley of pistol fire came from thirty yards away.

Spur took careful aim with his .44 and fired.

The first horse in the charge screamed, fell away to the left in front of the second horse and then went down, the rider spinning head over heels. The other horseman pulled up and turned sharply racing back out of pistol range.

For a moment Spur couldn't see the man on the ground. He jumped up then, dodging and darting one way, then the other as he raced back thirty yards to be away from the enemy fire.

Spur sent two more pistol rounds at them, then reloaded. He could not identify the gunmen. He saw through the darkness that the second man was lifted on the horse, then they rode off double on the nag, heading back to town.

Spur made sure they had left, then he searched in the small stand of cottonwood until he found his bay chomping on some late Spring grass. He caught him, lifted on board, and then moved north again. He would ride quietly through the prairie so the newspaper man could not know he was coming.

He pondered the attack. The only explanation he could think of was that somehow Hans knew he was being followed, or *would be followed*, and set up the two guns to come after him.

Spur moved slowly, nearly silently through the no-moon Texas night. He could not hear nor see the wagon. The agent stayed two hundred yards off the main trail. Ahead he saw a small grove of trees upstream on the tiny Johnson Creek. There was enough water in it to flow year round, but in the Texas summer, it was only a trickle.

Spur moved up silently within a hundred yards of the woods and kept his hand around his mount's muzzle. He listened, and at last heard the jangle of harness. The wagon was in the woods waiting for someone. It would make a good meeting place.

Spur pulled back along the trail for a quarter of a mile and stepped down from the saddle. The Big Dipper sank lower in the western sky, but not to the midnight point yet.

The Secret Agent watched, listened and waited. A half hour later he heard a rider moving up the trail. He could not recognize the horse or the man on its back. Spur ground tied his mount and ran softly behind the rider and to one side.

He moved cautiously as he entered the grove of cottonwoods and black oak. There were dozens of wild pecan trees there and they left pods that crunched under foot. He worked through them and ahead saw a small fire.

A voice barked through the darkness.

"Put out that damn fire! You think this is a church picnic?"

Spur recognized the voice. It belonged to Town Marshal Garth Ludlow.

"Jeeze, I like a fire," Hans said.

Spur eased closer as the fire died under a storm of kicked dirt.

"You see anything of McCoy?" Hans asked.

"Met my two men on the way back to town. They told me they put at least three slugs in McCoy and run off his horse. They promised me he was either dead or would be by morning. They wanted the other half of the pay."

"You didn't pay them?"

"Hell no! I told them when I saw the body, they'd get the rest of the money. I don't hand out a hundred dollars without getting my money's worth."

"At least he won't bother us tonight," Hans said, sounding relieved. "I heard a dozen or more shots behind me. I know they had a set-to back there toward town."

"You bring some food?" Ludlow asked.

"Damn right, I get hungry, too, you know. In the wagon. But that's for after the digging."

"Where are the others?" Garth asked.

"Not time yet. They got fifteen minutes. Can I smoke?"

"If you got the makings."

"Hell no more of that. I splurged and bought cigars. Have one."

A moment later Spur saw matches flare and then two red glows as the cigars caught fire. He eased back out of the woods and found his horse where he left him. He tied his kerchief around the bay's muzzle so he wouldn't talk to the other horses as they came by.

The two men came together, ten minutes later. Spur let them get into the woods, then swung up on his horse. He started toward the trail when he sensed more than heard another rider. He waited. The horse came out of the gloom slowly and only at the last moment did he realize who it was.

"Beth! What the hell you doing out here?"

"Oh, God! I'm glad it's you, Spur. I was following Dr. Greenly as ordered. That's him up there with Zed Hiatt. They came out together."

"That's the four of them. Two dead and four to go." He paused. "You did fine, now ride back into town."

"Not a chance. These men killed my father. I want to know why. I've got that right."

He paused. She had. "But what if they catch us? They would kill us just as quickly as they did your father. I don't know why, but something out here is damned important."

"That's why I'm coming with you."

He saw the upthrust of her chin, the tight lips, the determination flashing out of her eyes even in the faint light.

"I guess the only way I can stop you is to run off your horse and hogtie you to a tree."

"You wouldn't do that."

"No, but I should. If you get yourself killed out here I'll just be mad as hell at you."

She laughed softly. "I'll be furious about it myself. Let's get going. Did they meet in the grove?"

"Yes. We'll go around this side, slow and easy." He tied both horse's muzzles with bandannas. "We don't want any horse talk if they smell the other mounts."

She nodded and they walked the horses forward slowly. When they were at the far side of the grove, they heard the jangle of harness as the two plow horses tugged the heavy wagon out of the trees and angled north on the trail again.

"Any ranches out here?" Spur asked.

"A few farther on. Another two miles or so is a ranch my granddad owned. I guess it's mine now. It was burned out thirty or forty years ago and never built back. Indians I guess. But I still pay county taxes on it."

A half hour later they knew the wagon was headed for the old Johnson ranch. When they saw the wagon pull up near the shell of a barn on what Beth said was the old place, Spur and Beth dismounted and ground tied their horses about a quarter of a mile away. Spur took his rifle and all of his shells and then moved up cautiously.

By the time they got there, all four men had lit lanterns in the old barn and were busy lifting the floor boards of the unburned part.

"Beth, did your father ever mention anything happening up here during the war? Any kind of action, or a fight, or maybe some Yankees camped out here?"

"He didn't say anything like that. I do remember somebody said he found a Yankee army wagon wrecked below a cliff around here somewhere." She frowned in the soft night light. "Seems like there was some talk about a patrol of Yankees around here once about at the end of the war, but I can't remember."

They had moved up within fifty yards of the men in the old barn.

"You stay right here," Spur told her. "Did you bring a gun?"

She showed him a small caliber six-gun, maybe a .32 caliber.

"Good, can you use it?"

She nodded. "Daddy wanted me to learn how to

shoot it. I can."

"Good. Stay right here or I'll spank you. I'm going to sneak up closer and find out what's going on. I'll be back."

She caught his sleeve. "Spur McCoy, you be careful. I don't want any bullet holes in that wonderful body of yours."

He grinned and slipped away.

Spur moved to the old well, then forward again until he could see into the open door of the barn. They had half the two-inch floor board planks lifted off and the two men were digging. Spur waited. Soon all four men were in the hole throwing out dirt.

"Damn, I hit something hard!" Hans shouted.

"Me, too!" Zed yelled. "We must be almost there."

A few minutes later as Spur watched, the two men lifted out a long narrow box. It was the kind of crate the army used to ship rifles.

The men heaved the heavy box onto the side of the hole and eagerly opened the heavy hasp. For a moment all four stared into the box. Then Garth picked up something.

Spur saw it gleam in the lamplight. There was no question what it was.

Gold!

Spur had seen a bar like that before. It was a ten pound gold bar in its purest form. Had they found a wagon full of gold?

Spur lifted the rifle. Strategy. They would be well armed.

Doc Greenly took out a bar of gold and hoisted it. He sat down quickly. "Christ! This one little ten pounds of gold is worth over three thousand, three hundred dollars! That's more than I take in in three years!" He shook his head. "Damn, I've got to piss before I wet my pants."

"You're rich enough you can take a leak anywhere you want to!" Zed shouted.

"Rather do my privates in private," Doc said. He put the gold bar back in the box gently and headed into the darkness. He came toward Spur.

Spur tracked the short, red-haired doctor and when he stopped and turned away from the barn, Spur moved toward him silently. Doc was totally relaxed letting the urine flow when he heard something behind him.

Before he could turn, Spur McCoy's left arm wrapped around his throat, jerked him off his feet and dragged him away from the barn. Thirty yards back from the diggers, Spur let up the pressure on Doc Greenly's throat. He rasped for breath.

Spur whispered in his ear. "Not a word, Doc, or I slit your throat ear to ear, you understand?" The man nodded.

Spur tied his big handkerchief around the doctor's mouth gagging him. Then he tied the man's hands behind his back with rawhide and his feet as well.

Beth slid up out of the gloom.

She stared at Doc for a moment then slapped his face so hard his head jolted to one side. Spur grabbed her.

"Not now!" he whispered to her sharply. "He'll have his day in court, then he'll hang. Don't make any more noise. We've got three more of them to capture. Agreed?"

The anger faded from her eyes, and she nodded.

When Spur got back to his vantage point, he saw the three men hoisting box after box out of the hole. How much gold was there?

He lifted his rifle, went into a prone position and sighted in. He had two of the men in the open. Quickly he fired one shot over their heads.

"Freeze right where you are, otherwise you're all dead." Spur bellowed.

Garth dove into the hole out of sight. Zed lifted his hands.

"Don't shoot, oh, God, don't hurt me!"

Hans Runner went for his six-gun at his hip. Spur moved his sights slightly and drilled a .52 caliber slug through Runner's right shoulder. The force of the round knocked him backwards over the boxes of gold. He sat up holding his shoulder.

"Damn you, McCoy! You're supposed to be dead!"

"They missed me, and lied to you. The easy way out."

There was no comment. "Doc is all tied up out here, don't expect him to help you. Give it up, Garth."

"Not a chance, McCoy. We figure we've got a ton of gold here. And it's ours. War loot. Finders keepers. We'll kill you if we have to."

"Big talk for a man pinned down and nowhere near his rifle."

"Been in worse spots," Garth spat.

"Hiatt!" Spur yelled. "Get out of there. Throw down your gun and get out here in the dark."

"No!" Garth screamed. He lifted and fired a shot at Hiatt but the big man was already running into the darkness.

Garth shot out two of the lanterns. Spur ran forward to the very edge of the barn. He could see into part of the hole. He spotted Garth's legs. Spur sighted in. One leg moved. He changed his sighting and fired. The bullet smashed into Garth's right leg, slicing through muscle and tissue but missing the bone, bringing a wail of anger and fury from the town marshal.

"Damn you, McCoy!" Garth screamed. He shot out the last lantern and the darkness was complete inside the barn shell.

Spur closed his eyes for a moment, then opened them. He turned his head with his right ear toward the hole. Someone moved. He forgot where Hans Runner was.

"You'll never make it, Garth. Give it up and have a chance to live."

"A jury in this town? No chance in hell I'd make it." He fired twice over the lip of the hole. Spur drew his revolver and put three rounds into where he thought the hole was. One slug hit a wooden box.

"Not even close!" Garth bellowed.

As Garth spoke, Spur sensed that he had moved. There was an open space beyond the hole and the pile of boxes that he guessed must be filled with gold. If Garth tried to run he would go out through that open space. It showed a lighter sky behind the dark sides of the barn and the interior.

Garth would silhouette himself against the sky if he tried to run that way.

"No chance you can make it, Garth. I've got a posse of fifteen men coming out. I figured on midnight."

Garth did not reply. Spur listened. He heard the scrape of a boot on a rock or a timber. Yes a timber. Garth was moving toward the light. Spur concentrated on the lightness of the far opening where the barn side had burned away. He brought up his sixgun to cover the area and held it with both hands, his left locked around his right wrist.

Another scrape.

"You don't have much time left, Garth. Where will you run to?"

The ex-soldier took advantage of the sound of

Spur's voice to make his try. His feet skidded on a rotted timber, then one toe caught and he was up and running for the burned out side of the barn.

It was twenty feet. Spur caught him the moment he lifted from behind the pile of timbers. Ten feet toward the door he was a black blob against the lighter sky. Spur fired twice so fast the shots sounded like one roar.

Spur saw the effect of the first .44 slug. It caught Garth in the shoulder high up on his back and drove him forward. The second round lanced through the middle of Garth's back and he went down with a faint skidding sound that was drowned out by the pistol shots inside the old barn.

Spur stood as still as a stone pillar. He held his breath listening.

A groan drifted back to him. The man had not moved. Slowly, with his weapon up, Spur McCoy edged forward toward Garth Ludlow. In the pale shaft of light from the night sky that slashed into the barn through the opening, he saw Garth spread eagled on the far part of the barn floor that had not been torn up.

"Help me, McCoy!" Garth said.

McCoy saw the growing pool of blood under Garth. He wasn't faking. Spur knelt down beside the wounded man.

"I'll help you, if you tell me about the gold. It was a Northern detail bringing in gold from California?"

"Our best guess," Garth said softly.

"And you hit them before or after you knew about the gold?"

Garth told him.

"You four and Harry Johnson and Father Desmond?"

"True. It was just one last jab at the Bluebellies.

Oh, God that hurts!" He swore for a minute. "Roll me over, Spur. Don't cotton to dying staring at the dirt."

Spur eased him over, saw blood on his chest.

"Passel of stars out there," Spur said.

"Whole shit pot full," Garth agreed. He coughed and spit out blood.

"Damn we had it worked out. We figured a ton of gold. That much gold is worth six hundred, sixty one thousand four hundred and forty dollars!" Garth looked at Spur. "That's one thousand three hundred and seventy-eight years of pay for a cowhand at forty dollars a month wages and found."*

"Was it worth the try?"

"Damn right! I grew up dirt poor, McCoy." He coughed again, a great gout of blood spewed from his mouth.

"Dying, McCoy. I'm dying, you know that?"

"True."

"Worth a try for more than a half million dollars! Damn right. I'd do it again. And the war was still on. It was our patriotic duty to kill them Bluebellies."

He looked up at McCoy.

"Gold . . . McCoy. A ton of gold!" He coughed again, then blood filled his mouth, he let out one last rush of air and his eyes stared at the stars that he would never reach.

Spur ran back to where Beth waited. She had Zed Hiatt lying face down on the ground, his hands behind his back.

---

*Ton of Gold at $20.67 an ounce (1837 to 1934) equaled $661,440.00. 16 ounces to a pound.

"That's three," Spur said. "What about Hans Runner?"

"Over there, damn near bleeding to death," a soft reply came not ten feet from them. Spur moved cautiously.

"Got no gun, get over here and try to stop this damn blood!"

Spur found him leaning against the pump house. His arm was a mass of blood. Spur felt for the wound. Pressed a piece of Hans's shirt against the gash and bound it with another strip of his shirt.

"You'll live. Where's your gun?"

"Out there somewhere."

Spur searched him, found a small derringer and pocketed it.

"Stand up and move up by the barn. I'll get one of those lanterns working. Lucky he didn't burn down the rest of the barn."

Doc Greenly and Zed Hiatt looked at Spur in surprise when he told them what they were going to do.

"Don't think I'll do that," Zed said.

Spur pushed the muzzle of his .44 hard up under Zed's chin where the fleshy part is tender.

"Zed, you do like I tell you, or I'll blow your head off right here, right now! Is that a good enough reason for you?"

20

Spur untied Doc Greenly and led him and Zed up to the barn. He found a lantern that would work, and put the two men to carrying the boxes of gold to the back of the freight wagon.

"Stack it in there close and tight," Spur told them. "Just like it was yours, which it isn't. It belongs to the United States Government."

The two men grumbled and complained. Beth came up and watched them, her eyes angry as she held the six-gun in her hand. It was enough to keep the workers moving.

Spur picked up a shovel and dug out the last four boxes of gold and hoisted them to the top of the pit.

Spur opened one of the boxes and counted the bars of pure gold in it. There were ten bars. He counted the boxes, twenty of them. If each box had ten bars that would be a ton.

A ton of gold! It was almost enough to make a man forget his loyalties, to forget about the Secret Service and high tail it into the mountains of Colorado and live a life of luxury.

Almost enough.

When they had the twenty boxes spread over the floor of the freight wagon evenly, Spur tied Doc's hands and told him to crawl on board. They lifted Garth's body into the wagon and wrapped it in a canvas. Spur put the wounded Hans Runner in the box, too, and tied their horses on behind.

The sun was just beginning to taint the eastern horizon when they washed up in a bucket of well water and headed back toward town.

At the small cottonwood grove just north of Johnson Creek they parked the wagon, put the prisoners on horses and draped Garth Ludlow over his mount and tied him on.

Beth was amazed. "You leaving a ton of gold sitting in the wagon that way, unprotected?"

"I'll be back in about twenty minutes." Spur said. They rode quickly into town, Spur appointed one of the town men as a deputy to watch the jail and he deposited the three men in one cell. Then he rode back to the wagon of gold.

At the cottonwood grove he cut three fifteen foot tall trees with lots of branches and tied them behind the wagon. Then he drove off toward a draw he had seen on the ride in. He backed the wagon next to a steep wall that looked like it was ready to collapse. Spur unhitched the horses and drove them away from the wagon, then he climbed the wall with one of the shovels and began creating a landslide.

He worked for twenty minutes before he had the first fall started. Then he made another, and within a half hour he had loosened enough dirt and rocks from the side of the bluff to surge down and completely cover up the freight wagon. Spur drove the horses off, used the cottonwood branches to dust out all sign of the tracks, and then mounted up and led the draft horses as he rode back to town.

He turned in the three animals to the livery and said he would take responsibility for the added rent on the freight wagon that Hans took out. The livery man lifted a brow, but said nothing.

Spur went up to his room and washed up, put on clean clothes and then went down to the jail.

Doc Greenly had asked for supplies from his office to fix Hans's arm. It was bandaged and he was in good shape.

Spur sat down with the town's only lawyer, and stared at the three prisoners in their cell.

"I need to know exactly what happened the night Harry Johnson was murdered," Spur said.

Hans laughed. "You asking us to put a noose around our necks? Not a chance."

Doc Greenly shook his head. "You'd have to prove anything that might have happened. Going to be extremely hard."

Zed Hiatt asked to go to the outhouse. The newly appointed deputy unlocked the door, but once outside the cell, Zed went to Spur instead.

"Put me in a different cell, and I'll tell you exactly what happened to Harry. I don't care any more. It's bound to come out anyway. I'll tell you precisely what the five of us did. How we shot Harry Johnson."

Hans screamed at Zed, swore at him in three languages, at last slumped down and shook his head.

Doc Greenly laughed without humor. "It was a gamble, the biggest I ever took in my life. It almost worked. They can't hang me, I didn't fire the first shot. All they can convict me of is conspiracy to cover up a murder. He died instantly when Garth shot him the first time. I touched his throat. I know. All the other four of us did was shoot into a dead man. I don't recall that as being a crime."

Spur had been expecting some such defense. "The conspiracy charge will get you five or ten years, Doc, as well as Zed and Hans. You'll all be old men when you get out. If you get out. I think Harry would have liked the punishment."

"What about the army wagon?" Zed asked.

"I don't know anything about an army wagon. If there's an army wagon around here somewhere, the army will come and claim it." Spur looked at the other two prisoners. "Have either of you seen an army wagon around here lately?"

They both shook their heads. "I didn't think so. If there was a wagon it's hidden so well it would take an army to find it. Certainly there is no chance that three men in jail could tell anyone on the outside where it might be."

Spur tapped the lawyer on the shoulder. "Get those complaints of murder and conspiracy drawn up and over to the county seat this afternoon. Let's move on this quickly. I can't be in town more than another week."

Outside Spur stretched. He needed a good night's sleep. First he had to send an official letter to the army post outside Dallas. He needed an escort of twenty-six troopers. He got paper and pen from the desk clerk and wrote the letter, asking the Post Commander to check Spur's credentials with Gen. Wilton D. Halleck in Washington D.C.

He asked for the mounted escort at the earliest possible time, no later than seven days from receipt of the notice which would arrive by stage. He dated it, signed it, added his title, U.S. Army Colonel, retired, and his Secret Service number and sealed it.

The letter left on the morning stage for Amarillo and points East.

Spur had just finished his noontime meal in the hotel dining room when a young boy handed him a note. It was sealed in a pale pink envelope that smelled of rosewater.

Inside in a delicate hand was a note, also on pale pink paper.

"McCoy. I'm bathed, and rested, I'm hungry but not for food. How fast do you think you can pack your bags and move your things up to my guest room? If the guest room doesn't sound good enough you can have half of the master bedroom.

"Can't wait to have you in my clutches again. Oh, yes, I also want to know the last of the grisly details, and where you hid that wagon." It was signed, President Grant.

Spur folded the envelope and slid it in his pocket. He left a tip for the watiress and went upstairs and packed. He checked out and hired a boy to take his bag to the Johnson house. Then walked up the street.

The army would arrive, dig out the gold and return it to the U.S. mint in Philadelphia which is where it was probably headed for four years ago.

The army would demand an investigation into the death of the patrol, which would be duly recounted as an act of war before the end of the conflict, and it would be laid to rest.

Spur picked a rose from a convenient rose bush on the way to the Johnson place, and held it out as he was let in the door.

Beth smiled at him and led him upstairs to the master bedroom.

"I hope you're going to stay for the trial," Beth said after she kissed him on the cheek. "The judge won't be through town for another month on his circuit."

Spur smiled.

"I'll need at least a week to find out exactly what those men did and how they killed Daddy. And then you have to tell me how you put it all together. That will take a week . . . or . . . so."

Spur McCoy was thinking along the same lines. But he could count on a week, maybe eight days, before a telegram caught up with him by stage and he would be off on another assignment.

But until then . . .

He bent and kissed Beth Johnson's saucy lips. "You are a tease," he said. "A real Texas Tease."

She caught his arm and fell backwards on the big, soft featherbed, pulling him with her.

"Sir, I may be a tease, but at least I know how to deliver."

"You shall," he said, easing down on top of her. "You may be so sore you won't be able to stand up. You said you wanted to try that as I recall."

"Yes, let's try!" she squealed.

They did.